THE CONCERT

ISMAIL KADARE, born in 1936 in the mountain town of Gjirokastër, near the Greek border, is Albania's best-known poet and novelist. Since the appearance of *The General of the Dead Army* in 1965, Kadare has published scores of stories and novels that make up a panorama of Albanian history linked by a constant meditation on the nature of the human consequences of dictatorship. Kadare's works brought him into frequent conflict with the authorities from 1945 to 1985. In 1990 he sought political asylum in France, and now divides his time between Paris and Tirana. He is the winner of the inaugural Man Booker International Prize.

ALSO BY

Ismail Kadare

Fiction
The General of the Dead Army
The Palace of Dreams
The Pyramid
The File on H
The Three-arched Bridge
Three Elegies for Kosovo
Spring Flowers, Spring Frost
Broken April

Ismail Kadare

The Concert

A NOVEL WRITTEN IN ALBANIAN
AND TRANSLATED FROM THE FRENCH
OF JUSUF VRIONI
BY
Barbara Bray

Harvill *Secker*
LONDON

Published by Harvill Secker, 2005

2 4 6 8 10 9 7 5 3 1

Copyright © Librarie Arthème Fayard, 1989
English translation copyright © HarperCollins *Publishers*, 1994

Ismail Kadare has asserted his right under the Copyright, Designs and Patents Act 1988
to be identified as the author of this work

First published in France with the title *Le Concert*
(Albanian title, *Koncert në fund të dimrit*)
by Librarie Arthème Fayard, 1989

First published in Great Britain by Harvill,
as an imprint of HarperCollins *Publishers* 1994

HARVILL SECKER
Random House, 20 Vauxhall Bridge Road
London SW1V 2SA

Random House Australia (Pty) Limited
20 Alfred Street, Milsons Point, Sydney,
New South Wales 2061, Australia

Random House New Zealand Limited
18 Poland Road, Glenfield,
Auckland 10, New Zealand

Random House South Africa (Pty) Limited
Isle of Houghton, Corner of Boundary Road & Carse O'Gowrie,
Houghton 2198, South Africa

The Random House Group Limited Reg. No. 954009
www.randomhouse.co.uk/harvillsecker

A CIP catalogue record for this book is available from the British Library

ISBN 9781846550065 (from Jan 2007)
ISBN 1846550068

Papers used by Random House are natural, recyclable products made
from wood grown in sustainable forests; the manufacturing processes conform to the
environmental regulations of the country of origin

Printed and bound in Great Britain by
Mackays of Chatham plc, Chatham, Kent

THE CONCERT

I

THE WINDOW LOOKED DOWN on the street, where the passers-by, all muffled up, seemed to be hurrying along as fast as they could. A three-wheeled delivery van pulled up beside a tobacco kiosk, where drivers often stopped to buy cigarettes.

It struck old Hasiyé that the van was attracting a lot of attention. She wiped a space in the misted windowpane to get a better look.

Yes – three or four people had paused to stare at what the van was carrying: a tub containing a lemon tree. She could imagine the questions they'd ask the driver as he got back into his seat. "Where are you taking it?" "Where do they sell them?"

Suddenly the old woman thought she recognized Ana among the crowd. She was just going to tap on the window to attract her attention, when she remembered that Ana was dead – had been dead for a long time.

She sighed. More and more often lately she found herself not only getting the order of events mixed up, but also confusing real facts with things seen only in dreams. She tended to mix up the living and the dead, too, but she didn't mind too much about that. Most females of her age had the same problem: it was supposed to be typical of old women. Sometimes she thought that was why people treated them with respect.

She looked out into the street again. Ana was still there. Beautiful as ever, she was standing somewhat apart, gazing with a melancholy smile at the people hovering around the lemon tree. Why don't you just go on sleeping peacefully under the ground where you were buried? thought Hasiyé.

She could hear her grandson learning his lessons in the other room: "Sing, O goddess, the wrath of Achilles, son of Peleus!" Would there never be an end to all this anger? she muttered to herself. Of late it had been getting worse instead of better.

She picked up her coffee cup and examined the grounds. They

were muddy and hard to read, but that didn't surprise her. What future could an old crone like her expect?

"Sing, O goddess, the wrath . . ." She felt like yelling at her grandson, and at the world in general, for that matter, to go to the devil and take their wrath with them – there was far too much of it already!

Enough, enough! Don't keep dinning it in our ears!

She glanced outside again, but this time she couldn't see any van, or any lemon tree, or any people staring. I must have been seeing things, she thought. Or perhaps I fell asleep for a moment.

Then she nodded off again, but now what she seemed to be looking at were the bowels of the earth. Not underground caverns or catacombs which man really may see, but closely packed geological strata unvisited by light, impenetrable to the human eye. Nearby, invisible too, lay latent earth tremors and other nameless, formless menaces.

There was a faint rumble of thunder in the distance. Then the whole sky was rent by a long, sickly roar.

"Strike! Strike!" muttered old Hasiyé, not knowing who she was talking to, or why.

The bell had rung loud and long, and as Silva opened the door she prepared a smile of welcome for the first of her guests. But instead of them she saw a man with a tub on his shoulder, and emerging from the tub – a barrel sawn in half – the branches of a lemon tree.

"This is Gjergj Dibra's house, isn't it?" he said.

"Yes," she answered, taken aback. "Is that for us?"

"You ordered it, didn't you?"

And without more ado he walked into the hall.

"Where shall I put it?" he asked impatiently.

The tub must be pretty heavy.

"Careful!" she said. Then, opening a door: "In here, please."

The man stumped across the room as Silva opened the French window on to the balcony.

"Anywhere here will do," she said. "We'll find a better place for it later on."

The man put the tub down, straightened up, and paused for a moment to get his breath back.

The phone rang in the hall.

6

"A lemon tree is all I needed!" thought Silva.

The man began to drone out instructions.

"You'll need to spray it with insecticide every three months, and change the earth every six. And if there's a frost, cover it over with cellophane or it'll shrivel up in a single night."

But Silva didn't pay much attention. Her guests would be arriving at any minute, she hadn't prepared the salad yet or carved the roast, and she still had to change and tidy herself up.

The man seemed to notice her impatience.

"I'm sorry," he said. "I've come at a bad moment."

"Oh no – it's quite all right!" she said penitently. The man had hauled a heavy load all the way up to the third floor. She might have made more effort to conceal her irritation.

"Can I offer you something?" she said, trying to make amends as they went back through the hall.

"No, thanks."

"Oh, you mustn't refuse," she insisted. "It's my daughter's birthday."

When at last the door closed behind him, Silva went back to check the dinner table. She was tempted to add a few finishing touches, but in fact did nothing but stare absently at the coldly glittering array of plates and glasses. Then the doorbell rang again and roused her from her daze. She recognized her daughter's ring.

"Would you be a dear and make the salad and carve the meat while I have a shower and change? I'm sure I must smell of cooking!"

"Leave it to me, Mother!"

Silva looked at herself in the bathroom mirror as she undressed. Had she put on weight round the hips? She stood there pensively for a moment, as if she'd forgotten where she was. Then the phone rang again in the hall and roused her from her reverie.

She turned on the shower, anxious to get on as fast as possible now before the guests arrived. They were all friends, apart from a couple of Brikena's teachers, so they hadn't been asked to come at any definite time.

She came to a halt again back in her bedroom, wondering what to wear. But she soon felt cold, and settled for a mauve dress that she knew Gjergj liked. It still fitted perfectly: she must have been wrong about putting on weight. "I don't understand why you keep fussing about your figure," her husband sometimes complained. "A

7

woman doesn't really blossom until she gets to your age!" (She was well aware he was being tactful in putting the emphasis on flowering rather than on ripeness, and she was secretly grateful.) "I may be old-fashioned, but I don't see why a woman in full bloom has to be as skinny as a rake!"

Silva smiled to herself as she looked in the glass. As often happened on birthdays and other festive occasions, the putting on of the dress had suddenly divided the day into two. Amid the seemingly never-ending rush of preparation there always came a moment when fluster was transformed into celebration. As she buttoned the neck of her dress, Silva realized the magic moment had arrived.

She didn't take long over her hair, just doing it the way Gjergj liked it, despite or perhaps because of the fact that he was away and wouldn't be able to see it.

"Oh, Mother – you do look lovely!" cried Brikena when Silva emerged into the hall.

Silva smiled at her, threw a casual look at the table, and for some reason she herself didn't quite understand, began to wander aimlessly round the flat. Usually she liked to sit down and wait for her guests, but today that pleasure was spoiled by not knowing exactly when they would come.

Her daughter's voice came from the kitchen:

"I've done the carving, Mother – do you want to see?"

Finally Silva sat down in an armchair in the living room with her eyes half closed. It had been a really exhausting day, with her husband not there to give her a hand. A good thing I had that shower, she thought. The statuettes on the bookshelves, relics of her days as an archaeologist, loomed through the October dusk like a row of ghosts foregathering to exchange some secret. But the slightest noise or interruption would be enough to deprive them of their mystery and turn them back into figures of clay and stone.

Brikena, slender and tall for her age, appeared in the doorway.

"It's all ready! There's nothing more for you to do!"

"Thank you. Come and have a rest."

Brikena sat down opposite her mother.

"I wonder where Father is now!" she said.

Silva shrugged.

"Up in the sky over some desert, I expect! Or else in an airport waiting for another plane."

8

Brikena was going to ask another question, but her mother, lying with her head against the back of her chair, looked as if she needed some peace after her harassing day. So Brikena went and got a photograph album from the bookshelves, then sat down again and started leafing through it.

Silva could hear the rustle of the pages, and although she was trying to make her mind a blank she couldn't help imagining the photographs her daughter might be looking at. A montage of years and seasons – especially summers – rose up in her memory. Her family had always been fond of taking snaps, and Silva enjoyed spending a quiet afternoon sitting on the sofa as Brikena was sitting now, looking through one of their many albums.

The sound of pages turning stopped. Silva could guess which snap her daughter's eyes were resting on.

"Which picture are you looking at?" she asked, her own eyes still closed.

"The one of Aunt Ana."

So she'd been right – she'd been almost sure of it even as she asked. She went cold inside, transfixed by the fierce pain she still felt whenever her sister was mentioned, although it was eleven years now since she died.

At last the pages began to turn again, and Silva took a deep breath, perhaps to free herself from the vice in which her daughter had unknowingly caught her.

The doorbell rang again. This time it really was some visitors. First came Silva's mother, followed by her brother and sister-in-law. Her mother, never very talkative, had scarcely spoken at all since Ana died. She might be at a family dinner or some other such gathering for hours without uttering a word, though she never inflicted her grief on anyone else. And unlike most people's vehement mourning, hers seemed so muted and so evenly spread over the whole of her life as to be quite bearable. Silva often thought this was the way Ana ought to be mourned.

Silva's mother kissed Brikena and handed her a parcel. Then she embraced Silva, went silently into the living room, and sat down in her usual chair.

"Is there anything I can do to help, Silva?" asked her sister-in-law.

"No, thank you. Brikena and I have seen to everything."

The sister-in-law and her husband settled down on the sofa. Silva sat on a chair facing them.

9

"It's freezing cold out," said her sister-in-law.

"Is it?" said Silva, getting up to put a log in the tiled stove.

Then there was a silence, during which Silva, surreptitiously studying her brother's handsome face, thought she detected signs of anxiety. Sensing that he'd noticed her looking at him, she turned away, but a little while later, seeing that he wore the same expression as before, she wondered why he had always passed so unnoticed among their small circle of friends. Had any but herself remarked his present worried look? He was a graduate of the military academy and at present an officer in a tank regiment; but people were always surprised to hear that Silva had a brother at all. This state of affairs had been even more marked when Ana was alive: Silva and Ana, universally known as the Krasniqi sisters, had seemed to monopolize everyone's attention, to the exclusion of the rest of the family. Whenever the girls mentioned their brother in conversation, people would stare and say, "Have you really got a brother? A real one, I mean, born of the same mother as both of you?" "Yes, of course!" they would answer, greatly amused.

Even now that Ana was dead, many people still thought of the two sisters together, just as they had done in the early sixties, when they were nearly always together, despite the fact that Ana was already married then and Silva still single. But everyone persisted in regarding their brother as practically non-existent.

"When did Gjergj leave?" he asked Silva, in the hope of cutting short her scrutiny.

"Four days ago."

"How inconvenient!" said his wife, referring to Brikena's birthday.

Silva knew that all her guests except her mother would make the same remark.

"It couldn't be helped," she said.

There was another ring at the door: two of Brikena's teachers and their children, bearing gift-wrapped parcels. As they took their coats off in the hall they too asked about Gjergj's trip, and they were just exclaiming "How inconvenient!" when the bell rang once more. Timidly this time.

"Who is it, Brikena?" Silva called out, not hearing any sound from the hall.

"Veriana," her daughter called back.

Silva jumped up. By the front door, struggling out of her raincoat, her cheeks red from the cold, stood her only niece. A frail figure – the very image of Ana.

Silva went over and kissed her fondly.

"Father says he's very sorry, Aunt Silva – something cropped up and he couldn't manage it."

"What a pity! But did you come all on your own?"

"Yes. On the bus."

Silva took her niece's hand and led her towards the living room. Silva herself just stood in the doorway.

"Good evening!" said the girl to everyone in general.

They all looked back at her with a mixture of curiosity and pity.

"Isn't she like her poor mother!" whispered one of the women.

Veriana went straight over to her grandmother, who made room for her on her chair and began stroking her hair affectionately.

"Besnik's been unexpectedly detained and can't come," said Silva from the door, answering her guests' unspoken question.

Silva thought she heard someone say "What a pity!" Unless, thinking the same herself, she'd only imagined it. She drew back into the hall for a moment.

She really was sorry Besnik wasn't there. It was because of him she hadn't invited Skënder Bermema. She liked them both equally, but always made sure they didn't both come to see her together. Besnik Struga, her brother-in-law, who hadn't remarried after Ana's death, was naturally closer to her, but Skënder Bermema was closely linked to the memory of their youth, the rapturous years the two sisters had shared before Ana's divorce from her first husband. Moreover, before Ana met and married Besnik, there'd been a friendship between her and Skënder which even after all these years was still something of a mystery to everyone, including Silva.

An ideal time for going over all these memories, Silva had thought an hour ago. On autumn afternoons like this, just before some festivity, she liked to sit on the windowsill and, as darkness came down like a theatre curtain, forget present preoccupations and conjure up the past: the scandal of Ana and Frédéric's divorce; the endless conjectures about the reasons for it; the mysterious attitude of Skënder Bermema, whose name had been closely linked to the whole business even in the courtroom, which people had likened to a literary jury. For at the husband's request – though it had only made him seem even more ridiculous – the judge had pored for days over certain pages of Bermema's books which Frédéric insisted were dedicated to Ana. Then came the unexpected twist when it turned out that Ana's decision to get a divorce had nothing to do with Bermema, whose own marriage was going through a difficult patch, but was really due to her relationship with Struga, and to their sudden decision to get married as soon as possible. No one ever knew whether, in view of the fact his jealousy had been concentrated for years on Bermema, this lessened Frédéric's fury, or whether his anger at being betrayed was increased by the entrance on the scene of a third man.

Silva had never tried to get to the bottom of the matter: she preferred it to be forgotten. The aspect of the business that had upset her most, apart from the divorce itself, was the coolness that grew up between Besnik and Skënder. This grieved her not only because she liked and respected them both, but also because they were the people most intimately connected with her sister's memory.

Strangely enough, the breach between Besnik and Skënder had opened up when you might least have expected it: after Ana's death. Was her death the cause of the rupture between the two friends? Silva would have thought it quite natural if it had been brought about by Ana herself, or by the break between Besnik and his fiancée, who happened to be the niece of Skënder's wife. But neither of these theories held water, because Besnik and Skënder had gone on seeing one another after Besnik had broken with Zana, and even after his scandalous liaison with Ana, which had swiftly followed.

But although it seemed that neither explanation was correct, Silva had a feeling it was no use looking for one elsewhere. After cudgelling her brains for some time she'd come to the conclusion that while neither her sister nor Besnik's ex-fiancée was responsible separately, together they had been enough to cause the breach between the two men. Skënder's wife might have put up to some extent with a vague rumour about her husband's relationship with Ana, just as later on she might have tolerated his seeing Besnik after the latter had quarrelled with her niece. But when the two considerations came together, and Besnik married the woman whose name had long been linked to that of her husband, Skënder's wife, perhaps understandably, had decided that the pill was too bitter for her to swallow . . .

Silva suddenly remembered she'd left her guests to fend for themselves in the living room, but when she got near the door she could hear a lively conversation going on: no one seemed to have noticed her absence. She tiptoed over to the French window opening on to the balcony, beyond which the darkness was now rapidly deepening. The lemon tree brought by the unexpected delivery man from some unknown nursery was there in its tub, spending its first evening in its strange new home . . . The doorbell interrupted Silva's meditations: it was Gjergj's four sisters – the "herd", as he called them. Three of them were married; the single one was studying medicine.

The hall was full of voices, arms flailing to get out of coatsleeves, children rushing about with parcels.

"Brr – it's so cold!" said one of the sisters.

"Really?"

"There's been a sudden drop in the temperature. But it's nice and cosy in here!"

"What a shame Gjergj's not here! Couldn't he put his trip off?"

"No," Silva answered. "It wasn't up to him."

"Of course not," said the youngest sister. "And the way things are going with China . . ."

"Won't you come through?"

Silva shepherded them into the living room.

The atmosphere in the flat had all at once become cosy and cheerful. Back in the hall, Silva felt like smiling at the sight of all the clothes heaped on to the hall-stand. Some of the children's fur jackets looked as if they were riding piggyback on the grown-ups' overcoats; Silva took them down and put them on a divan in her daughter's room.

Then she went and inspected the table in the dining room. The quiet brilliance of the glass and silver seemed very remote from the commotion that had invaded the rest of the flat. The children had already established a route for chasing one another about, from the living room through the hall to Brikena's bedroom and back. Conversation in the main room was now so lively there was no longer much danger that the little party would fall flat. Silva, standing in the doorway, noticed that her brother was the only one not joining in. She drew up a stool and sat down beside him.

"Is something the matter, Arian?" she asked gently. "You look rather out of sorts."

"No, Silva – I'm all right."

From close to he looked quite drawn.

13

"What do you mean, you're all right? I can see something is wrong."

He smiled up at her with a look of sadness tinged with surprise, as if to say, "Since when have you started bothering about me?" Silva felt an almost physical twinge of conscience. She could see he was now in real trouble, though in the past the perpetual personal problems and dramas of his two sisters had seemed to deny him the right to any worries of his own.

Then Silva was called to the telephone.

She heaved a sigh of relief when everyone was sitting down at the table and the continuous clatter of knives and forks showed that the meal was well begun. She realized she was sitting next to Arian. Perhaps she oughtn't to press him any more about why he looked so glum. Besides, by now she was beginning to wonder whether that wasn't his usual expression: didn't men have plenty of reasons for feeling fed up? She would probably have let the matter drop – this was supposed to be a party, after all – if out of the corner of her eye she hadn't noticed her brother down two glasses of raki one after the other without stopping for breath. This was very unusual for him – not so much the actual drinking as the way he threw back his head after emptying his glass, and even more the way he set the glass down again on the table. His whole attitude suggested he had made up his mind about something and was prepared to take the consequences, whatever they might be!

"Have you got something on your mind?" Silva whispered.

"What if I have, little sister?" he answered calmly. "Even if I had a real problem, you wouldn't expect me to tell you about it in the middle of an occasion like this, would you?"

Silva was put out not so much by his answer as by the sardonic gleam in his eye. Such a mixture of annoyance and sarcasm can be hurtful even if it isn't directed against you.

"And why not?"

Now that he wasn't actually looking at her she could feel all the more clearly how vexed he was.

What in the world could have happened to him? she wondered, with another pang of conscience: did her brother have to be threatened by serious misfortune for her to act as if he really existed?

14

"I don't want to bother you with my troubles," he said at last. "It's something I haven't told anybody."

Silva looked swiftly at his wife, who was laughing and clinking glasses with Gjergj's youngest sister: was it something to do with her? She studied her for a moment. Yes, of course, she thought. He's jealous, though she probably doesn't suspect it. Otherwise, how was it she didn't seem at all bothered by her husband's sulks?

"It hasn't got anything to do with Sonia, has it?" asked Silva, for some reason regretting her question as soon as she'd asked it.

"Sonia!" exclaimed her brother in amazement. "What an idea!"

So it must be something different, something more serious, she thought. She was surprised at herself for imagining that anything could be more serious, for she'd been brought up in a family where the wives were always the source of any complications.

A wave of toasts swept round the table.

"Well, whatever it is, you shouldn't hide things from me," said Silva, leaning her head briefly on her brother's shoulder.

She was getting more and more anxious about him.

He turned towards her, and the look of pain in his eyes struck her like an electric shock.

"I'll tell you if you insist," he said, "though I'd made up my mind not to talk about it to anyone."

He twisted his glass round in his hand, gazing at it as if it were an object of wonder.

"I'm probably, perhaps even certainly, going to be expelled from the Party some time in the next few days," he said. "And from the army too, needless to say."

Silva nearly dropped her fork.

"What?" she stammered. "But why?"

"Please don't ask any questions. It's very complicated."

"But how is it possible?" she murmured, as if to herself.

"It's a very complex business," he repeated. "And there's nothing to be done about it. But at least it can't hurt the rest of you."

"How could you imagine we'd think of ourselves?" Silva protested. "You ought to be ashamed!"

He gave a wry smile, stabbing with his fork at a piece of meat that he'd picked up and put down again several times already.

"But why?" said Silva again. "What's it all about?"

Arian stared in silence at his almost untouched plate, as if he expected to see something there that would help him decide whether or not to confide in his sister.

"As you know, there were some army manoeuvres recently," he said at last, "Well, in the course of them I disobeyed, or rather refused to obey, an important order."

So that's all, said Silva to herself: at first blush it didn't seem as awful as she'd feared. But her brother went on, as if he'd guessed what she was thinking:

"When there's a war on, that's enough to put you in front of a firing squad. But as it's peacetime I shall just be thrown out of the army. And out of the Party too, of course. That's all. I don't think there'll be any other consequences."

Silva sighed. But of course . . . what other consequence could there be? Wasn't it bad enough already?

Arian made another attempt to pick something up from his plate, but his fork seemed incapable of dealing with it. Silva felt terribly sorry for him.

"Is anybody else being punished?"

"Four out of the six officers in our unit. All those who refused to obey."

He made another stab at his plate, but gave up and refilled his glass.

"So why did you do it?" asked Silva.

"Do what?"

"That order – why did you refuse to obey it?"

He turned his head away abruptly. His eyes were blazing with anger.

"Don't ask me about it. I shan't tell you."

"All right, all right," said Silva. "What's done is done. Don't torture yourself."

He picked up his glass and drank.

"Just one last thing," Silva went on. "Do you feel guilty about it?"

"Absolutely not!"

Silva glanced absently round the table. She couldn't make up her mind whether his not feeling guilty was a good thing or not.

"Forget it now," he said, raising his glass. "Here's to all of you, and to Brikena's very good health!"

"And the same to you!" Silva replied.

He waved his hand dismissively, as if to say "For me it's all over – you'd do better to concentrate on other people!"

Silva set down her glass and looked round at her guests. The dinner party was going on just as it had before her attention was distracted from it. Perhaps her brother's problems weren't as bad as all that, she thought, and made an effort to dismiss it from her mind. Everyone was in the best of humours; the red wine sparkled in the glasses; the peaceful buzz of conversation and laughter was punctuated only by the sound of bottles of mineral water being opened. It was hard to believe evil could go on claiming its victims after such a gathering.

Silva woke up with a start. At first she thought the brightness flooding in through the window was the dawn, but then she realized it was the cold glow of moonlight. Brr, she was freezing! But of course – that was what had made her wake up! She stretched out a hand and switched on the bedside lamp. A quarter past four. She lay there for a moment, staring at the bare ceiling. Then she felt cold again. All the glass in the room was covered with frost. It must be freezing hard outside. She thought of Brikena and Veriana, asleep in the next room.

She got out of bed, pulled a woollen cardigan round her shoulders and went quietly out into the corridor. The door of the other bedroom was ajar. She pushed it open cautiously and went in. By the bluish light filtering in from outside she could see the two girls' hair mingling on the same pillow. No doubt because of the cold, Veriana must have left the divan and snuggled into bed beside her cousin. Smiling to herself, she went over and looked down at the two serene faces. Then she remembered her mother's injunction: never look at anyone while they are asleep. She pulled the covers up over the girls' shoulders, fetched another blanket from the divan and spread it gently over them, then tiptoed out into the passage.

But there, instead of going back to her own room, she felt somehow impelled to take another look at the scene of the dinner party. When she switched on the light she was dazzled at first, but her eyes soon adjusted. The table was just as it had been left at the end of the meal. Plates, glasses and dishes stood empty and half-empty where the guests had abandoned them to go and have coffee in the living room. Silva looked at it all, trying to remember where everyone had been sitting. It all seemed very far away. She noticed Arian's almost untouched plate, and sighed. She didn't feel in the least sleepy now, but couldn't concentrate properly, either. Reviewing the plates and glasses, she recalled scraps of the conversation that had ebbed to and fro over them, interspersed with jesting and laughter. But during part of the discussion – the debate over Albania's relations with China – laughter had been only an outward mask disguising inner anxiety. One of the guests believed that these relations had worsened lately, as they had during the Cultural Revolution some years back, but that the deterioration was only temporary and the dark clouds would soon disappear. Someone else had answered that things looked more serious this time, and the crisis wouldn't be overcome so easily. There was no way we Albanians could approve of the rapprochement between America and China, so a certain amount of tension was only to be expected. Silva scanned the table as if imagining the trajectory of these exchanges. The opinions they expressed had been over-simplified and not very interesting, and two or three times Silva had caught Arian smiling rather condescendingly. It was the smile of someone who is in the know, and prefers not to join in the conversation of those who are not.

The crisis was only to be expected, repeated the husband of one of her sisters-in-law. But someone else reminded him that relations with China, unlike those with the Soviet Union, which were over for good and all, were subject to ups and downs: this last hitch was merely one of a series. Don't you remember? – we went through it all before, when the National Theatre proposed to put on Chekhov's *The Seagull* in the middle of the Cultural Revolution!

Silva remembered it very well. It was a winter afternoon: it looked as if it was going to snow. All Tirana was in a high state of excitement; no one could talk about anything except the play. People were feverishly getting ready to go to the theatre; telephones kept ringing. Was the opening really going to take place this evening? – there was talk of cancellation . . . Then the theatre itself, and more discussions with friends in the cloakrooms. It was rumoured that the Chinese had tried to have the production suspended (Chekhov, like Shakespeare, was banned in China), and some officials at the Ministry of Education and Culture were on their side. Nevertheless, to the satisfaction of everyone there, the performance did take place . . .

But ever since then, Sonia herself had pointed out last night, it had been evident that our ideas were diverging from those of the Chinese. If I had my way, Gjergj's youngest sister had put in, we'd break with them altogether – I can't stand the sight of them! It's not as simple as that, answered one of the men; and what they look like has got nothing to do with it . . . I agree, said another: I think it's shocking the way so many people have started looking down on them. There's no denying they're a great people with a marvellous culture . . . Yes, indeed! was the reply, but, say what you like, China will always be an enigma. Zhou Enlai once said that if you want to understand Chinese politics you should go and see the Peking Theatre . . . But that's full of incomprehensible symbols, monkeys and snakes and dragons . . . !

Silva started to clear the table, as if she were trying to get rid of the remains of the argument too. She soon disposed of part of the débris, but when she came to Arian's plate she felt another qualm at the sight of his helping of roast meat, with scarcely a mouthful missing. "Oh, I do hope he manages to get out of this scrape all right!" she thought.

The familiar sound of water running into the kitchen sink cheered her up a bit. She had started automatically on the washing up. Then it struck her this was an idiotic thing to do at half-past four in the morning, and she left it.

By now she was feeling cold again. She buttoned up her cardigan. The kitchen windows too were covered with frost. It must be well below zero, she thought. Then she suddenly remembered the lemon tree that had been delivered the previous afternoon, and what the man from the nursery had said: If there's a frost you must cover it up, otherwise it can shrivel up in a single night. It seemed crazy to think of going out on the balcony in this temperature, yet as she switched the hall light off and made to enter her bedroom, she paused. After all, why not? It wouldn't take long to go and cover up a little plant. She went on into the bedroom, opened the cupboard over the wardrobe, and felt around for a big cellophane bag she'd stowed away there at the end of the summer. Here we are, she exclaimed, tugging at it. Then she remembered that it was full of clothes, the kind of thing you probably won't ever wear again but can't bring yourself to throw away. With some annoyance she started to pull the things out of the bag. There were frocks and blouses that Brikena had grown out of; a loose jersey dress that

Silva herself had worn when she was pregnant; bits of lace; skeins of embroidery thread; different-coloured balls of wool; scraps of knitted sweaters started and left unfinished; and various half-forgotten frills and flounces made of materials pleasant to the touch and triggering off vague memories.

Silva tipped them all out on to the carpet, meaning to put them away later in the day, then, throwing a coat round her shoulders, went out through the French window on to the balcony.

It really was very cold, and the pale yellow light of the moon, together with the utter silence, made it seem colder still. The wan brightness seemed to have cast a numbing spell on the leaves of the lemon tree, as on everything else. Looking up, Silva saw a terrifyingly smooth sky which seemed to belong to another universe. At the thought that at this very moment Gjergj might be winging his way across that treacherously featureless expanse, a shiver ran down her spine.

The lemon tree would certainly have died in the night if I hadn't remembered to cover it up, she thought. She arranged the cellophane bag carefully over the little bunch of leaves, glad to find that it came down not only over the tree itself but also over part of the tub. Through the film of plastic the lemon tree looked nebulous, like something seen in a dream.

As Silva was about to go inside, something held her back: the waxen mask of the moon. She almost had to tear herself away from the pull of it.

Back in her bed, which still retained some warmth from her body, she found she was still trembling, not so much from the cold as because of that terrible emptiness. She couldn't get back to sleep. Snatches of the evening's conversation, the arguments about Albania's relations with China, and thoughts about her brother's situation kept whirling about in her mind in ever-increasing confusion. If you want to understand anything about China, go and see the Peking Opera . . . But it's full of fearful symbols, monkeys and snakes and dragons . . . Silva tossed and turned. Monkeys and snakes, she murmured, trying to remember something. Oh yes – it was something she'd been told years ago by Besnik Struga. He'd said how, just as snakes appear to people in dreams as a sign of misfortune, so he had seen some in the Butrin marshes just before the break with the Soviet Union. "As you know," he'd said to her, "I'm not and never have been superstitious, but afterwards, when things went wrong between us and the Soviet Union, I couldn't get those snakes out of my mind. And oh, I almost forgot – do you know what happened to me a few months after the break?"

Then Besnik had told Silva how he'd been out in the street on the night of the first reception held after the rupture.

"Everyone was waiting to see a firework display, with rockets that had just arrived from China: they'd been the main topic of conversation for days. The whole sky suddenly erupted, and people looked up in delight and astonishment. For these were no ordinary fireworks – they were foreign, and as they fell they let out an eerie whistle that seemed to say, What crazy sort of a world is that down there? And as if that wasn't enough, another kind of rocket followed, producing shapes like mythical Chinese serpents: first they all hung in a kind of curtain or fringe, then they disappeared one by one, leaving the sky black as pitch. People started shouting, 'Snakes! Snakes!' and my own heart began to thump. 'What, more serpents?' I thought. 'Another evil omen?' Because, don't forget, Silva, this was the first public celebration after the crisis . . ."

Silva, huddled under the blankets, remembered all these incidents, and for the umpteenth time asked herself why Gjergj's journey had had to take place just now. In her mind's eye she saw again the black briefcase containing the secret documents he had to deliver – documents that were keeping the two of them poles apart tonight. What was that briefcase Gjergj was carrying across the sky without even knowing what was inside? And this journey . . . She remembered the sudden notification, the summons to see the minister, the rapid issuing of the necessary visa. The mere thought that her husband had been sent on a special mission was unnerving. He shouldn't have gone, she told herself. And as she felt herself dropping off, her mind was filled again by visions more vivid than ever of Besnik Struga's rockets, her brother's imminent expulsion from the Party, and Gjergj's mysterious briefcase. She woke up again several more times, and always those images seemed linked together by threads invisible in the darkness of the room. But soon the first gleams of an autumn dawn began to creep in through the window.

2

THE SKY WAS UNIMAGINABLY EMPTY that late October night. A few hundred planes landing at or taking off from airports, some millions of birds, three forlorn meteorites falling unnoticed into the immensity of the ocean, a few spy satellites orbiting at a respectful distance from one another – all these put together were as nothing compared with the infinite space of the sky. It was void and desolate. No doubt if all the birds had been rolled into one they'd have weighed more than the planes and taken up more room, but even if every plane, meteorite and satellite were added to those birds, the result still wouldn't have filled even a tiny corner of the firmament. It was to all intents and purposes empty. No comet's tail, seen by men as an omen of misfortune, blazed across it this autumn night. And even if it had, the history of the sky, rich as it was not only with the lives of birds, planes, satellites and comets but also with the thunder and lightning of all the ages, would still have been a poor one compared with the history of the earth.

Against such immense vacuity the signals sent out by a certain spy satellite seemed desolate indeed. It was relaying in their most recent order, as drawn up for some official ceremony, the names of the members of the Politbureau of the Chinese Communist Party: Mao Zedong, Zhou Enlai, Wang Hongwen, Ye Jianying, Deng Xiaoping, Zhang Chunqiao, Wei Guoqing, Liu Bocheng, Jiang Qing, Xu Shiyou, Hua Guofeng, Ji Dengkui, Gu Mu, Wang Dongxing, Chan Yonggui, Chen Xilian, Li Xiannian, Li Desheng, Yao Wenyuan, Wu Guixian, Su Zhenhua, Ni Zhifu, Saifudin and Song Qingling. In comparison with the size of the sky through which they were travelling, these names, despite their attempts to ape the names of gods, were just a wretched handful of dust, and those on the complete list of senior officials which wafted with them through space were no better. Nevertheless, hundreds of people in scores of ultra-secret offices studied the list as carefully as the world used to

22

scan fiery comets, double stars and other celestial signs, trying to penetrate their mystery. As the experts pored over the handful of ideograms which had just dropped out of the chilly darkness, they compared them with the previous list, seeking portents concerning the future of a large part of the human race, if not the whole of it.

Meanwhile the Earth and all the bodies gravitating around it rolled on regardless. Two or three meteorites plunged, as if trying to escape pursuit, into a remote stretch of sea, leaving no trace behind. In different parts of the sky, hundreds of lightning flashes discharged their electricity. Birds dropped down exhausted. And through it all sped a letter addressed by a small country to a large one.

The letter was in the briefcase belonging to Gjergj Dibra, a diplomatic envoy travelling on the night plane from Paris to Peking. For some time now he had been flying over the Arabian desert. If it had been so dark that you couldn't see anything, Gjergj would have found the resulting sense of isolation quite bearable. But it was a clear night, and the moon revealed not only the empty sky stretching out beneath the plane but also the equally arid expanse of barren sands below.

Every so often Gjergj would turn away from the window, resisting the lure of all that emptiness, but after a few moments he couldn't help turning back again. Thousands of feet below, the moon seemed to be wandering over the surface of the desert like a lifeless eye – a coldly mocking eye holding the image of the sky prisoner, just as the retina of a dead man is said to retain the image of his murderer. And indeed, thought Gjergj, the sky had killed this part of the earth, turning it into a wilderness.

He drew sharply away from the window, and for want of anything better to do asked the stewardess to bring him a coffee. It was his fourth, but what did it matter? He had no intention of trying to sleep.

When he'd finished his coffee he had to make an effort to prevent himself from turning back to the window again. But even without actually looking down at it, he could feel the pull of the desert. For the umpteenth time he tried to distract himself by imagining himself back in his apartment, among the guests at the little party his wife was giving for their daughter's birthday. He looked at his watch.

They must have left the table by now, he thought. But he could still conjure up the various phases of the dinner itself: the comings and goings from room to room of Silva and Brikena, the vase of flowers on the table, the cheerful bustle of the guests' arrival, the clinking of glasses. They'd certainly have thought about him. He tried to imagine what they'd said, but that was difficult – it was easier to imagine their smiles and laughter. He reviewed the probable list of guests: his sisters, their husbands, the children, Silva's brother, his own mother, his niece Veriana, and either Besnik Struga or Skënder Bermema. He spent some time wondering which of the two had been there. It didn't seem possible that either should be absent. Perhaps they'd both come, he thought – and before he could stop himself he found he was looking out of the window again. The empty darkness gaped beneath him, wanly lit by the moon, like an X-ray photograph. Yes, Besnik and Skënder probably both went to the party, he thought dully. All human passions seemed small and trivial compared with that great void.

He sat for a while with his eyes closed. Every so often his hand brushed against the metal lock of his briefcase, reinforced by the red seal of the foreign ministry. Throughout this whole dreary journey he hadn't let the briefcase out of his sight for a second. He knew it contained an official document of the utmost importance, though he hadn't the faintest idea what it was about.

Drowsy though he was, he made another attempt at summoning up his daughter's birthday party in his mind's eye, but something prevented him from actually entering the flat. Every time he tried, he found himself lingering wistfully outside the door, like a stranger. At the thought of suddenly appearing in the doorway with all those people eating and drinking and talking; of all the familiar gestures he'd have to go through to ring the bell, kiss Silva and their daughter, and then greet the guests, his fingers grew numb and powerless. He realized this was because he was still gripping his briefcase. What is it, Gjergj? their eyes all seemed to be asking. What have you got in that briefcase?

He shook his head and opened his eyes. He must have dozed off, and his hand, clutching on to the handle, had gone to sleep too. He sat on for a while without moving, trying not to look out at the void, then briefly nodded off again, though more lightly now than before. The same sequence of images as before, but swifter this time, led him back to his daughter's birthday party.

Once again the briefcase prevented him from going in and mixing with the guests. I shouldn't have kept it on my lap, he thought – then remembered the iron rule decreeing that he must always have it with him wherever he went. It had been decreed that there was nowhere else in the whole world for the briefcase to be except with him.

Opening his eyes again, he saw a kind of break in the sky, ahead of the plane and on the same level, but far away in the distance, perhaps over central Asia. The dawn.

He asked the stewardess where they were, and she told him they were already over China. The sun was rising. Below them, hidden by a layer of mist, lay the largest and most ancient country in the world. Gjergj gazed out of the window. The sun, a ruddy patch strangely resembling the wax seal on his briefcase, seemed to be struggling over the horizon. Two or three times he thought he glimpsed the earth, but he couldn't be sure. The engines of the plane throbbed as if with great effort. Still staring out of the window, Gjergj asked himself how was one supposed to deliver a letter to a country like this? Surprised by his own question, he felt like some mythical envoy of antiquity, charged with delivering a message to an empire that was deaf. He went on trying to catch a glimpse of the earth, but in vain: he almost doubted if it still existed.

More than a thousand metres below the belly of the plane lay the land of China, with its population of nearly a billion. Other billions lay beneath the land itself, most of them changed long ago into handfuls of mud. But that autumn morning, out of the billions of Chinese still alive, one had chosen for his own peculiar reasons to be under the earth already, hidden away in a cave. This one was Mao Zedong, Chairman of the People's Republic of China.

He had gone back to his underground isolation some days before. He knew very well that every time he did so the people always found out about it eventually, and that they wouldn't rest until they found out why he was there. His enemies said it was because he was in a blue funk, as he had been when he hid here during the Cultural Revolution. That was understandable enough at the time, others argued, but why was he down there again, now that things had settled down? Perhaps in order to get used to the idea of death, suggested a third group: hadn't he sensed its approach a long time ago? Others shrugged their shoulders: that might be the correct explanation, but then again there might be some other reason known only to Chairman Mao himself . . .

One thing was certain: for some time he had resumed this old habit: perhaps he himself didn't quite know why. He scoured reports on the rumours circulating about it so eagerly you might have thought he'd forgotten why he'd gone down there, and fully expected to read the explanation in the reports. In fact, he'd come to believe that a head of state's most useful actions were those which remained incomprehensible not only to others but also to himself. They lent themselves to such a vast range of different explanations. There were always people ready to suggest a meaning for some enigmatic piece of behaviour, while others sprang forward to contradict them and offer another interpretation. Then came another group who thought they were the ones who knew best. And so on and so forth *ad infinitum*. Meanwhile the action in question was kept alive precisely because it was veiled in obscurity, while hundreds of others, clearer, more logical and more useful, were consigned to oblivion.

The reports informed Mao that many of the rumours put forward religious or mythological reasons for his retreat. One view was that as he already knew all that was said about him on earth, he wanted to find out what was whispered about him underground, where his supporters were no longer in the majority. On the whole he preferred the mythological theories to those that stuck to fact. He liked to think of himself sleeping under the earth for a while and then, like some ancient god, reawakening with the lush new grass of spring.

To tell the truth, the half-death he seemed to experience down in that cave struck him as the state that suited him best. The strange days he spent there, divided between existence and non-existence, enjoying the advantages of the one and avoiding the traps of the other, partook of both heaven and hell. His thoughts became clear and strove to pierce to the uttermost depths of consciousness. He was surrounded by nothing but mud and stones; the only things present were the earth and himself – the leader of the biggest country in the world in direct contact with the terrestrial globe, without any intermediaries, theories, books or officials between them. Where else could the expression "Middle Kingdom" be better understood? As time went by, mornings and evenings merged into

26

one, whole days were reduced to a single afternoon, and a night might vanish altogether, or else consist only of midnight itself, like a dish containing only the choicest parts of the most delicious fruits. He slept and woke, drowsed and dropped off again. There were times when he felt as if he were dead; others when he felt as if he'd been resurrected, drugged, or made into a saint or a god.

He had given orders that he was not to be disturbed on any account, but now through his half-sleep he became aware of a kind of whispering coming from the entrance to the cave. The guards must want to tell him something. What could have happened? he wondered. War? An earthquake? The murmur came nearer. It must be something important for anyone to dare to come and spoil his peace and quiet.

"What is it?" he asked, without opening his eyes.

He heard them mumbling something about a letter. Didn't they know he didn't receive mail down there in his cave? But they went on muttering, and he eventually distinguished the name of Jiang Qing. So the message was from her.

"Leave the letter with me, then," he said. Or rather thought he said. In fact he'd formed the words only in his head.

A letter from out there, thought he, as if it were a missive from another world. What are they up to? Aren't they tired of it all yet?

There in the depths of the earth, amid the rocks of the cave, the letter seemed like some alien object, charged with hostility. If it hadn't been from his wife he'd never have opened it: as it was, it was some time before he made up his mind. The message was brief, informing him of the latest events in the capital and of Zhou Enlai's illness, and ending up with the information that the president of Albania had written to him . . .

Featherbrain, he thought to himself, averting his eyes from his wife's writing. Who ever heard of anyone sending letters underground?

> Letters go to every corner of the Universe,
> But nobody ever saw one go underground . . .

He wasn't sure if he'd read these lines somewhere or if he'd just made them up.

"How often have I told you the thing I hate most when I'm down here is getting letters! And now, not content with writing yourself, you have to tell me about another letter from someone else! . . . The world must be going mad up there!"

The rustle of the paper in his hand made him look at it again.

So the president of Albania had written to him, had he? An official letter, it seemed, but without any of the usual pleasantries. On the contrary, the whole thing was downright disagreeable. Outrageous, even.

The concluding phrases were the most caustic. Albania objected to the U.S. president's forthcoming visit to China, and was more or less openly asking for it to be cancelled.

Mao Zedong fumed. Why hadn't the stupid woman told him that to begin with? The anger which in other circumstances would have filled him by now seemed merely to hover around him like some chilly breath, not knowing how to gain admittance. The earth and the rocky cave had done their work.

A letter from Albania, eh? It must have taken some time to get here. H'mm . . . He realized it would take him at least thirty-six hours to get really angry. That would give him time to think about it. So – he said to himself yet again, trying to get his thoughts in order – this is a letter from Albania. He must consider things as simply as possible. Not that he could have done otherwise down here, even if he'd wanted to. Sometimes he would speak his thoughts aloud as if to explain them to the earth and the rocks. That was one of the reasons he liked coming here: being able to expound things in the most elementary fashion to the cave, making it understand the affairs of the world . . . So this letter came from a long way away. From Albania. A little country on a contemptible continent called Europe, inhabited for the most part by white men who dislike us as much as we dislike them. The one exception is Albania, our ally. Our only ally on that evil continent. And now Albania, a mere one-thousandth of the size of China, has the cheek to write me a letter. Not an ordinary letter – a positively belligerent one, in which that tiny country not merely refuses to obey but actually tries to impose its will on me. Albania is asking for punishment, and I shan't fail to oblige.

Mao Zedong was getting a headache. All this thinking, after several days of virtual unconsciousness, seemed to have exhausted him. I ought to have read the letter more slowly, he said to himself. He tried to be detached, to transport himself mentally to the plateau of Tibet, which seemed to him all the more uninhabited because he himself had never been there. "You really ought to pay a visit to the Roof of the World," his wife had suggested several times. "It would be really appropriate." He had joked about it and accused her of vanity, but deep down inside he did consider making such a visit. So much so that he'd spent some time reading the works of the Tibetan hermit Milarepa. And now Milarepa's poems, full of the terror inspired by the Himalayas, began to come back to him, together with the names of the caves the hermit lived in. He even remembered some of the phrases he'd learned in preparation for the journey: *shos-dbying*, for example, the Tibetan name for that primal state, beyond being and non-being, which had always fascinated him; *dje-be*, the ten goods, and *mi-dge-beu*, the ten evils, the first of which he'd later made use of in his instructions to Communist youth, while the second were included in army regulations.

Shi-gnas, he said aloud. But he realized that the more he tried to follow the hermit's teachings and strive for serenity, the more the letter preyed on his mind. *Shi-gnas*, he said again, and then repeated the same thing in Sanskrit: *samatha*. But still to no effect. It was the same as with sleeping pills: either they put you out like a light or else they kept you awake indefinitely.

It was all of no use: in the end he just gave in and lost his temper. The letter seemed more and more monstrous. Relations with Albania had been deteriorating for years through that country's own fault, but hitherto he had turned a blind eye. His colleagues had grown increasingly irritated: how long, they said, are we going to put up with their whims and fancies? But Mao had been patient, ignoring Albania's coldness during the Cultural Revolution, their attitude about Shakespeare, and lots of other nonsense. When the Sino-Soviet frontier crisis blew up, his colleagues had come to see him, blue in the face with rage at the Albanians' intolerable attitude: instead of coming out directly and unequivocally in support of us, their allies, they'd actually said there were faults on both sides, and that China's territorial claims smacked of nationalism. That crowned all! They were setting themselves up as knights errant, nobly committed to their principles, like characters out of the *Chanson de Roland*! Ugh, what cheek! "*Now* do you see?" they had demanded. But again Mao had turned a blind eye. "Just wait," he'd said. "I'm saving it all up. One of these days they'll get into a row with Yugoslavia over . . . what's it's name? . . . Kosovo, and then we'll pay them out."

29

He'd known Albania would go on being restive – but that it would actually get to the point of giving him orders . . . ! It was inconceivable. Yet it had happened, unless his wife had gone out of her mind and what she'd written was just a figment of her imagination. But that was highly unlikely. There was little doubt that the letter had come: the thing had happened, and if the Chinese people got to know of it he'd be reduced to grovelling humiliation. Mao realized he was getting angry more quickly than he'd expected. I'll show them! he thought. I'll teach Albania a lesson it'll tremble to remember for a thousand years! I'll play with it like a cat with a mouse!

He hadn't yet decided exactly how. For the moment only one word whirled around in his head: economy. He dimly felt that was the beginning and end of everything, but the vagueness only increased his vexation. As a matter of fact he had given orders during previous periods of dissension for policy to be angled on economic considerations, but the idiotic officials whose business it was had evidently misunderstood his instructions. Their way of doing things was obvious, their tricks stuck out a mile. They thought there was only one way of going about it: by slowing down ships carrying machinery and cutting off aid. How often had they come to him and said: "We oughtn't to deliver that steel works – let's leave them to stew in their own juice!" But he would always say: "Really? So they can get what they want from Sweden instead, and thumb their noses at us? . . . No, we'll send them the goods, but it'll be the sort of stuff that'll make them curse the day they took delivery of it!"

When he explained what he meant they all had a good laugh. That steel works would be more like a blacksmith's forge! Then he explained that such measures needed to be accompanied by others in different sectors. The idea was to drive the Albanians crazy little by little. It was in such terms, many years ago, that Mao had defined the policy to be adopted towards Albania. He had gone into it in the minutest detail. But obviously the idiots in charge of carrying it out hadn't understood a word. And now, instead of China having atrophied Albania's whole brain-centre, Albania was trying to tell China what to do. How horrible! he cried. Now he really did feel angry. Memories about the relations between the two countries were beginning to come back to him; conversations with his colleagues; plans. Not long ago he, Jiang Qing and Lin Biao had studied a letter from a middle-ranking Chinese official who had spent some time in Albania. His account was full of bitterness and repining. Their standard of living was much higher than ours, he said. The people lived in apartments; the shops sold lipstick, armchairs, and all kinds of other degenerate objects; young women and girls frequented cafés and drank whatever they liked; there were no curtains at the windows; the women reeked of perfume; you could buy novels, and as much bread as you liked. The question was bound to suggest itself: why should Albania still be receiving aid from poor old China? To help it wallow even deeper in luxury and extravagance? Cut off all aid, dear Chairman Mao, said the official, ending his letter, or else find some other way of putting an end to this scandal.

Samatha, he muttered to his unknown correspondent: calm down. But he didn't feel at all calm himself. The first letter from the irate official, which he hadn't answered, had been followed by a second that painted an even more sombre picture. Punish me if I've done wrong, wrote the official. Denounce me as an agent provocateur, an agitator, drag me through the mud, gouge my eyes out – but reply! He must have realized his first letter had been completely ignored: Chinese aid to Albania, far from being reduced, had actually increased. In his second letter he tried to express himself more calmly, attempting a description of the Albanian national psychology. It was a tiny little country, he wrote, and there was nothing more horrible than seeing a place like that in the grip of a mania for expansion. According to him the Albanians, in the past, unable to wrest a single inch of territory from their neighbours, who were just as tough as they were, had hit on a novel way of extending their influence: by flirting with the countries that occupied them, offering their services as allies. After they'd been beaten by the Turks, or rather when they finally admitted defeat, they offered their help to the victorious Ottoman Empire, acting just as their Illyrian ancestors had done towards Rome. (These forebears too were not only rough and excitable but also feeble-minded, and had taken about a hundred and fifty years to accept that they'd been conquered by the Romans.)

These potty little countries! thought Mao. He'd often wondered how he'd have seen things, how he'd have judged events, even what his reaction would have been to the depression that sometimes swept over him, if China had been smaller, or if it had been an archipelago, like Japan. Once, in Tchangsha, he'd been afflicted by a really deathly fit of dejection, a boredom so monstrous it would have overflowed the boundaries not only of any little European country but of half the whole continent! Yes, he sighed, he really was made to measure for China, just as China was specially created for him!

He remembered a dream in which Mongolia had been transformed into a lake. His officials had all run hither and thither in such agitation, telephoning and transmitting his latest decisions, that he'd grown impatient: what are you getting so worked up about? he'd asked. They'd been abashed. It's not easy, you know, Chairman Mao: there are all sorts of problems, and all the files and archives need to be altered. For example, that business of Lin Biao's plane going up in smoke in the Mongolian desert . . . Oh yes, he'd said – I remember. But all you have to do is change "bursting into flames" to "sinking into the waves" – no need to make such a fuss! But it isn't as easy as that, the others insisted. It's common knowledge that Lin Biao was ill and what's more had a horror of water. And what were they supposed to do about the burned wreckage of the plane and the bullet-marks on its fuselage? That'll do! he'd snapped. It's up to you to take care of the details. And then he'd turned his back on them.

His thoughts returned to the letter from the official. For some obscure reason, the man had said, the Turks accepted the Albanians' services, and this resulted in one of the strangest phenomena in the whole history of the Ottoman Empire: in 1656 an Albanian was made prime minister, and five of his compatriots succeeded one another in the post. And you can easily imagine the long string of ministers and generals and admirals that went with them. They'd converted to Islam, blithely exchanging Christianity for influential posts without the slightest trace of remorse. Their possessions extended from Hungary to the Sea of Azov; they controlled provinces and cities, armies, governments, whole nations. Some of them became so powerful they had the impertinence to set themselves up as rivals to the Sultan, to disobey him and sabotage his foreign policy; some of them even founded dynasties of their own, in Egypt for example.

What chaos! thought Mao, though not without a tinge of envy. He made a face every time he heard the word mentioned. "Chaos in Cambodia, in Chile, in Ireland . . ." Pooh, he'd sneer: what sort of chaos could you get in those petty little countries no bigger than the palm of his hand? Genuine chaos could only occur in states of some size, and super-chaos only in China itself.

Shos-dbying . . . He'd always been fascinated by great upheavals. What he liked best in the works of the ancient poets were the descriptions of chaotic political convulsions. Li Po or Du Fu – he couldn't quite remember which – had written passages like that. The Mongol armies sweeping over the country. The imperial armies put to flight. Couriers' steeds roving about without their riders. Wolves and jackals with tufts of human hair between their teeth . . . But the biggest upheaval ever had been the one produced by him: the first state of chaos in which the opposing sides both acclaimed the same name. His. They vied with one another in adoration of him at the same time as they set about one another, slaughtering and reducing one another to ashes for him, while he stayed aloof down in his cave, listening to the sound of the tumult above. All he had to do now was get them used to the idea of his death . . .

Shos-dbying . . . Oh yes, the famous letter! God, what a screed! Was he remembering it in slow motion or was it really as long as that? The Albanians could easily have broken away from the Ottoman Empire, wrote the official, but after a certain point they themselves didn't want to any more: they didn't want to lose the enormous state which they'd partly transformed into their own. The ruled were acting as rulers: they'd acquired a taste for power, a power wielded not over the mere square inch of territory that was their own country but over great expanses of Europe and Asia. Needless to say, all this, together with their pride in their Illyrian origins, produced an arrogance as ill-founded as it was extreme.

Pooh! said Mao. The end of the letter was what he remembered most clearly. Early in the twentieth century the Albanians actually had won their independence, though the country they found themselves confined to seemed as small as a baby's cradle. The dream was over. So this horde of tattered and deluded Don Quixotes set out in search of another occupying power, or at least of some new and powerful ally they might lead up the garden path, pretending to submit only in order to exploit him more easily. And that was how these dreamers, whose pride the Germans had exacerbated by proclaiming them a master race, had, after ogling the countries in their immediate vicinity and coming to grief first over the Yugoslavs and then over the Soviets, turned their attention to us, to China.

And it must be admitted their cunning plot is meeting with great success. The whole world regards Albania as a satellite of China, and perhaps even we ourselves feel flattered to hear such a thing said about a country in Europe. Meanwhile the Albanians have every reason to laugh up their sleeves at us. Our ships queue up in their ports to unload their cargoes. Our standard of living is low in comparison with theirs. We go on calling Albania a satellite and its people the lackeys of China, but since when did lackeys live better than their masters? Wasn't it all just a tragic farce?

Mao Zedong, his eyes half closed, remembered almost word for word not only the end of the letter but also the note that Zhou Enlai had written underneath: "What he says about relations between Albania and the Ottoman Empire is factually true, but that's only one side of the case – the side concerning their pride. However his interpretation of the facts in general is quite naive and misleading. The analogy between us and the Soviet Union doesn't hold water. As for the standard of living in Albania, I don't believe it's so enviable as our provincial correspondent supposes. Things are much more complicated than that. Still, the letter does contain some small points worthy of notice."

"'Some small points'!" exclaimed Mao. Zhou was brilliantly clever, but sometimes he failed to spot certain aspects of a situation. That letter was nothing short of prophetic! Not content with having exploited China as if it were their own back yard, the Albanians were now openly trying to lay down the law. Incredible as it might seem, the Albanian president's letter had actually been dispatched. Unless Jiang Qing had gone crazy and made the whole thing up. According to her, the Albanian president not only commented on the American president's visit – he went so far as to ask for it to be cancelled! How abominable! thought Mao to himself. The Albanian leader telling him what to do! The leader of Russia himself had never dared try that on. Just wait, fumed Mao. I'll soon show you who's boss!

He tried to laugh through his wrath, but it was too soon for that. You'll see what the old man's still capable of ! he muttered stoutly. Don't imagine I didn't foresee this when I made you a present of all those factories and industrial complexes. Comrades were always coming to me and complaining, The things we're sending those Albanians, whereas they . . . ! Just wait and have patience, I told them. I knew they were very annoyed; perhaps the letters purporting to come from the official were really written by my assistants, or by Lin Biao, or even by Jiang Qing – they've always been impatient, that lot. I, on the other hand, have always bided my time, in accordance with the old Chinese proverb, "Don't worry: wait by the bank of the river, and it will bring you the head of your enemy." And now the time has come. We couldn't really teach the Albanians a lesson a few years ago, before they'd started laying the foundations of their chemical factories, their steel complex and their big hydro-electric plants. No – now's the time to twist their arm, when they're in the middle of building them. But the comrades couldn't wait: every time we sent Albania a new turbine or the equipment for a new factory they sweated blood, their eyes flashed. "What are we going to ask for in return?" they kept demanding. "Wait till they really get started building and then we'll see," I told them. This exasperated them, though of course they didn't show it. Perhaps they muttered among themselves that the old man was getting past it, or even that I was frittering away our country's heritage. While I was just thinking: Wait a bit longer . . .

Finally the laughter broke through. Mao propped himself with one hand against the wall of the cave and nodded. The moment has come, he thought. The building work is in progress, and all the sites are as vulnerable as open wounds. A half-finished steel complex or an abandoned hydro-electric dam are no better than ruins. When everything's left high and dry, that's the time to start thinking about dictating terms. Now I can torment them just as I like. For every factory I shall demand a sacrificial victim. For every chimney, for every turbine, for the smallest bit of funding. You're going to have to pay back something in return for everything you've had, I'll say. You're going to have to strip away your insufferable pride, your history, your art, your intelligentsia . . . I know you quail at the thought of an impoverished intelligentsia, of writers abolished by a stroke of the pen. Perhaps you don't feel you can wipe out your literature as we have wiped out ours? Perhaps you shrink from sending pen-pushers to prison, or out into the rice-fields, or forcing them to clean the latrines? I'm such a kind old gentleman I'll show you how to manage by a completely different method, apparently diametrically opposite from ours. Have a vast renaissance! Create hundreds of novelists a year, and thousands of poets, by calling any report containing a bit of dialogue a novel and any rhymed petition a poem, and you'll see that after a few years your literature will have vanished without trace. No one will accuse you of doing anything wrong. On the contrary, you'll always find admirers ready to acclaim you for nurturing all those writers. What an unprecedented flowering! . . . And you must do the same with all the rest: give and it shall be given unto you. For every turbine, every credit, give something: for every electronic brain, give part of your own brain. But wait – that's nothing compared with what I'll ask you for next. For you'll have to give your Party too! I know how unacceptable that may sound to you; how barbarous and sinister. I realize it's your dearest, most inviolable and undisputed possession, and that you've based all your security, your present and your future upon it. I know all that. But wait: I may be an old man, but I'm not so stupid as to ask you to violate the inviolable or question the unquestionable. No, not at all. Far be it from me to do such a thing! Besides, what good would it do me? Without your Party your whole country would go down the drain and I'd lose you for ever. You'd move away, you'd drift off. So I wouldn't dream of entertaining such an idea. We must act with the Party, always with the Party, my pets -- but with a Party that's slightly more . . . what shall I say? . . . more open! Wait – hear me out! It's not as bad as it may sound. If I'm not mistaken, you've got a flag with a two-headed eagle on it, haven't you? So why should the idea of a Party with two lines strike you as so terrible? It's unacceptable and barbarous, you say? Very well, let's say no more about it – we'll think of something else. We're not short of symbols, thank God.

He'd discussed it with Zhou Enlai. He himself had made a few suggestions, and Zhou had met one of their ministers, a general, and was preparing to get in touch with various important elements in the Albanian economy. Zhou had come round to his own way of thinking: you couldn't do anything in Albania without the Party. In fact, you had to start with it. And if you managed to mould it, to manipulate it a bit, everything else would follow. Things would take a new course, the ramparts of the citadel, as they liked to call their country, would be no more than camouflage, and their pride would turn into its opposite, their disobedience into docility. And from then on out they would never again dream of writing a letter to oppose an invitation to an American president.

For a few seconds Mao lost the thread of his thoughts, but then he managed to find it again. All right, keep your Party then, he said aloud, but on one condition: make a few alterations. I'm not asking anything very difficult – just a bit of a change, a little mutation, as the scientists say. You refuse? In that case the factories will stop going up, the blast furnaces will go out, the dams will crumble, everything will shrivel up into a skeleton. Usually, when a country is reduced to rubble, it's because of a war, but in your case it will be the débris of peace, than which nothing is more horrible: bodies unburied, souls on the scrap-heap, epidemics, death itself . . . And Tartar hordes, wolves and jackals with scraps of fur and women's finery in their jaws . . .

Mao Zedong let himself burst out laughing at last, and went on stroking the wall of the cave as if he was trying to wheedle it. The time was now ripe for blackmail. Our people on the spot could exploit the situation. According to reliable sources, China had open or covert supporters inside the Albanian government, on the Central Committee even. The "sleepers" could finally emerge from their slumbers. The real game was about to begin. Now you're going to pay all your outstanding debts. I'm going to tighten the screw – slowly, week after week, month after month, season after season. Sometimes I'll pretend to slacken off for a bit, so that it'll hurt all the more when I tighten up again. And so it will go on until you're at your last gasp, and you yourselves offer me more than I've ever asked of you. Ha ha!

Unhurriedly, as if savouring a good wine which one keeps in one's mouth as long as possible to enjoy the bouquet, Mao imagined the future Sinization of Albania. First the abolition of the intelligentsia and the downgrading of education, then the erosion of history, the consigning of heroes to oblivion, and the emergence of the first new men, the Albanian Lei Fens (what were the first new tractors in comparison?) Rumour had it that they'd already introduced some Chinese elements into the choreography of their ballets. Such portents were still as rare as the first spring flowers, but they would gradually multiply. After the deeds would come the words, and after the words the thoughts. Their reservations about being European would slowly dry up, like water in a citadel under siege. Then one last onslaught and Albania would surrender . . . It was inevitable . . . Asia first set its heart on Albania some seven centuries ago. And having acquired it, kept it for five hundred years. Early in the twentieth century, though, Albania, the cunning lynx, managed to escape. But that was the last time it did so, and now there

37

was nowhere for it to go. Little by little, quietly, without any clash of swords, it would come back to Asia, this time for ever. It would be a magnificent moment in the age-old history of China. The first country in Europe to be "Sinified". And like a patch of leprosy, "Sinification" would gradually spread northward, first to central Europe and then still further. It would be the first victory of Asia over Europe – a victory fraught with consequence. An epoch-making revenge. Therein lay the real significance of Mao's own achievement. Unfortunately very few eyes were capable of perceiving it. But great achievements are never seen from close to: only from a distance of years or even centuries can they be appraised justly. So moan away, you benighted fools, and write your anonymous letters: your sight is still as dim as that of a month-old baby. Whereas I am about to enter my eightieth year!

Once again Mao lost the thread; once again, after some time, he found it again. He pondered about how long the process of "Sinification" would take. Perhaps the first results wouldn't be apparent until he was ninety years old, or a hundred and forty; but that didn't matter. Even if the change wasn't complete until he was a hundred and eighty or three hundred and twenty years old, it still didn't matter. He'd started seeing life and death as indistinguishable long ago. In his opinion there was only a trifling difference between the two: until a certain year he would go on breathing and moving about. Afterwards . . . But this was of no more importance to him than moving to a new house or a new job was in the life of an ordinary individual. He saw his life, or perhaps rather his life-and-death, as one and indivisible. Perhaps that was the main reason why every so often he buried himself underground.

Again his mind wandered, and when he collected his thoughts it was the letter from Albania that came to mind. His anger seemed to be concentrated in his extremities, especially his hands. The one still leaning against the wall plucked at the stone as if to pull it down. Every time he did this he thought how earthquakes were caused. How silly of the Greeks' god Zeus to think he could bring them about from a distance, from up in the clouds. The globe had to be shaken from below, from down among its foundations.

Mao's hand was still on the rock, as if he had no doubt that the earth had begun to tremble and that a cataclysm was about to take place up above.

That's the whole difference between you and me, said he, looking in the direction where he supposed Europe, the ancient Greeks, and the whole of white humanity to be.

3

THOUGH SILVA WALKED as fast as she could, she still arrived at the ministry slightly late for work.

Greeting, as she rushed past, a porter almost invisible behind his window, she hurried on up the stairs, and in the first-floor corridor almost collided with Victor Hila, an old acquaintance she hadn't seen for a long time.

"How are you?" she asked him, still out of breath. "To what do we owe the pleasure?"

He looked at her rather vacantly, and only then did Silva notice how tired and depressed he looked, and how ill-shaven.

"I'm here on business," he muttered with a vague wave of the hand. "Can you tell me where the chief vice-minister's office is?"

"I'll take you there. Come along."

She led the way, glad to be of help. Though she didn't see him very often now Ana was dead, she tried to be nice to him, as to all the friends whom the two sisters had once had in common and who now represented a subtle link with the past.

"Here we are, Victor," she said kindly.

He mumbled his thanks and knocked at the door without even offering to shake hands.

He must be out of sorts or upset about something, she thought as she made her way to her own office. Such behaviour would have offended her, coming from anyone else; but not from him . . .

"Good morning," she said as she opened the door.

"Good morning, Silva," answered her boss.

His addressing her by her first name suggested he hadn't noticed she wasn't on time, but as she hung up her raincoat she apologized anyway.

"I'm afraid I'm a bit late . . ."

Linda, looking over from her desk, treated her to a mischievous wink. She'd done her hair differently, and looked even younger

40

than before. She's only twenty-three, thought Silva as she opened a drawer and took out the files she needed. Why must she try to make herself seem younger still?

No one spoke. It was now, first thing in the morning, that the silence that usually reigned in government offices weighed most heavily on the people that worked there, preventing them from exchanging a few words about what they'd done the night before, repressing their comments on the latest interesting bit of news. The panes in the tall baroque windows seemed to filter out all the interesting whims and fancies of the weather, admitting only such light as was needed to work by. Beneath his sleeked-back hair the boss's smooth expanse of brow hung motionless over his desk. Silva, sitting close to Linda, could feel almost physically how eagerly her friend longed to turn and talk to her.

As the morning wore on, Linda's impatience communicated itself to Silva, and every time the phone rang or someone knocked at the door they both waited with bated breath for their boss to be called away.

But though he answered several phone calls they never heard him say, "Very well – I'll be right along." Then, when they'd almost given up hope, he just got up of his own accord and left the room.

"Thank goodness!" said Linda as soon as he'd gone. "I don't feel a bit like work today."

"I like your hair-do – it suits you!"

Linda's face lit up.

"Really?"

"When I came in just now I thought to myself, 'Why does she want to look even younger than she is?'"

"I'm not as young as all that!"

"You don't know how lucky you are!" Silva exclaimed. "My God, if you're not young, what am I?"

Linda looked at her.

"Well, I wouldn't mind changing places with you," she said.

"What?" exclaimed Silva, feeling herself start to blush for some reason or other.

Linda smiled.

"I said I wouldn't mind changing places."

"You must be joking!"

"No – I mean it."

41

Silva knew her cheeks were still flushed. Why was she being so foolish?

Luckily the door opened, and in came a plump secretary from the protocol department.

"Brr! Isn't it cold today!" said the newcomer. Then, putting her hand on the radiator: "Your heating's working! It's freezing in our room! Where's your boss?"

Linda kept her eyes on the door until it was safely closed behind the intruder, then turned back to Silva again.

"Curiously enough," she said, "I really did mean what I said just now. But it's not all that strange."

"I think we'd better drop the subject," Silva answered, who really had no idea what she was saying.

"Why?" asked Linda, with a mixture of cajolery and regret.

There was another knock, a more peremptory one this time, and without waiting for an answer a head appeared round the door.

"All Party members to meet at ten!" it announced. "Oh, sorry! There aren't any here, of course!"

The door was briskly shut again, and the voice could be heard receding along the corridor, repeating, "Short meeting of Party members at ten . . ."

That's how they'll announce the meeting at which Arian is expelled, thought Silva, and was immediately engulfed in a wave of sorrow. He'd said it was bound to happen soon; he didn't think there was any hope of avoiding it. You know, Silva, he'd told her, expulsion is the mildest possible punishment in a case of this kind. There had been neither regret nor resentment in his voice – that was what had frightened her most. "A case of this kind" – she kept repeating to herself. But what kind of case was it? "What is it really all about?" she'd asked him for the umpteenth time. But his answer had been as reticent as ever.

From the corridor there came the muffled sound of doors opening and shutting. Perhaps it was the official still going round calling the meeting. Silva felt a pang. What if, unknown to her, the meeting dealing with Arian's case had been held already, and she knew nothing about it? No, that was impossible, she thought. Even if Arian himself hadn't let her know, Sonia would have done so. Unless . . .

The door opened and the boss came in, looking even more gloomy than usual. He couldn't help assuming this expression whenever a Party meeting was announced during working hours. He wasn't a Party member himself, and it was common knowledge that this stood in his way. "What do you expect? – I haven't got a red one," he would say to his friends, referring to the Party card, whenever the question of his promotion came up. Caught up in the routine of office life, absorbed in the giving of orders to his subordinates and by his own position as boss, he could usually forget that he wasn't a member of the Party, and thought others forgot it too. But when, as today, someone announced a Party meeting, he felt horribly uncomfortable. His embarrassment lasted all the time the meeting was in progress, for he was afraid of coming face to face with someone who'd exclaim in astonishment – and this had actually happened several times – "Good heavens, why aren't you at the meeting? Oh, sorry – I was forgetting . . . You're not a member, are you?"

These really were his worst moments. He never knew what to do. To avoid being found in his office he would go and wander round the corridors, sometimes managing to disappear altogether. He felt worst of all at open meetings of the Party, when, after the customary pause, the secretary would say, "Would comrades who are not Party members kindly excuse us? We have a few internal matters to discuss." Then, wishing that the ground would open and swallow him up, he would hang his head and slink out with the rest, the picture of dejection and humiliation, as if to say, "You'd have done better not to ask us to come at all." After such scenes he would go on feeling mortified for a couple of days at least.

He was now poking about crossly among the papers strewn over his desk.

"Where's the report from the planning office got to?" he demanded at last.

"You must have put it away somewhere," said Linda affably.

It was obvious he wasn't looking for anything in particular: he was just opening and shutting drawers at random. In desperation he got out a packet of cigarettes and a lighter – for some strange reason he kept them in a drawer – put a cigarette in his mouth but didn't light it, then left the room.

"He looks furious," said Linda.

Then Silva went out, to take some papers to the minister's secretary. All was quiet in the corridor. A phone was ringing unanswered in one of the offices: the person concerned must be at the meeting.

Once again Silva thought fleetingly of the meeting that would seal her brother's fate, but she repressed the idea. But she made up her mind to phone him that day.

Back in her office she found Linda in conversation with Illyrian, from a neighbouring room. They were laughing over something they'd been saying. Why didn't they see more of each other, Silva wondered. They'd make a handsome couple.

"I was telling him about the boss," explained Linda. "And how he's all on edge whenever there's a Party meeting."

"Today's is probably about our relations with China," said Illyrian.

"Really?" said Linda.

"I think so. Because of the visit of the American president. In some ministries the subject's already been raised with members of the Party, and even with executives who aren't members of the Party."

"Our attitude on the subject was made quite clear from the outset," said Silva. "You've only got to look at the papers to see that."

"Absolutely," said Illyrian. "Everywhere else in the world the press and the radio hyped the trip up like mad, while our own papers dismissed it in three or four lines. Our television didn't show a single shot of it."

The sound of doors opening and closing came faintly from the direction of the corridor. A telephone, perhaps the one Silva had heard earlier, shrilled insistently in the distance.

"In other words," observed Linda, "all we've heard about China lately is true."

"Apparently," said Illyrian.

"And it could actually come to a breach?"

As Linda spoke she blinked incredulously.

Illyrian shrugged and turned to Silva as if for her opinion.

"I don't know what to think . . ."

She gazed at the top of her desk.

". . . Perhaps a peaceful severing of relations. Which is quite different from –"

She was interrupted by the entrance of Simon Dersha from the office next door.

"May I use your phone?" he asked. "Ours is out of order."

"Of course," said Silva.

She was just about to turn back and resume her conversation

44

with Illyrian when she realized they couldn't discuss a subject like that in front of the newcomer. Although he worked in the adjoining office he'd always remained a kind of stranger: they never noticed he even existed except on payday, when he sat beside the accountant, subtracting the union dues from everybody's wages. His presence didn't make any difference to them one way or the other, but even so Silva didn't like talking about anything whatever when he was there. So she just sat watching his hand as it dialled its number, and she could have sworn Linda and Illyrian were doing the same.

"Hey, Simon!" said Linda. "You're wearing a new suit! It *does* look good on you!"

"Thanks," said Simon, pressing the receiver to his ear, "but I've had this suit for ages!"

"I haven't seen you wearing it before."

Simon smiled faintly and hung his head. The dark blue of his suit made his face look even more gloomy than usual.

It was the first time Silva had really looked at him. He had always struck her before as narrow-minded and withdrawn, and she was surprised to see on those wan features, drawn after what had probably been a sleepless night, what looked like a flash of joy. Was it love? Silva wondered, almost with disgust at the thought that Simon Dersha could ever have anything to do with such a feeling.

The room had fallen silent except for the distant ringing of the phone at the other end of the line, in some other, empty office. Then Simon finally hung up, thanked them, and left.

"He tried the same thing on in *our* office a quarter of an hour ago," said Illyrian, who had shown no sign of moving.

"He has his own life to live," said Silva.

"Yes – he has a perfect right . . . But what were we talking about? Oh yes – the Chinese. And a peaceful severing of relations with them . . ."

"Not like the rupture with the Soviets!"

"Why? Was that more dramatic?" asked Linda.

"No comparison!"

Illyrian had gone over to the window and was looking outside.

"Come and have a look," he said.

"What is there to see?"

"Chinamen in Skanderbeg Square!"

The other two got up and went over to the window. There were indeed groups of Chinese scattered all over the broad pavement of the square. Some were still arriving, while others were standing near the marble columns of the Palace of Culture or the Skanderbeg monument not far away.

"I've never seen so many Chinese all at once," said Illyrian.

"There are more of them still coming," Linda observed. "Look, over by the main boulevard!"

"Perhaps there's a meeting at their embassy," suggested Silva.

"Yes, that must be it."

They stood for a while, gazing at the scene without speaking.

"The square's absolutely full of them," said Linda. "What a peculiar sight!"

Silva looked uneasy. That sudden mysterious mass of humanity surging slowly around the square somehow filled her with deep misgivings.

"When they see the new Chinese Embassy starting to go up, people think history is repeating itself," said Linda. "It was the same with Moscow – our relations with the Soviets worsened while they were building their new embassy."

"True," agreed Illyrian.

"Just now you were saying this was a peaceful severing of relations, Silva," said Linda. "How was it different before?"

"With the Soviets, you mean? . . . Oh, there was a sort of threat hanging over everything. A sort of anguish. It was another kettle of fish altogether."

"And how was it in the case of Yugoslavia?" said Linda – and immediately could have kicked herself for asking. The break with Yugoslavia had happened a quarter of a century ago, and the question seemed to underline the difference in their ages. She felt herself flush slightly. "But maybe you don't remember?" she added, trying to cover up her blunder.

"Yes, I do," Silva answered. "I remember quite well." An inward smile seemed to light up her face. "I was still in primary school. It was a cold, rainy morning, and we were all standing in line in the playground waiting for the bell to ring. Then the headmaster came to the door and said, 'Children, I have an announcement to make. Tito has betrayed us!'"

"It was the same when we broke with the Soviets," said Illyrian. "When that happened I was still at school too." Then, turning to Linda: "But I don't suppose you can remember either occasion?"

46

"No," she said, sounding rather puzzled. "All I can remember is something about Krushchev . . ."

"You must still have been in kindergarten then," said Silva with an attempt at a smile.

Linda admitted it, flushing guiltily.

"I suppose you two think I'm still just a kid," she said. "I remember us taking down the portrait of Krushchev from the classroom wall. One of the other children wanted to trample on it, but the teacher said there was no need to exaggerate."

"Do you really remember, or did you just read about it?" said Illyrian, teasing her.

"Don't be so horrid!" replied Linda sulkily, sounding as if she really was still just a kid.

"You couldn't have been more than seven in 1960," Silva reckoned.

Linda shook her head.

"A bit older than that."

"Well, *I* got married soon afterwards!"

"Really?" exclaimed Linda.

Silva gazed dreamily out of the window.

"It was just at the beginning of the blockade. And it was then that I gave up archaeology and went into construction."

"If I remember rightly, lots of engineers were directed into construction about then, weren't they?" said Illyrian.

"Yes. Construction was the first sector to be affected."

Silva went on looking through the window. The memory of the ancient theatre at Pacha Liman came back to her cold and clear, as if from another world. With it came the image of the deserted excavation site, and the thought of how jealous she had been of a good-looking Russian girl who'd suddenly fallen for one of the male archaeologists in the team. "There's nothing more awful than being jealous while you're working on a dig," she'd told Ana, later. "You feel as if all the trenches are being carved in your own flesh."

Her sister had listened rather absent-mindedly. Silva knew Ana didn't know the meaning of the word jealousy, and so was unaware of the suffering it could bring. Even so, she had tried to help. "The Soviets will go away now, so it'll be all right again," Ana had said. But that was no consolation to Silva: she thought the sudden parting would only make the man love his Russian all the more. "I just don't understand you," said Ana. "Well, go on suffering, then, if

47

that's what you really want." But she'd been glad later on, when Silva met Gjergj and forgot her anguish overnight. Ana herself had just met Besnik ... But why, Silva wondered, was *she* thinking about Besnik more and more often these days?

"So it was all quite different then," said Linda.

Silva nodded.

Steps now approached along the corridor, and the door opened to admit the boss. Though his attitude was still gloomy enough, he also looked somewhat relieved. The meeting must be over, and, thought Linda, he'd probably adopted the expression of some Party member who'd just been released and whom he'd passed in the corridor. He seemed to want to speak, but something was holding him back. Illyrian, who knew he was persona non grata, tiptoed out.

"I was right about the meeting," said the boss, without looking up from the papers on his desk. "It *was* about China."

"Really?" said Linda.

"It seems they're changing their policy." Then, turning to Silva: "I expect your husband will give us some first-hand information on the subject. When will he be back?"

Silva shrugged.

"I don't know," she said. "I haven't heard from him."

She hadn't sat down at her desk again yet, and for some reason or other she found herself straying back to the window overlooking the square.

"Linda!" she said, putting a hand on the girl's shoulder. "Look!"

Linda turned round and pressed her forehead against the glass.

"How strange!" she exclaimed.

"What's the matter?" asked the boss.

"A little while ago the square was full of Chinese, and now they've all gone ..."

"As if the earth had opened and swallowed them up!" added Linda.

"You can never tell what they're going to do next," said the boss. "It was the same with Nixon's visit. They kept it secret right up to the last minute."

"Better to break once and for all with people like that," said Linda.

The boss looked up.

"Easier said than done. This isn't one of your cheap romances,

48

where if one character hurts another person's feelings they have a row, say they wish they'd never set eyes on one another, and flounce off . . ."

"I don't know what you mean," said Linda, looking him straight in the eye.

"I mean foreign relations are not like people's private affairs: you love me, I don't love you any more, and so we part . . . This sort of thing goes much deeper. There are objective considerations and all sorts of other factors to take into account . . ."

"Do you think I'm such a feather-brain that I reduce everything to the level of a domestic row?" asked Linda icily.

The boss stared at her, taken aback.

"Calm down! I didn't say that!"

"But that's what you were insinuating!" she replied, her eyes flashing angrily.

He waved his hand vaguely, then turned to Silva as if to seek her help. But, unsure she was willing to come to his aid, he threw up his arms as if to say, "That's all I needed!"

For a few moments he busied himself opening and shutting the drawers of his desk, as he usually did when he was nervous. Then he lit a cigarette. And promptly stubbed it out again.

"Right, that'll do," he said mournfully. "I didn't mean to be disagreeable, for heaven's sake! I suppose, at the end of the day, I'm allowed to make a bit of a joke! I am the boss, aren't I?"

He leapt up, stuffed his packet of cigarettes into his pocket, and left the room.

"He really is a case," said Linda. His annoyance had displaced her own. "I'm the one who ought to have been annoyed!"

Silva smiled indulgently.

"Shall we go down to the cafeteria?"

"Do you think I went a bit too far?" Linda asked as they went down the stairs.

Silva smiled at her again. Vaguely. She was thinking of something else.

The cafeteria was in the basement, and the stairs leading down to it were crowded with people coming and going. This was the time most of the clerks took a coffee break. Silva noticed Victor Hila at the far end of the counter with a glass of brandy. He looked worn down.

She went over.

"Did you get to see the vice-minister?" she asked.

He waved his hand.

"Yes. Much good it did me!"

"Do you know each other?" she asked as she introduced him to Linda.

"Delighted to meet you," said Victor, still staring into space. "May I offer you a drink? Sorry, I'm like a bear with a sore head today . . ."

"What's the matter?" asked Silva. "I noticed something was wrong when I met you first thing . . ."

"I didn't take it seriously at first, but now I see I'm in trouble. I've been running around all morning trying to find out what's up, but no one will tell me anything definite . . . Anyhow, what'll you have?"

"Perhaps it would be better to leave that till another time," said Silva. "You look a bit low."

"All the more reason for you to help cheer me up! Come on, do have something! I insist!"

Linda glanced at Silva, as if to ask if Hila was quite right in the head.

"All right," said Silva. "Coffee for us, please."

Victor Hila emptied his glass. Then:

"I'm in trouble over a Chinaman," he said.

"What?" exclaimed Silva.

"We were just talking about the Chinese," said Linda, looking at Victor curiously.

"Yes," he went on. "A Chinaman! A particularly lousy Chink!"

Linda put her hand to her mouth to stifle a laugh. Victor went and fetched their coffees from the counter and set them down in front of them.

"I was told yesterday that I'd been suspended. Do you realize what that means? I'm neither still employed, nor sacked! Just suspended! And all because of this Chinaman! I've spent all the morning combing the ministry trying to sort it all out, but it's no good. I'm absolutely fed up. You'd think they'd all gone deaf."

"But what happened with the Chinaman?" asked Silva, after taking a sip of her coffee. "Did you have a row with him?"

"Worse! I trod on his toes!"

This time Linda wasn't the only one who couldn't restrain her mirth.

"Are you serious?" she chuckled.

"Yes," growled Victor, "I thought it was funny at first, too! Then I found out the Chinaman had lodged a complaint, and now the fact that I laughed is being held against me!"

Linda was still so amused she had to put her cup down on the counter to avoid spilling her coffee.

"And then what happened?" asked Silva.

"Don't talk about it!" sighed Victor. "The Chinaman alleged I'd trodden on his toes deliberately. Of course I swore black was blue I hadn't done it on purpose. But the whole business went up to the Ministry of Foreign Affairs, and the Chinese Embassy insisted I must be punished. When they heard nothing had been done to me, the Chinks protested again. Apparently they've sent the file to Peking, together with an X-ray of their citizen's foot. We're still waiting for the reply. So you see what a jam I'm in?"

"But it seems our relations with China are not what they used to be," said Linda, wiping away tears of laughter. "That may work in your favour . . ."

"Oh, I know how it is with affairs of this sort," said Victor. "Of course, all kinds of things may happen. Someone might set fire to the Chinese Embassy. But no one will ever forget I trod on those toes. Just my luck!"

He looked around the room.

"The worst of it is, everyone tries to give me advice. 'Keep calm, Victor, and don't criticize the Chinese – it'll only make matters more difficult for you!' The Party secretary, the director – they all say the same thing: 'The Chinese people are like this, the Chinese people are like that . . .' 'Right,' I tell them, 'I haven't got anything against the Chinese people. I haven't even got anything against China itself. All I want to know is, what's going to happen to me?'"

Still the same as ever, thought Silva. Impulsive, hot-headed, a magnet that attracted every kind of trouble – just as he'd been when she first got to know him at the time of the break with the Soviets, when she and Ana used to go to some of his famous dinner parties. If she remembered rightly, it was on one of those occasions that Ana had met Besnik . . .

"X-rays of the chap's foot, diplomatic notes – you get the picture?" Victor went on. "For a whole week I've been waking up in the middle of the night in a cold sweat! And why?" He lowered his voice. "Because of a lousy Chink! A saboteur!"

"What?" cried Linda. "That's the first time I've heard anyone call a Chinaman a saboteur!"

Victor looked from one to the other of them.

"I suppose you both think I'm exaggerating a bit. Perhaps. I was reprimanded once for being too excitable. Maybe I'm wrong – I admit it's quite possible. The government knows more about these things than I do. But as far as I'm concerned, the Chinese . . ."

"Be careful! Don't go putting your foot in it again!" teased Linda.

He smiled.

"I know I must seem a bit crazy. Instead of concentrating on things that really matter, I just keep wondering if that confounded X-ray has got there."

The other two started to giggle again.

"Why should you worry about that?" said Linda. "If you really trod on his foot by accident, it couldn't have left much of a bruise . . ."

Victor lowered his eyes and smiled into his beard.

"That's the trouble," he said. "I did it on purpose."

Linda's peal of mirth made two or three people turn round.

Victor knocked back his glass of brandy.

"What else could I do?" he said, glowering. "For a whole month he'd been driving me up the wall, the swine, keeping me waiting for some papers I needed. Every day he had some new excuse for putting it off. 'I didn't have time yesterday,' he'd say. 'I was busy reading the works of Chairman Mao . . . And today I have to think over what I read yesterday . . .' I don't know how I kept myself from strangling him! That's right – laugh! It's obvious you two have never had to deal with a Chinaman!"

As they laughed, Linda kept her eyes on his drawn, ill-shaven face.

"Ping – that's the bastard's name," said Victor, "comes and walks round the factory every morning with his foot done up in a bandage or a plaster or some Chinese old wives' concoction. Can't you just see him, pacing up and down for everyone to see? Perhaps he expects someone to put up a statue to Ping the hero, victim of Victor Hila, the Albanian bandit? You think that's funny? Well, it leaves me suspended – do you hear? – suspended! Neither on earth nor in heaven. And no one will answer my questions! . . . Still," he sighed, "perhaps it's not the government's fault. I suppose the Chinese keep pestering them about what they've done to punish me. A few days ago my boss said, 'What got into you, Victor? A nice mess we're in because of what you did . . .'"

The women finally said goodbye and left the cafeteria.

"A nice chap, isn't he?" said Linda as they went upstairs.

Silva nodded.

"He's been like that all the time I've known him. He's hardly changed at all."

Silva's face wore a hesitant smile.

"Really nice," she murmured, as if to herself.

Back in the office, the boss still hadn't returned. Linda collected some papers and took them along to the typists. Silva sat for a moment with her elbows on her desk. She didn't feel like working. She got up and went over to the window, looking out at the square with its surrounding ministries and the grey, rainy day. She moved across to the radiator. It felt only lukewarm. "I only hope there won't be any shortages . . ." Why had that phrase come back to her? From what recess of her consciousness had it arisen, the hope that Ana had so often expressed at the beginning of that inauspicious period when the future had seemed so unpredictable? It was a hope doomed to remain unfulfilled, for shortages were to become part of their way of life . . . And if history were to repeat itself, then they might expect more of the same gloomy medicine . . . But still, it couldn't have happened as fast as all that! And it was common knowledge that the boiler responsible for the central heating was unreliable – there'd been talk once or twice of replacing it. No, she was letting her imagination run away with her, she decided, going back to her desk. This time everything's different. It's all so quiet.

The door opened and the boss came in, followed by Linda. Strangely enough, the boss looked quite cheerful now, and when Linda asked Silva something, he volunteered the answer himself – a tacit sign of reconciliation. He started to talk about the Chinese, and Linda told him about Victor Hila. He was still roaring with laughter at the story, his mirth punctuated with his characteristic yelps, when there was a knock at the door and Simon Dersha reappeared.

"May I use your telephone for a moment, please?" he asked.

Still laughing, the boss nodded towards the phone, and Dersha went over and dialled a number. Silva and Linda exchanged glances. At each turn of the dial, the boss's laughter grew less. Finally, as before, they heard a phone ringing at the other end of the line, but again there was no reply. Simon's face, though anxious, still wore its previous blissful expression. It looked as if it had been left there by mistake. At length he hung up.

"So what did he do then, this Victor?" said the boss. "That is his name, didn't you say?"

Simon Dersha was still sitting there as if trying to make his way into the others' universe, but the unwonted expression on his face prevented Silva from speaking freely. She made an effort and made some comment on Victor's plight, at which the boss began to laugh louder than ever. Stealing a glance at Simon, she thought she now saw a tinge of irony in his happiness.

He slipped out of the room unobtrusively when the boss's hilarity was at its height.

"What's the matter with him, wandering around all morning like a sleepwalker?" said Linda, not even bothering to lower her voice.

"Don't pay any attention."

"No, but did you take a good look at him? I've never noticed that navy blue suit before, and I think it makes him look very weird!"

Silva nodded.

The boss sighed, as he usually did after he'd been laughing. Then the whole office lapsed once more into silence.

"You think you're so wonderful, don't you?" said Simon Dersha inwardly in the neighbouring office. And he indulged in a condescending smile. As recently as yesterday the laughter still ringing in his ears would have made him feel lonely and excluded. But now the mirth, the larking about that had once tortured him like something precious for ever beyond his reach, seemed tarnished and worthless. He felt completely free from the inferiority complex he'd always suffered from in relation to his colleagues. And this miracle had come about in a single night, like something out of a fairy tale.

If they only knew where I was yesterday evening, he thought. All morning he'd been torn between the desire to tell them where he'd dined the previous day and a kind of inexplicable reticence. He'd seen from the way they looked at him that they were wondering what was the matter. And at the thought that what had happened to him was beyond anything they could possibly have imagined, he was filled once again with delight.

The previous evening he'd been to dinner with one of the best-known members of the government. It was like a dream; sometimes he couldn't even believe in it himself. Perhaps that was why, this morning, he'd tried three times to phone the friend who'd intro-duced him to the minister in the first place, and then taken him to the dinner party: he just wanted to exchange a few words with him about it, in order to convince himself that the miracle really had happened. But as ill-luck would have it, he hadn't been able to get through.

The miracle had taken place in stages. It had begun a week before with a phone call from a man with whom Simon had remained on friendly terms since they'd worked together in a commercial firm, and who had since risen to become a vice-minister. The man had told him that one of these days – he'd tell him the exact date in due course – he'd take him to dinner in a place he'd never even dreamed of. When the two of them had eventually met for coffee and the other man had said what that place was, Simon had been dumbstruck. Was it really possible, he kept stammering, that an ordinary pen-pusher like him, a person of no importance . . . ?

"But that's just it," the other had replied. "Ordinary people, honest unassuming workers, are the very backbone of both the Party and the State. Do you see, Simon?"

Then, lowering his voice:

"I don't mind admitting I don't know myself why the minister suddenly felt the need, or the desire, whichever you like, to set up more direct relations, outside ordinary office routine, with workers from various areas of activity. If you ask me, politicians think that kind of contact helps them keep their finger on the pulse of public opinion. Well, a few days ago he told me he'd like to meet someone from the Ministry of Construction, an ordinary worker, not a senior official – he was already up to his eyes in senior officials! In short, when he told me he wanted to find out what went on from just a humble, honest, ordinary worker, I thought straight away of you."

As he remembered these words, Simon felt as if his eyes were still misty with tears. He'd spent days afterwards waiting anxiously for a phone call from the vice-minister. Sometimes it seemed to him their conversation had never taken place. Other doubts followed. What if the minister had changed his mind? What if he really had said that about wanting to get to know ordinary people, but had only been speaking generally, and Simon's friend had been mistaken in trying to involve *him*? At one point he decided it was all wishful thinking on the part of his friend, and foolish naivety on his own. He'd almost given up hope when his friend finally phoned. Not only had he thus kept his promise, but he also gave Simon the exact date and time of the dinner party they were to attend together. Even now, several days later, it gave Simon a pleasant glow inside to think of that phone call.

He was alone in his office now. He could hear the sound of doors opening and shutting along the corridor, but they seemed very far away. He thought again of his colleagues in the other office, and it filled him with sardonic satisfaction to remind himself that from now on it was they who should be envying him, and not the other way round. Henceforth he could look down on their humdrum existence, with its chatting and joking and noisy laughter over their morning coffee. Up till today, when they passed him – greeting him, if they did so at all, as if he were almost beneath their notice – they'd probably asked each other how the devil the poor wretch managed to get along, apparently devoid of any object in life. The contrast was so striking he'd often agreed with them: "They're quite right, really – I wonder, myself, why I'm alive at all." And he used to reflect thus quite humbly, with a resignation untinged with resentment, placidly accepting the rôle of unobtrusive spectator of other people's lives. Sometimes, seeing them burst gaily in and out of one another's offices, he'd try to imagine the relationships that existed between them. If one of them looked especially bright or tired first thing in the morning, he scented a special significance in the fact, as in the tone of his colleagues' voices when they exchanged furtive phone calls. Sometimes his imagination ran away with him even further, and he had visions of them naked in one another's arms, their faces buried in shadow and mystery. Then he would heave a sigh, and say to himself under his breath: "No, I can't be cut out for that sort of life."

But now the situation was reversed. A single dinner party, and everything was turned upside down as if by an earthquake. And he could feel within himself not merely a combination of euphoria and scorn, but also the first stirrings of blind rage. He couldn't have said whether his anger was directed against the others or against himself. It was a frustrated wrath, provoked by the length of time he'd been living in a kind of limbo because of his own submiss-iveness and lack of jealousy. And it was accompanied by the dim stirrings of a desire for revenge. But this feeling was still very faint indeed: it was alien to his nature, and found it hard to take root there.

They'd been talking about China, he mused. He'd heard other discussions on that subject lately: it had been mentioned at the dinner party itself, though he hadn't been able to concentrate sufficiently to catch exactly what was said. Everything seemed dim and vague, apart from what had actually been happening to him, which he couldn't get out of his mind. It must be like that, he thought, when you were in love. Not that he'd ever been in love himself, but other people were always going into such raptures on the subject it must be pretty wonderful. But he was sure his present feelings were more wonderful still, and more lofty, because more rare.

Most people, if not all, had been in love. But very few had had the experience of dining with a minister.

Yet again he recalled what he'd felt like just before it was time for him to set out. He'd decided to wear a navy blue suit which he'd had made some years back out of some expensive Polish material. He'd kept it for special occasions, and in due course it had come back into fashion again. He remembered trying to select a shirt, and how his wife had hovered around him with an expression that struck him as somehow disagreeable. Looking at himself in his dressing-table mirror, he'd been struck by something rather pitiful about the rawness of his carefully scraped cheeks and the redness of his neck inside its stiffly starched collar. Just as he was leaving, his wife asked him for the umpteenth time if he'd remembered to take a handkerchief, and all the way to his destination he'd worried about what he would do if he suddenly sneezed in the middle of dinner. He tried to dismiss the incongruous thought from his mind, but it was no good: he kept remembering a story he'd read at school, about a minor official who sneezed in the presence of some bigwig. The grown-up Simon quickened his pace and told himself he was a civil servant in a socialist country: his situation had nothing in common with that of a bourgeois pen-pusher who swooned away in terror because he'd sneezed in the presence of a superior.

Simon Dersha's nervousness subsided somewhat when he was

joined on the way to the party by the vice-minister, then grew again as he noticed that his protector too had lost some of his usual self-assurance. The nearer they got to the minister's residence the more their conversation languished, until at last the only sound to be heard was that of their footsteps. Several times one of them said "What?" though the other hadn't said anything. The street was only faintly lit, which made the damp surface of the road and the iron railings round the gardens look even darker than usual. "This is it," said the vice-minister in a scarcely audible voice as they came to a two-storey villa.

Memory is governed by laws of its own. Simon's mind was a blank as to the time between the moment when the vice-minister said "This is it" and the moment when they entered the villa. But he could remember the dinner itself quite plainly: some parts of it seemed engraved in his memory for ever, while others were still suspended in a kind of mist, a tantalizing cloud of vagueness.

There were four or five other guests, all distinguished officials who would have been the centre of attention at any public gathering, but who were here reduced to mere ciphers in comparison with their host.

Alone in his office, Simon Dersha lit a cigarette. No, he really couldn't recall the miracle in its entirety. It was like something you can only swallow if you break it up into pieces; otherwise it might choke you. Simon sighed. Fortunately, he thought, it all passed off without my dropping any bricks. And he was right. The minister had turned to him a few times, asking how the building of the big factories was getting on, especially the power stations in the north where the Chinese were working. Simon had answered as best he could.

He would have been hard put to it to endure any more particular attention, especially as, during the dinner, he had a feeling that every dish was a trap. He couldn't relax until they came to the cheese and the fruit: then, thank God, the problems were over – he was in no further danger of splashing himself with some elaborate sauce. He hadn't needed to use his handkerchief, though he'd taken it out of his pocket a couple of times and pressed it mechanically to his nose: the smell of clean, well-ironed linen was pleasant and reassuring. Yes, things really couldn't have gone any better. Not the slightest thing had happened that might have made one say, as is so often the case, if only this or that hadn't happened;

perhaps I ought to have answered such-and-such a question differently.

There'd been only one incident, but it was nothing to do with him – so far from it, indeed, that even now he couldn't have said whether it was a good thing or a bad. It consisted of a telephone call. At about half-past ten, just as they had finished the second course – the one that was the most difficult to handle without any spills – one of the phones had started to ring . . . Even though so much time had elapsed since, Simon had the feeling, every time he recalled the phone conversation which had followed, that recalling it was his last hope of jolting his memory into lucidity, for it must have been the most significant part of the whole evening. But it hadn't seemed so at the time, and his memory of it was as of something distant and irrelevant.

When the phone rang, the host had risen from the table to answer it, leaving his guests still laughing at some pleasantry.

"Yes . . . Hallo, Comrade Enver . . ."

The guests exchanged glances. It must be Him. This would anyway have been an important, an unforgettable occasion. But such a phone call, at such a late hour, made it doubly important. A memorable dinner, during which Comrade Enver had rung up . . . Even now Simon felt his heart miss a beat at the thought of it, though he wondered whether something significant really had occurred, or whether it was merely the product of his own anxiety. But no, he decided: his uneasiness had been a reaction to something outside himself. The first thing that had alerted him was the way the minister spoke. His voice had been quite calm to start with, but then there'd been a sudden check, and he'd looked as though he'd suffered a shock. The change in the minister's voice produced an even deeper silence among his guests, so that the belated clatter of a fork on a plate made every head turn towards it. As for the phone conversation itself, it had apparently concerned the most unremarkable of subjects: the caller was asking for explanations about the expulsion of certain tank officers from the Party. This was a subject of relatively minor importance, certainly not enough to render the minister speechless. Still, as Simon had reflected later, on his way home, it was rather astonishing that the leader of the Party himself should phone up so late at night on so insignificant a subject. But then perhaps it wasn't so surprising after all. The fact that he'd rung up at that hour might just as easily mean that the subject of the conversation was one of those minor matters one puts off till the end of the day – maybe it had suddenly occurred to him after dinner.

Throughout the rest of the evening Simon had done his best to dismiss that phone call from his mind, and it seemed to him that everyone else, including his host, was doing the same. The minister was still very affable and vivacious, but every so often, in the midst of the conversation, he seemed to freeze, and his eyes went dull and vague – like Simon's recollections. But when he took the trouble to think things over for a moment he felt reassured. The phone conversation and the minister's twinge of anxiety seemed quite normal. The sort of thing that happens all the time, he told himself: you'd need to be really looking for trouble to think it unusual. And that, though his first reaction was always one of doubt and resentment, was the conclusion he always came to eventually whenever he looked back on the incident.

Walking home with the vice-minister, his general state of euphoria was disturbed two or three times by the memory of the phone call. He even allowed himself to refer to it once, but his companion only said, "Yes, quite . . ." This made Simon think his own experience hadn't been purely subjective. But after a little while he managed to put it out of his mind.

And now, here in his office, he did so again. I really am hopeless, he told himself. I had that incredible stroke of luck, that wonderful opportunity, and all I can do is look for complications! All his calculations about the phone call seemed utterly absurd. Waves of exultation swamped his uneasiness yet again, and he started to think once more of the office next door and the trivial conversations of its occupants. Even his official superiors all seemed less important than before. And this time his feeling of triumph lingered: everything seemed easier, more within his reach. At one point, though, his eye lighted on the telephone that wasn't working that morning. He remembered the unanswered ringings in the vice-minister's office, and sighed.

The day's work was nearly ended. He went over to the window and stood for a while looking out at the comings and goings in the square. The air felt damp, but the weather looked too bright for rain.

He heard a key being turned in the lock of a nearby office. Footsteps echoed along the corridor. He looked at his watch and took

60

his own keys out of his pocket. And a few minutes later he was walking across Government Square as usual, another anonymous pedestrian amidst the crowd of clerks hurrying home.

4

ALTHOUGH THE RAINS WERE LATE, it was already autumn. Every morning, clouds would appear on the horizon and fill the sky with pointless peals of thunder, only to vanish at the end of the afternoon without having shed a drop of moisture. After this had gone on for a whole week, people reconciled themselves to the idea that it was going to be a dry autumn. Meanwhile all the other seasonal changes took place as usual: the leaves turned colour, the temperature dropped, the birds migrated. As usual too, painters flocked to the headquarters of the Writers' and Artists' Union to get their annual permits to concentrate on autumnal themes.

But even before anyone noticed the first fallen leaf or the growing scarcity of birds, most people had started to be aware of something else: an obvious fall in the level of seniority among the delegates attending Sino-Albanian meetings. The change might well have begun earlier, but as the national days of both China and Albania fell in the autumn, it was then that it became unmistakably evident.

No doubt about it, the Chinese delegations were not what they had been. Almost all of them were led by lesser officials than usual: vice-ministers instead of ministers, seconds-in-command instead of generals, assistant directors instead of heads of technology, and so on. And of course these lesser Chinese delegates were met at Tirana airport by members of the Albanian Party who had never appeared before at any official ceremony. As if this were not enough, the composition of the delegations themselves became more and more peculiar, not to say outlandish. Thus a delegation of popular orchestras from South-East China, led by the assistant editor of agricultural broadcasting, was succeeded by a ceramics delegation led by an assistant director, and this in turn was followed by another described merely as a delegation of peasants.

Since it was difficult anyway to find Albanian institutions corresponding to those to which the Chinese delegations belonged, the relatively lowly officials sent to meet them tended to be from bodies that were almost irrelevant. A team of workers from a collective producing Mao Zedong badges had to be welcomed by the assistant head of a ferro-nickel factory, much to the annoyance of the Chinese, who lost no time in pointing out that workshops which turned out badges bearing portraits of Chairman Mao had nothing whatever in common with ordinary factories. Thereupon the organizers tried to find someone else to preside over the official dinner at least, and came up with the assistant head of the Mint.

Another problem was presented by the toasts which had to be proposed at banquets and receptions. Not only had it become necessary to modify their form, but it grew more and more difficult to match the wording of the guests' own toasts. Adjectives were weakened, adverbs strengthened, among many other adjustments. All the guests were constantly on the alert – especially the interpreters, fearful of getting some nuance wrong. Things were even more complicated when it came to reporting these occasions in the newspapers. Whenever a banquet was held in honour of a Chinese delegation, the official in charge of press coverage had to stay on in his office till late at night waiting for the copy to be phoned in. He happened to be on a strict diet, and his colleagues joked that these parties were just as bad for his liver as if he'd actually attended them.

The Chinese were the first to modify the formula used to round off accounts of receptions and banquets given in honour of the delegations. Such occasions had previously been said to have "taken place in a very warm and friendly atmosphere." At first the Chinese omitted "very", then they left out "warm", and finally they replaced the closing words of the communiqués altogether with the phrase, "those present were observed to exchange smiles in the course of the evening."

The Albanian press stuck to the old formula, except that "warm and friendly" was replaced by the one word, "cordial".

None of this was lost on the reading public, though some people predicted that this period of coolness would eventually wear off as others had done a few years earlier. Just as trees lost their leaves in winter but flowered again in spring, so the delegations would eventually flourish anew.

Yet at the same time everyone talked of how work had slowed down on many big construction sites, especially those building hydro-electric plants in the north. This was because of hold-ups in supplies of equipment from China. Freighters now took an unconscionably long time to reach their destination, and when they did arrive they might be carrying the wrong cargo. On two occasions ships had turned back without even entering Durrës harbour. All this was said to be part of China's famous "turn of the screw". Cafés in Tirana were full of stories about this tactic: no one realized that one day the whole country would be its victim.

The Chinese press made no mention of the subject. For weeks their newspapers and airwaves concentrated on accounts of the Spartan life-styles of two of their country's own leaders. One hadn't worn any new clothes since the liberation of China; the other, to save the people unnecessary expense, had no furniture except a couple of barrels, one used as a bed and the other containing his only food – chick-peas. It seemed that the first of the two, easily recognizable from the towel he wore round his head in magazine photos, was engaged in some sort of argument with his opposite number, though exactly what it was about no one quite knew. Some rumours had it that their rivalry, comical as it might appear, was really nothing to do with the two men themselves, who in fact merely symbolized two important factions engaged in a power struggle. Incredible as it might seem, some people were prepared to take all this quite seriously, and to debate it at length. During one television account of the arrival of a Chinese delegation in Mexico, led by the turban-wearing member of the Politbureau, the camera, as if trying to solve the enigma, dwelt for several seconds on the arrangement of the towel round his head.

Such things had apparently so little to do with the late arrival of the freighters that the Albanian ministers concerned about these delays just shook their heads in bewilderment. Meanwhile, foreign press agencies announced that Mao Zedong was seriously ill, if not as dead as a doornail, and that the man who'd been seen at public receptions recently was merely one of his doubles. Some people even said Mao had been dead for ages, and everything that had been going on in China since then was the result of quarrels between two of his doubles, each claiming to be the great man himself.

Some saw a connection between reports of Mao's illness and the recent deterioration in Sino-Albanian relations, and hoped that when he, or one or both of the doubles, got better or died, the situation would be cleared up, things would go back to normal as they'd always done before, and this period would be no more than a disagreeable memory. And so that autumn, the delegations, though diminished, went on coming and going; for the first time in years, an invitation even went out to a delegation of writers. But any lingering optimism was roughly extinguished by a rumour to the effect that the Chinese ambassador had asked for an audience with the Albanian foreign secretary on the subject of an X-ray: if the matter at issue wasn't actually a brawl, it was said to be the bruising of a Chinese foot by an Albanian one.

Linda had a bath and then started to wander aimlessly around her apartment. Ever since breaking off the affair she'd had with a government television engineer the previous year, she'd found the afternoons terribly long. Now and again she would pick up a half-read book from the settee, but she soon threw it down again. Finding herself in the hall, she stopped and looked in the glass. Still undecided as to whether to go to the dressmaker's for a fitting or call on one of her workmates at the Makina Import office, she started to do her hair.

For some reason or other she couldn't get out of her mind a poem she'd read a few days ago, waiting at the hairdresser's:

> Ever since you left
> I can feel myself gradually forgetting you,
> Feel your eyes dying in me,
> And your hair, and all.

She took out a hairpin and adjusted a couple of small combs. Forgetting someone's hair, she thought as she fiddled with one of the combs. "I can never forget you," he'd said in his last letter, his last attempt to revive their affair. "I can never erase anything about you from my memory – your words, your eyes, your hair . . ." And yet, writing in that magazine, there was someone strong enough to say he *could* forget. "Feel your eyes dying in me . . . and your hair."

People said that when you died it was your hair that died last. Linda smiled, in spite of the comb she was now holding in her mouth. Then she dropped it, put on her raincoat and opened the door, still not knowing where she was going.

The late afternoon was still warm beneath the dull autumn sky, as if ignoring the seasons. Several times Linda almost went into a shop to buy some material, but each time she changed her mind. She felt relaxed and at ease with herself. For no particular reason, Silva's words came back to her: "I got married during the blockade." As a matter of fact, her thoughts had lately been turning more and more often to Silva and things connected with her. The surge of happiness she'd felt when she first met her, eight months ago, kept recurring. She now rejoiced in her good luck at working in the same office as Silva, and shuddered at the thought that one of them might be moved. Every so often she found herself adopting one of Silva's expressions or gestures, and while she did her best to avoid copying the older woman, she didn't feel guilty about it. She liked everything about Silva – her face, her way of dressing and doing her hair, the way she spoke on the telephone, the atmosphere around her and the relations she created with everyone, from her fellow secretaries to her superiors. Linda also admired Silva's relationship with her husband, and had even, on the basis of just a few glimpses, taken a liking to the husband himself, with his stern-looking and yet not forbidding face, and the deeply etched lines on his forehead that seemed signs of youth rather than age.

"'I got married during the blockade,'" she repeated, smiling. Would she herself get married during this second blockade? She turned towards a shop window so that no one would see her smiling to herself. She certainly liked doing as Silva did, even at the risk of seeming like a pale imitation of her friend. Anyhow, mightn't anything happen during a blockade? Hadn't Silva got married, while her late sister got divorced in order to marry Besnik Struga, and Struga himself, a person still shrouded in mystery for Linda, had broken off his engagement? She'd met Struga, Silva's former brother-in-law, only once, by chance, in the corridor, when he'd come to the ministry to see Silva. But -- perhaps because Linda had heard so much about him – he'd made a strong impression on her. Most of the people Silva knew were somehow out of the ordinary: her brother, the tank officer, who'd come to see her two days ago, looking distraught; Skënder Bermema, the writer, an old family friend who'd had a rather enigmatic relationship with Silva's sister; and other cousins and acquaintances whom Linda had met or whose voices she'd heard when they'd called in at or rung up the office to speak to her friend. All were interesting; almost all had something in their lives – some phase, some act or some episode – that was connected with the Soviet blockade. Linda was growing more and more fascinated by that period, and by anyone who'd been directly involved in it.

And why shouldn't I too get married during a blockade? she joked to herself as she made for the Makina Import building. But then she'd have to find someone to marry. And furthermore, was this really a genuine blockade? By all accounts the other one had weighed down on everyone like lead: a period harsh in itself had been slashed through as by an icy abyss. But it was still hard to say how serious the present crisis might prove. You needed to be a code-cruncher to deduce anything from the articles in the press. But things might not turn out so badly as that: there mightn't be a blockade at all. And detecting a tinge of regret in this thought, as if she could only get married if there was a blockade, she smiled at her own absurdity.

"If anyone suspected the idiotic notions that go through my mind!" she thought. It was a good thing Tirana was big enough for one to daydream as one walked along without bumping into people one knew. Then, paradoxically, she had a feeling someone was watching her. She turned, and thought she recognized a face. The man just nodded vaguely. Where have I seen that ravaged face before, she wondered. And then she remembered. It was in the cafeteria at the ministry.

Linda smiled at him. They both walked on a little way. Then he spoke.

"You're Silva's friend, aren't you? We've met before, if you remember."

"Yes, indeed!" Linda exclaimed. But he didn't take the hand she'd half extended.

"How did that business about the X-ray turn out?" she asked, laughing.

But he remained serious.

"No developments," he said. "Nothing."

"Really?"

She gave him a sidelong look, and her own smile faded. If she'd met anyone else in the street like this, she would have walked on without more ado, but there was something about his downcast expression that made him seem different from other people.

"Perhaps things will sort themselves out faster than you think."

Victor Hila shrugged, as if to say it was better not to talk about it. They'd been walking along together for some time now, and it seemed to make both of them uncomfortable. Linda had noticed before how disagreeable it is being overtaken in the street by someone you know, rather than just meeting them coming towards you and passing by. Although the man looked even gloomier than he had the other day at the ministry, she resolved to give him the slip at the next shop they came to. Then he, as if reading her thoughts, asked her point-blank:

"Are you in a hurry?"

"Yes," said Linda, though she spoke rather uncertainly. "I'm on my way to see a friend."

He looked at her closely for a moment.

"Would you mind if I asked you something?"

"Not at all," answered Linda, staring straight ahead.

"Please don't misunderstand me," he said, "but I feel so depressed this afternoon that you really would be doing me a kindness if you'd have a drink with me."

Linda stood still for a moment, hesitating. The man's expectancy was almost tangible.

"All right," she said, surprised at how faint her voice was.

"It's very kind of you," he murmured. "Thanks."

Linda didn't know what to say. They went across a square to a little café. "But I was right to say I'd come," she thought as they went in. "He really did look down in the dumps."

There weren't many other people in the café.

"What will you have?" he asked.

"A coffee, please," said Linda.

They sat with their elbows on the table for a while without speaking.

"I'd been wandering around for an hour," he said. "I'm really out of work now, you know. It wasn't so bad the day I first met you – I'd been suspended, but I could still go to the factory, see my friends, turn my hand to something. But now, with the Chinese on the watch all the time, I can't go anywhere near the factory. You can't imagine what it's like when those devils have got their eye on you."

Linda felt she might risk a smile. Victor's drawn face relaxed.

"I'm just a figure of fun," he said. "Do you see what I mean? I've dropped out of time. In the past I might have been punished for what I did; in the future I might be praised. But in the present

68

situation between our two countries, it's neither one thing nor the other. That's the worst of it. I'm suspended between two different periods of time. Which means I don't belong to either. To any. Do you understand?"

"Perhaps that just makes you a man of today," said Linda.

"Do you mean I'm typical of our own age?"

"Who can say?" replied Linda, smiling. "Perhaps. A hero of our time!"

Victor gazed at her for a while as if meditating a decision: should he or should he not forget his pain and smile with her? He had a vague feeling it was his sorrow that had made Linda interrupt what she was doing and come here with him, and that if he showed less of it she might feel no further moral obligation and go off with an easy conscience, her mission accomplished, leaving him alone again.

He hadn't worked this out clearly: he just sensed that she'd come with him because she felt sorry for him, and would go away again as soon as she saw him feeling a bit better. But in fact, apart from the pleasure of sitting here in this charming girl's company, he didn't feel any relief whatsoever: on the contrary, Linda's presence, by reminding him that life went on normally regardless of his distress, just made him feel further pangs. So it wasn't a pose when he went on looking sad.

Linda's smile faded first from her lips, then from her cheeks, and then from her eyes, leaving her with a sense of guilt. She picked up her cup, only to realize at the last moment that it was empty.

"Some witticisms are very amusing to quote after the event," said Victor, "but sometimes they're rather painful at the time."

"I wasn't trying to be funny," replied Linda. "I sympathise with your trouble, and as a matter of fact . . ."

She'd been going to say, "that was why I agreed to come here." But she didn't finish, partly out of annoyance, partly perhaps because of some sort of inhibition.

"I wasn't referring to you!" cried Victor. "The thought never entered my head! On the contrary, I'm very grateful to you for giving me your company on a day like this. It would be really boorish of me to bother about such trifles . . ."

"Anyhow, it's of no importance," said Linda.

Another silence fell between them, unrelieved by the clatter of their empty cups or the sound of Victor's lighter as he made several unsuccessful attempts to light a cigarette.

69

"Have you been working in the same office as Silva for long?" he asked at last.

Linda perceived that the best way of relieving the tension was to talk about a third person. She spoke of Silva with a warmth, almost a passion, which she herself found hard to explain.

"Have you known her long yourself?" she asked.

"Yes, for a very long time," Victor answered.

He stared for a moment at the whorls of cigarette smoke, then added:

"I was closer to her sister, though. Perhaps Silva has told you something about it?"

"Yes."

"She was a remarkable woman. We'd known each other since the time of her first marriage. Then she divorced and married one of my friends – Besnik Struga. I expect you've heard of him."

"Yes. Didn't he act as Enver Hoxha's interpreter in Moscow in 1960?"

"That's right. He was an extraordinary person, too. But such is life – their happiness didn't last long."

"Besnik Struga was a friend of yours, was he?"

Victor nodded.

"I met him when he came back from Moscow," he went on thoughtfully. "As chance would have it, it was through him that I was one of the first to hear what had happened there."

Now Linda was listening with bated breath.

"He wouldn't say anything about it even to his fiancée. Some people say that was one of the reasons why they broke up."

Linda longed to hear more, but didn't like to ask questions for fear of seeming inquisitive.

But she could see how restlessly his hands were moving about on the table. The man sitting opposite was one of the people who'd been involved in the first blockade. And one of the first, perhaps the very first, to be involved in the present one.

"Well, there it is," he said suddenly. "A Chinaman turns up from the other side of the world and ruins your life for you."

He waited a moment to see if she was going to laugh again. Then, as she hadn't even smiled:

"The worst of it is," he went on, "having to explain it to people. They all take it as a joke. No one seems to understand, not even one's nearest and dearest."

At the first part of this sentence she had almost protested, but at the second she decided to hold back.

"Were you going to say something?" he asked.

"No . . ."

"So that's how it is," he said, tossing his lighter from one hand to the other. "Not even the person closest to you. Not even your own wife . . ."

Linda looked at him.

"She seems more and more fed up lately," he explained. "She says the whole business has been dragging on too long, and she'd never have dreamed it would turn out like this. She acts as if I was making it out to be worse than it is – as if we'd agreed to treat it as something comic, and it was my fault that it's degenerated into tragedy."

"I suppose, if there are money worries . . ."

He smiled bitterly.

"Of course," he said. "We've lost more than half our monthly income. I'm not joking!"

"I believe you," said Linda.

"Sorry to bother you with all this. Why should you have to listen to my tale of woe? I shouldn't have asked you to come here. But I really did need to talk to someone. My wife's been away on a mission in the north these last few days, and I was feeling pretty lonely . . ."

"No need to apologize," said Linda. "I'd be only too glad to be able to cheer you up a bit. We're only human, after all . . ."

She turned towards the window so he shouldn't see she was blushing.

Outside it was as dull as ever – that time of an autumn afternoon where everything seems becalmed. She went on staring at the window. The glass is nice and clean, she thought vaguely.

"I expect I've kept you too long," he said. "We can leave whenever you like."

Linda smiled and nodded.

"Yes, it is getting a bit late."

Victor summoned the waiter. She couldn't help glancing at his wallet. It contained a few 100-lek notes. Remembering he was out of work, she was tempted to offer to pay for their coffees herself, but the fear of giving offence, together with a new surge of pity, was so strong it made her feel quite faint. For some reason or other, the sight of him handing over the money made her feel guilty. If it hadn't been for the risk of being misunderstood, she'd have liked to say: "Let's stay on for a while, if you like." But even though she hadn't opened her lips, and though it was she who led the way out of the café, her lack of haste revealed what she had been thinking.

By now they were walking along in a direction that was neither hers nor his, and still Linda found herself hesitating. Should she say she meant to go and see her friend now, or even merely go home, or should she just let herself be led aimlessly along? It didn't yet commit her in any way . . . She couldn't make up her mind, and to set aside her own uncertainties she asked him about the Chinaman again.

"What?" he exclaimed.

"The X-ray," she said. "What will happen when it comes back from China?"

Victor shrugged and smiled.

"How should I know? They'll certainly attach the Chinese doctors' reading of it. Unless they ask for another X-ray altogether. I've no experience of that sort of thing."

"What a nasty business!" she exclaimed.

She could feel him looking at her.

"The X-ray of a Chinaman's foot flying from one country to another!" he said. "Macabre, isn't it?"

She looked up involuntarily. For a moment, the fate of the man walking along beside her seemed linked to a vast expanse of sky being crossed by the long-awaited image of a foot. This brought back to her mind the X-ray her father had had to have a couple of years ago: the hazy white bones on the cloudy background . . . The future of the man beside her depended on a similar image.

She couldn't help sighing. A Chinaman's foot, she mused. The shop windows on either side of the street, the passers-by, all seemed to withdraw, giving way to that macabre image flying between the continents, a combination of Asian and European myth. Any man who was hand in glove with that phantom foot must certainly be out of the ordinary.

"Oh, this is where I live!" she heard him say. But his voice sounded far away.

He'd stopped, and was pointing to the third or fourth floor of a block of flats. Linda looked up, but absent-mindedly: she still felt strangely languid.

"Shall we go up for a minute?" he asked rather hesitantly. "It's too soon just to go home, don't you think?"

The afternoon seemed to be dragging on for ever. Linda's mind refused to take anything in. She gazed idly at the little garden in front of the flats: the grass was starting to wither; there was a sketchily painted red seesaw.

"It's so pleasant, talking to you. So peaceful," he said. "Couldn't we stay together a little while longer?"

Linda's mind still dwelt on that still life with sky and the X-ray of a foot. In such a context, his suggestion seemed quite natural. After all, why not? she thought. He's so unhappy!

"Why not?" she murmured. And head bowed, without looking at him, she began to walk in the direction of the flats.

What am I doing? she asked herself several times as they went along. She'd agreed to go up to the apartment of a man she hardly knew before this afternoon. She asked herself the same question yet again. But she felt as if she'd been snatched up into some vast space in which she would soon dissolve.

Linda left Victor an hour later. It was dark by now, and she looked into the shop windows, which for some reason were not lit, to see if her hair was dishevelled. In fact, as she well knew, her hair was as tidy as ever. If there was any disorder, it lay elsewhere. Looking back on what had just happened, beginning with the sudden embrace which struck her as more insane with every minute that passed, quite apart from the fact that it had probably surprised her companion as much as herself, she wondered what sort of girl he must have taken her for.

"Goodnight," she said suddenly when they came to an intersection. "I'm almost home."

He made as if to say something, but then just murmured goodnight, almost as if to himself.

I never ought to have read any Russian literature, Linda thought as she covered the short distance to her own place, hurrying as if for dear life. It was all because of her own damned soft-heartedness, she thought, patting her hair again as if the misunderstanding – she was now convinced that this was all it was – lay there, like a burr she was trying in vain to disentangle.

Victor was woken up by the telephone. It sounded unnaturally long and loud (ever since he'd been suspended from his job, Victor had felt that even the ringing of the phone sounded scornful and cold). He was wanted at the factory. What? Why? he asked. Would it be good news or bad? Come and find out, said the head of personnel.

As he dressed he wondered, almost aloud, "Why am I so calm?" Then, as if a load had fallen from him, he remembered the afternoon with Linda, their walk, and then, in his flat, the amazing way she'd instantly put her arms around him. He'd thought about it over and over again, lying on his bed till midnight lighting one cigarette after another, as if trying to shroud in smoke something which was anyhow nebulous, inexplicable and vague as a dream. Curiously enough, what he remembered most clearly, better than all that had followed, was that first impulsive gesture of Linda's. Sometimes he saw it as sisterly, sometimes as something quite different. He remembered learning at school than in the old Albanian ballads men called their sweethearts "sister", and wondered whether it wasn't his unhappiness that had made him so sentimental. I'd never have had such tender feelings about an incident like this in the past, he thought. But then, in the past, it would never have happened. That soft hair on his cheek, the gentle touch of her lips, and above all those arms round his neck – it was all as fragile and fleeting as a rainbow: one vulgar word or gesture might destroy it. And even though that which people call vulgar had happened, the original rainbow remained intact . . .

He felt the only way he could keep the memory safe was to disappear. That was what he must do. He wouldn't phone Linda; he would set their moment apart from reality, let it be sublimated by oblivion. Even if he happened to meet her by chance in the street, he'd pretend not to remember anything, perhaps not even to know her.

As he walked to the bus stop he thought now of the events of the previous afternoon, now about the reason for his being summoned to the factory. The man at the gate gave him a cheerful wink.

"Back again, are you, lad? Good!"

74

"I don't know about that, Jani. It depends what they tell me in personnel."

"Go ahead," said the old man. "There aren't any Chinks in the corridors. They're all on the factory floor."

Victor smiled sadly. How had things got to the point where he had to enter his workplace almost surreptitiously? In his last days at the factory, before he was suspended, his friends had kidded him about what had happened, suggesting he should come to the factory in a theatrical wig and a false moustache so that the Chinese wouldn't recognize him.

When he came out of the personnel office, Victor couldn't decide whether he ought to lament or rejoice. They'd told him he was to leave straight away for a new job at the steelworks in Elbasan. "In other words, I've got to leave Tirana just to please that swine?" he'd exclaimed, surprising even himself by his sudden rage. "Watch what you say, comrade," the head of personnel had answered sternly. "Hundreds of comrades and Party members consider it an honour to work at Elbasan. And don't forget you're in the wrong. The Party told us not to react to any provocation on their part, and you had to go and . . ."

"What a fool I am," Victor thought then. "I ought just to be glad the matter's being wound up without more ado . . . You're right, comrade," he told the head of personnel, who was still scowling at him disapprovingly.

But, once out in the corridor, he felt suddenly empty. He was going to have to leave here for good. No matter how much he told himself it mightn't really be for ever, that the Chinese might eventually go themselves and he be able to come back – you never knew – it didn't make him feel any better. He walked across the yard not bothering to avoid attracting the Chinamen's attention. His case was settled now; he had no reason to skulk. He'd even have liked to meet them and say right to their faces: "Well, I'm going. Satisfied?"

He stopped at the refreshment stall for a coffee. Everyone said, "Oh, so you're back at last, are you?" But he just shook his head.

Before he left he made one last round of the huge factory where he'd spent part of his life. Everywhere voices called out, "Back again, engineer?" But he either shook his head or merely smiled. Pain at having to leave this place was like a growing weight inside him. The wall newspapers, to which until now he'd paid little attention, the graphs recording socialist endeavour, the photographs of outstanding workers, even the mere announcements dotted about the noticeboards – "Union meeting tomorrow at 4 o'clock," "Choir practice today" – all seemed different now.

As he prowled around he could feel people looking at him. "There are all sorts of stories being told about you," said an electrical engineer who kept him company for a while. "You're a real legend! More than a legend! There's talk of demonstrations against you in Tienanmen Square, protests at the U.N., and I don't know what! Are people letting their imagination run away with them, or can it all be true?"

Victor smiled as he listened. As a matter of fact, the business of the X-ray wasn't all that different from such fabrications. As he passed through the workshops the female workers on either side gazed at him admiringly. Every so often he would remember Linda's embrace, and he would feel as if he were weightless, borne along on some invisible wave. Then ordinary consciousness returned, and he could feel the ground under his feet again.

At last he came to the place where he had stood on the Chinaman's foot. He shook his head as if to drive away the idea of those cloth shoes, more like slippers, so symbolic of the Chinaman's stealthy approach. The softness of those shoes contrasted with the cynicism which had made their wearer call for a stoppage in two of the workshops and almost bring the whole factory to a standstill. For a moment Victor had felt as if all the hypocrisy in the world were concentrated in that pair of cloth slippers. Moved not only by anger but also by the desire to tear away the mask of deceit, he'd gone up to the man and trodden on his foot as if by accident.

"Yes, a real legend – you're the hero of the hour," the other engineer went on. "Do you know what Aunt Nasta says? She says it's a shame to lose a good man just because of one of those short-assed Chinks!"

He guffawed as he spoke, but Victor found it hard to join in.

An hour later he left the factory and walked towards the bus stop, gazing blankly in front of him and still deep in thought. He looked back one last time at the chimneys, belching black smoke. He'd recently dreamed of seeing others like them, only they were all upside down. Perhaps, with his transfer, his life would get back on the right lines. As the proverb said, every cloud has a silver lining. He went on musing as he looked back at the chimneys, thinking of the engineer's jokes but still not finding them funny. The way the smoke rose into the sky struck him as somehow alien to and supremely scornful of the human race. Not for nothing did interpreters of dreams regard smoke as a bad omen.

5

HIGH ABOVE THE SURFACE of the earth, faint traces of life sped steadily across the sky. In the deepening chill of autumn, spy satellites transmitted from one to another a list of the members of the Politbureau of the Chinese Communist Party, arranged in the same order as for the committee appointed recently to organize a state funeral. There was only one slight change from the order as it had been three weeks earlier: the member who wore a towel round his head, the One in the Turban, as sinologists now called him among themselves, had risen from thirty-fourth to thirty-third, thus changing places with his colleague with the two barrels. Insignificant as the change might seem, the experts who were no doubt already rushing to interpret the signs would scrutinize it for the slightest indication that the balance was swinging, even temporarily, in favour of one faction rather than the other. Unfortunately, despite their untiring efforts, the experts had never been able to make out which school either of the two members belonged to. A novice might have thought their rivalry reflected a preference for developing the textile industry on the one hand and the food industry on the other (the towel and the chick-peas), and that the change in the list meant that the first had been given priority over the second. But the explanation was probably to do with something more profound, such as the Chinese economy as a whole; or, more important still, some change in foreign policy or in the state of the class struggle at home. Meanwhile other experts pored with equal zeal over Ming dynasty encyclopaedias and learned treatises on poetic symbolism in order to puzzle out what the towel and the chick-peas might stand for in themselves, and what they might mean when placed in a dialectical relationship.

The spy satellites made no mention of other events. But just before dawn, one of them transmitted the following: "As far as is known, no reply has yet been sent to the Albanians' letter. This

78

information is derived from a reliable source. It may be that no such letter exists." In the morning the satellite received a message in reply: "There certainly was a letter from the Albanians. Do everything possible to get hold of the answer." But there hadn't been any answer. Though the attaché-case belonging to Gjergj Dibra, now on a flight from Peking via Karachi to Paris, did contain some important papers, these didn't include any reply to the letter. It was now eleven in the morning. The heavy aircraft was flying over the plains of southern China, above thin clouds touched by the autumn sun. Every now and then the sound of the engines reached the ground. "Couldn't they have re-routed the plane a bit?" grumbled Mao Zedong, a few thousand metres below.

He was quite alone in the midst of the vast plain (his guards were crawling on all fours through the bushes, so as not to be seen). The horizon shimmered in a reddish haze. Mao looked up, trying to see the plane. He was worried not only about his own peace and quiet, but above all about security. These plains grew marihuana, and foreign secret services had apparently got wind of it: the international airlines all seemed to be trying to fly over the area, at low altitudes whenever possible because of what they alleged were difficult atmospheric conditions. But his own idiotic foreign minister and home secretary didn't understand about this, and spent all their time trying to keep atomic secrets, as if the drugs being grown all over the plains were of less importance. They found it quite natural to concentrate all their attention on the sophisticated sciences of electronics and nuclear technology, ignoring fields and crops, the work of mere peasants. Mao let out a growl, in the access of blind rage that gradually swept over him whenever he thought anyone was daring to underestimate or even despise any work to do with the country. He always regarded such indifference or disdain as directed against his own peasant background, and his elderly brain, instead of dismissing it as a matter of taste or principle, saw it as the sign of a desire to take his place.

Let them guard their little aristocratic secrets. He had more faith in the fields of Indian hemp than in all the bags of tricks produced by electronics, atomic power, and all the other confounded sciences.

This was the fourth day that he'd walked in the fields, and he'd rarely felt as he did now. He'd been right to come here straight from his cave. His eyes half-closed against the light, he gazed over the quivering ruddy surface of the plain.

The red ceremonial flags, the posters, the banners . . . The anthem, "The East is red" . . . All the little red books brandished by millions of people . . . "Do you think I take all these red whatsits seriously?" He laughed to himself at the thought of this question, then suddenly stopped and tried to remember where he'd asked it and of whom; but he couldn't. "Do you think I take all this seriously?" Oh, now it was coming back to him. It was one of the questions he asked himself in imaginary conversations with important people – politicians, kings, presidents, his own colleagues, his enemies. Deep inside himself he'd accumulated heaps of such questions, all waiting to emerge one day. Or perhaps they'd given up hope of ever doing so; perhaps they were quite dead, and lay there within him only in the form of corpses.

But the one that had just occurred to him was still alive and kicking, and needed only to be spoken. "Do you think I take all this scarlet seriously?" He tried to summon up the laughter of an interlocutor whose face he'd seen recently in a newspaper. Laughing eyes, a strong jaw . . . It was the face of the American president. The phrase that had taken shape in his mind somehow or other in order to be addressed to someone or other – perhaps Chiang Kai-shek, or Tito, or Haile Selassie, or the Pope – had now fallen to the lot of the American.

"Do you think . . . ?" No, he didn't really believe in all that red. If it came to that, he preferred the ruddiness of the marihuana to the riotous colour of the flags. It was still too soon to say so yet. But it wasn't too soon to think it. It might even be a bit late.

He swiftly looked around. The guards were nowhere to be seen. He could almost believe they didn't really exist, and that his rural existence was protected only by plants – maize, cabbages, soya.

Fields sown with dreams, with senselessness . . . Not so, gentlemen! he exclaimed inwardly. When people can't sleep, don't they take sleeping tablets? But what we were dealing with was the disturbed mind of a whole planet. A lot of nonsense was talked about the way human affairs should be ordered, but no one really bothered about it seriously. People went in for every kind of philosophy, but forgot that what was necessary to one man was equally necessary to a thousand, a million, to the five billion inhabitants of the world. They agreed that one individual whose mind was overwrought might need tranquillizers, but when the mind of the whole race was involved they condemned these fields as full of dreams and senselessness . . .

As for Mao himself, he wasn't very impressed by all those -isms. He had his own opinions about the evolution of things and the future of the world. Unlike most people, and in contrast to what he himself had thought a few years ago, he'd recently come to the conclusion that the world had developed further than it ought to have done: this was one of the causes of mankind's present ills, and of the catastrophes that would overtake humanity in the future if something wasn't done. It was urgently necessary to take steps to bring the mind back within its former limits. If the human brain were not restored to its elementary simplicity it would destroy the world. This was one of the universal truths that Mao had discovered.

One day when he was having tea with Guo Mozo, Guo had told him the debate about the human mind was one of the oldest in the world. Didn't Greek legend present it as the origin of the quarrel between Zeus and Prometheus?

"So you might say," Mao had answered almost jokingly, "there were two party lines on the subject on Olympus?"

"Exactly, Chairman," said Guo Mozo. "Zeus wanted to replace humanity by another species with a less complex brain; in short, as we say nowadays, to create a new man." (Mao had a fleeting vision of Lei Fen.) "Prometheus took the opposite point of view."

"Let those who want to go along with Prometheus," answered Mao. "We're on the side of Zeus."

Guo Mozo had looked at him reverently. "And who more suitable than you, Chairman," his eyes seemed to say, "to play the part of Zeus?"

Mao's narrowed gaze encountered no obstacle on all the vast expanse before him. These glowing plains would be part of the arsenal in his great campaign. The reports he'd read four days ago on China's secret exports of marihuana had been encouraging. Hundreds of tons had already been sent to Europe, and hundreds more were on their way there. But more still was needed. How many tons would it take to drug the whole population of the world for twenty-four hours? No one yet knew. But start with Europe, Jiang Qing had advised him a little while ago, and the whole world will be high: it's Europe's brain that is the most dangerous. That's what I'm trying to do, he'd answered, but it's not as easy as it

looks. If sown on a soil composed of sobriety and wisdom, hundreds
of tons of dreams or nonsense – call it what you like – would
melt like snow in the sun if not backed up by other, more devious
measures. The brainwashing of the human race was a titanic under-
taking. If you didn't destroy the things that fed and stimulated the
mechanisms of the mind, it would be like trying to drain a lake
without stopping up the rivers running into it. Then he'd told her
about his plan to destroy the existing educational system, to close
the universities, to reduce the number of books and go back to the
era when they were copied by hand. No one needed to read more
than a dozen books in a lifetime, and most of those ought to be
about politics. Mao had managed to do all this in China itself
during the Cultural Revolution, but what was the good? – he hadn't
been able to carry it further. True, he'd done so in Cambodia, and
tried – unsuccessfully – to do the same in Ceylon, but those two
countries were still only in Asia. And his dream had been to extend
his policy much further. Into Europe. Yes, Europe . . .

He would rather not have thought about Albania on a day like
this, but it came into his mind unbidden. He'd had such high hopes
of Albania! But be patient, he told himself: all things come to him
who waits . . . It was too soon to give up hope. He'd issued new
instructions, and there was to be a complete overhaul of the official
attitude towards Albania. Something must be done; the lynx would
soon be tamed.

In Cambodia, on the other hand, things were going quite well –
better even than he'd expected. And all over the world his followers
were supporting him and had gone over to the attack. For the first
time ever, the thrones of such supreme masters as Shakespeare and
Beethoven were toppling. Someone had suggested that a Chinese
pianist who had played a Beethoven sonata should have his arms
cut off. That might sound barbaric, but it was not. Monsters like
Shakespeare and Cervantes were more harmful than any emperor.
They wielded absolute power; they were tyrants of the mind,
colonizers of the brain. Kings could easily be overthrown, decapi-
tated, or relegated to oblivion; but those other scourges managed
to survive through the ages with their power unscathed and even
enhanced. But now their supremacy was about to end. He, Mao
Zedong, had come into the world to challenge them. Their time
was up. Like the kings and the tsars, they would be given their
marching orders: Chairman Cervantes, Prince Beethoven, General-

issimo Shakespeare, Count Tolstoi, and so on . . . Compared with him, Mao, what a poor figure other, minor world-changers cut: they had merely overthrown some monarch or prime minister, while he alone had stood up to the evil Titans and would deliver the whole human race from the unwholesome spell of art.

He'd had scores of thousands of individuals put on trial and punished, but he still wasn't satisfied. Some had been sent to the provinces, consigned to muddy ditches and rice-fields. They'd been beaten and spat upon. They'd been made to forget they'd once been writers, and then terrorized by being reminded of some novel they'd written, as if it had been a crime. As for those who couldn't forget, they'd been driven to suicide. And yet he felt he hadn't done enough.

Every so often he would rehearse in his mind, like a kind of play, a meeting which resembled sometimes a gathering of the Greek gods on Olympus and sometimes a session of his own Politbureau. For the next point on the agenda, I call first upon Prometheus . . . Then on Chen Pota.

In any case, Zeus had been wrong to chain Prometheus to a rock. That only made a martyr of him. Marx himself had said so, thus spreading confusion among the world proletariat.

If he had been Zeus, Mao wouldn't have put Prometheus in chains or hurled down thunderbolts upon him. He would have sent him to the rice-fields, amid the mire and the people.

The ancient Greeks knew plenty of things but they didn't know the power of the paddy-field. The paddy-field, with its mud and its night soil . . . Nothing like it for destroying a man and making him disappear without trace.

Mao had a file, perhaps the one he cherished most, labelled "Letters from the Rice-fields". In the last few years he'd received letters of every kind from all sorts of people: from prisoners on the eve of execution, from widows, from fallen ministers begging him for clemency, from unemployed embalmers, and so on. But those from the rice-fields were the only ones he enjoyed looking through again from time to time. They were from writers deported for a period of re-education in the provinces or in out-of-the-way villages. "Thousands of us here in the water and the mud thank you, O God, for delivering us from the demon of writing . . ."

Mao liked to get out the file and compare recent letters with earlier ones. He noticed that they grew more and more scrappy, their sentences thinner and thinner, akin to the dullness of the earth. Lord, he thought one day, soon they'll only be sending me senseless ramblings like the blatherings of someone with apoplexy. And after that I shouldn't be surprised if one of them just dispatches a piece of paper smeared with mud, a few scattered characters like grains of rice miraculously left behind after a flood.

He smiled at the thought of it. Then he *could* be said to have got the better of the writers! He'd always felt a deep aversion for them, but after he married Jiang Qing, and especially after she began to get old, his dislike had become almost unbearable. He knew, as the foreign press had recently reminded him, that she was influenced by her past as a third-rate film actress, and the jealousies, failures and permanent humiliations she'd undergone, though she probably hadn't told even him about the worst of them. He knew or could imagine the real reasons why this belated settling of old scores had become an obsession with her, but as it chimed with his own ideas he didn't disagree with it. One day he went so far as to tell her so.

"You're an out and out egoist, and it's a personal matter with you. I'm a poet myself, but I don't hate other poets out of jealousy or spite. It's because they do harm that I can't stand them, not out of any personal animosity. And when I've got rid of them all I'll even feel a certain regret, as one might after having to pull up a beautiful but noxious weed. You, on the other hand . . . But you're a woman, so I suppose one mustn't be too hard on you . . ."

He well recalled that unforgettable July night in Shaoshan when they'd sat up till dawn talking about the future of the world.

It was an oppressive, damp night, stifling the end of every sentence into groans. They'd both been excited at the thought of the world of the future, purified of art and literature. "How marvellous it will be to purge the world of such delusions and unhealthy emotions!" she had cried, though she cracked her knuckles with a certain amount of apprehension. She knew it was a difficult task, and kept asking him, as if for reassurance, about the chances of success. He duly reassured her, and she replied, almost as if she were actually drunk: "And music too – on another night such as this we'll rid the world of that too, so that the whole planet is as deaf as a post!" The theatre, the novel, poetry – they were all to be dealt with in the same fashion. The only subject left for the imagination to work on – she didn't say this explicitly, but he could guess what she meant – would be their own two lives. Or rather hers. And was it such a wild idea, after all? What other woman since Creation had had the leader of a billion men for a husband?

All these things could be brought about somehow or other. Autos-da-fé had been common throughout the history of mankind, and it was quite feasible to close theatres, smash pianos, drag thousands of writers through the mud, and even return the human brain to a less complex state and make the imagination wither away. These things were all interconnected: the elimination of one brought about the destruction of another, just as the fall of one beam can lead to the collapse of a whole roof. But there was still one thing more difficult to dispose of than all the rest. Twice, almost trembling, she had asked him: "What about life itself? What are we going to do about what people call the good life, with its after-dinner conversations, and love . . . ?" More out of fear than anything else she'd had to make two attempts at explaining what she meant by love. After much beating about the bush she'd finally brought it out: she was talking about love in the usual sense of the word – the relationship between men and women. Mao had listened to her in silence, then, with the same deliberation as before, he explained that all the aspects of life she had referred to, not excepting love itself, would eventually fade away. After-dinner conversations would disappear, if they hadn't died out already, for the simple reason that there wouldn't be any more dinners (you couldn't describe a mere bowl of rice as a dinner!). As for love, that was only a question of time . . .

Except that his ideas were untinged by any personal ambition, their views had recently tended to grow more and more alike. True, Mao had been very much in love with his first wife: when he dedicated one of his most moving poems to her, Jiang Qing had responded with hysterical tears. But in the course of the last few years his opinions about love, as about a number of other things, had changed.

Jiang Qing, glad to see love relegated at last to a place among the other undesirables, began to talk more passionately, more fanatically even, than before, for hours and hours which he would always remember as *her* night. She whispered in his ear that love was their personal enemy (she no longer bothered to call it the enemy of China or of the Revolution), as ruthless as the rest and in many ways more unrelenting than they because more insatiable. She maintained that this wretched relationship between the sexes used up a large part of the world's total resources of love, thus depriving him and her of their own due share: it hijacked the love that should rightly come to *them*, she went on tearfully. Again he interrupted her calmly. "Don't worry, Jiang Qing," he said, "love will be abolished too." And he explained that love wasn't as powerful as it might seem: it hadn't even existed until comparatively recently. In the ages of barbarism it took the form of mere sexuality, and even in classical times its affective content was limited. It was the European Renaissance that had fostered the disease and turned it into the most widespread epidemic in the world. But the winged monster would eventually die as rapidly as it had been born, after having already said goodbye to the things that had nurtured it – the arts, literature and all the other nonsense. He described the various stages of the war to be waged against it: the first thing to do was reduce love to what it had been before the Renaissance. The second phase would deliver it a fatal blow by reducing it to sexual relations pure and simple. Thus the danger would be to all intents and purposes eliminated. "But how long will it take, for God's sake? How long will it take to finish it off?" she asked impatiently, almost in anguish. He had given her some sort of limit, he couldn't recall exactly what, but he did remember her sighing because she didn't think they'd live to see it. Soon afterwards, when he first heard of lovers in Cambodia being summarily executed after being found talking about love instead of politics, he'd reminded her of her sceptical sigh that hot damp night . . .

They'd talked till dawn, that strange summer night, discussing subjects that had probably never been debated before since the world began. "Anything that might encourage love must be abolished," she murmured. "Women's shoes, jewellery, dresses, hair-dressing . . ." "But we've done that already, practically!" he answered. "Such extravagances haven't existed in China for a long time." "Not in China, perhaps," she complained, "but we must look much further – the rest of the world is full of them!"

Then she suddenly stood up and went into another room. After a while she came back wearing a uniform that was half military and half more like that of a prison warder. For a moment he had to shut his eyes: he couldn't stand the sight of her got up like that, with that wretched cap covering her sparse hair, those trousers clinging to her body – it was horrible, as if there were nothing left of her, not even the bones. He was well aware why she adopted his ideas on the reform of mankind so eagerly, but seeing her like this he realized she would go on trying to translate that dream into reality until she died. "From now on," she whispered, "I shall dress like this not only when I'm with you, nor even just at meetings of the Politbureau, but everywhere – in public, at the big parades in Tienanmen Square, and even at official receptions, under the very noses of the foreigners." Her words convinced him that if her sacrifice was going to be complete, the reward she expected would be no less so. I must be careful, he thought: this woman is consumed with ambition. But she shall have her reward! He couldn't remember very clearly now what he'd actually said at the time, nor even what he'd thought. No doubt he'd made a few half-joking, half-serious remarks: "As you faded, so beauty too faded from the world;" "the world must mourn for your lost youth;" "it's not you, but the world, that has grown old" – that sort of thing. And: "I once heard of a book about a young man whose face remained unchanged, while the effects of time could be seen only in his portrait . . . Someone must pay for the passing of your youth, Jiang Qing. All the women in China aren't enough for you? I knew you'd say that! Very well, let all the women in the world pay, then!"

He reminded her that some women in Europe thought as she did.

She listened eagerly, feverishly. "Some women," he said, "have lost no time in adopting my ideas, even in the heart of Europe, in Paris – people call them Maoists. Don't you think that's wonderful?"

"Of course," she answered, "but there aren't very many of them – just a drop in the ocean. What a task it will be to change all the others! Perhaps it would be a good idea to start with the women in Albania? The alliance between our two countries would make things easier."

"Yes, you're right," he answered. "That's what we'll do. The Albanian women will be the first ones in Europe to be de-feminized. I'm told they managed to throw off the veil after being forced by Islam to wear it for five hundred years. But we are much stronger than Islam!"

As dawn approached, their conversation grew more and more incoherent: sometimes he would nod off, sometimes she sounded as if she were talking in a waking nightmare. She would get into a rage, then a moment later be overcome by an icy wave of doubt. "Unsex all white women, master!" she cried out once as in a dream.

Then became cast down again at the thought of how long it would take. She was afraid everything would peter out when he died. She feared he himself might not be determined enough. He reassured her as best he could. "Don't worry! Once we get the thing started there'll be no stopping it." If it hadn't still been in the future, he might have quoted the example of Cambodia: "Look at Cambodia – it started there with hatred of culture and ended up with hatred of everything else. Now they're even allergic to buildings in their cities!" As it was, he just had to listen to her breathless fretting: "What if this? Supposing that?"

It was getting light when he started talking about marihuana. Perhaps the rosy gleams of dawn made him think of it. Perhaps he thought it was time to put an end to her ravings. At any rate, he suddenly heaved a sigh and said: "There's another way I can achieve my ends." Then he told her of what his enemies called the latest bee in his bonnet – his marihuana plan.

"When I gave orders for farmers to start growing it, a couple of months ago, everyone thought it was for the four or five billion dollars it might bring in. The idiots! My reasons were quite different . . ."

She listened open-mouthed.

"I'd have told you about it before," he said, "but I was waiting for an opportunity like tonight."

Then he rambled on about the waves of red that would eventually spread out over the whole earth like ripples on a pond, and about the hallucinations that would fill all those gradually softening brains. A few years' addiction to the drug brought about a weakening of the mind, while a few years more produced further deterioration, and so on until the persons concerned had lost about half of their mental faculties.

"And that's the key to the whole thing," he murmured. "That's what will make all the rest quite easy – do you see?"

And so they began a new day, hovering between sleep and waking. All that was needed was the hoot of an owl to complete Jiang Qing's resemblance to Lady Macbeth, as there lay in the next room, with their throats cut, Shakespeare, the Ninth Symphony, the Mona Lisa, and all the drunken governments who, like King Duncan's drugged grooms, woke too late to prevent the murder . . .

Mao Zedong took a deep breath as if to drive away the memory of that night. Some time had gone by since then, and what had once been a dream had long since turned into fact. So much so that foreigners had begun to smell a rat. He froze again, thinking he heard the sound of another plane. But when he looked up the sky was empty except for clouds dotted here and there, as before. I must have been dreaming, he thought. Then, a moment later, growled: "They sniff around my marihuana like a pack of hyenas." But let them fly as low as they liked, let them take photographs, make films, even analyse samples of soil, they would never guess his ultimate object. Their minds are too stale too discover our secrets, he told himself. Even Marx couldn't have done so, explaining everything in terms of economics and politics as if that were all! He'd have like to remind Marx of Genghis Khan – there'd been no economics or politics, no profits or surpluses, in his tide of conquest: only violence, annihilation, the grinding of everything to dust. How do you explain that, eh, Herr Marx? Your mind can't cope with our Asian ardours. That's why you were doomed never to succeed with us.

He realized his thoughts were becoming confused. Europe, marihuana, the need to strengthen the dose again – the various ideas were not combining into any sort of order. "Mari-hua-na," he mumbled. "Mao-mari-huana." He laughed. "The thoughts of Maorihuana! Laugh, the rest of you! You'll still be the first to come crawling to me for mercy! Ave Mao-Maria!" And he laughed to himself again. But this time it was more like a sneer.

They'd say he was raving. It was a word they were very fond of. They were always in a hurry to stick labels on any ideas their sluggish minds couldn't understand, any concepts a bit larger than what they were used to. "Cosmic ravings", indeed! Of course, if someone's mind isn't capable of standing back and regarding the world impartially, everything strikes him as crazy. But *his* mind *was* capable. He could stand a thousand yards back from the world and examine it closely, even though he was only a tiny particle compared with the whole cosmos. Not for nothing was he the spiritual leader of a billion men. It was this multitude that conferred on its guide the power of seeing the world in its true proportions. You had only to look at it properly to see a tiny globule revolving in the heavens like millions of others, inhabited by at most four or five human beings: one white, one yellow, one red and one black. The white is physically the strongest, with a well-nourished brain that enables him to dominate the other three. These submit to him because they have neither the physical nor the mental strength to oppose him. And so the days (the centuries) go by, until the yellow man happens to discover a plant, which he slyly boils and gives to the white man to drink. The white man swallows it, has sweet dreams, and his mind is weakened. He goes on drinking the potion for years. And then comes the day (the century) when the yellow man, seeing the white man at the end of his tether, seizes the opportunity to wrest his power from him. Now, thinks he, it's my turn to rule the world. What a pity it's not a bit bigger!

That's all. The rest was just stuff and nonsense. This was the whole history of the globe, past and present. A waste of time to discuss it further. To complicate things was mere foolishness. And now he was brewing the potion for the whole of mankind.

Mao blinked, then looked out over the landscape. This was the cauldron in which he brewed his philtre. The red steam rose to the brim. Was the world troubled? Then its fever must be soothed as soon as possible. This was what he'd been working towards for a long time: he was going to give the world a sleeping pill of his own making.

He felt drowsy too. Again he thought he could hear a plane, but once more when he looked up the sky was empty. "That's how the problems of the world might be settled," he thought. "It's too small a one to be worth any more bother. I could have dealt with a world that was much bigger."

The roaring sound returned. But this time Mao didn't look up. "It must be just a buzzing in my ear," he thought.

Gjergj Dibra's plane had been flying for ages over the Arabian deserts. The return journey seemed so long it was as if the desert had grown larger since the journey out. He'd given up looking out of the window a long while ago: the monotony of the scene below only made the time creep past more slowly. He tapped nervously at the locks on his briefcase, which as always he was holding in his lap. It was a bit fatter than it had been on the way out, but sealed in the same way. Yet, though he knew nothing of its contents, his intuition told him that even though it might look heavier, its contents were in a way less weighty than they had been.

And he was right. The briefcase didn't contain any reply to the letter from Albania to China. At first sight the papers it did hold had nothing to do with the letter. Some of them dealt with economics: four reports trying to explain the freighters' delay. The fifth document was a long memorandum, accompanied by maps and sketches and drawn up by seven Chinese experts, warning that the main compensating dam serving the northern hydro-electric power stations might burst if there was an earthquake. Work on the site should be halted at once in order that the necessary precautions might be taken. Documents 7 and 8 were accounts of a long series of negotiations between the two economic delegations, strewn with misunderstandings arising largely out of language. The ninth document was the X-ray of a Chinaman's foot, together with two interpretations of it – one by a group of surgeons at the osteology centre in Peking and the other by a group of barefoot doctors – together with a note from the ministry for foreign affairs. The last paper of all was a detailed report on the evidence collected concerning the murder of Lin Biao, with various theories as to who was responsible. This was the only document with whose contents Gjergj Dibra was more or less familiar, since in the course of the tedious evenings he'd spent in Peking he'd often discussed the rumours about Lin Biao's disappearance with his friends at the embassy. During the flight home he'd been turning what was said over and over in his mind, perhaps because these comments had disturbed him, or perhaps because Lin Biao's end had involved a plane journey. As soon as Gjergj had set foot on the steps leading up to the aircraft, he couldn't help imagining the marshal in some secret airport, hurrying towards a plane over which the shadow of death probably hung already. He was with his wife and son, and all three looked terrified. So much so that at the last minute, just as he was about to enter the plane, Lin Biao appeared to halt, as if petrified, and had to be dragged inside . . . It was a strange and senseless journey, aboard a plane without a crew – was it possible that his son, a squadron leader in the Chinese Air Force, would have chosen such an aircraft, let alone one with insufficient fuel aboard? It was all very hard to believe, as was the alleged phone call from Lin Biao's daughter, who betrayed her father by telling Zhou Enlai about his attempted escape five hours beforehand. Not to mention Mao Zedong's words, "Let him go," and the suggestion by one of the marshal's fellow-conspirators that the plane should be brought down by rockets so as to remove all traces of the plot. Then Mao again: "You'd better let him go, so people won't be able

91

to say we murdered him." And then the plane crashed and caught fire in Mongolia . . .

Gjergj Dibra gave the briefcase a shake and scrutinized its complicated locks. Things probably hadn't happened like that at all. This doubt had been expressed several times during his long evenings with his embassy friends. None of the foreign diplomats in Peking ever talked about anything else. Most of them inclined towards some other version of the story.

And every night what Gjergj had heard, instead of fading from his memory, merely grew clearer before he fell asleep in his hotel room. What has it got to do with me, he would ask himself – to hell with them and their mysteries! But in spite of himself he would always lie awake revolving all kinds of theories.

In all probability Lin Biao hadn't boarded the plane in order to flee, but simply to fly to Peking – and he'd been killed on the way. He must have quarrelled with them about something. Perhaps about the visit of the American president . . . And so they'd hatched a plot against him. They sent for him – said it was urgent. On the plane, seeing that the flight was lasting an unexpectedly long time, he became suspicious and asked where they were going. Through the window he could see a landscape that resembled the Mongolian desert . . .

Although he had made up his mind not to look out, Gjergj couldn't help leaning towards the window. Below, through the gathering dusk, the deserts of Arabia were still visible. Not unlike Mongolia, he thought. "Well, where are we going?" Lin Biao had asked. And then, recognizing the country below, he and his men had taken out their guns and shot themselves.

The light was fading swiftly, as if drawn down by the sands. On an evening such as this a few Soviet soldiers, struggling through the desert, had found the wreckage of the plane. Among the débris was the charred body of the man who had once been the second glory of China, Mao's expected successor. The man of all those presidiums, those meetings, those appearances on colour TV, was now reduced to ashes, a blackened ghost like the image on a photographic negative. After a thorough inquiry, during which spent cartridges were found in the wreckage of the cabin, the question immediately arose: who had fired the shots, and why? The theory of attempted escape was now eliminated.

Gjergj went on fiddling with the handle of his briefcase. Perhaps the Soviets held the key to the mystery. But how could they know? Was it Lin Biao who had fired first, as soon as he realized he was being removed by force from China; and had the others fired back? Or had the others shot him when he asked where they were going? Or had both groups – if there really were two groups – opened fire at the same time? Gjergj Dibra no longer tried to extricate himself from the maelstrom of hypotheses in which he was plunged once more, as in his sleepless nights in Peking. He just let out an oath from time to time, wishing them all to the devil. But he did so only mechanically – he knew this nightmare would last throughout the journey.

Well, someone had fired shots inside the aircraft. And then the plane had crashed. Why? Because of the shots? (Perhaps some vital piece of mechanism had been hit. Or had the pilots been killed?) Anyway, the drama had taken place prematurely, unexpectedly.

But what would have happened if no shots had been fired? Where would the plane have gone to? And, most important of all, where and how would the drama have ended?

As often happens when one dreams that one is flying, Gjergj's imagination was drawn towards the earth.

Apparently the plan was that the matter should be settled on the ground – on foreign soil, evidently, to make people think Lin Biao had been trying to escape. Otherwise, there were plenty of deserts in China where he could have been eliminated without any difficulty.

So the intention was that Lin Biao should be found on foreign soil (Soviet soil, as it happened). Aboard the plane on which he'd fled. Dead.

The plan implicit in this hypothesis was clear. The plane was to land somewhere in Mongolia. Before the Soviet frontier guards arrived, the killers would have plenty of time to shoot the marshal, either inside the plane – they could pepper the body with impunity now it had landed – or outside, on the ground.

In the latter case the marshal and the people with him would have been made to disembark, and then shot beside the aircraft. When the Soviets came on the scene they'd have been told: "This is Lin Biao, our minister. We were his guards. He was trying to escape. We are loyal to Mao. So we shot him."

But this fine plan had been foiled by Lin Biao himself, with his question about where they were going, the shots, etc. Unless what

93

triggered things off was the guards' attempt to disarm him ("As soon as you cross the frontier, take away his gun!").

Gjergj shook his head. Was it likely the meticulous Chinese would embark on so crude a plan? The perfunctoriness of it was obvious, but quite apart from that it involved enormous risks. There were two groups of armed men aboard the plane, and Lin Biao's escort was at least as likely as not to get the upper hand. Then he would have got clean away.

No! Gjergj told himself. It couldn't have been like that. Such an unsound plan could only have been set up by someone certain that whatever happened inside the plane – even if Lin Biao did get temporary control – the end of the story would be the same. For the simple reason that both parties would be burned to ashes.

The plane would be shot down. Someone was sure of that.

Gjergj leaned his forehead against the window, but the vibrating of the glass only made him more agitated than ever.

There were two groups on that plane, and each group thought it knew the truth. Lin Biao's party thought he was being flown to Peking. His potential murderers knew they were going to murder him in Mongolia. But over and above all this there was someone else, not on the plane, far away even, who really knew what was what: who knew that the plane was doomed to be burned to ashes.

H'mm, thought Gjergj. So they planned to shoot the plane down. Easy to say, but not so easy to do. If the marshal had been summoned to Peking he would have travelled either on his own plane, or on a government aircraft, or on one belonging to the general staff. Whichever it was, all such aircraft were guarded day and night: it was unlikely anybody could plant a bomb aboard them or interfere with their landing gear. Even if that were possible, it would still be difficult for the killers to get themselves aboard. Lin Biao's escort would challenge any unknown faces and order them to be thrown off the plane without more ado.

H'mm ... Not really very plausible. Even if such a plan had gone smoothly to begin with, how could the bomb be timed to go off at a precise moment, after the plane had crossed the frontier? The marshal was the second most important man in China, and in charge of his own comings and goings. He could have delayed his flight by an hour, by two hours even, if he felt like it. No, it must have happened differently. Or perhaps all the theories reflected the facts in some way, only in a different order and in pursuit of a completely different purpose.

But what does it matter anyway? thought Gjergj to himself in a last effort to get the business off his mind. There was no point in cudgelling his brains over something that was bound to remain a mystery no matter how much one tried to puzzle it out. He was already depressed enough after spending all that time surrounded by mask-like faces inhabiting a seemingly lifeless world. He'd felt his own vitality draining away as the days went by. And now he was leaving it all behind he meant to forget those empty countenances and all the stress he'd endured. To hell with them and their mysteries! Anyway, this might be his last trip there.

He tried to imagine himself back at home among his nearest and dearest, but some obstacle seemed to stand in the way. The entrance hall of the flat, the doors into the rooms looked different. There was something strange about the familiar sound of Silva's footsteps going from their bedroom to the bathroom. There was even a mist over Silva's and Brikena's faces. What was going on? he thought worriedly. The spell of Asia seemed to envelop him still.

He beckoned to the stewardess who was patrolling the narrow passageway between the seats, and ordered a cup of coffee.

"Where are we?" he asked her when she brought it.

She gave the usual automatic smile and told him. But he didn't hear: his mind had substituted the words, "Over Mongolia."

"Where are we going?" Lin Biao had asked on the fatal plane, as it speeded towards an unknown destination. "Oh, hell!" cried Gjergj, realizing he couldn't tear his thoughts away from that other aircraft. He'd heard so much about it during those dreary evenings in Peking —it was going to take time to get it out of his system.

So for the moment he gave up trying. He just tried as best he could to clarify his ideas on the subject, as if drawing up a report on a press conference. He hoped this might calm him down.

Clearly there had been no attempt at fleeing the country. Nor had the plane been piloted by Lin Biao's son. Admittedly the marshal's wife and son had been with him (perhaps all three had been invited to Peking together), but everything had been arranged so as to make the theory of escape seem plausible. And indeed everyone would have believed it had it not been for the shots. Who had fired them, and at whom? Had the son shot his father? Had they both

95

fired at one another? Was it conceivable that the betrayal attributed to Lin Biao's daughter had really been committed by his son? . . . Not very likely.

There must have been others on that plane. But who? They must have been hostile to Lin Biao, since, whoever fired first, shots *were* indeed fired. So that made two opposing groups aboard, though at least one of the two parties – the one charged with killing Lin Biao – knew the other wouldn't emerge from the journey alive. The plane took off. One hour, two hours went by. Peking, whither Lin Biao was supposed to have been summoned urgently, was still not in sight. It was then that he asked: "Where are we going?"

Up till then everything was more or less clear, but after the fateful question all became obscure. Including the shots.

But you've just said it was practically impossible for the presumed murderers to get on board the plane, whether it was a private or a government aircraft! Gjergj reminded himself. This is torture! Then suddenly he realized who it was that might actually ask him these questions. He even knew where the interrogation would take place: in the Riviera Café, where Gjergj often went and sat with Skënder Bermema. That's it! thought Gjergj – it's because of him I keep turning these thoughts over and over in my head. He knew that as soon as he got back Bermema would bombard him with questions. In particular about the murder of the marshal. The two of them had talked about it several times before. Bermema probably meant to write about it.

It was not a soothing thought, and Gjergj relapsed once more into a morass of conjecture. If ever there was a gleam of light, it vanished before he could examine it . . . Had there been a miscalculation? Had the plan been thrown off course by the marshal's question about where they were going? He must have looked anxiously at his watch. Recent anxieties and suspicions must have played their part. His nerves were bound to have been on edge. He must have asked himself a dozen times why he'd been summoned so urgently. And so, when there was no sign of Peking . . .

Or maybe none of all that happened at all: he neither looked at his watch nor asked any questions. They could have just shot him as he drowsed in his seat. "If anything unforeseen happens, kill him on the plane . . ." But, to be on the safe side, the killers didn't wait for any hitch. So it was all over sooner than expected, and inside the plane all was deathly silent. The murderers were now escorting the cooling corpse of their master, little knowing that they, as well as it, would soon be burned to ashes.

But you just said . . . What would have happened if . . . All right, all right, I know what you're going to say. It's a very curious scenario. So many complications. The most sensible approach was put forward by a senior official who suggested simply shooting the plane down with rockets. That would have dealt with the matter nicely. But according to official spokesmen the suggestion was made by one of the marshal's own accomplices, in order to "destroy the evidence"! Evidence of what, if you please? . . . Oh, that's enough! Gjergj imagined himself saying to Skënder Bermema as they sat in the Café Riviera.

Gjergj struggled to stay there. He saw in his mind's eye the low seats by the misty plate-glass windows, the rain on the pavement outside, the slim figure of the waitress, who'd seemed even frailer to him after he heard she was living with a wrestler. Ever since he'd met Skënder Bermema they'd gone to the Riviera every so often to have a coffee together, usually sitting in the corner overlooking the airline offices. An anonymous letter had brought about the beginning of their relationship, several years ago. Gjergj had received the letter just after he and Silva got engaged. It was the usual sort of thing: Silva was a capricious young woman, pleasant enough as a mistress, no doubt, but most unsuitable as a wife. Both the Krasniqi sisters, the unknown writer went on, were very free in their ways (it was clear that, on second thoughts, the writer had used the word "free" instead of "loose" throughout). There were all sorts of rumours – some of them might be unfounded – about them: they were supposed to swap lovers, or else be fiendishly jealous of one another, and so on, though all this was probably exaggerated. But what was true and common knowledge was that one of the sisters was having an affair with the famous writer S.B. . . . It was no secret that his novel, *Forgetting a Woman*, was dedicated to her.

There the letter ended. What perturbed Gjergj was that its author didn't say anything precise. He'd turned the letter over in a rage to see what was written on the back, as if he expected to find some accusation about Silva there – for example that she'd had an affair with an archaeologist on the site at Pasha Liman. She'd told him about that herself. But the writer of the letter didn't mention it, and Gjergj was more upset by what he hadn't said than by what he'd set down in black and white. The swine, he felt like yelling –

why doesn't he mention what everybody knows? The answer was clear. The writer of the letter had foreseen that if he referred to that well-known liaison, Gjergj would have read the allusion with a sigh of relief. As it was, the "well-wisher" gave the impression of scorning gossip, turning a deaf ear to some of it, thus making the contents of his own letter more plausible. Similarly, having made the allegation about lover-swapping, and spoken of the affair between Ana and Skënder Bermema, he could leave Gjergj to think: if Ana and Skënder Bermema, why not Silva and Skënder Bermema?

Gjergj had let some time go by before mentioning any of this to his fiancée. But one day he did ask her if she knew Skënder Bermema. He'd prepared himself for a painful moment in order to see her reaction. But her reply, instead of reassuring him, left him more troubled than before. "Yes, I know him," she said. "We both do, Ana and I." "Both of you?" There hadn't been the slightest indication, either of guilt or of innocence, in her expression. Just something vague that was neither one nor the other. Then he showed her the anonymous letter. Silva read it calmly. Her cheeks did flush a little when she came to the part about exchanging lovers, but she didn't flinch. She thought for a moment, then looked up at him and said: "What do you expect me to say? That it's all just slander and tittle-tattle?" Gjergj was lost for words. "Of course it's meant to be malicious," she said. "Still, there is a grain of truth in it."

Gjergj's mouth went dry.

"But even if the letter's right about Ana," she continued, "do you think what it refers to is so shameful and immoral that it reflects on me . . . ?"

"What are you saying, Silva?" he broke in. "I didn't mean that at all! I just showed you a letter. A horrible anonymous letter."

She told him she herself had questioned Ana about Skënder Bermema, but the answer had been so evasive she hadn't raised the subject again. That was the only time Ana hadn't confided in her. But it hadn't changed Silva's opinion about her sister in the least, she insisted. And Gjergj had replied that it wouldn't change his either.

One evening later on – at the theatre, during the interval – Silva had introduced him to Skënder Bermema . . . She was with Ana . . . After that the two men had come across one another on several occasions. But it wasn't until after Ana's funeral that they had their

98

first coffee together . . . It was strange, Silva had said. Her sister, with her great beauty, seemed to have been sent on earth to stir men up one against the other. But strangely enough she had had the opposite effect. As if in accordance with some mysterious pact, those who'd desired her had always avoided anything that might embitter their relations.

Gjergj tried to linger on these reminiscences, but it wasn't long before they were swept away and replaced by the sinister affair of Lin Biao. Gjergj groaned, clutched his brow, and longed for the journey to end.

As soon as he'd landed in Tirana he would meet Skënder Bermema and unload this agitation on to him. Transferring it to someone else was the only way to get rid of it.

But for the moment he had to cope with it alone.

His nervous tension seemed to have given him a temperature, which was made worse by the sound of the engines . . . One of the marshal's accomplices had suggested shooting the plane down with missiles . . . God, it's started up again! he whispered. But there was no resisting it. So . . . One of the marshal's accomplices, as yet unidentified, had suggested shooting the plane down. To do away with the evidence, the Chinese spokesmen had said. But that didn't make sense! What evidence did the accomplice mean, the one who had remained on the ground? Whether the marshal managed to escape or got shot down, his plot would be exposed. And in either case the conspirators would be unmasked. The marshal's supporters would be arrested one after the other, and those interrogating them would only have to tug on one thread for the whole skein to unravel. No one could save anyone else. So the idea of shooting the plane down, and for the reason alleged, was nonsensical if attributed to one of the marshal's accomplices.

But it would all – including the phrase "destroy the evidence" – make perfect sense if it had been suggested by others, and for a completely different purpose. While the fateful plane was still in the sky, the secret telephone network used by those following the escape must have echoed and re-echoed with the words: "We must shoot it down – otherwise how are we going to destroy the evidence?" Getting rid of the evidence – a perfectly natural preoccupation after such a murder. In this case, "evidence" meant details of the trap: the summoning of the marshal to Peking, the sabotaging of the plane, not to mention the disposing of the witnesses. During those feverish hours the phrase "destroy the evidence" must have been used over and over again: and something had to be done to explain such a compromising expression. So they attributed it to a conspirator who had been unmasked. Then it was all right. All those who had heard it occurring again and again during the incident could stop worrying: it had indeed been uttered, but by a traitor.

But in fact, as everyone knew, the suggestion was rejected. Mao wouldn't agree to having the plane shot down. Why? The answer went without saying: he didn't share the anxiety of the others, for the simple reason that he knew something they didn't know. Then another question arose: what *did* the others know? And what *didn't* they know? Were those who suggested shooting the plane down so ill-informed as to think such a solution was possible? Didn't they know that the plane of the marshal supposedly invited to Peking was doomed never to land? You'd have to be very naive to believe they were ignorant. No, they were all perfectly well-informed: after all, it was they who'd prepared the trap in all its details – the take-off, the re-routing towards the Mongolian frontier, the bomb placed on board or the sabotage of the landing gear, designed to cause a fire. They knew all this. But still they suggested shooting the plane down.

Every so often Gjergj was consoled by the thought that he wasn't the first person to rack his brains over this affair. Hundreds of people must have followed that flight. To make the theory of attempted escape more plausible, all the airports in China had been put on alert. But just as on the plane itself those who were leaving or thought they were leaving all had different notions about what was really happening, so too did those who were still on the ground. Most of them – officers in charge of military airfields or rocket launchers, pilots ready for take-off, radar experts and so on – had been informed about the marshal's attempt to escape. But one thing they couldn't make out: why had there been no order from Peking to pursue his plane or even shoot it down? Even when the plane appeared on the radar screen the order didn't come. The pilots had difficulty holding themselves back – they longed to fall on their prey and tear it to pieces, and were afraid other pilots from another base might be given the chance instead. But soon, through some channel or another, the explanation came: Chairman Mao hadn't allowed the plane to be shot down. Apparently he'd said: "Let him go if he wants to!" This information filled some people with admiration (the great Mao dealt with a traitor as calmly as he might have brushed off a fly), and others with amazement (this was no joking matter, and the marshal, far from being a fly, knew all the state secrets . . .).

But a much smaller circle was in possession of quite a different set of facts: the summons to Peking, the attempted escape to Mongolia, and above all – yes, above all – the setting fire to the plane by means of a bomb or the sabotaging of the landing gear. They'd also had wind of the possibility that the marshal might be executed in the air. "If anything unforeseen happens, kill him on the plane!"

As soon as they heard the plane had taken off they heaved a sigh of relief. Thank goodness the whole business would soon be over now. That's what they thought at first. But soon, as the flight continued, they began to be assailed by doubts: wouldn't it be more efficient to bring the plane down with rockets? What if the time-bomb didn't go off, or the pilot managed to land the plane safely despite the sabotaged landing gear? (Hadn't there been many such cases?) How could they bear to let their prey slip through their fingers?

They probably went and told Mao about their anxiety. One of them added: "Even if Lin Biao were already dealt with – should the witnesses be allowed to survive?"

Mao heard them out patiently, but showed no sign of going back on his decision. Finally he answered curtly: "As I said before, let him go. If he's lucky enough get away in spite of the bomb and the sabotage, it means fate has decreed that he should live!"

They exchanged glances. This was his new style. They weren't used to it yet. It must be due to his spells down in the cave – they joked about these sometimes.

But their anxiety only increased. Mao had assured them the plane had been doubly sabotaged, by the planting of the bomb and the damaging of the landing gear, but they couldn't suppress their doubts. It wasn't that easy to sabotage a plane Lin Biao was travelling in!

Mao himself was perfectly at ease. For the simple reason that he knew another secret. Never mind the bomb and the damage to the undercarriage – Lin Biao was dead already. Killed not in mid-air, as their feeble brains might imagine, nor in the Mongolian desert, but on Chinese soil.

As they dithered around him trying to tell him their worries, Mao looked them over sardonically. They always forgot he came from a peasant background – and a peasant always trusts terra firma better than the sky. Could he possibly have been so reckless as to let Lin Biao fly around before he was killed? He couldn't afford such a luxury. That was why he'd said "Let him go!" so placidly. He'd known he was talking about a corpse.

So Lin Biao and his wife and son had died, like the vast majority of human beings, on earth. On a landing strip or in a hangar in some remote airfield. Or else they were liquidated even more cold-bloodedly inside the marshal's official residence, as they were taking a stroll round the garden after breakfast. They were shot with a machine-gun through the iron railings, and their bodies were put in a van and driven to the little military air-base. There the bloody corpses were lashed to their seats in the waiting plane.

If Mao was so calm it was because he knew all that. But he had never confided in anyone except Zhou Enlai. The reason for his silence was simple: he was protecting his own prestige. He felt that the planting of a bomb on a plane and the sabotage of its landing gear were strategems which might have damaged his reputation, whereas a ground operation was something quite different. He hadn't even spoken about it to Jiang Qing. Zhou was seriously ill and hadn't got long to live, so the secret was safe with him. As for the killers, they would soon follow their victims to a place where they could tell no tales.

Meanwhile the little army plane was flying over northern China. Deep silence reigned on board. No questions were to be heard, no gunshots – only the monotonous purr of the engines. The bullets which were soon to put the whole world in a turmoil were already in the bodies. Every so often the corpses, now beginning to cool, would slip down off the seats. One of the killers had probably thought it enough to fasten them into their seat belts.

Gjergj felt a tremor go through the giant plane, and leaned towards the window. The lights had gone on asking passengers to fasten their seat belts. They were apparently about to land. Night was falling; the tiny purple-glinting windows far below seemed to belong to another planet. The plane was bumping more often now. Gjergj's ears were hurting. The ground was coming closer and closer, and he found himself glancing towards the place beneath the wings where the landing gear would soon emerge, with a faint jolt that would run right through the fuselage.

What a relief! This torture would soon be over. He was sure that as soon as the plane had touched down he would be free of all these chaotic obsessions. But the landing was taking a very long time. The mauve lights of the airport building vanished to the right, as if they'd fallen into an abyss. Was he still going to have to keep churning up the same old jumble of thoughts in his skull, when after all the whole affair could be reduced to the story of a dead body being thrown over the Chinese frontier?

Yes, that's it, he thought, his temples throbbing as the air in the cabin was depressurized. The story of a dead body being dumped. In the old days, bandits used to leave the bodies of their victims at their enemies' door. Mao dumped them at the door of the nearest super-power. Tossing corpses into forts and citadels in order to terrorize the defenders was a custom as old as time. He remembered, too, how the ashes of the false Dmitri of Russia were shot over the Polish border in a cannonball. All quite typical of such countries. And hadn't Mao threatened them in exactly those terms when he said, "I'll scatter your corpses in the air"?

The body of the plane creaked loudly as it descended through the semi-darkness. Gjergj was still holding his briefcase on his lap. The metal buckles gleamed faintly. The Soviets had been just as mysterious over Beria. He'd vanished more than twenty years ago, and his disappearance was still an enigma. People said there wasn't even any trial or firing squad – he was just killed at a meeting of the Politbureau. One version said somebody had strangled him with his bare hands. Then the body was hastily buried. Whereas he, the amazing Mao, airily tossed corpses from one country to another as if with a catapult.

Why can't I get these images out of my mind, thought Gjergj. Again he peered out of the window, but all he could see was the damp impenetrable darkness. Where had the earth gone? How much longer were they going to have to wander around in space? He leaned his head against the cool glass, feeling the plane's vibration run right through him. Then suddenly, a long way in front of him, he saw a multitude of little lights, not only mauve but also red and green and blue, winking and flickering in the darkness. He felt his heart grow warmer, he was filled with a delightful languor. The plane's wing blotted out the lights on the ground for a moment, but he sat on with his forehead pressed to the glass as if he could still see them. His thoughts had drifted home again to his loved ones. Their faces, wreathed in smiles, succeeded one another in his memory until for some reason or other it came to a halt on an episode he hadn't remembered for a long time. What he recalled was his first moment of real closeness to Silva, in an avenue strewn with dead leaves – he still didn't know its name. It lay between the main boulevard and Elbasan Street, and they'd just come away from an evening party – they hardly knew one another as yet. Under the streetlights the yellow leaves stretched out like a sumptuous expanse of gilding glowing with the patina of time. They noticed a scrap of paper amongst the leaves – a piece from a musical score, with the notes still legible. He pointed at it. "Look, some Mozart!" he said. She laughed. He glanced at the dark buildings bordering the avenue: "I think this is quite near the hostel for music students."

The memory of this interlude was almost painful. Gjergj thought of the moment just before they made love, when her eyes were about to cast off sight just as her body was about to strip itself of clothes. Then came the moment when he was bending over her white belly and that which was waiting, unbearably intense, below . . .

The heavy fuselage jolted when the plane touched down on the landing strip. The engines shrieked as the pilot throttled back. Multicoloured lights quivered frenziedly on either side. "How wonderful to be going back!" he exclaimed. In three days' time he would be in Tirana. The plane slowed down, panting heavily. What airport was this, then? He looked around in the hope of seeing some name among the lights, but they still jigged about drunkenly and were dumb. Anyhow, what did it matter? The main thing was that he would soon have left all this behind. Then he remembered that he hadn't even sent his family a telegram. How could he have forgotten? But never mind, it still wasn't too late. He peered out of the window again in search of a name. The stewardesses had just announced something . . . But how did one write a wire in these parts – in Latin characters or Arabic?

The plane came to a stop at last, and the passengers got ready to disembark.

Gjergj smiled to himself as he stood up. He was going to send that telegram anyhow, even if it had to be written in Egyptian hieroglyphics.

* * *

Silva got the telegram the next day. It was growing dark and she was tidying up the refrigerator when there was a ring at the door. Then she heard Brikena calling from the hall:

"A telegram, Mother! I think it's from Father . . ."

After a moment's surprise she straightened up and ran out into the hall. Brikena had already opened the envelope and they both pored over the wire, reading it out almost in unison: "Arrive Thursday German plane. Fondest fondest love."

"How lovely!" cried Brikena, clapping her hands.

At first they could think only of the message, reading it over and over and scrutinizing the date-stamps which said when it had been dispatched and when received. Then they rushed to consult Brikena's atlas to find the town it had been sent from.

"He's still miles away!" said Brikena when they'd located it.

A few moments later their apartment, which had been so quiet lately, suddenly came to life again. The lights were on in all the rooms. Silva went from refrigerator to stove and then to the cupboard in which she kept the crockery, where she promptly forgot what she'd come for. "What sort of cake shall we make?" Brikena asked. Of course, that was what Silva had gone to the cupboard for! But it was still too soon – he wouldn't be home for another couple of days. They had plenty of time for everything. But if Brikena wanted to they could make the cake today. Silva was so happy she didn't know what to do with herself. At one point she found herself wandering aimlessly around the apartment. Then, rather than starting on something that needed to be done and then putting it down again unfinished, she just picked up the telegram and went through it again slowly, as if to trying to read something between the lines. Her smile froze when she came to the words, "Fondest fondest love", wondering why they made her feel vaguely anxious. What does it mean? she thought – and found herself crying out to something deep inside herself: "What's the matter with me?" Nothing, replied the gulf within. But the uneasiness remained, distant, vague. Anyhow, that fit of sentiment wasn't a good sign . . .

In the end, the gulf within delivered its answer. Silva hadn't been able to repress the memory of a very distressing funeral. The man being buried had died in a plane crash on the way back from China, and the man's wife had said to Silva: "I don't know – his last letter was so emotional I was quite disturbed . . ."

Nonsense, Silva told herself – the post-office people often

duplicate words in a telegram. She knew this wasn't really true –
they only repeated dates or figures. But why was she letting herself
get upset like this?

"What's the matter, Mother?" asked Brikena.

Silva took herself in hand.

"Nothing, dear. I was just trying to think of something special
we could cook for your father."

And she started bustling around the apartment again.

On Thursday morning Silva asked her boss to let her leave the office
at eleven, though the plane wasn't due until three in the afternoon.
In any case, she couldn't concentrate on any work. Linda kept
glancing at her with a curious look in her eyes.

"Have you missed him very much?" she asked, the first time the
boss left the room.

"Yes, very much," answered Silva, without looking up from her
desk.

But she could tell Linda was still looking at her. It felt stiflingly
hot in the office: had they turned the heating up too high, or was
it just her imagination?

"What do you feel like when he comes back from abroad?" her
young friend asked, hesitantly. "Are you very happy?"

"Of course," said Silva, glancing at her.

Linda's cheeks were slightly flushed, though she was pale around
the eyes.

"Of course," said Silva again, feeling her own cheeks going pink.

Does Linda really not understand? she thought. But that was
probable enough. Marriage altered everything – especially what
people felt after a separation.

There was a knock at the door. Illyrian. He'd heard Gjergj was
arriving that day. Silva felt rather self-conscious. She had the feeling
everyone was trying to imagine what she and her husband would
be doing that afternoon and evening. As a matter of fact she kept
thinking about it herself. Sometimes she thought about what under-
clothes she'd wear; sometimes she thought about the moment when
she'd slowly take them off. He liked watching her do that.

She began to wonder if it wasn't she herself, with these thoughts
of hers, who was making the others imagine her consumed with
desire. She almost believed that if she stopped thinking about it the

awkwardness between her and them would disappear. But no. The others were meeting her more than halfway. When she'd asked the boss if she might leave early, he'd laughed roguishly and said, "Oh yes! – today's the day, isn't it?"

Illyrian didn't take any such liberties. Dressed as elegantly as ever, but more serious than usual – almost solemn, in fact – he'd come to ask if she'd heard about the change in the plane's time of arrival. And she, though she had in fact been informed, thanked him without telling him she knew already.

There goes someone, at least, who knows how to behave, she thought as he shut the door.

At a dance nearly a year before, just after he'd been taken on at the ministry, Illyrian had paid her some very meaningful compliments. Silva was used to masculine admiration and paid no attention, but when, a little later, he returned to the charge more insistently, she responded so tartly she surprised even herself. What had made her fly out was the thought that his boldness might be due to some image about her, and especially about her sister Ana, that he'd acquired from somewhere else. After that incident she'd expected him to bear her a grudge, but apparently he'd concluded it was his own fault, and had swallowed her snub with surprising dignity.

At eleven o'clock, as she was going down the stairs, she met Simon Dersha. He was still wearing his navy-blue suit, and his face was as drawn as before. One of these days this chap's going to go off his rocker, she thought as she greeted him. The registry clerk in the planning department, who saw and heard everything, claimed that Simon had been invited to dinner one evening by minister D—, and that ever since then he'd been wearing his only smart suit in the hope of being invited again.

As soon as she was outside the ministry, Silva breathed in a gulp of fresh air and felt much better. It was a dreary, drizzling day, but Skanderbeg Square suited her cheerful mood. You could stroll along the pavement in front of the ministry, and facing you was a garden laid out in the form of an amphitheatre. The road overlooking the garden was wet, and shrouded in a seasonal veil of mist. But she had no time to waste. At half-past one, two o'clock at the latest, she and Brikena must leave for the airport, and she still had a few things to do. But nothing very important. Perhaps she should buy two or three bottles of wine and some cakes to be on the safe side, as a few friends might very well drop in in the course of the evening. But everything else had been ready since the day before.

As she went by the local greengrocer's shop she noticed some very fine apples on display outside, and went in. As usual the greengrocer, a great beanpole with a voice like disc jockey, was holding forth to the customers as he served them. There were eight or so of them, men and women, awaiting their turn. The greengrocer was tipping some apples into a string bag held out by a man who was rather carefully turned-out.

"How's the Chinese coming on?" asked the greengrocer, rummaging in the cash register for the man's change.

"I beg your pardon?" said the other.

"I asked how the Chinese was coming on," the greengrocer said again.

"Well!" exclaimed the man, pursing his lips indignantly at the other's lack of discretion.

"I don't reckon all the trouble he's taken learning Chinese will do him a bit of good," said the greengrocer when the man had left the shop. "He lives near here – one of those ex-bourgeois types who've changed their tune," he explained as he weighed out apples for one of the women. "He used to be a translator from Russian – he'd learned it in prison. But after the break with Moscow he abandoned Russian for Chinese, and managed to learn it in two years! But what's the point? It doesn't look as if Chinese is going to be much use to him now!"

"Those bourgeois devils could learn to talk in stomach rumblings if it suited them," croaked an old man.

"Still, poor chap," said the greengrocer. "Imagine toiling away for years to learn a language, and then practically overnight it turns out to be no use any more! He must be seething with rage!"

"That's what you get for trying to be clever," grunted the old man. "Why did he want to go and learn Chinese?"

"He must have thought there'd be plenty of translation going," said a young man.

"Well, he thought wrong!" crowed the ancient.

Several of the bystanders laughed.

Silva bought some apples and left. As she did so she could hear the old man saying something else, and the others laughing again.

How strange, she thought. The people in that shop hardly knew each other, but they talked about China more or less openly. She walked on faster. In the last few days, preoccupied with Gjergj's return, she hadn't paid attention to what was being said about relations with China. So the conversation in the greengrocer's had in a way taken her by surprise. Such comments would have been unthinkable at the beginning of the break with the Soviets. And now everything's so quiet, she thought, shifting the heavy string bag from one hand to the other. Well, so much the better, I suppose. And she started thinking about Gjergj's return again.

At home Brikena was waiting impatiently. Silva asked her to stay by the telephone while she herself had a bath. As she lay in the water she couldn't help remembering her boss's arch remark and Linda's pink cheeks and questions about her feelings. These recollections mingled with an acute sense of imminent happiness.

At the airport there was a small crowd, but they were almost all foreigners.

"Mother, did you see all those Chinese?" Brikena exclaimed in surprise as their taxi drew up outside the customs building.

The taxi driver smiled.

"The place has been full of them, the last few days," he said. "They seem to take it in turns."

"What do you mean?" asked Silva, handing him a 50-lek note.

"The usual thing – the first lot go and the next lot take their place," said the man, feeling in his pocket for change.

Silva thanked him and got out. The concourse was crowded with Chinese too.

"We're early," she murmured. "We're going to have quite a long wait."

"Never mind, Mother – I like it here."

They managed to find a free table and sat down. But between then and the moment when a female voice announced over the public-address system that the Berlin–Budapest–Tirana plane would be arriving in a few minutes, the time passed more quickly than they expected. Standing at the windows overlooking the airfield, they watched the plane land, the steps being wheeled up, and the first passengers begin to appear.

"There he is!" cried Brikena, the first to spot her father among the small group of passengers, most of them Chinese. Gjergj started to walk in their direction: his bearing was as usual – upright, deliberate, his briefcase in his hand. He hadn't noticed them yet, probably because of the reflections on the glass. It wasn't until he was quite close that he saw them, and waved.

"Did you have a good trip?" Silva asked while he was still hugging them both.

"Yes, thanks. How've you two been getting on?"

"Fine. Except that we were worried about you."

"Why?"

"Well . . ." Silva pointed to the apparently endless crowd of Chinese.

He laughed.

"You look tired," she said when they were in the taxi.

He stroked her cheek with the back of his hand.

"Well . . . I must admit the journey was exhausting. And then there's the time difference . . . Did you get my wire?"

"Yes."

He smiled to himself, as if remembering something.

"Everybody's talking here about the difficulties with China," Silva said.

"Are they? I rather expected they would be."

"It's the only topic of conversation!"

"Where do you live?" the driver asked as they were reaching Tirana.

Silva was going to tell him the address, but Gjergj spoke first.

"I'd like to stop at the foreign ministry first, please, just for a minute."

He smiled and pointed to his briefcase. Silva leaned her head on his shoulder.

He left them outside at the ministry, but they didn't have to wait long, and a few minutes later they were home. Gjergj wandered around the apartment while Silva and Brikena laid the table.

"Good gracious, the lemon tree's flowered!" they heard him exclaim when he came to the French window.

"Do you like it?" asked Silva.

"It's lovely."

When Silva came out of the kitchen a little while later to say the meal was ready, she found him standing in their bedroom gazing absentmindedly at the curtains.

"A penny for your thoughts," she said.

He nodded towards the windows.

"I was looking at the curtains," he said. "I can't get over it. Out there they don't have any."

"Really?"

"Strange how much one missed them! It was as if the windows were blind. Or dead ... But that isn't all. One day a Chinaman told me, 'The reason why we've abolished curtains is that that's where the trouble begins – the desire to keep private life secret.'"

Silva kissed him.

"Stop thinking about it," she said tenderly, leading him out of the room. "Come along, the meal's ready."

"You're right," he said, following her. "I must get it all out of my head as soon as I can."

By the time they'd finished eating it was getting dark. One of those dusks in which day and night merge in perfect harmony.

Silva glanced at her husband.

"Would you like a little rest?" she asked.

"Yes, that would be nice."

"You go and have a lie-down too, Brikena."

"But I'm not tired!"

"Have a rest anyway ..."

"All right."

Brikena stood up, went over and kissed her father on the cheek, and disappeared.

Silva and Gjergj looked into one another's eyes, exchanging smiles as misty and mysterious as the approaching evening. Then, one after the other, without a word, they stood up and walked through the corridor – now quite dark – into their bedroom.

In the distance, as if from another world, the telephone rang and rang. "What can that be?" asked Silva plaintively. If Brikena didn't answer, she must have gone to sleep, she thought ... Finally she got up and went to the phone, not stopping to put on a dressing gown.

"Who was it?" asked Gjergj when she came back.

"Your sisters. They wanted to know how you were. They're coming round this evening."

The phone rang again.

"Leave it – they'll get tired and hang up," he grumbled.

She was tempted to let it ring, but, as if under some compulsion, got up again. It was her other sister-in-law. As she spoke into the phone she stammered a little: it had just occurred to her that Gjergj might have made her pregnant. A girl friend had once said it always happened at times like this.

"Why didn't you disconnect it?" he asked when she came back again.

"It wouldn't be polite," said Silva, shivering and cuddling up against his chest – it had been cold out in the hall. "People want to welcome you back."

He didn't answer.

The phone rang several times more, and in the end they both got up. Silva put the coffee on. Brikena, who'd fallen asleep in her room, woke up too. The smell of coffee made the warmth of the apartment more delightful still.

"How I've missed it all," Gjergj said, looking round.

When they'd had their coffee Silva started on the washing up from lunch, which she'd left in the sink. On the stroke of six, two of Gjergj's sisters arrived. They were followed by other visitors, relations mostly. But fortunately, after a while, they all said, "Now we'll leave you – Gjergj must be worn out after that long journey."

By about ten o'clock the three of them were alone again. After dinner Brikena put some discs on the record player, every so often asking her father if he liked what she was playing or if he'd rather listen to something else. Meanwhile, Gjergj looked from one object to another with a strange expression on his face, as if he was seeing them all for the first time.

"It feels so strange to be home again," he kept saying, in a tone that made Silva and Brikena exchange surreptitious glances.

After midnight, Brikena retired to bed and Silva and Gjergj went to their own room. The voices of late passers-by wafted up from the street.

"I *have* missed you!" he whispered, stroking her hips.

They lay for a long while in one another's arms. In the silence, punctuated by their breathing, she thought again about the possibility of his having made her pregnant, but she soon dismissed the idea. Anyhow, it wouldn't be so tragic. A dreamy procession of those who had phoned or dropped in passed through her mind. Her brother Arian hadn't shown any sign of life. He was gradually drifting away from those he used to know, as people usually did when they were expelled from the Party. This thought caused her a pang. She sighed, and hesitated for a moment. Should she talk to Gjergj about it? It was two o'clock in the morning. The pillow where their hair lay intermingled was inviting. She brushed his cheek lightly as if to check whether his eyes were still open.

"Gjergj," she whispered in a low voice that was more like a strangled sigh. "I didn't mean to mention it this evening, but I can't help it. A week ago Arian was expelled from the Party."

"What!"

She repeated what she'd said. He lay still for a moment, staring up at the darkness.

"But why?"

"I don't know. He hasn't said."

"Very odd," he said. "I suppose it couldn't be anything to do with the Chinese?"

"The Chinese? You must be joking!"

"Not at all."

He moved his arm from around her so as to turn and look at her.

"It may sound ridiculous, but things like that can happen when there's a crisis. You know what I mean . . . It happened before, with the Soviets . . . Some people weren't very keen on making a break . . . Though in this case, of course, it would be crazy to suppose . . ."

"You mean he might have sided with the Chinese?" Silva exclaimed. "Never – you can be sure of that! The idea never even crossed my mind. I'm sure it must be something else – probably nothing whatsoever to do with the Chinese."

"Maybe," he said.

"I'm sorry, Gjergj – I probably shouldn't have mentioned it, especially this evening. But I've been so worried . . . for days and days . . ."

"No, no," he interrupted. "You were quite right to tell me."

A clock they'd never heard before chimed somewhere nearby. All those clocks, in apartments full of human memories, thought Gjergj.

After a moment he said:

"No, I'm sure it's nothing to do with the Chinese."

6

EKREM FORTUZI DREW BACK the curtain and looked outside. It was a damp, grey day. I'd better wear my galoshes, he thought. He pondered for a while before a heap of shoes that he kept in a cupboard beside the bathroom door, then bent down and rummaged among a mass of sandals, slippers and boots, most of them with holes in the sole, broken straps or missing heels. Eventually he found his galoshes, dropped them on the floor, and was about to put them on when he heard his wife's voice calling from the bedroom.

"Ekrem – where are you going to so early?"

"It's not early, Hava – it's nearly ten o'clock. I'm going round to the ministries to see if there's any work."

"You still haven't given up hope?"

He didn't answer.

"I've lit the stove," he said after a moment. "And the milk has been boiled. So I'll see you later, my pet."

"All right, my love."

A feeling of relief came over him as he went out into the street. The shutters of the house opposite, warped and weatherbeaten by the rain, were still shut. Sunday, he thought – people are having a lie-in. But he had to do the rounds of government departments to see if anyone had left any translation jobs for him to do. So that his employers wouldn't need to seek him out, he'd got into the habit of calling at the various offices after working hours or on Sundays to pick up files containing documents to be translated from Chinese. They'd be left at the door for him to collect, usually with a note attached saying when the job was to be finished – in most cases far sooner than was reasonable. Nor did he go in and receive his fees personally: he waited for them to be sent by post. For his friend Musabelli had given him some useful advice when he first started to translate from Russian, in the days of the Soviets: "Be careful not to be seen too much around government offices – the communists don't like falling over us ex-members of the bourgeoisie every time they go out into the corridor."

Ekrem had stuck to this rule. Whenever he came upon a crowd of people outside a ministry or other government building at the end of the day, he would turn away and not come back until everyone else was gone. Sunday was usually the best day. Not only could he pick up the files then without any bother, but he could even exchange a few words with the man on duty. They all knew him now. Most were ex-servicemen, and though Ekrem felt rather shy with them, he was grateful for their friendliness. Some even seemed to admire him. One day the man at Albimpex said, "You must be pretty clever, eh? How did you get to be so good at Chinese?" "Somebody had to, I suppose," he'd answered. "You're right there," said the man, gazing at him respectfully. "Good for you, comrade!" Ekrem blushed, but any kind of display embarrassed him and he hurried away.

It was almost with affection that he thought back now to those afternoons, those snatches of conversation by the porters' lodges and the smell of the chestnuts the inmates roasted over their little electric stoves. Work had grown scarcer and scarcer lately. And now the demand for translations had almost completely dried up.

Ekrem had reached Government Square. The wide grey pavements, more sombre than ever in the rain, were deeply depressing. The lofty portals of the Ministry of Construction, with their heavy bronze door-knobs, stood ajar. He peered through the opening at part of the cold, empty, dimly lit hall, then slipped inside. The man on duty was in his usual cubby-hole, warming his hands over a stove. "Good morning," said Ekrem. "Chilly, isn't it?"

"Good morning," answered the man. "Yes – it's the time of year. Is it raining?"

"Just spitting."

"There isn't anything for you, I'm afraid." Ekrem felt his heart miss a beat. "I'll have a look in the drawer to make sure, but I don't think there's anything."

For a few seconds Ekrem looked on dully as the man fumbled in the drawer among a few odd papers.

"No, nothing," said the man.

"Right, then. Goodbye," said Ekrem.

"Goodbye. Better luck next time."

"Next time . . . ," Ekrem thought to himself as he went out into the square. He trudged on for a while without thinking. Where should he go next? To Agroexport or to the Ministry of Trade? But wait a minute! If he went to both those places, mightn't that be seen as a kind of investigation, as if he were checking up on things? He had a sudden vision, a memory of the prison yard on the day parcels were handed out, together with, for some reason or other, the dirge-like singing of a common law prisoner convicted of incest. But the next moment: how ridiculous, he thought. Why should anyone need to be checking up? For days people had been talking about it almost openly. To hell with precautions! Not only would he go and ask if there was any work for him at the two places he'd just thought of, but he'd also present himself at Makina Import and Albimpex, and even the Planning Commission. He'd go the whole hog. He realized he'd started to walk faster . . . He began to calm down. Perhaps he wouldn't go to the Planning Commission for another couple of days, he thought, but he'd certainly go to the other places.

Isn't all this just my luck! he said to himself as he made his way towards the Agroexport building. He felt very down, though he did try to tell himself all wasn't yet quite lost. But in fact he was sure he was the unluckiest person in the world. He'd just arranged to do a new translation – from the original, this time – of the libretto of *Tricked by Tiger Mountain*, when the first rumours of disaster had started to spread around. It had been the same with Russian: just as things had seemed to be going better than ever, the catastrophe had happened. But it was much more annoying to see his Chinese going to waste: thousands of people had known Russian, but he was one of the few Albanians who knew Chinese, and he'd gradually emerged as the best. That opera translation would have opened up new possibilities for him. But now everything was collapsing. When he'd told Hava about the first hints of a break with China, she'd said casually, "Don't pay any attention to such gossip! Weren't you disillusioned enough after the break with the Russians?" "That's not what bothers me," he'd replied. "I'm not crazy enough to have any hopes about politics! What I'm worried about is my knowledge of Chinese – it won't be any use any more!"

The Agroexport offices, with their hermetically sealed shutters, looked far from inviting. Ekrem went and stood just inside the great door.

"No, nothing for you," called the man behind the little window brightly.

"I thought I'd just take a stroll, to see," said Ekrem, almost apologetically.

"No, not a thing."

"Of course not," said Ekrem, cursing himself for not being able to shut up. What a fool he must look. "I didn't really expect to find anything, but I just dropped by in case. You can easily call in for nothing, but then again, sometimes a translation's needed just when no one shows up to do it!"

He forced a laugh. The man seemed surprised. Ekrem tried to look unconcerned.

"Well, goodbye, then."

"Goodbye."

Once outside he gave way to his dejection. There was nothing. No point in trying anywhere else. No point at all . . . Just the same, he felt his legs carrying him back towards Government Square. He was just going round in circles. Like an ass on a threshing floor.

The man at the Ministry of Trade was new, and took some time to understand what he wanted. Then, mortifyingly, he didn't even leave Ekrem time to invent an excuse: he just said no one had left anything to translate into any language. Ekrem even got the impression the man suspected him of being up to no good! That was the last straw! he thought as he left. He probably ought to have stayed and explained that he came here regularly to collect work. But he didn't go back. What was the good? Let the oaf think what he liked! But Ekrem couldn't help shuddering at the thought that the man might have picked up the phone and spoken to a colleague at the Ministry of Construction: "Hallo? Has a shady-looking individual been there asking if you still need translations from Chinese?" In other words, had he been there trying to find out the effect on international relations of the recent rumours – rumours well-known to have been put about by ideological agitators.

He shivered and came to a halt. Should he go on? Then he started walking again. Let the oaf phone his colleague! The other man would sort it all out and there wouldn't be any problem. What an idiot I am! It'll be all to the good if he *does* phone!

The Albimpex and Makina Import buildings were both in the same street. Ekrem hadn't yet decided which he'd go to first. He could feel the damp air chilling him to the bone. He'd never imagined that one day he'd be reduced to running from one government office to another begging for a bit of translation. In his wildest dreams he'd never imagined his Chinese ending up like this! All those friendship meetings and delegations going back and forth had seemed to promise just the opposite.

His Chinese . . . When he thought of all the sarcasms, the sneers and the bitchiness he'd had to put up with from his acquaintances! One day Hava Preza had said, "There's no harm in learning Chinese, but I don't like to see you putting all your eggs in one basket and using up all your spare time on that gibberish. Supposing – God forbid! – they put you in prison again? The last time you learned Russian. What would you do this time?" "Don't be so spiteful!" his own Hava had answered. "My Ekrem certainly won't be going to prison again!" "You never know," retorted Hava Preza. "As the unfortunate Nurihan said, anyone can land up in jail whether they've been there before or not." After that, she would sigh and add: "Still, there are plenty of other languages left to learn, I suppose!"

At first even his own Hava had made fun of Ekrem, but at least she'd also been the first to understand the point of his efforts, and had even begun to encourage him. When he'd managed to learn the first eight hundred ideograms they celebrated by going out to a restaurant for supper. There, as she looked at him with a mixture of excitement and regret, Ekrem, his cheeks slightly flushed with wine, described what their future would be like under the new dispensation: how successful his first translations from the Chinese would be; how celebrated he'd become as the best in the field; the fat fees he'd earn; how he'd probably be asked to do a new version of the poems of Mao Zedong. These would no doubt be followed by invitations to the Chinese embassy, and then – why not? – after he'd done some particularly important translation, for instance Chairman Mao's complete works, he might be sent on a trip to China, with stop-overs – heavens above! – in Paris and Rome . . .

She went on looking at him with the same despondent eyes, almost tragic with their heavy mascara and puffy, painted eyelids.

"Why are you looking at me like that, my darling? Don't you believe me?"

"Yes, I believe you," she answered. "I'm just sorry all these things won't be happening to us because of a more civilized language –

English or Spanish, say. Chinese strikes me as – how shall I put it?
– a dud sort of language."

"Never mind," he'd answered cheerfully. "One can find happiness even with the language of the devil!"

Later, when he'd begun to receive his first fees, Ekrem realized that his involvement with Chinese brought him a certain amount of political security as well as material advantages. It brought him closer to officialdom and to the régime in general. Not for nothing was Chinese called the language of friendship. As soon as people found out what he did, a feeling of mutual trust was generated which wiped out his bourgeois past. But now, alas, all this was being reversed. He would be made to pay dearly for that partial rehabilitation. The excellence of his Chinese, of which he had been so proud and which had acted as an antidote to his past, would now turn into an exacerbation, if it hadn't done so already. Henceforward he would be doubly undesirable, as a survivor of two detested eras – that of the bourgeoisie and that of the Chinese. People would point at him in disgust as the worst of time-servers, the most servile and shameless of turncoats. God! he groaned. Suddenly everything looked black. Every door was closed to him. And to think he'd still had the heart to go begging for translations out of that accursed lingo! He'd do better to shut himself up at home and never go out again, in the hope of being left in peace and forgotten.

He shouldn't have let himself crawl from door to door like that. It would have been wiser to go to the opposite extreme: even if anyone offered him some translations left lying about by mistake, he ought to have said, "Sorry, I gave up that sort of thing a long time ago. I don't feel sure of myself now. The ideograms have impaired my sight, and although I've had two sets of new glasses I still can't see them properly any more."

That's what he ought to say even if they came and implored him. Instead of going looking for trouble! "Take yourself off while there's still time," he exhorted himself, "and shut the door in their faces! The break with China is the signal for you to make a break of your own."

He felt like bursting into tears. A day like this was enough to make you weep, anyway. The bare rows of trees lining the streets made the grey frontages of the ministries look even more dreary than usual. Ekrem imagined the porters and duty officers inside, warming their hands over their stoves. He noticed he was passing the vast offices of the Makina Import company, and began to walk faster as if he were guilty of some crime. Take yourself off! he told himself. Go away, you wretch, before it's too late!

As he slunk along with his chin sunk in the fur collar of his coat, his attention was caught by a familiar symbol on a poster. No, not a symbol – a line of ideograms. He slowed down to decipher it: "Exhibition of Porcelain". What's this, he wondered, going nearer. Yes, it was Chinese all right, though underneath the text there was a translation into Albanian. The poster looked as if it had been there for some time, but the wind and the rain and the street cleaners had failed to tear it down.

But it didn't look as old as all that. An elegantly dressed couple had stopped in front of it. The man, whom Ekrem thought he'd seen somewhere before, was smiling and talking to the woman as he examined the words on the poster.

Ekrem looked at the pair. He felt as if the man's smile invited him to join in their conversation, as often happens when strangers meet by chance at some unusual sight or incident. He felt an almost irresistible desire to speak to them. To say, for instance: "Fancy leaving that poster up now! What a joke, eh!" And in spite of his natural shyness he might actually have spoken, but for the feeling that he'd seen that face before. On the way up to the Kryekurts's first-floor apartment? Or somewhere else? On television, perhaps?

He moved a step forward. Perhaps I should look at the date? he thought. Abandoning all precautions he peered closely at the poster. He thought he must be seeing things. Could it be possible? He took off his glasses and got another pair out of his pocket. Then he read the date, first in Chinese and then in Albanian, then in Chinese again. No doubt about it. The poster bore today's date. It also said where the exhibition was being held. The Palace of Culture. Impossible!

"Today?" he asked the man, his voice faltering with emotion.

"Yes," replied the other, looking him straight in the eye. "Today."

Ekrem thought he could discern a kind of amused mockery in the man's voice and expression – a mockery aimed not only at him. But this was of no interest to him now.

"Thank you," he said. And then he made his way back across Government Square towards the Palace of Culture. A surge of pleasure made him almost stagger. He felt his chest suddenly expanding – his old lungs couldn't cope with it. So things weren't as bad as all that, he thought. One of the tunes that generally came back to him in moments of euphoria tried to make itself heard. But this time it wasn't *O Sole mio*. No, it was *The East is Red*. He recited the words to himself in Chinese as he approached the Palace of Culture.

Skënder Bermema looked after the stranger for a few moments, then turned back to the poster.

"Just look!" he said to Silva, whom he'd met by chance in the street a little while ago. "An exhibition like that at a time like this! How exciting! I love it when this sort of thing happens on the eve of great events. Come on, let's go and have a look."

"All right," said Silva. "I'm late already, but I can't resist!"

The Palace of Culture, where the exhibition was being held, was quite close by, and on the way Silva told Bermema some details about Gjergj's recent trip to China. He was highly amused.

"He's dying to see you," Silva told Skënder. "He tried to phone you but you weren't there."

"Really? Well, I'm eager to see him, too . . . I say, look at all the people!" They had almost reached the Palace of Culture, and Skënder was pointing to the crowd around one of the entrances.

The atmosphere was much as he had expected. The exhibition was probably attracting far more visitors now than it would have done six months ago. Most of their faces wore a strange smile, an unnatural mask-like expression of curiosity mingled with bewilderment. Among the rest there were several Chinese and some officials from foreign embassies.

"I've noticed that just before a breaking-off of relations they always put on an exhibition," said Skënder, turning his own smiling mask towards Silva. "Or perhaps 'mystification' would be a better word for it."

Silva, finding it hard to concentrate, was gazing at a mass of terracotta objects, unenticingly displayed. Her companion's warm bass voice reached her through loud background music. Chinese music.

"Someone told me," he was saying, "that in accordance with their habit of conveying political messages by means of symbols,

121

the Chinese have placed a couple of pots in a particularly significant position here."

"Really?" said Silva. "Where?"

Skënder laughed.

"Ah, there you have me! First we have to find them, and then, if we do, we have to try to guess what's meant by their placing."

"Could it be those?" asked Silva after a while, pointing out a couple of vases of unequal size on which a weedy little man seemed to be feasting his eyes.

They both burst out laughing and let themselves be swept along by the crowd.

"There's a pair of yesterday's men," said Skënder, indicating two visitors wearing off-white raincoats as wan as their smiles. "I shouldn't be surprised if at least one of them didn't still cherish the hope of our getting together with the Soviet Union again. I don't believe in argument by analogy, but they remind me of the time when we broke with Moscow. Do you remember? – everyone was asking when were we going to take up with the West again."

"Yes, I remember."

"Just watch their faces when they look at some Chinese vases. They seem to be saying, 'Did you really think these objects were ever going to take the place of *Anna Karenina* and Tolstoy?'"

Silva put her hand over her mouth to stifle a laugh.

"I don't know why they don't just say it outright. And look at the way they dress. Always in the same colours the Soviets wear on their rationalist Sundays – pale grey and off-white. I don't know if you remember the first New Year after the break – the idiotic way some of them behaved?"

"Yes, I remember," said Silva again. For some reason or other she was thinking of Ana. Perhaps he was too, for he was silent for a while. Then:

"Look, there's one of our China fanciers – a genuine connoisseur!" he exclaimed. "I knew we'd find examples of every species here!"

"I didn't know there were such people."

"Oh yes," he said, his tone suddenly harsh. "They're rare, but they do exist . . . Do you know that one over there?"

"No," she said. The person he meant was short and swarthy.

"That's C— V—, the critic."

"Is it? I've read some of his articles, but this is the first time

I've seen him in the flesh. Does he really like the Chinese?"

Skënder's grey eyes went cold.

"After the break with the Soviets he was all poised to step into the breach and fill Albania with Chinese theories on literature and art. And he was the first to suggest our adopting the Chinese habit of not putting authors' names on the books they write."

The crowd seemed to have grown since Silva and Skënder arrived. It was quite difficult now to move about the long room, which every so often was lit up by a camera flash.

"Two years ago in this very hall," Skënder said, "they exhibited the famous sculpture, *Outside the Tax Office* – a real piece of rubbish, as you may imagine. There were plenty of sarcastic remarks about it, but in those days the people who swallowed Chinese art hook, line and sinker were still in the ascendant."

Silva's smile told her companion she thought he was overdoing it a bit.

"And look at them now," he went on, "prowling around those vases, or whatever they are, making disparaging remarks. The whole thing is a cold-blooded war in which neither side really gives a damn about anything. But of course, in present circumstances, the enthusiasts are in the minority . . ."

"Look over there," said Silva, interrupting him.

A group of people were gathered around a showcase. A press photographer, who from his equipment looked like a foreigner, kept crouching down to take pictures.

"I should think that's where the fox is lurking, shouldn't you?" said Skënder.

But when they got near enough to see, the vases the group was looking at turned out to be quite ordinary.

"Sorry I interrupted," said Silva. "You were saying the China enthusiasts are on the wane . . ."

"Ye-e-es . . . But that sort of riffraff don't give up easily. To start with, they still hope the rift with China can be mended. But the main thing is, they think that even if the Chinese do go they'll leave a useful amount of their jiggery-pokery behind."

"How can they possibly hope such a thing?" said Silva indignantly.

"Because they're swine!" he answered. "Still, you ought to know there's a difference between the two camps. The first lot's love of Russia was to a certain extent understandable – it was connected to a part of their life that they'd spent there. To Russian literature, the Russian winter, and so on. And especially Russian girls – as you may have heard, Russian girls are very charming. But the other lot's love of, or rather craze for China is completely base. It hasn't got anything to do with China really, with Chinese art or the Chinese view of the world ... It's inspired by ignoble considerations that have only to do with themselves ..."

Silva shrugged – a gesture he liked, because it reminded him of Ana – to indicate that she couldn't quite follow.

"Let me put it another way," he said. "While those who felt a kind of nostalgia for things Russian stayed loyal out of conviction, or misapprehension, or sentimental attachment, those – a smaller group – who went crazy about China did so not out of love for the place but because things Chinese provided them with something that disguised their own deficiencies – inefficiency, lack of talent, envy, inferiority complex and spiritual poverty. It provided them with an outlet for their fundamental wickedness, and I don't know what else!"

"Phew! You don't mince your words!"

"Perhaps, but such are their motives, and that's why it'll be difficult to turf them out, even after the Chinese have gone ... Just look at C— V—!" he said, turning towards him. "The perfect embodiment of ..."

Silva turned round, but the shoulders of other visitors hid the critic from view.

Skënder leaned closer.

"I expect you think I'm fanatically anti-Chinese. Be frank – you do, don't you?"

"Well ..."

He stifled a laugh.

"Well, you're quite wrong!"

She rolled her eyes mockingly.

"I'm serious," he exclaimed, looking at her evenly as if waiting for her to stop smiling. "In fact I'd regard myself as an ignorant boor if I did entertain such views!"

Two or three people nearby turned to look at them.

They think we're quarrelling, thought Silva, and tried to draw him away. Someone must have accused him of being anti-Chinese before, she thought. There was no other explanation for this sudden outburst.

"I have a great respect for their culture, as anybody must have if they're in their right mind," he said. "We've talked about their culture before, haven't we?"

"Of course."

"And who created that culture, that poetry, and so on, but the people you thought I was denigrating?"

Silva felt like saying she'd never thought any such thing, but knowing what he was like she restrained herself.

"If I get worked up and talk like this, it's because it's the Chinese people who suffer most when things go wrong."

"I do understand, Skënder," said Silva soothingly.

He was talking now without even looking at her.

"People in this country are always telling stories and jokes about the Chinese, and I expect they always will. But it's got nothing to do with racism, whatever some may think."

"No . . . Good heavens, what a crush! It's like being packed in a tin of sardines!"

The visitors were cruising around in complete disorder. They seemed to have come there to meet one another rather than to study Chinese ceramics. Everyone was beaming, contributing to one great meaningful smile. They came and went, eyes sparkling, ready to burst out laughing at the slightest excuse.

"And there's the old guard for you!" said Skënder.

"So what's their position?"

"They're gaga. If they still had all their faculties they'd be lamenting now instead of exulting as they did when we broke with the Soviets."

"But why should they be downcast?" asked Silva. "Perhaps they're cherishing some hopes, now as then?"

"They've no reason to hope. We're drawing away from China at the very moment China's moving towards America. And so . . ."

"Yes, you're right."

"But they're completely past it, and can't understand the situation. Unless they're only pretending . . ."

Silva started to laugh.

Then, from their right, there came a sudden noise, followed by cries of "What is it?" "What's happening?" Heads turned, but no one could make anything out from a distance.

The crowd drifted towards the centre of interest. The more impatient elbowed their way forward. Others could be seen coming

125

back in the other direction, wearing smiles of satisfied curiosity.

"What's happened?" Skënder asked one of these.

"Someone's broken a vase."

"Good gracious!" Silva exclaimed.

"A Chinaman knocked it over by accident," said the man. "I don't know what would have happened if it had been one of us!"

Silva thought for a moment of Victor Hila. Scraps of conversation could be heard all round: "That beautiful vase – smashed to smithereens!" . . . "I was sure someone had knocked it over!" . . . "What? Who'd have dared?" . . . "Well, I never!" . . . "It was very valuable, too!" . . . "Still, I suppose it's a good sign" . . .

Silva, turning round to see who'd spoken the last few words, was surprised to see the man they'd noticed a little while ago, looking at the poster. He was rubbing his hands, and his face was flushed with satisfaction.

"Let's slip away," said Skënder.

And after having strolled around for a little longer, they left. He went with her for part of the way, and as they parted she could feel on her lips a trace of the collective smile worn by the visitors to the exhibition. It was colder now and she walked faster. As she strode along she wondered if she'd been right not to tell Skënder Bermema that her brother had been expelled from the Party. Perhaps he might have been able to give her some explanation? Anyhow, she'd contrive to mention it to him another day.

As she was passing the Café Riviera, where the lights were on because of the overcast sky, a sudden intuition made her turn and look in through the window. And her whole being was invaded by a deep, burning sensation, spreading like ripples when a drop of water falls into a tank. There, sitting on a bench near the front of the café, Gjergj was sitting with a young woman. "What could be more natural?" she told herself. And then, as if to check the waves of pain that were pulsing right through her body, "So what?" So what if he was sitting in a café with a woman – that wasn't the end of the world! But some blind force, stronger than her own will, made her do something that offended against her own code of conduct and her own dignity: she looked again. The young woman – or girl – sitting with Gjergj was pretty. In the course of the two or three seconds that Silva had spent looking at her (I only hope I didn't look *again*! she thought later), her mind took it all in: their pensive look, the way the girl was toying with her coffee cup, the

126

smoke from his cigarette, and, worse still, the dangerous silence that reigned between them. How shameful! Silva reproached herself, swiftly turning her head away. How horrible! But between "shameful", which applied to herself, and "horrible", which applied to what she'd just seen, there was an enormous distance. "How horrible!" she said again, forgetting her own unseemly behaviour. It seemed to her a mere drop compared with that other ocean of evil.

The farther she left the café behind, the more irreparable seemed what she had seen there. The long light-brown hair, the whirls of cigarette smoke lazily enfolding them both . . . She'd have to be very stupid not to see there was something between them. She realized how fast she was walking by the sound of her own heels on the pavement. It seemed to come from far away. Then she felt a temporary calm descend on her, though she was well aware it was false respite, a grey, barren flatness bound in the end to emphasize the underlying pain. This was the reason, then, for his over-affectionate telegram. For that over-insistent "fondest". Of course, a part of that effusion, perhaps the main part, was really directed towards the other woman! She saw again in her mind's eye the intimate moments of their first night together after his return, moments cruelly lit by the thought that he'd done the same things the next day, or the day after that, in some anonymous room with the other woman.

She was overwhelmed by a jealousy all those long years of happy marriage could do nothing to modify. She made a last effort to throw it off, contain it. Wait – perhaps it isn't really like that, perhaps it was only a coincidence. But the stronger, the dominant part of herself soon stifled that appeal to wisdom. You had to be very naive not to suspect Gjergj and that woman were up to something. Blind as she was, she'd told herself that sort of thing happened only to other people, never to Gjergj and herself. She'd believed like a fool in her happiness, and all the time it was rotten to the core. She'd shut her eyes to all possibility of danger, smug as the most empty-headed of women. All the signs had been there, but with an unforgivable lack of shrewdness she hadn't even noticed them. Hadn't she found him, several times lately, lying on the sofa reading love poetry? Once she'd even asked him, "What are you reading that for? I've hardly ever seen you open a book of poems . . ." He'd answered, "I don't really know why . . . No

127

particular reason . . ." She must be quite bird-brained not to have thought about what might lie behind such a change. Nor was that all. After he got back from China, not content with reading poetry he'd also taken a liking to chamber music. Quiet pieces mostly, the kind that promotes daydreaming. Yesterday evening she'd found him lying on the sofa, his head leaning on his right arm, listening to some Chopin. What more did he have to do to proclaim that he'd fallen in love? she raged inwardly. All there was left for him to do was draw hearts and arrows on the walls of the apartment. If he did she'd probably ask: "What are those funny symbols, Gjergj? Could they have anything to do with your feelings?"

If at least the two of them had been cowering at the back of the café, she wouldn't have seen them, she thought bitterly. But no, regardless of what anyone might think they'd sat right by the window, as if to exhibit themselves to the whole of Tirana. The anger she'd been feeling against herself now turned on him. He might at least have refrained from trying to pull the wool over her eyes with his sham affection, his sugary telegrams and what followed. He ought to have had the guts to show his indifference openly, to go off the deep end, throw scenes, make all the neighbours come running – it would have been more honest than that deceitful calm.

It wasn't as if *she* hadn't had the opportunity to deceive *him*! Her jealousy suddenly mingled with a thirst for revenge. Against her will she imagined herself hurrying to a secret rendezvous. Some day as full of treachery as today, she would take off her clothes for a man, swiftly, impetuously, without shame, to make her vengeance more complete. Scenes followed one on another in her mind, but they gave her no satisfaction . . . She knew she could never behave like that. But what else could she do?

She was no longer heading for home. She'd changed direction, as if working out another, more cruel way of punishing him. And she did have an idea now. It only remained to put it into action. She soon found herself near a bus-stop. She was still in a state of shock, and didn't ask herself why she was waiting there. It wasn't until the bus came and she got on it that she realized where she meant to go. To the cemetery. To Ana's grave.

Her tear-filled eyes distorted everything that passed before them. She felt as if she was about to burst out sobbing, not so much because of what had just happened as at finding herself in one of those periods in her life when Ana's absence seemed particularly terrible. How irreplaceably wonderful Ana would have been in such circumstances! Silva imagined herself having a cup of tea with her sister in some shop, and telling Ana her troubles. She would have been ready to endure much worse sufferings if only she could have told Ana about them.

The bus was full and drove along slowly. Silva was impatient. She thought she glimpsed a familiar face amongst the crowd, and turned her face to the window to avoid being spoken to. For many of those she knew, she was still one of the inseparable Krasniqi sisters, and their names were always linked together in people's conversation. Today Silva didn't want to talk to anyone.

The bus arrived at the terminus. The cemetery was only a few minutes' walk away. Once through the iron gate, Silva almost ran along the path leading to Ana's grave, as if her sister were waiting for her. The cemetery was almost empty, but Silva slowed down so as not to attract attention. At last she came to the grave: its pale marble tombstone seemed to contain the last gleams of day. A bunch of fresh pink roses had been placed beside the faded ones from last week. Who could have brought them? Silva bit her lip with vexation: her mind was in such a whirl she'd forgotten to bring any flowers. She sighed. Some scattered white rose-petals, languishing on the grave, seemed to have melted into the marble. Everything was quiet. A few paces away to the right there was an old woman whom Silva had noticed there several times before: as usual, she had brought her dear departed a cup of coffee. She'd put the cup on the top of the grave, and was either weeping or just bowing and lifting her head. Silva knelt down, and for something to do used the handkerchief crumpled up in her hand to polish the porcelain medallion on the headstone. It acted as frame to a photograph. Ana smiled out at her, her hair blown slightly by a wind off the sea; you could see the waves in the background. Besnik had taken that snapshot the first summer they spent together at the beach, at Durrës. Yet again Silva felt her eyes brim over, and tears as well as petals now patterned the marble slab. She couldn't take her eyes off the petals: for some reason or other they conjured up more strongly than anything else could have done the idyllic affair between Ana and Besnik. Ana had often told her about that perfect felicity, during thrilling hours they'd spent together in the tea-shop on the third floor of the palace of Culture, when Ana came to collect Silva from the reading room of the library. Later on, after Ana's death, seeing Besnik facing life's ups and downs with such calm indifference, Silva had wondered whether this was because he had already had his full quota of happiness.

Whenever she visited her sister's grave Silva recalled parts of the story of Ana's second marriage. It wasn't because of the grave, with its pale marble vaguely suggesting a bride's veil, the wreath of flowers, and the traditional handfuls of rice. These things belonged to Ana's first marriage rather than her second, for which she had dressed very soberly. No, it was because of something else, something that in a curious way erased the memory of the interminable days of Ana's illness, the months in hospital, the anxious waiting, the operation. Ana's first marriage, to Frédéric, had somehow been swallowed up in those sad memories – had been stripped of its veil, its lights, of everything that was joyful, and had made way for Ana's second marriage as one house may give up its contents in order to furnish another.

"Silva, I'm going to divorce Frédéric . . ." She well remembered hearing Ana say that. It was on a cold grey day like today, without mercy for anyone who stepped out of line. Ana's face had been paler than usual as she spoke. Before Silva had time to get over her astonishment, her sister had continued, even more amazingly: "I'm going to marry someone else." "Marry someone else?" gasped Silva. Then she tried to speak more moderately. "Have you gone out of your mind? Haven't you said yourself that for you men are only interesting at a distance, and as soon as they get near you they lose most of their attraction?" "Not this time," said Ana. "I've been with him – or rather I've been his, as they say – for a week." "I can't believe it!" Silva had cried. She seemed to say nothing else all those icy weeks. "Fred thinks I've betrayed him lots of times," said Ana, "but I never did, as you know. Never. Except perhaps once, in circumstances where I . . . where we both . . ."

Silva had sat staring at her sister. She was probably referring to her relations with Skënder Bermema which had been the talk of the town but which no one – including Silva – really knew anything about. Silva was tempted to say, "What's all the mystery about Skënder Bermema? You might at least tell me! You're always making enigmatic references to it . . . Unless you only met him in a dream, or vice-versa, or unless the gossips themselves dreamed it all up . . ." But that day Ana had been talking about somebody else, a third man, and that wasn't the moment to try to find out about Skënder Bermema. Nor did a suitable occasion present itself later. Ana never told Silva her secret; she was to take it with her to the grave.

Anyhow, that day, the subject of conversation was somebody else. "Who is it you want to marry?" Silva had asked, finally. And then, for the first time, Ana had uttered the name of Besnik Struga.

"The man who was in Moscow and has just broken off his engagement?" Silva asked.

Ana nodded.

"Yes. Perhaps you remember me going to dinner with Victor Hila a few weeks ago? Well, it was there I met him."

"And what are you going to do now?"

"I've told you. I'm going to marry him."

Silva, perched now on a corner of the rose-strewn marble slab, huddled up to keep out the cold, felt a great emptiness inside her. Scraps of memories whirled around her indistinguishably; none emerged more distinct than the others. Then vaguely, distantly, they formed into a kind of television film with the sound turned off: first came the scandal caused by the announcement of Ana's divorce; then the legal proceedings, with Frédéric coming into court carrying an armful of books by Skënder Bermema in which he'd marked all the passages he alleged referred to the author's affair with Ana; the gossip; Ana's dignified behaviour throughout. The storm, which Ana, with her talent for making everything around her light and airy, transformed into a spring shower, was followed by a flat calm: her marriage to Besnik Struga; the little dinner party with just a few close friends. When, after the first few weeks, they assessed the damage this earthquake of theirs had caused among their circle, they realized there hadn't been any great upheavals, apart from one loss that affected them deeply: they couldn't see the Bermemas any more.

Silva remembered a bright rainy afternoon when she and Ana were walking past the puppet theatre, and her sister nudged her and whispered, "Look, Silva – that's the girl who was engaged to Besnik . . ." The girl was hurrying along under a transparent umbrella which cast pale mauve reflections on to her face. In that lavender light her expression struck Silva, who had never seen her before, as full of mystery. There was no trace of resentment in Ana's eyes or voice. She just said, "She's pretty, isn't she?", when the girl had gone past. Silva didn't know what to say. She agreed. When she saw the girl again later, after she'd got married to an engineer, she still seemed just as mysterious as on that first day, through that mauve mist. But perhaps this was because Silva had heard people say that although she was so attractive to men, she was also proud and self-willed; it was even whispered that she was very cold towards her husband. But Silva was rather sceptical about that. Perhaps because of all the tittle-tattle about Ana, she tended to discount rumours about women's infidelity. There was much more to be said about the infidelity of men.

Silva sighed. In the end, what did it all matter? She'd come here for something else. She stared at the wet marble; her eyes were so tired they hurt. What would she have said to her sister if she'd still been alive? "Ana, I'm going to divorce Gjergj"? She shuddered. Oh no, she thought. Never! She'd heard someone else use such words, and now she wanted to give them back, like something she'd borrowed that didn't suit her. Like most younger sisters, she'd often imitated Ana, but the time for that had gone by. They had been as one, like sisters in the ancient ballads, and they still were one. But now they were like twin water-lilies, the invisible roots of one of which were dead. Even though people still spoke of them together, the old symmetry was no more. The words Silva had been on the point of saying were quite alien to her.

She glanced around. No one. When she looked at her watch she couldn't believe her eyes: it was after two o'clock. At home they'd have been wondering where she was. She felt her lips curve in a bitter smile. Perhaps she'd smile like this when she first spoke to Gjergj. It was late, but she hadn't yet bothered to think what she'd say to him. She stood up, smoothed her skirt down, and started to make her way out of the cemetery. The worst would be if he tried to hide the truth, and degraded himself in her eyes with petty lies. How horrible! thought Silva, as if a new misfortune had suddenly been revealed to her. I only hope it won't be like that, she thought as she got on to the almost empty bus. Then she wondered what it would be like if he simply admitted he was having an affair; at this idea she wasn't quite so shattered. She sighed again. Whichever way she looked at it, she couldn't see any solution. What horrible chance made me go by that cursed café, she wondered. It would have been better for me not to know. I'd a hundred times rather not have seen anything.

The bus picked up passengers at every stop. It was almost three o'clock by the time she got off. She still hadn't thought what she would say to Gjergj. She ought at least to have an answer ready when he asked where she'd been. But she felt too worn out to think about anything. She was almost surprised to see a couple of young men unloading crates of mineral water from a lorry outside a bar in the street where she lived. They whistled as they staggered across the pavement to the shop, the bottles clinking. Was life really still going on as if nothing had happened?

She paused for a moment outside the apartment as if to muster her strength. Then she took her key out of her bag, and trying, heaven knows why, to make as little noise as possible, opened the door. In the hall she took her coat off and waited for Gjergj to come and ask where she'd got to. But a suspicious quiet reigned. What if he hadn't come back? It vaguely occurred to her that he might still be there in the café with the girl, or lunching tête-à-tête with her in some restaurant. Why hadn't she thought of that before? She snatched the scarf from round her neck almost violently – it seemed to cling on – and propelled by fury at the possibility she'd just been considering, she burst into the kitchen. And there was Gjergj, standing by the French window that opened on to the balcony. She was so astonished she almost cried out, "You're here!" He was smoking. The face he turned towards her, though it showed no surprise, wore a frown. What was he looking like that for? Perhaps he knew . . . Perhaps he'd seen her though the window of the café . . . And now . . . Attack was the best form of defence! All this flashed through Silva's mind in less than a second. Then something made her look at Brikena, who was busy at the dresser: she wore the same sullen expression. The explanation must be worse than that, she thought, stunned. But what could it be? That he had indeed seen her and had no intention of defending himself, even by attacking her, but would calmly, cruelly, lethally tell her he loved someone else, and . . . and . . . that he'd told his daughter about it . . . so that she could choose between her father and mother . . . So there *was* something worse, much much worse ("Fondest fondest love") . . . Perhaps . . . perhaps . . . (the word "separation" came into her mind with the harsh tearing sound of someone ripping a length of cloth). And all that had taken no more than another second . . .

"What on earth has happened?" she managed to stammer. Exactly what she had expected *them* to say to *her*.

133

Gjergj looked back at her fixedly. He too looked rather surprised, but his main expression was one of consternation. He seemed to be saying, "Never mind about us – what about you?" He glanced towards the sofa, and it was then that Silva realized there was someone else in the room. Sonia, her sister-in-law, was sitting on the sofa, white as a sheet and with tears streaming down her cheeks and even into her shoulder-length hair.

"Sonia!" said Silva, starting towards her. "What's happened?"

Sonia's brimming eyes seemed to have aged suddenly.

"Arian . . ." she murmured.

Silva nodded encouragingly.

Yes, but what, she wondered, half wanting to know and half too worn out to care. Had her brother had an accident? Committed suicide? For a moment she thought this might be the answer, but no – if so, Sonia would have stayed at home . . .

"What?" she repeated.

"Arrested," sobbed Sonia.

"What!"

Silva turned first to Gjergj and then to Brikena, as if to ask them if she was in her right mind. Of all the possible misfortunes, this one had never occurred to her. What a day!

"When?" she asked, trying to keep calm.

"This morning at ten o'clock."

Just when she was laughing at Skënder Bermema's comments at the exhibition, and while Gjergj . . .

He went on smoking, standing by the French window leading out on to the balcony. Brikena was now setting the table. The mere idea of eating struck Silva as barbarous. But as if she found some temporary respite in catching up with duties she'd thought she'd skipped, she started coming and going with unnatural assiduity between the table and the stove, where the meal had got cold and been heated up again several times.

"I don't suppose you've had any lunch, Sonia?"

"I haven't even thought about it!"

"Anyhow, sit down and eat something . . ."

"It was frightful!" Sonia groaned. "Fortunately Mother and the children weren't in!"

"I was just going to ask you what had become of them," said Silva.

"They don't know anything about it. Aunt Urania had called for

Mother to go and see some friend of theirs. The children were out."

"They mustn't know!" said Gjergj. "Tell them he's been sent on a mission."

"This is the last straw!" Silva exclaimed. "Come and have something to eat now, and we'll talk about it all later."

She was about to start serving when she remembered the salad hadn't been prepared. She asked Brikena to see to it, while she herself went to the refrigerator for the cheese, and something else out of a tin which she then replaced. She performed all these actions feverishly, her mind in a whirl. These plates wouldn't do for taking food to a prisoner --- you're only allowed to use tinfoil containers . . . Snap out of it, she told herself, grabbing a handful of forks from the dresser.

Sonia was still weeping silently on the sofa.

"When they expelled him from the Party," she said, "I thought that would be the end of it. Who would ever have thought things would go so far?"

"Don't cry, Sonia," said a voice Silva recognized as Gjergj's.

She felt she hadn't heard it for a long time . . . ever since . . . ever since the disaster. But this wasn't the moment to think about that; it would be indecent.

"I'm not just saying it to console you," Gjergj went on, "but I'm sure it's only a misunderstanding. Besides, Sonia, being arrested when you're in the army is not the same as if you're a civilian. It's not nearly so serious – not a catastrophe at all. Any soldier can be put under arrest for disobedience or some such offence, and afterwards go on just as before. It's in the regulations – you must have heard about it . . . You've seen it happen in films, don't you remember? Some trifling misconduct, five days in clink, fall out!"

"Gjergj is right," said Silva. "To be put under arrest in the army is nothing! When our colleagues at the ministry come back from reserve training they're always full of stories about it. Arian has merely committed some minor offence for which army regulations prescribe arrest!"

"But they came to the house to arrest him!" cried Sonia. "And I don't know if it was done according to the rules – I've never seen an arrest before. But it didn't look like a disciplinary matter."

"Did they have any authorization?"

"Yes, of course. They had a kind of warrant, and one of them showed it to me as well as to Arian. Not that I could read what was written on it, I was so upset. There was someone else with them – a member of the local committee of the Democratic Front."

Gjergj and Silva exchanged a surreptitious glance. Sonia noticed it, but she still didn't know whether the warrant and the member of the Democratic Front were good signs or bad.

Gjergj finally moved away from the French window, but to Silva he seemed to do so more rapidly than was natural, and this added to her uneasiness. He too started coming and going around the kitchen, helping to get the meal ready.

"Don't worry, Sonia – I'm sure my explanation is right. Sit down and have something to eat," he said, shifting chairs about noisily. "Brikena, where's the pepper? Come along, Sonia . . . Why were you so late, by the way, Silva?" He sounded as if he wasn't sure it was possible to say anything so ordinary here any more.

Silva stared at him for a moment.

"I'll tell you later on," she said, lowering her eyes. "Come on, Sonia – come and sit down."

"I don't want anything to eat! I couldn't swallow a mouthful!"

"Don't be silly," said Silva. "I'm sure it'll all be explained. We mustn't give in. And don't forget the family, Sonia . . . Most of them are senior Party members . . . It's not as if we hadn't any influence any more . . ."

But it seemed to her that the more she said the less she believed it. Take those stupid remarks about the family. She knew the arrest of a member of a communist family was just as serious as the arrest of someone connected with the old guard. More serious, in fact, because it was so unusual. As for the warrant and the member of the committee, they showed this was no routine matter.

But it was precisely what Silva said without believing in it herself that persuaded Sonia to come to the table.

During the meal, though everyone did their best to avoid long silences, they couldn't find much to say. So they made much play with china and cutlery. When they'd finished, Silva made coffee – the only thing that was welcome to everyone.

"I must go," said Sonia. "Heaven knows what's going on at home."

"In any case, don't say anything to his mother or the children," Gjergj advised her.

"But how long can it be kept from them?" replied Sonia. "It's impossible!"

Impossible, thought Silva . . . Gjergj, for all his advice to Sonia, knew that as a Party member himself he would have to inform the next meeting of his cell that his brother-in-law had been arrested. Out of the corner of her eye, Silva could see Brikena's hair almost falling in her plate, as she ate without looking up at the others. She hadn't uttered a word throughout the whole meal: heaven knew what she might be going through . . . Her textbooks were full of enemies of the people who were finally unmasked and arrested, and now that world, which had been as distant for her as ancient myth, was irrupting into her own life. And this wasn't all! Silva bit her lip at the thought of the forms her daughter would have to fill in to join the youth movement, then to go to the University, and so on throughout her career. To the question, "Has any member of your family been arrested or imprisoned under the present régime?," most of her friends would be able to write "No," but she, with a trembling hand, would have to write, "I have an uncle who . . ."

Sonia stood up.

"I *must* go," she said.

They saw her to the door, with flustered reassurances which, though they may have soothed Sonia, had the opposite effect on themselves.

"Phew!" exclaimed Silva, collapsing on to the sofa when Sonia had gone. She wept for a moment in silence, while Gjergj went over to the French window again and stood with his back to her, smoking a cigarette.

"I'll have one too," she said, between sobs. She asked Brikena to go to her room, and the girl went without a word.

"Do you really believe what you said about the arrest?" Silva asked.

Gjergj still didn't look round.

"I'm more inclined to think it's a misunderstanding. One soldier does as he pleases, and his superiors give him the boot . . ."

"Do you really think that?"

"I did wonder whether it hadn't got something to do with the Chinese question . . . It may seem ridiculous, but at times like these the key to the inexplicable often lies in current events . . . And if this particular business were connected, even indirectly, with China, I'd be tempted to think it was very serious. But I can't see any evidence for it. Especially as he was expelled from the Party for disobedience – in other words for being a bit of a rebel. And the reason for his arrest must be the same as the reason for his expulsion from the Party."

"That would make it just an ordinary detention, as you said from the beginning."

"But being expelled from the Party makes it worse," said Gjergj, "and other things may get drawn into it too. When the charge of disobedience is being examined, perhaps the officers inquiring into it will discover aggravating circumstances – insubordination towards his superiors, or insolence . . ."

The phone rang. Silva shuddered. Gjergj answered, and as soon as he spoke she sensed that the call had nothing to do with what had flashed through her mind. As he went on talking, it occurred to her that the time might come when they'd call or be called by her brother much less often, or not at all, and of course stop seeing him. And it wouldn't end there. If Arian was in prison for long, it wasn't impossible that Sonia would divorce him. There were cases where not only a prisoner's wife but all his relations too dropped him completely.

Gjergj hung up and went over to the French window again. They remained as they were for some time. Silent. Outside, time seemed suspended.

"When you came in just now I thought you knew," said Gjergj. "You were so pale."

Silva looked up.

"No. That was for another reason."

She didn't want to talk now about her anxieties that morning.

"What reason?"

Silva plucked at her brow, where her eyebrows met. If he insisted on knowing why she had come home looking distraught, she was going to have to tell him. But perhaps this was the moment to have it all out. Now or never. At any rate it would take their minds off the other business.

"I saw you this morning in the Riviera," she said finally, giving him a sidelong glance. "You were with a young woman."

He didn't flinch. He was still looking out through the window. The mist on the panes made the grey of the late afternoon more dismal still.

"Perhaps you're going to tell me you met her by accident," she said, unable to bear his silence any longer.

He didn't answer straight away. Then:

"Not exactly," he said.

Silva felt her heart thumping. Perhaps she was probing too far. Wasn't all this too much for a single day? She'd been sure he would stammer out something to deny the facts, or minimize them, or . . . But now, instead of justifying himself, by lying if necessary, he was telling her he hadn't been with that woman in that café by accident. That's all this awful day needs, she thought: my husband calmly admitting he's deceived me!

"This isn't a very good moment for me to explain," he went on.

"Perhaps not," said Silva, feeling a great icy wave sweep over her. "Maybe it would be better to leave it till another time."

She'd spoken quite sincerely. All she wanted now was for the matter to be closed. She was even ready to ask him not to mention it again.

"You're right," she added. "It's not the right moment. I shouldn't have started it."

"Not at all," he answered. "Perhaps it's just the right moment . . ."

Just the right moment, she murmured to herself, shattered. What did that mean?

"Gjergj," she murmured faintly. "Please . . . I'm terribly tired . . . Why do you want to add to my torment?"

"I want exactly the opposite. I want to explain, to relieve you of any kind of doubt . . ."

What a ghastly day – would it ever end? thought Silva. But she felt just a twinge of relief.

"It's not easy to explain, but I'll try," said Gjergj. "It all began in China . . ."

What all began in China? Had the girl been there too? Had they met in a hotel? The anguish Silva thought she'd thrown off gripped her again.

"I've already mentioned the spiritual barrenness you can experience there, but you know I don't talk much – I didn't want to go into detail." He was still staring at the window. "You feel a kind of void, an indescribable panic. It's impossible to have a genuinely human conversation. You begin to long for simple, authentic phrases – 'It's raining,' 'How are you this morning?' But they don't exist. As soon as you remark on how windy it is, the person you're talking to says, 'The wind from the East is stronger than the wind from the West.' If you complain that it was foggy, he'll answer,

139

'Chairman Mao says fog suits the imperialists and the revisionists.' "

Gjergj shook his head as if dismissing further examples put forward by his memory.

"Empty words and tedious slogans everywhere. 'Though far apart, our peoples are friends' – that's what they say instead of 'good morning'. One monotonous refrain peppered with endless quotations. Wherever you looked there was nothing but placards with ideograms scrawled all over them ... For nights now I've been dreaming the world has been invaded by billions of Chinese characters, like ants. How I used to long to hear a human sigh over a cup of coffee. What was the name of that chap who went through the market in the daytime, carrying a lantern and looking for a man? Diogenes, I think ... Well, in the middle of that ocean of banners and placards, we were looking for a man ... Not that there was any shortage of people, but we didn't really have any contact with them. We were isolated from them by a cordon sanitaire of guides, officials, and all those wretched slogans. If we ever had a normal conversation with someone on our embassy staff, it was immediately swallowed up in that sloganomania. What I clung to in my mind was our life here. I told myself, as soon as I get back I'll do this and that, and above all I'll live closer to other people. I was dying, dying to talk to human beings – even if they were surly or exasperating, so long as they were human beings! That was why when I got back I wanted to stay with you as long as possible, with you and with our daughter. Do you remember the first night I was home, when I was half-dead with fatigue and yet I asked you to talk to me a bit longer, and you said, 'Don't be so childish – do you need a fairy-tale to send you to sleep?' "

Even if she couldn't quite manage a smile, Silva could feel her face relaxing. It had all happened just as he'd said, and he had dropped off to sleep while she talked to him about something she'd now completely forgotten.

"I expect you remember finding me reading a book of poems the day before yesterday," said Gjergj, "and the day before that, listening to music. That too was because of my craving for warmth. The cold had penetrated so deep inside me – to my very bones – that I felt nothing could ever warm me up again. So I wanted to build up reserves, just as someone who's been through a famine hoards bread. That's more or less how I felt. And then, this morning ..."

Gjergj paused for a few seconds, lit a cigarette, and started to describe that morning, his first Sunday since he got back from China. He'd gone to a café, then strolled along the main boulevard as far as the avenue Marcel-Cachin – near the Dajti Hotel and the bridge with a marvellous view of the falling leaves. Then he suddenly felt an urge to visit the cemetery. For no reason at all he'd got it into his head that the Chinese had abolished cemeteries! He'd bought a bunch of flowers to put on Ana's grave, and then he'd set out.

"Pink roses," said Silva.

"Yes," he answered, with no sign of surprise. "Were you there too, then?"

She nodded.

"There were quite a lot of people at the cemetery," he went on. "I stood by Ana's grave for some time, remembering things about her life, and about ours. Then I came away. When I got back into town it was still early and I felt like having another coffee. But not alone, nor with a mere acquaintance – no, it had to be someone with whom I felt a bond. In China I'd come to think no one ever remembered anything: of course that couldn't be true, but it was the impression you got from the outside. So I felt like having a coffee with someone who did remember things."

Silva recalled the old woman in the cemetery, with *her* cup of coffee.

"I don't know how to explain it, but that was what was missing from my Sunday. So I did what I haven't done for a long time – I phoned an old student friend whom I hadn't seen for years. I tried to explain to her over the phone what had made me call her up, and she somehow managed to understand my ramblings. She was a very nice girl, the girl-friend of one of my fellow students – we'd had a brief romance in our first year. She's married now. That's all, Silva – neither more nor less. I just wanted to talk about another part of my life . . . I was like someone who's been ill and is on the brink of convalescence . . . I don't know if I've managed to make you understand at all . . . I'm afraid I probably haven't."

Silva couldn't take her eyes off his face: it looked suddenly haggard. Her own expression was full of tenderness.

"How awful it must have been for you over there," she said gently. Then, to herself: "But perhaps the situation that caused his suffering will soon be over?"

Outside, it was getting dark. In the dusk, everything was growing

141

distant and insubstantial: the balconies of other apartments; the first lights lit inside them and twinkling faintly; the pigeons swooping over the roofs, their grey and white wings merging into the general pallor.

Silva gazed at the man standing there by the window: he was not only her husband but also a mythological messenger, raised into immortality, bearer of a missive to a terrifying foreign state. A letter severing relations . . . She suddenly felt an irresistible desire to comfort him after his journey into that alien universe.

As if he'd read her thoughts, Gjergj left the French window, then came slowly and quietly across the room and sat down beside her on the sofa. She ran her fingers through his hair and down to the nape of his neck. Then started to stroke his hair rhythmically. And so they sat on, side by side, through the end of a day that might well prove to be the beginning of an era.

7

THAT NIGHT SILVA tossed and turned, her sleep broken by dreams of which, in the morning, she could remember nothing. When she got up, her face looked drawn. Gjergj was up already – the hum of his electric razor could be heard through the half-open bathroom door.

In the kitchen, Silva automatically turned on the tap, then remembered she'd done the washing-up the night before, and turned it off again. The growing brightness in the dark-blue sky, which she could see through the window, made her feel a bit calmer. Things are bound to sort themselves out, she thought dimly – she still wasn't properly awake. It'll all come right in the end.

It seemed to her Gjergj had never taken so long to shave. But finally the sound of the razor stopped, and Gjergj appeared in the doorway.

"Good morning," he said. "Did you sleep well?"

She shrugged.

"So-so."

"Don't worry. I'm sure it's just a misunderstanding."

"There's nothing worse than waking up in the morning with a worry like that on your mind."

"He was the first thing *I* thought about, too."

"Really?"

"Yes."

Silva felt relieved, somehow.

"It's especially awful when you wake up . . ."

"Yes," he agreed. "Particularly the first morning."

She was on the point of asking him when he'd been in a situation like this before, but restrained herself. He might be referring to quite a different kind of ordeal. She'd felt something similar herself during a youthful love affair.

Silva's hands opened and closed the doors and drawers

of the dresser without even thinking about it. As she was cutting the bread she realized Brikena was still asleep, and went to wake her.

The three of them breakfasted in silence. It wasn't until Brikena had gone off to school that her parents began to talk. But all they could find to say to one another was more or less the same as what they'd said the night before. As she drank her coffee, Silva reflected that people under stress feel a need to keep repeating themselves, like children.

Gjergj walked with her to the ministry. It was very cold. People were flocking round the news-stands as usual to buy their morning paper. Nonsensical as it was, it always seemed to Silva they bought more of them when the weather was cold. Gjergj bought a paper too, folded it twice and put it in the outside pocket of his raincoat. Silva suddenly felt she couldn't bear to start discussing China again, though lately this had been one of her favourite subjects of conversation. As if he'd guessed this, Gjergj had avoided the topic since the day before. Had Arian's arrest got anything to do with these events? Though they'd asked themselves this question several times, and every time answered it in the negative, they both still harboured a slight doubt. But be that as it might, Silva didn't want to hear China so much as mentioned any more.

After she'd left Gjergj, she went up the steps into the ministry, calling out her usual greeting to the porter as she passed by his lodge. But inside the hall she couldn't help turning back to check up on his expression: had it been colder than usual, or had she just imagined it? This is getting to be an obsession! she exclaimed, and ran up the stairs.

Her boss and Linda had just arrived in the office. Silva said good morning, took off her raincoat, and sat down at her desk. But she didn't do all this in her usual manner. She told herself this odd feeling would soon pass. This misfortune of hers was connected with society, and her first encounter with other people after it had happened was bound to be difficult. But she couldn't imagine how she was going to get through all these hours at the office without unburdening herself to someone. Gjergj had advised her not to talk to anyone about it for the moment, but she could tell it was going to be hard for her not to. Suddenly people seemed to be divided into two groups – those she could confide in and those she couldn't. It wasn't a question of trust, but of something else which even she couldn't define. In any case, she couldn't make up her mind for two minutes together whether she wanted to talk to anybody or not.

She tried to concentrate on her work, but it was too much for her – what had happened was so much a part of her, she couldn't get it out of her mind for more than a moment. How painful this first stage was, when no one else knew about her trouble yet, and she had to spend hour upon hour alone with it. No, it would be better for the others to find out, whatever the consequences. Gradually she persuaded herself that she ought to speak out somehow, but she didn't know how or to whom. It was easier for Gjergj: the Party had definite rules for such situations. A Party member had to report such a thing right away to the secretary of his cell.

But ordinary citizens had no such guidance.

What Silva feared most was the beginning of the mysterious and inexorable process which took a person out of the category of ordinary people and put him into the category of those whose life is tainted. It was a process which began with the individual concerned, but as other people saw that individual withdraw into himself, so their own attitude changed, provoking another retreat in him; and so on until he became unrecognizable, no longer having anything in common with what he used to be.

Though she didn't make a show of it, Silva took a pride in her family's past. She'd always been conscious of it, and it had acted as a foil to the image of themselves she and her sister – especially her sister – had created in their palmy days: the freedom of their ways, their poise, the clothes they wore . . . She could foresee how much she would miss it if it were lost. I shall grow ugly! she thought. Then she reproached herself: "Selfish brute that I am! My brother's in prison, perhaps being interrogated at this very minute, and I . . ." But she couldn't quite suppress the thought that from now on she wouldn't be able to wear her most elegant clothes.

"What's the matter, Silva? Have you got a headache?" Linda whispered.

"No." Silva smiled gratefully. "Well, yes, a bit."

"Would you like an aspirin?"

"No, thanks, Linda. Later on, perhaps."

Heaven knows what she was going to have to face later on! It would almost certainly include the sarcasm, perhaps even the vengefulness, of people who didn't like her: "Oh, here's the

Biografibukura!" (God, why had she said that instead of *Sybukura*?)*

Silva shook her head as if to get rid of these thoughts. She knew that if even a fraction of what she'd been imagining came to pass, she'd go out of her mind. But she wouldn't let it get that far! She'd fight, she'd leave no stone unturned, she'd explain to everyone, beginning with herself, that she . . . But what? What? She nearly asked it aloud . . . Her thoughts were in utter confusion.

"Linda," she croaked feebly. "I'll have that aspirin now, please."

At any rate, she must do *something* before this mental turmoil got the better of her. Right. She'd tell Linda what had happened, straight from the shoulder. Then she'd see what attitude to adopt. She might even discuss things with her. But first their boss would have to clear off and leave them by themselves.

The prospect of talking to Linda calmed Silva down somewhat, but just as she thought the boss was about to go out of the room, it was Linda who walked over to the door.

Silva, taken aback, watched the door shut. Then she was thrown into a state of agitation again by the thought that she was now alone with someone she could talk to, even if it wasn't the person she'd have chosen. An opportunity had occurred which might not present itself again that day and which she'd better take advantage of before it was too late.

"Comrade Defrim!"† she found herself saying.

God, how could his parents inflict such a name on him? She and Linda hardly ever used it, and she now realized for the first time how inhibiting it was.

"Yes," said the boss, raising his eyebrows but not looking up from his papers.

"I'd like to talk to you," said Silva, in such a faint voice that now he did glance across at her. "My brother was arrested yesterday."

She felt him subside with all his weight on to his desk, and even thought she heard his body give out a groan as if he'd become a block of wood himself. She kept her eyes on his face, as if it might reflect the gravity of her brother's situation. After a moment of stupefaction, the boss broke out into a sweat. He didn't know where

* *Sybukura*: woman with beautiful eyes. *Biografibukura*: (by analogy) woman with a (politically) beautiful biography.
† *defrim*: amusement, pleasure.

146

to look. His whole being seemed to be groaning, "What have I done to deserve this?" He obviously wished she'd never opened her mouth.

"But your husband's a member of the Party, isn't he?"

"Yes, of course," she said. But why was he suddenly addressing her with the formal second person plural? And what had her husband got to do with it?

She watched him, waiting for him to go on. It didn't matter what he said so long as he said something!

"So how did it happen? I mean, what was the reason?"

He spoke reluctantly, as if to convey that he didn't want to discuss the matter: she could think what she liked about him, but after all she belonged to an influential family, and had a husband who worked at the foreign ministry and was sent on secret missions . . . And so on . . . So why didn't they just sort it out for themselves and leave him alone? – he didn't have a Party card or the advantages that went with it, and there was no reason why he should share the disadvantages.

"The reason?" Silva repeated. "It just happened – we don't know the reason."

So much the worse! said the boss's expression. Worse for the individual concerned, and worse for him too – having to listen to this rubbish, and so early in the day! He would probably have got up and left the room to avoid being left alone with her, but at that moment the door opened and Linda walked in. The boss felt reassured: Silva thought she heard his desk creak again as it was relieved of his weight.

It could have been worse, she thought. He might have lectured her or told her to disavow her brother, even though she still didn't know what he was accused of.

What had Arian really done? . . . How many times had she asked herself that? And what if he'd merely been detained for questioning as Gjergj had suggested, and all this anguish turned out to be unnecessary? That was what she'd wanted to talk about to someone, but she'd applied to the most unsuitable person. From now on she'd be able to tell the sheep from the goats.

She got up and went over to the telephone. Her boss watched her furtively as she dialled the number, as if trying to make out what unfortunate wretch was being drawn in now. He wouldn't be in *his* shoes for anything! A private conversation in the office was one thing, but the phone was a completely different matter. Other people might be listening in, and might even pass on a distorted version of what was said.

"Hallo? Is that the switchboard?" said Silva. "I'd like to speak to Besnik Struga, please. Extension four-four-five, if I remember rightly . . ." She was standing there with the phone resting against her cheek, staring into space, when she met Linda's inquisitive eye. It suddenly struck Silva that her colleague might be interested in her own former brother-in-law. "Hallo, is that you, Besnik? This is Silva."

Linda listened with a mixture of envy and resentment to her colleague making an appointment with the man she herself so longed to meet. Then suddenly she caught her boss's eye. What was the matter with *him*? She was tempted to laugh. Did the silly idiot think there was something immoral going on? She herself believed more than anything in the world in the integrity of the people who gravitated around Silva. Even Victor Hila, for whom, out of pity, she'd had a moment of weakness, had behaved very correctly, and far from trying to take advantage of her lapse he'd never made the slightest allusion to it since. Just once, a few days later, he'd phoned her up, apologizing over and over again for disturbing her, to stammer that he was calling to explain that he was on the point of leaving Tirana because of the business of the Chinaman's foot . . . Not that he had any right to bother her with all that, but just to tell her he thought she was wonderful, and that he felt the greatest respect for her – really, the greatest respect imaginable – and that she was absolutely peerless and unique. She'd been genuinely touched by his decency and selflessness, and had thanked him. But what was this Silva was saying? Besnik Struga was going to drop in here? Yes, sure enough – Silva was repeating: "All right, I'll be waiting for you in the office when you've left your meeting . . ." Now she had rung off.

"Is Besnik Struga coming here?" asked Linda, not trying to conceal her agitation. "Will you introduce me?"

"Of course," said Silva. "He's just leaving home to attend a meeting at the Ministry of Education, and when that's over he'll come on here."

Linda's hands reached out of their own accord for her handbag and mirror, then something held her back. The wave of pleasure which had swept over her at the thought of actually encountering

Besnik Struga, the man she'd dreamed of meeting for so long, seemed to call for some dissimulation, like everything else one holds dear.

Although it was Silva who kept looking at her watch, Linda waited just as eagerly as her friend for Struga to appear. At one point Linda almost asked her colleague why she seemed so anxious, but she was afraid this might reveal her own nervousness.

Besnik Struga arrived just after midday. Silva introduced him both to the boss and to Linda as "a friend of mine". The boss looked at him with a mixture of astonishment, contrition and irony. As for Linda, she didn't try to hide the warmth of her feelings. "I've heard a lot about you," she said as she held out her hand. "I'm very glad to meet you."

"Me too," said Besnik, looking at her with interest.

They immediately struck up an animated, even sparkling conversation, as often happens when two people take an instant liking to one another. She told him what she knew about him; it wasn't much. His trip to Moscow with Enver Hoxha, to attend the great congress of communist parties which she had had to write about in her history exam. . . . He interrupted to point out how this underlined the distance between them – he meant the difference in their ages. Blushing a little, she hastened to explain that this hadn't even occurred to her. On the contrary, he looked very young (at this she reddened again, but luckily this was partly camouflaged by her permanent smile). So young, in fact, that she found it hard to believe he'd met Krushchev. And since he'd taken part in that confrontation, it wouldn't be surprising, would it, if the present situation brought him face to face one day with Mao Zedong? Besnik laughed. As she must know, dialectical materialism – perhaps she'd sat for an examination in that too? – said that situations never repeated themselves in exactly the same form. As a matter of fact, according to Marx, what occurred first as tragedy was very likely to recur as farce.

"Do you think this business with China might be regarded as a comedy, then?" she asked. "Oh no, not at all. I was only referring to my own rôle."

Linda couldn't help noticing that Silva was following this repartee with a cold, almost constrained smile, as though its vivacity displeased her. This deflated Linda at once: her previous flow of words ended as suddenly as a spring shower.

"Shall we be on our way, then, Silva?" said Besnik, holding his hand out first to Linda and then to the boss.

The office seemed lifeless after they'd gone. But Linda's face still wore a smile.

"Funny to think he was at that historic conference, isn't it?" she said to her boss as if to justify herself. She felt she ought to try to explain the warmth of her welcome to their unexpected visitor. But the boss wore an expression of complete detachment. He was obviously thinking of something else. Linda felt reassured, and let her mind wander back to Besnik Struga. It was the first and most beautiful moment of an attraction between two people – the moment when nothing's yet settled, no decision taken, no habit formed, no timetable established . . . there isn't any hurry . . . Everything was as new as the creation of the world; time was eternal, free of the servitude of hours; all was vague, unconstrained by any material calculation.

Linda gazed thoughtfully at the faint gleams projected here and there by a meagre sun. The impression Besnik had made on her was no mere passing fancy. She'd felt attracted to him even before she met him, a month ago, in the corridors of the ministry. He was associated in her mind with a period for which she felt a strange fascination: he was that period personified. She opened her bag, and, seeing that the boss was buried in his papers again, got out her mirror and looked into it for a moment, trying to see her face through Besnik's eyes. But she couldn't.

Even before they'd reached the nearest café, Silva had told Besnik what had happened to her brother. They sat down in a corner of the Riviera, and Silva scanned her companion's face. He looked thoughtful.

"Strange!" he said at last. "Very strange indeed!"

She began to recount in detail her conversation with her brother, when she heard for the first time that he was probably going to be expelled from the Party. But Besnik, instead of asking for further explanations, just exclaimed again, "Very strange!" Nor did he comment on Gjergj's hope that the arrest was nothing more than an ordinary detention following some disciplinary offence. But he did convey that he didn't really agree with this interpretation. Silva felt despondent, almost offended. Besnik's mind seemed to be on something else. She was almost sorry she'd phoned him. But she didn't say anything – just looked at him curiously. Was he taking the same sort of line as her boss? She began thinking of how she would apologize for bothering him: she'd adopt an extremely sardonic tone, implying that this was the last time she'd ask him any favours . . . Meanwhile he spoke, in a low voice, as if to himself.

"A group of tank officers . . . I think I *did* hear something about that . . ."

"Really?" Silva almost shouted.

She was ready to burst out: "In that case, what are you waiting for? What was it you heard, and what are they going to do to them?" But she restrained herself.

"Yes, I did hear about it," Besnik went on, "but I didn't think Arian was involved. And anyway . . ."

She didn't want to interrupt, but the pause grew so long she was afraid he'd forgotten what he was going to say. Unless he'd deliberately decided not to go on . . .

"Anyway . . . ?" she prompted.

Besnik swallowed.

"Anyway, it's a very complicated affair," he said. "No one knows much about it, really."

Always the same! she thought. Incorrigible. The flash of exasperation in her eye didn't escape him.

"Silva, I'm not trying to hide anything from you," he said. "I did hear something by chance, but I don't know anything definite. It's a very mysterious affair."

"Mysterious?"

"I might have been able to find out more, but unfortunately I'm due to go abroad on a mission. As you can imagine, what's happening in China is turning the international communist movement upside down."

He looked at Silva for a moment.

"When are you leaving?" she asked.

"In three days' time. Not long enough to find anything out – you can imagine all the things I have to do before I go."

"Yes."

"But as soon as I get back – and I shouldn't think I'll be away long – I'll do all I can."

"Thank you," said Silva.

"It's really incredible," he went on, still rather abstractedly. "Especially to think that Arian might be mixed up in it . . ."

"That's what we all thought."

"As I said, I did hear of something of the sort. And at the time, without dreaming Arian might be involved, I thought . . . But just in passing, as you might about anything you heard about by chance . . . If I'd known he was mixed up in it, of course I'd have tried to find out more . . ."

The more Silva tried to puzzle it out, the more she felt she was missing the drift of what Besnik was saying. She was right: he'd just finished a long sentence, and she realized with horror that its meaning had entirely escaped her.

"Look, Silva," he said earnestly. "I'm not saying this just to reassure you, but I have a feeling – well, it's more than a feeling, but . . . forgive me . . . I can't tell you any more about it now – a feeling that it's all a misunderstanding and that it'll eventually be cleared up."

Silva suddenly felt as if a weight had been lifted from her shoulders. The look in his eye told her she could believe him.

"Thank you, Besnik. To tell you the truth, knowing Arian as I do, I find his imprisonment so inconceivable I expect him to be released at any moment, in a few days' time at the worst . . . But meanwhile he's *there*, and you can imagine how painful it is for all of us."

"I do understand, Silva," he said. "I understand perfectly."

After a little while they stood up, and he saw her back to her ministry. On the way there she felt reassured, but as soon as he left her, anguish closed in on her again. She seemed to have every reason to worry rather than to calm down. All Besnik had really told her was what anyone with the least consideration would say to a friend: he was sure it would all turn out all right, he had a feeling . . . But what else could he say, after all? The opposite?

Silva opened the door into the office. Linda and the boss were both there. They watched her as she went and sat down, the boss with a rather shifty eye, Linda inquiringly, but quite ready to smile. Silva, pretending not to notice, opened her drawer and took out a file. Neither of the others addressed a word to her for the rest of the morning.

✻　　✻　　✻

152

When Silva got home, neither Gjergj nor Brikena were back yet. She put the lunch on to cook and got vegetables out of the refrigerator, but just as she was about to start preparing a salad she put the knife down and went over to the phone. Luckily, Skënder Bermema was at home. She said she needed to see him urgently.

"Whenever you want," he said. "Now, if you like."

"This afternoon would be better. Are you free?"

"Yes, of course. What time would you like to come?"

Silva hesitated.

"You want me to come to your place?" she said.

She could hear him breathing at the other end of the line. He knew she was avoiding his wife because of the business with Ana.

"As you like," he said. "We could just as easily go somewhere else, but I'll be on my own here this afternoon."

"I'll come at five, then."

She put the receiver down slowly, as if she were afraid it might break.

As soon as she entered Skënder's study, Silva was submerged in a wave of nostalgia. How many years was it since she'd set foot here? How long since the days when she and Ana used to come and see him? The curtains were different, and so were some of the books on the shelves, but the chair where Ana liked to sit leafing through a book or a magazine was still in its old place, and the pictures on the walls were the same. Silva stood there for a moment, forgetting why she was there. Skënder too seemed absent, perhaps for the same reason: the memories they had in common.

"Sit down, Silva," he said at last. He sounded tired.

She took a chair. She'd hesitated about coming, even after she'd phoned. Should she really go to his place or not? Two or three times she decided to do nothing, to avoid giving the impression that it was only when she had problems that she thought of him. She wasn't the kind to go round begging favours. But, apart from Gjergj, Besnik Struga and Skënder Bermema were the people closest to her. If she didn't unburden herself to them, to whom could she speak? She'd said this to herself over and over again. Yet when she left her own apartment at a quarter to five, she didn't tell Gjergj where she was going.

"What's it all about?" Skënder asked eventually. "You sounded rather upset when you rang."

She felt her eyes starting to fill with tears.

"To tell you the truth, I *am* upset."

She set about telling him what had happened, and to her own astonishment – perhaps because *he* was listening to *her* so quietly – managed to express herself quite calmly. As she spoke he kept glancing impatiently, and more and more frequently, at the telephone.

"Very strange." he said as soon as she'd finished.

And this brief epilogue convinced her that her story must indeed be out of the ordinary.

He bounded up and pounced on the phone as if it might try to escape. He grabbed the receiver with one hand and dialled feverishly with the other. The ringing at the other end of the line seemed to reverberate in Silva's heart. No one answered.

Skënder hung up, then lifted the receiver and dialled again – whether the same number as before or another, Silva had no means of knowing. Then there was a click, and he said, "Hallo – Skënder Bermema here."

She'd have liked to shut her eyes and have a rest after all that tension. At first she didn't take in what was being said over the phone. It was comfort enough to know that someone was taking an interest in her brother, and someone else again was supplying relevant information. At least the general silence, the shrugs, the inability of anyone to explain anything, were over! How right she'd been to come here! She watched his lips gratefully as he spoke.

The conversation continued. Now she wanted to know what they were saying. Her agitation returned stronger than ever. How could she be so thoughtless as to be lulled by a mere exchange of words? What mattered was what was being said.

Chewing her lip, she tried to piece together the conversation, guessing at the part she couldn't hear.

"What?" Skënder almost yelled down the phone. He seemed as frantic as she was. "What?"

"What's up?" she wondered. He was frowning more and more heavily. The person at the other end must be telling him something terrible. She seemed to feel her pulse slacken.

"What?" he bellowed again, waving his free hand impatiently. "Frankly, I don't understand . . . No, really . . . If you're supposed to be in charge . . . What? . . . No! . . . No offence meant, but I'm sorry I bothered you . . ."

Silva felt a bit better again. If Skënder was ready to lose his temper the situation couldn't be all that bad. He was now holding the receiver away from his ear. And soon he hung up, looking at Silva with a distant smile.

"Very odd," he said. "This chap starts by giving me an earful of tittle-tattle, then tries to tell me we have to approach the matter theoretically! And to think he's an old friend of mine!"

"Didn't he know anything?"

Skënder shrugged.

"Who knows? I couldn't make him out any better than you could, and you didn't even hear what he said! He wriggled like an eel!"

Silva would have liked to ask him who it was, but by now he was flicking nervously through the telephone directory. Eventually he found the number he was looking for.

Silva didn't understand any more of the second phone conversation than she had of the first. Then Skënder rang someone else, who was out, but the person who answered gave him another number.

"Hallo – is that the Political Office?"

Silva felt she would never escape from this maelstrom of calls. Was she going to have to listen to them for hours without being any the wiser?

"How are you?" he was now asking someone. "You know why I'm calling . . ."

Silva held her breath as she listened to his brief preamble. The silence that followed at the other end was almost tangible. Then the other person spoke. Skënder listened, gazing abstractedly at the little table on which the phone stood.

"Why get into a state about them?" he said, obviously echoing what he'd just heard. "I don't know about anyone else, but I'm interested in him because he's a friend of mine. A very close friend, do you get me? These things happen in the army? What do you mean by that? . . . We civilians attach too much importance to them? . . . No, I don't think that's true . . . Anyhow, I get the message. You don't know much about it either . . . No, no – don't bother . . . Goodbye!"

He put the phone down and smiled at Silva as before.

"Funny they're all so vague," he said, as if to himself. "I'd almost say they're worried. Why are we civilians taking such an interest?

. . . Yes, very odd . . . One can't help thinking . . . It's almost as if . . ."

"Perhaps it's got something to do with China?" Silva said gently, to help him finish his sentence.

"China? No, no . . . I was thinking of something else . . . Ah well . . . Just theories . . . maybe they're all nonsense."

He lit a cigarette and started pacing round the studio. He seemed to be staring into space. The same as ever, thought Silva. But perhaps it was because they never changed, he and Besnik Struga, that they were still her friends.

As she watched him going over to the bookcase, his back now turned, she suddenly felt that an exactly similar scene had probably taken place before, here in this studio, in the silent dusk – between him and Ana.

Forgetting a Woman . . . She knew that story of his almost by heart. Frédéric had asked for it to be read out during the divorce proceedings. Everyone said Skënder had dedicated it to Ana. Although it was set in a hotel room, Silva was convinced the scene it depicted had taken place here in this studio.

Skënder turned and walked over to his desk as if looking for something, but gave up and came and stood in front of Silva with his hands in his pockets.

"What a pity I've got to go abroad. I'm sure I'd have been able to solve the mystery."

"You're going away?" she said, not sure she'd heard right. "Where to?"

He smiled almost guiltily.

"Can't you guess? To China?"

"China!" exclaimed Silva. "Really?"

"Really and truly. Apparently this is the last delegation. The last swallow of summer."

Silva stared at the fringe on the rug at her feet. The last swallow of summer, she repeated to herself as he went on about the make-up of the delegation. They're all flying away, she thought sadly. And heaved a sigh.

Almost as soon as she got to the office next morning, her boss told her she had to go on a mission to the north of the country. She concluded at once that this was the first act of reprisal against her, after the business about her brother. With a haste she was ashamed of whenever she thought of it later, she assumed it was the prelude to a transfer, or else to out-and-out dismissal.

"Me? . . . I've got to go to the north?" she stammered, frowning, as if to say, Why, what have I done?

Her boss looked back at her in surprise.

"Eh?" he exclaimed. "If you can't manage it . . . if you've got some good reason . . ."

"No," she replied coldly. Her tone implied that it was quite possible for her to go, but she'd like to know why she was being sent.

It was as if a huge mass had suddenly formed in her head, preventing all normal thought. But after a few seconds, something inside her struggled fiercely to escape from that lethargy. It wasn't the first time she'd been sent on a mission . . . No, it wasn't the first time . . . Perhaps that was why . . .

"If you've got some reason for not going, you can stay," her boss was saying. She'd have liked to interrupt: "You know the reason perfectly well!" But what would be the point? She herself would never have claimed that the business about her brother was a valid excuse for not going. A few seconds ago she'd been imagining just the opposite . . .

"As you wish," the boss went on. "It was Linda I was thinking of, mainly – she'll be lonesome all on her own . . ."

It was only then that Silva noticed her colleague's expression. Linda was gazing fixedly at her: it was plain she couldn't understand her friend's attitude, and was upset by it. How awful of me! thought Silva. If the others hadn't been there she'd have buried her face in her hands. Why had she flared up like that? The more she thought about it, the more ashamed she was. The boss had told her about the mission in a perfectly natural manner – why had she let her nerves get the better of her and dreamed up all that nonsense? Yet as the same time she did feel rather sorry for herself. At this rate she was going to end up with a nervous breakdown . . .

"I'm sorry – please forgive me," she said to her boss, without looking at him. "Of course I can go! I could go today! There's no reason why not."

The boss waved his hands. He seemed embarrassed, too.

"You needn't go if you don't want to. In fact . . . Maybe . . . I hadn't really thought of that, to tell the truth . . ."

"No," she said firmly. "That's no reason not to go. Perhaps the opposite. Especially as Linda will still be here . . ."

She turned to her friend, who smiled for the first time, though apparently she had no inkling of what lay behind these exchanges.

"As you like," said the boss. "Personally I've always enjoyed these trips to the hydro-electric power stations in the north. You see a new world, you learn about new things. You'll have two comrades with you from the planning office, and an expert on seismology."

Linda, her eyes still reflecting the hint of a smile, looked from Silva to their boss as if afraid their conversation might relapse into unpleasantness. But Silva's expression was peaceful again, and Linda could breathe freely.

Back home that afternoon, Silva thought over her brief set-to with her boss. She was ironing some sheets, but this usually soothing occupation, instead of driving away her worries, only made her feel more tense. It might have been more relaxing to do some crochet or embroidery.

"Brikena!" she called. "Will you check the phone? It isn't out of order, is it?"

First she heard her daughter's footsteps, then her voice.

"No, Mother. It's working."

I'll start believing in ghosts next, thought Silva. The phone hadn't rung much since the previous Sunday, but it was silly to think this was because of the Arian affair . . .

She glanced for some reason at the calendar. Tuesday the 17th. Then she looked at her watch. Five-thirty. Gjergj ought to have been home by now. She imagined him ringing at the door, taking off his raincoat, asking, "Any news?"

She shrugged. None.

Next day Silva felt disoriented. Her boss seemed to be doing his best to avoid being left alone with her. On the two occasions that Linda went out of the office, he found an excuse to absent himself too.

"Let him do as he likes," she thought. "I don't want to think about it any more."

After she left the office she took a bus to the cemetery. Gjergj's bunch of flowers, almost withered now, was still there on Ana's grave. Silva could scarcely believe only three days had gone by since the previous Sunday.

She didn't stay long by her sister's grave, but when she got home she felt better.

On Saturday, just as she was resigning herself to spending a tedious afternoon alone (Gjergj was at a meeting, Brikena at a friend's birthday party), there was a ring at the door. A visitor, she wondered, then was doubtful. It was her nature: the more she wanted something, the less she believed it would happen. It must be the woman who cleaned the stairs, asking, as she'd done the day before, to be allowed to fill her bucket with water. Or maybe a stranger inquiring after one of the other tenants . . .

She threw the door open with some impatience, as one does when about to tell an intruder they might have made proper inquiries before just knocking on doors at random. Her exasperation vanished when she saw she really did have visitors. But the relief was short-lived.

How on earth? And why? – the question was sharp and cold as the edge of an axe. Why had they come to see her after all these years?

As if reading her thoughts, the newcomers apologized for turning up without warning. "We said to one another, let's go and see her – it's ages since we met – people shouldn't just lose touch like that . . . Anyhow, here we are . . ."

"Do come in," said Silva half-heartedly.

She still felt stunned. As they took their coats off they chatted away airily (God, how could they be so self-satisfied?): How was Gjergj? . . . And their daughter? – she must be quite big now . . . They hadn't any other children, had they? . . . Sorry again for coming without letting them know . . . Perhaps she and Gjergj had arranged to do something this afternoon? . . . After all, it was Saturday . . .

"No, it's all right . . ." murmured Silva.

But in fact they'd just provided her with the best possible excuse for turfing them out: "Thanks so much for coming, but as a matter of fact a friend of my husband's is due in about twenty minutes."

It still wasn't too late for her to say that. But wait. You could always find a way of getting rid of unwanted guests; the important thing was to find out why they'd come.

"'You can guess why! We're all in the same boat now, so we can afford to go and see one another!' Can that be it?" she asked herself. Could that really be it?

Her brain was gradually emerging from its lethargy. She would do her best to find out if that was why they were here. Or if, worse still, they'd come to gloat over her unhappiness, to avenge themself for the long years of indifference and neglect which she'd inflicted on them ... She could still get rid of them if she wanted to by remarking, "It *is* Saturday, as you say, and unfortunately Gjergj and I have an appointment."

Some years ago one of Silva's two aunts had scandalized her nearest and dearest by marrying a member of the old guard, and thenceforward no excuse had been needed for steering clear of her. She had apparently found her husband's circle quite sufficient, and hardly saw her own family at all except at the occasional funeral.

"This way," said Silva, leading the way into the living room.

It was the first time she'd seen her aunt's husband close to. She examined him surreptitiously to see what her aunt could have seen in him. He had a very ordinary face, but with curious wrinkles which instead of making him look older than he was seemed rather to fix him at one age for ever. Silva vaguely remembered hearing that he'd worked for an Italo-Albanian bank during the Occupation, that he'd inherited money from Italy, and spent a few years in prison after the Liberation. But she could recall very clearly the uproar caused in the family by her aunt's escapade. There'd been endless comings and goings, after-dinner councils, plans to intervene, telephone calls, and harassing interviews with the prodigal daughter. You've covered us in shame for the rest of our lives – how shall we be able to look other people in the face? And, never mind about tarnishing *our* reputation – have you so much as thought about the memory of your sister? How could you trample it underfoot like this? Silva's other aunt, who'd died in the war, had never been invoked so often. She'd been extraordinarily beautiful (Ana took after her), and apparently it was because of her looks that the resistance group she belonged to entrusted her with an especially dangerous mission: she was to get herself up as an upper-middle-class young woman and infiltrate circles to which her

160

colleagues had otherwise no access. She had carried out her task brilliantly (it was said she'd learned to make herself up more skilfully than the models who occasionally showed up from Rome), until one day, in circumstances that had never been clarified, she was unmasked at an officers' ball at the Hotel Dajti. Although she was seriously wounded as she was trying to escape along an alley near the main boulevard, she managed to reach the safe house where her friends were waiting for her. She was still wearing her jewellery, though it was spattered with blood, and while her comrades were treating her injuries she kept making signs. But the others, trying to save her life, paid no attention to these gestures, which might well have referred to her brooches and necklaces, to her painted lips and eyes, or to the elegant gown which she would have liked them to remove. When she died, an hour later, they buried her in all her finery.

You have trampled your sister's memory underfoot . . . How often Silva had heard that phrase! One day, after the scandalous marriage had taken place which was never referred to except with horror, Aunt Hasiyé, an elderly relative, had said: "God moves in a mysterious way. As soon as Marie started dolling herself up and doing her hair like a hussy, I had a premonition. All this bodes no good, I told myself. That's why when I heard of her goings-on I realized all those frills and flounces were omens. Like those you see in dreams . . ."

One of her grand-nephews had protested at this ridiculous fatalism, but Aunt Hasiyé wasn't to be moved: "I don't know anything about fatalism or revisionism – that's your business. But I can read the signs of the Lord!"

Silva now covertly examined this aunt's profile. Her striking facial resemblance to the dead woman was emphasized by the way her hair was done, smoothed back stiffly as in a stained-glass window. The same style as that of the war heroine herself, in a photograph that had shown her dressed in the bourgeois fashion of the day.

Silva, suddenly remembering she ought to offer the visitors some refreshment, stood up. She mused on them all out in the kitchen, as she poured brandy into glasses. There were four visitors in all: her aunt, her aunt's husband, their daughter, and another woman, whom Silva had never met before and who must be the husband's sister.

When Silva came back into the living room the sister-in-law had lit a cigarette and was talking. Her voice was at once raucous and cooing, with little bursts like laughter. You could tell she got on very well with Silva's aunt.

She was the first to drink.

"Your health!" she said, raising her glass.

"And yours!" said Silva.

Her aunt looked at her placidly. It was three years, perhaps four, since they'd seen one another. The last time, they'd met by chance in the street. Silva thought she'd never seen her aunt looking so gaunt, but when she asked if she was worried about something the older woman had replied tartly: "As if you were interested in my worries! My dear niece, you have your own life with your husband. Everything goes smoothly for you two. And why not? Your day has come . . ."

Silva tried to interrupt and say, "But you wanted it this way . . . You were the one who insisted . . ."

"I know, I know what you're going to say, but I've had enough of being criticized! And I don't intend to listen to any more of it today!"

It had taken Silva some time to find out why her aunt was so sour: her son had been refused permission to go to the University. The reason was obvious: his father's past.

Your day has come . . . Silva repeated to herself. But now times had changed again: instead of belonging to one or other party, she now had a foot in both camps. So she and her aunt could now visit one another . . . Especially as none of your own folk come and see you any more. Haven't you spent all your time listening for the door-bell and the telephone this last week? But never mind – if they don't come, we shall. We shall come quite freely now there's no barrier between us any more. We're all marked men, but your mark is more painful than ours because it's more recent . . .

Silva's mouth was dry. Why didn't Gjergj come home? Or even Brikena?

The sister-in-law contributed most to the conversation. It suited her nicely. They'd probably brought her along for that very reason. Silva heard only scraps of what was said. They'd just collected a motorbike from the customs for their nephew, but it wasn't the make he wanted: what should they do? . . . Benedetto Croce? When she was a student they all had his books by their beds . . . In fashionable restaurants people sometimes ate chicken with their fingers . . .

The conversation was like something out of the Ark. Allusions to Hondas and Vestas only made matters worse, and the word "genetic", through some absurd association of ideas, made Silva think of Greta Garbo's profile.

They went over all the little dinner parties they'd invited one another to, together with trivial events quite free of any of the more serious emotions. Behind the veil of old-fashionedness one divined a completely self-contained and self-satisfied world.

Brikena arrived just as Silva was making coffee.

"What a big girl she is now!" exclaimed the sister-in-law, kissing her. Then, turning to her niece: "Vilma, come and say hallo to your cousin. Have you really never met before?"

Brikena blushed and looked inquiringly at her mother. Then the two girls awkwardly kissed.

Silva felt a weight at the pit of her stomach again. Now she understood why they'd brought their daughter with them. They wanted to get their claws on the younger generation too.

"Come and sit down next to Vilma," said the sister-in-law to Brikena, enjoying herself hugely.

The girls stared at one another like strangers. Brikena turned to her mother again. Why isn't Gjergj back yet, Silva groaned to herself.

She got up and handed round the coffee. She had meant to wait for her husband, but perhaps it was better if he wasn't there.

"I'm going to read the coffee grounds in my cup," said the sister-in-law, laughing noisily. "I'm very good at it," she told Silva. "Would you like me to read yours?"

Silva longed inwardly to put an end to this farce. But something forced her to do nothing, to see how far they would go. She secretly hoped the woman would snatch her cup, solemnly turn it round and round, and utter the ritual formula: "Someone near to you will soon be going on a long journey . . ." (Gjergj, obviously . . . Was he going to be sent abroad again?) "You see that dark patch at the very bottom of the cup? That's an illness or a great misfortune – probably a misfortune. But look at this V – that means the sorrow is starting to lessen . . ."

Meanwhile the sister-in-law was commenting half-seriously,

half-jokingly, on what she saw in her own cup, while the others listened, smiling.

"She's always been like that," the aunt's husband told Silva. He sounded apologetic. "She likes to look on the bright side!"

They've talked about everything except Arian, Silva noticed. It's as if he didn't exist. And yet, she said to herself as they were putting on their coats in the hall, hide it as they might, it was because of him that they'd come!

"Goodbye, Silva," said her aunt, kissing her.

"Goodbye, my dear," said the sister-in-law, doing the same.

When the door closed behind them, Silva collapsed on to the settee. She felt exhausted.

"Don't you feel well, Mother?" asked Brikena.

Silva didn't answer. She just looked at the cups and glasses on the coffee table, as if trying decipher, through them, the motives of her visitors. It was easier to think about it now that they'd gone. They didn't really seem to have come out of resentment or in search of revenge. Nor for the malicious pleasure of seeing her down and out. But neither had they come out of sympathy. At best, what they felt was closer to half-hearted tolerance than to pity. But then if they *had* felt sorry for her she wouldn't have been able to bear it! She had to hold back her tears. There was something repulsive even about their goodwill: welcome to our cosy little world, we've been expecting you, so just calm down and relax . . .

And that's how Gjergj found her – sitting with her face buried in her hands. Brikena, who had let him in, had evidently told him about the visitors. He looked for a moment at the cups, one sinisterly upside down in the middle, and without saying anything, not even his usual "Anything wrong?", he came over and stroked her hair.

As if she'd only been waiting for this sign of affection, which seemed to rise up from the happiest times in their lives, Silva burst into tears.

He let her give vent to her feelings for a while, then drew her close and whispered, "There, there, that'll do now. Won't you make me a cup of coffee too?"

8

AS AT EVERY CHANGE of season, the sky was now full of flocks of birds migrating. Billions moved from one place to another within the continents, other billions crossed from one continent to another. Millions of them died, some by drowning as they flew over the ocean, some from exhaustion over the land; others had their wings frozen; others again got lost. But there wasn't a mention of all this in any of the thousands of newspapers and magazines throughout the world, or on radio or television, or at any of the international meetings, seminars and conferences.

Perhaps it would have been otherwise if there hadn't been so much political tension, said a couple of rather senile old professors of zoology as they drank their morning coffee in the Clock Bar in Tirana.

As it was, the air was completely saturated. Dozens of press agencies were busy transmitting the list of members of the Chinese Politbureau, as issued on the occasion of a recent state funeral. The list was as follows, in that order: Mao Zedong, Zhou Enlai, Wang Hongwen, Ye Jianying, Deng Xiaoping, Zhang Chunqiao, Liu Bocheng, Jiang Qing, Xu Shiyou, Hua Guofeng, Ji Dengkui, Wu De, Wang Dongxing, Chan Yonggui, Chen Xilian, Li Xiannian, Li Desheng, Yao Wenyuan, Wu Guixian, Su Zhenhua, Saifudin, Song Qingling . . .

Hardly had the list been sent out than it was followed by the first comment: as compared with the previous list, two names were missing. There was another change too: the positions of the member with the turban and the member with the two barrels were reversed again, so that each occupied the place he had had on the last list but one. But this was only a minor alteration compared with the complete disappearance of two names.

Phone calls, ciphers, queries and requests for verification flew in all directions. But it wasn't an accidental omission or a mistake in decoding. Funerals provided the most reliable opportunity for checking up on the order of the hierarchy, and it so happened there had been plenty of funerals lately. So this anomaly couldn't be merely a matter of chance. Two names were really and truly missing. The names of Wei Guoqing and Ni Zhifu.

Signals from all the major press agencies, secret services and spy satellites purred through the heavens. The search was on for two men who'd got lost. Their names echoed round the globe like those of a couple of mountaineers who had fallen down a crevasse. But there was no answer.

"Let's leave it at that," said an observer at a station near the North Pole, taking his headset off for a minute to rest his buzzing ears. "Why should we wear ourselves out all night looking for a couple of sharks like that?"

He'd been working at this listening post for several months by now, and perhaps his perceptions had become rather dulled. There were plenty of reasons why they might have done so: the length of time he'd spent cut off from normal life; the isolation; the mountain range of ice all round him, the hopeless sky above, the earth below – all so smooth and featureless that there was nothing for the mind to catch hold of. It was a landscape that stripped you of everything and gave you nothing in return but solitude and unfathomable distance. No wonder he often oversimplified things. He only had to look down – as it seemed to him – at the world: most countries were riddled with debt, and that was why they were always squabbling and grumbling, slandering and accusing one another. Krushchev was dead, Mao was ill, and so was Franco: the ranks of the tyrants were clearly thinning out, and maybe the death of these spectres would eventually make the world go round more merrily. But for the moment all that arose from below was a tissue of nonsense.

He put his headset on again. The search for the two lost names was still in full swing. As if they'd really be missed! There wouldn't have been nearly as much fuss if they'd been a couple of innocent doves, like the ones children play with in spring! But what can you do? He was going to have to start listening to that idiotic buzzing again. Especially in a couple of hours' time, after midnight, when the diplomatic receptions were over and the ciphers started up again worse than ever.

*   *   *

In Paris on this evening in late November, twenty-seven diplomatic receptions were being held. It was nine o'clock. A fine rain was falling. The headlights of the last tardy guests swept over the railings in front of the various embassies concerned. In the Rue de la Faisanderie, Juan Maria Krams found a parking space just big enough for his car, slammed the door, and made a dash for the Cuban Embassy. It was clear the party was at its height. But he made his way round both the drawing rooms without finding anyone of interest to talk to. Two waiters, probably realizing he'd just arrived because of the drops of rain still sparkling in his hair, both offered him drinks and *petits fours* at the same time. He took a whisky, but just held the glass in his hand, without drinking. He'd wasted almost an hour at the Cambodian Embassy, where everything was very dead. There were plenty of people he knew there, but not a single conversation of any interest. All the guests had looked lethargic, and though he'd hoped things might improve in due course, they'd only got worse. It was very different here, though he was surprised not to see any familiar faces. Perhaps they'd drop in later, but he couldn't be sure, and he didn't want to fritter away the whole evening.

He was invited to three other embassies – the Albanian, the Romanian, and the Vietnamese – and he couldn't afford to waste time. He looked at his watch. A quarter past nine. Without more ado he made for the door. In the hall he realized he was still holding his glass of whisky. He put it down on a table, beside a telephone, and left.

It was still raining. As he got into his car he wondered whether to go to the Albanian or the Romanian Embassy next. It was the Albanians' national holiday, so their reception would probably go on longer than the others. The Romanians just had a kind of exhibition on, if he remembered rightly. But as the Albanian Embassy was quite close by, he decided to go there first. He had to call in on the Albanians anyway, even if it meant he wouldn't get to the other two receptions: they were the ones most concerned with what he wanted to know.

He drove round the Etoile without thinking, and found himself in the Avenue d'Eylau. But although it wasn't unusual to find out more about what interested you at a different embassy from the one directly concerned, Juan Maria Krams pressed on. When he reached the little Place de Mexico, he had to slow down as usual to find the turning that led to the Albanian Embassy. The narrow

Rue de Longchamp was wet and empty. He was soon in the Rue de la Pompe.

The reception was very lively, but with a liveliness he didn't care for. The guests seemed unnaturally cheerful, and couldn't stick to any one subject. He made several attempts to talk about third-world problems to some Albanians he knew, but got the impression they didn't want to get involved in that. If this had been due to lack of expertise he wouldn't have minded, but in fact they seemed irritated and made little attempt to hide it. One of them, after trying unsuccessfully to stifle a yawn, said playfully:

"Comrade Krams, couldn't we talk about something more serious? All those other problems are so boring . . . Typically Chinese discussions, I'd call them!"

"What!" exclaimed Juan. "Do you think discussions can be categorized according to . . . ?"

The other smiled broadly and gave a vague wave of the hand.

"Is is really worth cudgelling one's brains over things like that? You should take my advice and stop worrying . . ."

"Is that so?" said Juan coldly.

Well, that's putting it plainly enough, he thought. His last doubts were removed. For some time he'd been noticing the signs . . .

He made for a quiet corner, but even there he wasn't out of range of the hum of conversation, the flashing of jewels, the bursts of laughter. He gazed absently at the guests as they came and went, most of them brandishing a glass as if it were a candle lighting their way – the way to the abyss!

A hand on his shoulder roused him from his musings.

"Comrade Krams? Good evening."

The speaker's face looked even swarthier and more wizened than it really was under its mop of black curly hair.

It took Krams a few moments to remember who he was. They'd met for the first time a couple of years before at an international gathering at which the Moroccan had represented a movement involved in the Sahraoui question. Then Krams had come across him again at another conference, where he represented a completely different school of thought, which, though it still had something to do with the Sahara, advocated other views and put forward other claims.

"How're things?" asked Krams.

"Not too good . . . We've had lots of dissension lately. We're reforming hard now."

In other circumstances Krams would have been interested in a conversation like this, but when, about a year before, he'd studied a sheaf of documents about the Sahraoui movement, he'd got so muddled up he'd given up hope of ever understanding anything about it. It really was difficult to discern the logic behind all the changes of policy, and Krams had come to the conclusion that to look for it was as hopeless as trying to read the traces left by the wind on the desert sands.

To stop the other going into explanations of the inexplicable, Krams asked him if he'd heard anything about the U.S. president's projected visit to China.

"Yes," said the Moroccan. "I have heard some rumours. But as far as I can make out, it's only bluff."

"Bluff?"

The Moroccan nodded.

"Yes. You can say 'bluff' in French, can't you? Anyway, a great booby-trap, just like the business of the hundred flowers." He laughed.

"Who told you that?"

"A friend I can trust. Mao intends to find out who's pleased at the news and who's going to try to take advantage . . . And then – bang! Like the last time. They'll strike without mercy, obliterate, destroy. There'll be another Cultural Revolution even more terrible than the first. And those who escaped the typhoon last time won't be able to escape this . . ."

"Really?" said Krams thoughtfully. "So there's not going to be any visit?"

"I don't know about that," the Moroccan answered. "The visit may go ahead, but it won't make any difference – the trap will work anyhow."

For the first time Krams smiled faintly.

"You've given me good news, *Shkretëtirs*.* I named you that because of the Sahara . . . Sorry if I offended you. People sometimes give *me* nicknames, and I must say I couldn't care less."

He remembered the reception at the Romanian Embassy and consulted his watch. He probably couldn't get there in time,

---

* In Albanian, "man of the desert".

but anyway he said goodbye to the Moroccan, took one more short stroll through the main drawing room, then unobtrusively slipped out.

The rain still hadn't stopped. His hair was soaked before he got to his car. What lousy weather, he grumbled. It took him a good ten minutes to get to the Rue Saint-Dominique, where the last guests were coming out of the Romanian Embassy. They were still saying goodbye to one another as he came up. Then, after turning away, they would keep going back again for another few words. Juan Maria had noticed that when people got drunk their affability could be as irritating as their touchiness. So just as one of them beamed at him and opened his mouth to greet him, he turned tail, leaped into his car, and drove off in no particular direction. No question of going to the Vietnamese Embassy at this hour. Even if the reception there wasn't over yet, he didn't feel at all like going now. His evening had been completely spoiled.

He drove along slowly, still undecided what to do. The sidelights of the cars coming towards him cast what looked like pools of blood on the road. He'd wasted an evening of which he'd expected so much!

On he went, as fast as the traffic allowed, fidgeting in his seat and every so often thumping the steering wheel with impatience. How could he escape and whiz along freely, without being stopped by the traffic lights?

He was in one of those states of excitement where the spirit feels shackled by the body. Cramped limbs, the impossibility of speeding – everything conspired to frustrate him.

He'd heard that this happened sometimes when you were in love (at first he'd hadn't liked to admit that it hadn't happened to him – but after all, what did it matter?). It might occur if you were obliged to perform some trivial task in the presence of the unattainable beloved . . .

And he'd spent the whole blessed evening just tearing from one embassy to another.

It was only the second time he'd had this feeling quite so strongly. The first time was during the famous autumn when there was talk of a split within the socialist camp. As soon he'd heard the first rumours he'd felt, as a militant progressive, that his whole being was ready. It was something he'd been waiting for with the same eagerness as others, spurred on by puberty, or in erotic dreams or whatever, longed for a woman. He remembered that whole period as one of semi-delirium . . . Days and nights of endless conversation in cafés, especially the Madrid and the Cardinal. Heated arguments, sleepless nights, doubts, hesitations, a lightning trip to Tirana, other journeys to Moscow and Peking, then back to the Cardinal and more sleepless nights. And in the end, his choice: to be on the same side of the barricades as the Albanians and the Chinese, against the Soviets.

At the time a lot of people couldn't understand why he'd made that choice. To begin with it gave rise to all kinds of speculation, then some started to sneer. What could possibly have made him drop the Soviets and come down on the side of the Albanians and the Chinese? Could he have been motivated by mere self-interest? That wouldn't wash – everyone knew the Soviets had much more to offer careerists than little Albania and poverty-stricken China. In the end it had to be admitted that Krams's choice had been dictated neither by sordid nor by sentimental considerations. He must have had some other reason.

And now history is going to repeat itself more or less exactly, he thought, still smiling coldly. The split between China and Albania was an open secret, and the same people as before would try to puzzle out why he took one side rather than the other: self-interest, romanticism, a weak spot for the under-dog, loyalty to the party line . . .

The lights from shop windows, falling obliquely on his face, made his smile look enigmatic. He hadn't yet told anyone what he really thought, but on the whole he inclined towards the Chinese. And this not because of the logic of events, nor because of sentiment, still less out of cynical calculation. No, it was something over and above all that. Something which transcended even principle, and probably left Krams himself altogether out of account.

The mass of cars had come to a halt at an intersection, and their drivers, hunched up on their seats, separated from one another by thick windowpanes, their eyes fixed on the traffic lights, looked far away, out of time. Krams thought of the interpretations, supported by all kinds of ridiculous guesses at motive, that people were going to put forward to explain his decision to side with the Chinese. But no one would find out the truth. He was all the more certain of this because he knew he himself was incapable of putting it into words.

More than once, in the rare moments when his thoughts managed to reach, though dimly, the depths of his being, he'd wondered when this love – if it could be called that – had been born in him, this feeling which for some reason he thought of as *group life*. It must have happened when he was still only seventeen or eighteen – he'd forgotten by now the initials of the little group whose meetings he used to go to every evening after supper, as he'd forgotten lots of other details about it. But the unparalleled delight he took in debate, especially when it involved the possibility of a split, the regrets which a schism might bring, the pleasure of seeing a new group come into being, and the thrill of taking what often seemed a real risk – all this was still quite fresh in his memory.

And that had been only the beginning. Gradually the fascination grew: a universe hitherto unknown to him began to swallow up his whole existence. Not only did he first allow and then encourage the passions to die away in him – he also banished from his life every other object of desire: his boyhood craze for collecting things; winter sports; the sea; the theatre; the melancholy of autumn; the Greek gods; astronomy; history; his parents. Some of these things became quite alien to him, the rest grew merely meaningless. He now had quite new interests. He found a deviation from a party or group line more captivating than all his memories of summer holidays. His life was entirely filled with the congresses of the various parties, and of the new groups and sections which had come into being since the break-up of the Marxist-Leninist communist parties; with their plenums, their programmes, the fluctuations of their policies, the different tendencies that grew up in their midst; with the reformists, the syndicalists, the paths to socialism, the conflicting views about the use of force, about pacifism, intimidation, anarchosyndicalism, the historic compromise, the third world . . .

"Don't you find it all terribly boring?" a friend had asked him one day. Juan Maria had rarely been so furious. They'd argued till after midnight in the café where the Colombian leftists hung out, near the Place de l'Opéra, then gone on arguing in the street, then in another bar, and so on until daybreak. They'd hurled fierce accusations at one another, quoting Trotsky, Marx, Stalin, Lenin, Che Guevara and Mao Zedong one on top of the other. Krams had charged his friend with about seven deviations, and his friend, as day broke, cried, "Do you know what you are, Krams? You're anti-life, you're the Devil in person!"

"Yes, I suppose I am, in a way," he'd answered. "I reject this life in favour of another that is to come." "And what if this other life rejects *you*?" said the other. "Has it ever occurred to you that if you move so far away from ordinary human existence, from what you scornfully call 'the thirst for life', you might become so twisted that if you ever wanted to change your mind, life might refuse to let you come back, might drive you away as if you were a ghost?" "Rubbish," he'd replied. "Petty-bourgeois verbiage!" But the other had persisted: "A shadow, Krams, that's what you are!"

And they'd gone on wrangling in the damp dawn, the shapes of passers-by seeming indeed to move in a world other than theirs. When the two young men separated, perhaps even after they'd begun to walk away, Krams' friend had turned round and called after him: "Give it all up before it's too late, Krams! You'll find more history, philosophy and perhaps even economics in the tears of the old women in the Balkans than in all your plenums and your right, left and centre resolutions!"

Old women singing a funeral song in the Balkans . . . thought Krams as he drove along now, his eyes on the wet road. The chap was probably referring to something he'd seen on a trip to Albania. He must have been to one of those funeral ceremonies to which Krams himself had so far paid no attention.

Even after all this time, he still felt some of his original disillusionment about Albania. He'd rushed there hoping to see a new world inhabited by new men, and all he'd found was the same humdrum old routine of human life: people earning wages, buying furniture and lampshades just as they did everywhere else, putting money away in the savings bank, divorcing, inviting one another to dinner, getting drunk, and occasionally even committing suicide for love.

But where was the new man? On the third day he suddenly asked his guide this question. "The new man?" said the guide, somewhat taken aback. "The people you see all around you – in the café, in the street. They're the new men!"

They were strolling along Tirana's main boulevard. Krams felt he'd been had.

"Excuse my frankness," he said, nodding towards the passers-by, "but the last thing I'd call these people is new men! Look at the way they're dressed! Look at the way the boys move, look at the girls' eyes! I don't know how to describe them."

The guide laughed.

"They're just human movements, human looks. Why should they need any other description?"

"That's not the point," said Krams.

So they had their first argument about the new man out there on the boulevard. Krams hadn't minced his words. The new man was the foundation, the key, the alpha and omega of the whole thing. If he could be brought into being, socialism could be regarded as successful; if not, everything would be in danger of falling to pieces. Krams brought out an idea he'd heard somewhere before: you couldn't build a new socialism with old bricks. Otherwise, in your Palace of Culture there would be vestiges of the erstwhile Church; in your People's Assembly, the old Parliament; in your proletarian meeting, the former procession; in your military march, the waltz; and so on. But if one set about making new bricks, then the buildings, even if they sometimes adopted old forms, would be new in their substance and thus proof against the phantoms of the old world.

"Do you see what I mean?" Krams had asked the guide. "The new brick is the new man. If we get him, the rest will follow. If not, one fine day hotels will turn back into churches, and instead of playing the *Internationale*, orchestras will play the liturgy."

The guide had nodded thoughtfully. In theory he wasn't against what Krams had said, but he couldn't quite see what this new man was going to be like. "The Chinese are trying to create him," said Krams. "Oh yes," said the guide, "I've heard about that. I suppose you're referring to Lei Fen?" "Exactly. You don't seem to like him very much?" "I don't know what to say," said the guide.

Scraps of other arguments were coming back to Krams. Their discussions had become more and more heated. One day his escort said, "I can't understand you, comrade Krams. I've noticed you're not interested in the life the people live here, only in certain things . . . I don't know how to describe them – dry, theoretical things." "Now *I* don't understand *you*," said Krams. "I'll try to explain. By dry, theoretical things I mean, for example, that when it comes to the workers you're interested only in their unions, not in their daily lives – their pay, their living conditions and so on. When it comes to the intelligentsia, you only want to know the different ways they manage to do their quota of manual work. I don't know if I've made myself clear. And take literature: you've never asked me what it takes as its subjects, but you've asked me dozens of questions

174

about how writers get in touch with the grass roots in order to merge with the masses . . ."

Here Krams had interrupted, to tell the other he believed that the only great literary achievement of the age of socialism was precisely that – the re-education of writers. He thought it would be wonderful if Albania managed to set a similar example to the rest of the world.

"A horror like that?" said the guide, with a grimace of disgust.

"Do you call that a horror?"

"That's putting it mildly!" And without trying to disguise his irritation, he told Krams the Albanians had no intention of debasing with their own hands the life they'd managed by twenty centuries of superhuman effort to preserve against famine, war and plague. "And you surely don't suppose they'd do it just for the pleasure of illustrating somebody's theories?"

Krams was silent. The fact was, that was exactly what he *had* thought. He'd hoped the Albanians would be ready to sacrifice their country on the altar of his theories. Now this fellow was saying the opposite. But perhaps he didn't reflect the general opinion? As time went by, Krams acquired the conviction that a lot of people in Albania shared his own views.

Nevertheless, his disillusionment had never quite disappeared. In later years, whenever he heard of what was going on there he felt some of the old bitterness. And then one day he heard on the radio that Albania had banned religion!

He was staggered. The country which had once disappointed him so much was now giving him an unexpected happiness. It had taken a step no one had dared take before. Nietzsche's dream! His Antichrist! Night after night Krams dreamed of bulldozers overturning churches and cathedrals, campaniles truncated, crosses knocked down. And this had happened in a country which in the Middle Ages was one of the outposts of Christianity! Wasn't it on Albania that the first furious tidal wave of Islam broke? Wasn't Skanderbeg, Albania's national hero, called Christianity's last bastion in Europe?

The two religions met here in an infernal clash. Neither drew back, and in the end Albania adopted both, and her hero took two names, one Christian, the other Islamic: George and Skander.

And now that was all over. The temples of both sides would be razed to the ground as if by an earthquake. To tell the truth, when Krams imagined this happening he saw church steeples collapsing rather than minarets. This may have been because he had a soft spot for the latter, due either to his many friendships with people in the third world or to some unavowed sympathy with Islam.

But the abolition of religion wouldn't have pleased Krams so much if it hadn't been the prelude to something else. He was sure the churches would bring down all the rest of the old culture with them in their fall: centuries of literature transcribed by copyists in monasteries, medieval ikons, painters, poets, philosophers . . . But even that wasn't enough – there were still countless things left to abolish: ceremonies, modes of thought and ways of life, a vast body of manners and customs, including the traditional dinner parties that were Krams' own pet aversion. He'd spent some time studying this phenomenon, and had discovered that the business of eating and talking at the same time, especially in the evening – in other words dinner parties in the contemporary sense of the term, which according to Krams were one of the worst scourges inflicted on the human race – had been invented by the ancient Greeks. He really believed that, unless these indulgences were done away with, it would be quite impossible to bring what was called the new man into being. He had even sketched out an article on *Dinner parties, last barrier to the creation of the new world*, in which he would examine birthday parties, funeral banquets, Christmas dinners, New Year suppers, Maundy Thursday, late-night conversations and the rest, as variants of the one decadent institution. (In his view, it was no accident that dinner suggested the end of the day.) And the abolition as soon as possible of this custom was an indispensable condition of real human progress.

But all that could wait. The first thing he had to do was go and see – check up on these incredible events on the spot and with his own eyes.

His first awakening in Tirana without the sound of church bells struck him as quite marvellous. The thought that the sky had been rid of that nuisance kept coming back to him and filling him with amazement. He would never have dreamed that the great change could have started like that.

He longed to find his former guide and say, "Well, which of us was right – you or me?" But the guide was a different person now. This wasn't surprising – the other man had probably been denounced by someone. Krams himself would never have done such a thing, but he did think his former escort had only got what he deserved. Or rather, he thought so until he discovered that his new guide was worse than the one before. Their first set-to was over the two million Albanians living in Yugoslavia. Krams regarded the debate about Kosovo as quite out of date, a relic of romantic nationalism (R.N., he dubbed it mentally), and he was amazed to see Albanian communists bothering about such things. He'd imagined they'd risen above such chauvinistic prejudices. The guide lost his temper, and the argument moved from the subject of bourgeois and proletarian ideas about patriotism to that of outmoded national heroes (O.N.H.'s, thought Krams). Then came the Greater-Serbian Rankovic's genocide of the Albanians in Kosovo (Krams thought this quite unimportant compared with the daily exploitation of the working classes), followed by the events in Cambodia. "Nobody knows where Cambodia begins," said the Albanian guide viciously. "Is it on Khmer soil, in Peking, or in certain cafés in Paris?" Then he glared at Krams as if to say, "Maybe Cambodia begins in *you*!"

Juan Maria could scarcely contain his wrath, but back in his hotel he cooled off. After all, there was no real reason why he should take offence. Despite certain excesses, he wasn't basically against what was happening in Cambodia. Let people call him Juan the Anti-Lifer, a ghost, a demon, the incarnation of sterility – that, in his own way, was what he was. If he had anything to worry about it wasn't that, but rather the fact that being called such names still upset him. It only went to show that his inner evolution wasn't yet complete.

One day he saw a funeral procession in the street, and this reminded him of his friend's reference to the Balkan mourners . . .

He didn't set much store by manifestations of this kind, and if he asked his guide to take him to a funeral it was so that when he got back home he could phone his friend and say: "I went to one of those ceremonies you were talking about, and the tears were just ordinary tears, that's all."

But his escort said that instead of taking him to a funeral he was going to take him to a cemetery. Or rather to two – the ordinary city cemetery and the cemetery reserved for national martyrs.

Krams had visited the latter before, on his first trip, but now, compared with the city cemetery, it made a different impression on him. While the graves of the martyrs were all the same, standardized, right down to the inscriptions and even the tombstones themselves, the ordinary graves presented an infinite variety of size, shape, style, symbol and sentimental epitaph. Distinctions were at their most evident among the dead. Perhaps that's where the great change begins, thought Krams: in the sky, where you no longer heard the sound of bells, and in death. Yes, that might well be it, though as yet he'd never heard of the "new dead".

He could feel his thoughts getting hopelessly scrambled. This was one of his rare lapses from lucidity. He was jolted out of his preoccupation by the guide, who nodded towards a tombstone of white marble:

"My wife's grave," he said.

"What?"

"My wife's grave," said the guide again, pointing to a photograph set into the headstone.

"Oh . . . I'm sorry . . . I didn't know . . ."

"No need to apologize," said the other, his eyes fixed on a bunch of wilted roses lying on the grave. "She died a few years ago. Breast cancer."

Krams waved his hands about helplessly. He felt horribly embarrassed, and couldn't think of anything to say. So he kept on saying, "I'm sorry."

He'd felt ill at ease ever since he came. Human beings have good memories — it's one of the human race's worst afflictions, Mao Zedong had said to him during their one and only interview. And when Krams asked him if he thought there might ever be a relatively simple way of explaining the complex mechanisms of the memory, Mao answered, "That's exactly what I've been working on lately."

As he often did when his ideas were undermined or challenged from without, Krams shut himself up in his hotel room earlier than usual, and sat himself down amid all the papers he'd brought with him. It was only when he was surrounded by documents that he felt completely safe. There, away from noise, perfumes, and unwelcome phone calls, he would steep himself in work until his mind settled down again. His enemies might call this world of his a verbal desert, a wilderness of empty phrases, a political Sahara --- for Krams himself it was the only world worth living and fighting for. He liked to pore for hours over the notes he'd written about everything relating to it: parties, splinter groups of left or right, Trotskyites, communists, Euro-communists, Marxist-Leninists, Maoists; their theories, tendencies, sub-tendencies, strategies and tactics, transformations, conflicts, and international connections. He knew that small world as well as he knew the palm of his hand: he'd belonged to some of its movements and even to their leadership, and after taking part in endless discussions within one group after the other had ended up in "Red Humanity". But although he was affiliated to one group, he felt linked, if only through hostility, with the whole galaxy revolving around him: the Organizing Committee for a Revolutionary Movement (the O.C.R.M.), with Trotskyite leanings, a large proportion of Spaniards on its boards, and a considerable network of foreign relations; the Movement of the 22nd of March (M 22), which had anarchist sympathies and was against democratic centralism and the dictatorship of the proletariat; the Communist League (the C.L.), a large almost folkloric organization with Trotskyite leanings which made little distinction between Stalinists and revisionists, since it regarded the latter as Stalinists who'd changed their name to make it easier for them to betray the communist movement. Those who took part in this group's demonstrations had had to shout "Ho-ho-ho-Ho-Chi-Minh" when Ho Chi Minh was the current idol, and "Che-che-che-Che-Guevara" when Guevara was in vogue, and now members of "Red Humanity" were expected to hail "Ma-ma-ma-Mao-Zedong". Then there was Workers' Struggle (W.S.), also Trotskyite, which didn't always draw the line at almost fascist violence; the Centres of Communist Endeavour (C.C.E.), whose militants unfortunately enjoyed an authority acquired during the Second World War; the Proletarian Left (P.L.), which claimed to be Maoist and carried out acts of sabotage in order to promote unrest, in accordance with the Guevarist slogan "Provocation-Repression-Revolution!"; not to mention the United Workers' Front (U.W.F.), the Marxist-Revolutionary Alliance (M.R.A.), the Anarchist Groups for Revolutionary Action (A.G.R.A.), the Anarchist Federation (A.F.), the International Situationists (I.S.), and so on and so forth. All these groups, together with their platforms, their lines and their positions on the dictatorship of the proletariat, the Party, the state and the future, made up a seething microcosm of passions which Juan Maria Krams wouldn't have exchanged for anything else in the world.

His visit to China had been much less upsetting. There no outside force had threatened his own universe. He was surrounded by hundreds of thousands of official phrases designed to protect him against the trivial attacks of what people usually called life. Against harmless, humane utterances like "Cooler today, isn't it?" or "What a boring afternoon!" a great barrier had been erected of new sayings and slogans: the two just and the three unjust things, the four chief recommendations, the seven faults, the five virtues and the ten evils, etc. These all acted as patrols, keeping Krams' world from being infected.

When the first rumours began to circulate about a cooling off in the relations between China and Albania, the first question that occurred to Krams and his comrades was whose side they should be on. Since the worsening of the situation arose from the rapprochement between China and the United States, Krams and his friends should logically have sided with Albania, who could be relied on to stand up for pure and inviolable principle, and to reject any dialogue or compromise.

But a kind of sixth sense made Krams jump the other way. China might be moving towards the West, but his own universe – what his adversaries called the "Krams-world" --- would probably survive longer in China than in Albania. He hadn't yet identified the fundamental reasons that had led him to this conclusion (history, the geo-political situation, mental outlooks, ethnic origins, perhaps even the Albanians' racial characteristics), but he was sure his intuition wasn't leading him astray. He never forgot his visit to the cemetery in Tirana that memorable Sunday. The Albanians have very good memories. But Mao had told him clearly: "People who remember too much are a danger to us."

That was what Mao had told him during their one and only tête-à-tête, when they had spoken at length about the possibility of world communism.

Krams had listened fascinated as Mao said it might take ten thousand years. This, after the hare-brained Krushchev's assertion that communism would be fully realized in the U.S.S.R. by 1980, sounded like a Titanic challenge. Everyone knew the advent of communism lay far away in the future, just as they knew that nevertheless – distant and utopian as it might be, like any great hope – it influenced the destiny of the world. People were also aware that at the coming of the communist paradise after thousands of years of tension and hardship, the human race might grow soft and degenerate. But none of these considerations – especially the last – had ever been formulated by the communist leaders. Mao was the first to dare to do so. In his interview with Krams he had clearly intimated that communism not only was but *had to be* unattainable, and so would never be realized.

"Communism is like a star," he had said. "One of the most beautiful of stars. It looks as it does to us because it's so far away. Have you ever thought what it would be like if a star came close to us? The collision would be a catastrophe . . ."

So the star had to remain inaccessible. Anything that seemed to bring it close – wellbeing, culture, emancipation – only put it in greater danger. That was why those things must be attacked without mercy, together with all who tried to bring the star nearer. They must be sacrificed in order to keep it at a distance.

"It may seem tragic," Mao had continued, "to strike at the very people who are most – even excessively – devoted to your own ideal. But it has to be done. There is no other way."

"What about the enemies of communism, then?" Krams had asked. "Were its opponents better for communism than its supporters?"

"Yes," said Mao. "Communism has always needed enemies above all else. And it always will. So much so that . . ."

Then he'd smiled without finishing the sentence. But Krams knew what he meant: "So much so that if necessary it would have to create them."

How magnificent! thought Krams, every time he recalled that forgettable conversation. He even said it aloud, especially at the time of the Cultural Revolution. It was then that he was able to verify the perfect cogency of Mao's argument: the break-up of people's lives, destruction, brainwashing . . . The star was farther away, and thus safer, than ever.

Cambodia begins in you . . . Yes, he thought to himself, Cambodia, and probably lots of future crimes as well.

For a moment he was filled with euphoria at the thought that he himself was also a fundamentally tragic character.

He had now emerged into the Place de la Concorde, but he was still so much absorbed in his own mental state that he wouldn't have been surprised if someone had whispered in his ear, "Look out! there are three kings' heads on pikes in the middle of the square!" He'd just have steered the car around them.

He really did see himself as a tragic figure, but he accepted his fate. He knew deep down inside that he'd chosen what side he was on in this new schism. Even if the Chinese would one day disappoint him, he'd made up his mind to support them. The third world was territory where he could sow his ideas: and if they failed to take root in the towns and the country, he would take them into the desert, among the primitive tribes where it would take at least a thousand years to make people understand the meaning of "autumn sadness". Cambodia starts in you . . . "But what is it that starts in *you*, then?" he cried angrily, narrowly avoiding a collision with a car in the next lane. The other driver put his index finger to his forehead and yelled, "Are you crazy or something?" "It's all of you who are crazy!" Krams bawled back. "All of you without exception! Crazy and small-minded!"

He had never acted out of base self-interest! Even when, during his visit to China, the small community of resident Europeans had bristled with rumours, half amused and half sarcastic, that Mao Zedong was going to make him his *pao pe* or godson. The rumours weren't entirely without foundation, but even so Krams hadn't indulged in dreams of power or hoped for any other vulgar advantages. True, he had sometimes imagined or even hoped he might one day become a leader – but no ordinary leader. He agreed with those who thought a real leader shouldn't have any power: but he went further still. Marx, Christ, Buddha and Che Guevara hadn't wielded any power, yet they had ruled, in a way, through their books, their ideas or their words. Krams thought a leader should be without even those adjuncts: he should be a kind of demiurge of the international workers' movement, half committed but half anonymous, without books or ideas of his own, and if possible without a name. But this was all a long way off still . . . For the present he was just the militant leftist Juan Maria Krams, an ascetic according to some, for others the Don Quixote of the movement. Some people called him Huan Mao Maria, or Marihuana for short, since his trip to China and the first accounts of Mao's plan to subvert Europe through drugs. The nickname had been pinned on him out of malice, but all in all he didn't really mind.

He was now driving towards the *grands boulevards*. He hadn't yet decided whether to go to the Café de Madrid, where the Latin American militants usually met, or to the bar frequented by the Portuguese. But finding himself near the latter, he parked the car and went in. The place was fairly empty, and as he looked around for a familiar face he suddenly froze. It must be telepathy! he thought, going over. The other man looked up, seemed equally surprised, and came forward to greet him.

"Great minds think alike!" exclaimed Krams, holding out his hand. "Fancy finding you here! . . . I was just remembering some of our earlier meetings."

"How are you?" asked the other. "Well? I expected to see you at the reception tonight."

"I did drop in," said Krams.

"Really?"

"I only stayed for a minute. We must have missed one another."

"Probably."

"Well, I'm very glad to see you, comrade Struga," said Krams. "Have you been in Paris long?"

"Just a few days. How about you? Sit down for a while if you're not in too much of a hurry. These people are members of the reconstructed Portuguese Communist Party. Perhaps you know some of them? . . . This is comrade Juan Krams," he said, turning towards the Portuguese. "I acted as interpreter for him when he was in Albania."

Krams now looked at the others for the first time. He had met two of them before. The others were strangers to him.

"We came here straight from the Rue de la Pompe," explained Besnik Struga.

"A pity I didn't see you there, but it's a stroke of luck finding you like this," said Krams.

The others made room for him at their table.

"Sure I'm not disturbing you?" he said before sitting down.

"Not at all," one of the Portuguese reassured him. "On the contrary."

"We were talking about the third world," said another.

"Very interesting!"

As soon as he sat down, Krams realized this was the table he'd been looking for in vain the whole evening. The discussion soon turned into an argument, chiefly between Krams and Besnik Struga. The Portuguese only put in a word here and there, until finally the other two held the field alone.

"Well, it's as I expected," said Krams, after a pause. "All the rumours about China and Albania disagreeing on a whole lot of fundamental questions are true."

"Apparently," answered Struga. He gazed at his coffee cup, picked it up, put it down again in the saucer, then went on, with a sidelong glance at Krams: "And I suppose the rumours about you taking China's side in all this are true too!"

"Apparently," said Krams, smiling.

The argument then flared up again, but the courtesy which had restrained their debates the year before was now abandoned.

Krams insisted that it was crazy and unforgivable to deny the existence of the third world. Struga maintained that the division of the world into three was a myth which flew in the face of scientific objectivity.

As Krams listened to Struga he felt a twinge of jealousy. This man was present at the Moscow Conference, he thought. He'd have liked to forget that this lent Struga a certain superiority, but there was no denying it. What wouldn't he himself give to have been there! Would there be other meetings like it in the future? In other words, meetings where everything was smashed to bits and then rebuilt as if after some apocalyptic catastrophe in which the fault line ran through the whole cosmos.

The discussion moved from the third world to the Sino-American rapprochement and back again. Krams tried hard to keep calm. He could bear anything except people denying there was such a thing as the third world. Again the exchanges grew heated.

"That's what your Mao Zedong says!" Struga interrupted at one point.

Krams looked at him in surprise.

"*Our* Mao Zedong?" he said with a bitter smile. "You mean he's not yours any more, if I heard you correctly?"

"You heard right," said Besnik. "Yours."

Krams shook his head.

"How strange," he said. "I'd never have thought it could come to this."

"What's so surprising?" asked one of the Portuguese. "Everyone has to make his own choice . . ."

"Of course, of course," said Krams placatingly. "And I choose Mao. With pleasure!"

Then he picked up his cup, and drank down his now cold coffee in three gulps.

☆   ☆   ☆

"What ravings!" exclaimed the observer on duty at the station near the North Pole, taking off his headset for a moment. "My God, what ravings!" He rubbed his ears as if to get rid of the painful buzzing, then put his earphones on again. It was the busiest part of the day and he couldn't take more than a few seconds' rest without the risk of missing an important signal.

The diplomatic receptions being held in the various European capitals had just ended, and most of the radio messages reported the comments the guests had exchanged in the midst of the hubbub, between whiskies. Such circumstances naturally enhanced the stupidity of their remarks, though these would have been stupid enough anyway. The radio officer laughed whenever he came upon the same conversation reported differently by two different embassies. The whole hotchpotch seemed to belong not to a number of different receptions but rather to a single long one which had been going on from time immemorial and would continue until the end of the world . . . Don't you think there'll be great upheavals in Yugoslavia when Tito dies? . . . As many as there will be in Spain after Franco . . . But Tito's different! . . . Of course, of course! . . . Have you seen who's on the Chinese committee for the funeral? . . . Romania . . . Romania's foreign policy . . . "Hell, I missed that bit!" said the radio officer. But he wasn't too worried – he knew he'd hear the same phrase again, probably so many times he'd get sick of it . . . Hey, here were our two lost pigeons again . . . Then came something, apparently not very important, about Portugal. The European parliament . . . N.A.T.O. interests in the Mediterranean . . . Spain doesn't intend . . . If the price of oil goes on rising . . . My God, how often must they go on repeating the same thing?

The observer's job was to record only messages relating to the communist world; all the rest were of no interest. But he was supposed to monitor everything. And apart from the fact that the communist world had poked its nose into all the problems of the human race, it sometimes happened that an apparently harmless conversation – about religious violence in Ireland, for instance – had some sort of relevance to Soviet missile bases in the Arctic. No message was negligible – that was the essence of the monitor's instructions. "Don't go telling yourself that a message missed by you will be picked up by one of your colleagues. Act as if you were the one and only monitor in the world . . ." And another thing. Uncoded messages were often as interesting as those sent in cipher. Some countries, especially the smaller ones, afraid their codes might be deciphered by their larger neighbours, sent highly important messages in clear in the hope that they might thus escape notice.

In the Middle East ... Soviet interests, of course, but ... So apparently Albania was never a satellite of China ... A rapprochement with Moscow couldn't be excluded ... N.A.T.O. in Greece ... Now that the bases in Greenland ... Have you seen who's on the Chinese committee for the funeral? Naturally, old boy – the make-up of those committees is always frightfully significant ... And what do you think's going to happen in the Persian Gulf? ... And the Dead Sea?

Tell yourself you're the only person listening in the whole world ... He shook his head to try to keep himself awake. One of these days I'll go out of my mind! he thought. Hearing your neighbour's blatherings through the bathroom wall was enough to drive you barmy – if you had to listen to those of the whole world! The "world's murmuring" ... He vaguely remembered reading somewhere, or perhaps he'd heard it in a conversation, that some authors had tried to write the total book, which would contain all the truth in the world in a condensed form. Sometimes people cited examples, in which the author had almost succeeded, as in a novel called *Finnegans Wake*, which the radio officer hadn't read.

He started to giggle. How could anyone write the Book of the World in a two-roomed flat? He was the only one who could write it, or even write a single chapter of it, up in the solitude of this icy waste where there was still hardly any difference between night and day, as in the time of Chaos. And its title ought to be the Ravings of the World, the "World's Delirium"!

The signals went endlessly on, sometimes interspersed with bits of popular radio programmes ... Germany will fulfil its responsibilities towards Europe ... If the Russian tanks ... The Balkans, troubled as ever ... *Non, je ne regrette rien* ... Talking of the Dead Sea ...

They can't get away from the Dead Sea this evening, can they, he thought, lifting his hand to take off his headset ... But just as he did so ...

"That's what your Mao Zedong says," said the Albanian communist. And this took the European leftist leader aback. "Does that mean he's not *your* Mao any more? ..."

That'll do for now, growled the monitor, writing all this down on his notepad. Still on about the cooling-off in relations between Albania and China ... He took off his earphones, and imagined what his head must look like without his headset. Small and insignificant ...

From outside came the howling of the wind over the snow. It sounded like a primitive cry. He sat for a moment gazing at his headset almost in surprise, then slowly donned his magic ears again and went on listening.

9

SIMON DERSHA KNOCKED, then put his head round the door. Linda and Silva exchanged glances.

"May I use your phone?" he asked. "Ours is out of order."

He was wearing his navy-blue suit, as he had been a few days ago, when he came to phone before and couldn't get any answer. As he dialled, Silva thought back to that day. How time flew!

"But you've only dialled three digits!" said Linda, who'd been watching him.

When he hung up and turned to look at them the two women were astonished at how haggard he looked.

"Just like me!" he said almost guiltily. "I can't think why I'm so absent-minded!"

"You can always try again," suggested Linda.

"What? Oh yes, of course . . . But . . ." And he waved his hand as if to say there was no point.

Linda looked at Silva again. Simon made as if to go out, then changed his mind and came back to the phone. He reached out for it cautiously, as if it were red hot, and was just about to dial when the door opened and in came the boss. Simon immediately put down the phone.

"Go on, go on," said the boss jovially, sitting down.

"No, thank you," stammered the other. "I was only bothering you because our phone's out of order."

"Please! Make yourself at home!" the boss insisted. "You can come here and phone as often as you like. *We* don't hesitate to trouble our friends if *our* phone's on the blink!"

"Of course! Thanks very much," said Simon, still edging towards the door.

"But you haven't made your call! And all because of me! Am I such an ogre?"

"No, on the contrary! It's my fault . . . But it isn't important . . . I can phone later . . . It's not urgent."

"As you like," said the boss.

Simon Dersha quietly let himself out. Linda and Silva smiled.

"A bit touched," said Linda, putting a forefinger to her temple.

"Do you think so?" said the boss. "I thought it was me that put him off."

"No. He'd been hovering around the phone for ages, not daring to call properly. He just dialled three digits and made up some excuse."

"How odd!" said the boss. "People really are funny!"

"I've noticed he acts a bit barmy whenever he wears that blue suit," said Linda.

The boss guffawed.

"You have some peculiar ideas too!" he said, surreptitiously checking on his own jacket. He was just going to say something else when the phone rang.

"Hallo?" Then his voice grew cold, as it always did when the call was for Linda or Silva. "Yes, she's here."

And he held the phone out to Silva.

It was Besnik Struga. Silva's face lit up, as did Linda's when she knew who was calling. Besnik's voice was warm, but a little deeper than usual. Perhaps he had a slight cold. Anyway, it was very attractive. He told her he'd got back from abroad the night before, but wouldn't be able to see her for two or three days because he had to write a very urgent report.

"It doesn't matter," said Silva. "When you've finished the report and had a bit of a rest . . ."

"What's been happening about that . . . business? No news? H'mm . . ." A pause. "We'll talk about it when we meet."

"Yes, of course," she said.

"Silva, I do hope you understand . . . I really can't . . ."

"I quite understand, Besnik," she said.

But he kept on as if he wasn't sure she did, especially now he knew her brother's situation hadn't changed.

"I've been longing to see you. I thought of you over there, and I can prove it!"

He's brought me another little present, thought Silva, smiling to herself. He did this every time he went abroad. Silva had noticed there was no one to beat him for bringing back souvenirs for his friends, especially his women friends.

"Is he back from Paris?" asked Linda when Silva hung up.

Silva nodded. After she'd sat down again at her desk her conversation with Besnik remained suspended over her for a while like a small cloud. She could remember his every word, the barest inflections of his voice, including a certain guilt when he spoke of her brother. Finally, the rest faded and this was the only impression that was left. As for what had happened since Besnik left, that could be described in one word: nothing. Skënder Bermema's delegation had been postponed four times and he was still in Tirana: he had phoned her several times to say he hadn't been able to get any further information.

One day he'd come back from China too, and he'd phone her as Besnik had today, to ask if anything had happened while he was away. And she'd say no. Nothing. She sighed.

"What did he say?" asked Linda. "What did he tell you about his trip?"

Silva looked at her blankly for a few seconds.

"Nothing," she said.

Linda felt herself blushing. She shouldn't have been so indiscreet. After a while, seeing her friend's cheeks were still pink, Silva was afraid she might have offended her with her brusque "Nothing." Yet she didn't feel like explaining, especially as that would have meant telling Linda all about Arian's problems.

But not long afterwards the boss was called out of the room, and no sooner had the door closed behind him than Silva prepared to say something to show Linda she hadn't taken any notice of her indiscreet inquiry. Linda, however, kept her eyes fixed on her desk, and Silva was still trying to think of a way of beginning when the door opened and Simon Dersha reappeared with his customary hangdog expression.

"Look who's here!" Silva whispered. Then: "Come on in, Simon! What's wrong?"

"Nothing," he answered, with a grimace. "I'd just like to use the phone, if you don't mind."

"Haven't you tried again anywhere else since you were here?" said Silva, winking at Linda, whose sulks now disappeared as if by magic.

"All the other phones are being used," said Simon. "And then . . ."

"It looks to me as if you don't really want to make that call," observed Linda. "You were very hesitant the last time . . ."

"Oh . . ." he quavered.

"What's the matter, Simon?" Silva asked again.

"Perhaps it's private and you'd like us to leave you alone?" Linda suggested.

"I didn't say that!" Simon protested.

"And I noticed that when you asked to use our phone the other day you were wearing the same suit as now!"

"Oh, you're diabolical!" growled Simon, heading for the door. "Absolutely diabolical!"

The door closed. They laughed.

"I think he must be a bit deranged!" Linda exclaimed.

"Hush," said Silva. "He might hear."

As a matter of fact Simon heard quite clearly what Linda said, but though in other circumstances it would have made him furious, today it didn't bother him. This was quite simply because he'd heard the same words applied to himself several times in the past twenty-four hours. He'd used them too, not only about other people but also about himself. "You must be off your rocker!" his wife had shouted yesterday after he'd broken the news that his sister-in-law (his brother's wife) might be leaving Tirana to go and live with her husband, who'd been posted to another town a year ago. This meant that Simon's mother, who had been living in the brother's house in Tirana, would have to come and live with Simon and his wife. "You must be mad even to think of it!" said his wife. "We're already squashed together like sardines in this apartment, and now you suggest adding one more?" "Where's she supposed to live then? In the street?" cried Simon. "Why in the street? Why can't she go and join your brother with the others?" "Oh, that's what you have in mind, is it?" "I don't see why any of them has to move," his wife went on. "It's quite usual for a man who's posted to have to leave his family behind." "But it's a serious matter now," Simon objected. "Haven't you read the article in *The Voice of the People*?" "It's always serious! That doesn't stop other people from leaving their families behind." "No, no – this is different!" And heaven knows how long the argument would have gone on if Simon's brother hadn't suddenly turned up, accompanied by his wife. They both looked extremely downcast.

"What's going to become of us?" moaned the sister-in-law, bursting into tears. Her husband sank into a chair and buried his head in his hands. Simon was taken aback. Only his wife was as energetic as ever. She stuck to the idea that Simon's brother shouldn't take his family to live with him, and the more blankly the others listened to her the more vigorously she sought new arguments and examples. She actually quoted the Constitution, not once but twice!

"Don't go!" she adjured her sister-in-law. "I know it's a question of one's attitude to society and the socialist conscience and so on. But just admit your conscience isn't very developed, and don't go. It would be different if you were a member of the Party, but someone like you isn't obliged to go. It's not the same for Benjamin – he's been posted and he has to obey. He's got a duty to the State, it's a question of administration – but taking wives too is another matter, a question of ideology, you might call it. Aren't I right, Simon? Officials themselves may have to set an example by going and living among the grass roots, but their wives are not under any such obligation – it's only a matter of individual conscience. And our consciences are not very developed – there's nothing we can do about it, is there, Benjamin?"

She carried on like that, addressing now one and now the other, until finally she made them listen to her. As might have been expected, the first person she persuaded was Simon's sister-in-law. After that, the two women had no difficulty in convincing Simon himself that the only solution, even if not an ideal one, was to leave his brother's family where it was. It was imperative that, in this impasse, some issue should be found. Only Benjamin didn't come round, and just sat miserably on the sofa with his head in his hands.

Simon's wife made coffee, and as they drank it the previous arguments were gone over again, slightly more optimistically. Cases were quoted where families had been left behind but, what with reasonableness on the one hand and consideration on the other, instead of their lives being wrecked, things had gradually sorted themselves out.

"Yes, but it's precisely such cases that the article in *The Voice of the People* was about the day before yesterday," objected Simon's brother. "All the reasons alleged for not taking your family with you – illnesses that can only be treated properly in Tirana, a mother who needs help, a paralytic father – all these things have been denounced!"

"What does that mean – 'denounced'?" exclaimed Simon's wife. "Are people supposed to change their attitudes just because a newspaper says so? If you ask me, it may produce the opposite effect, and people who never thought about it before may adopt the arguments the paper decries."

"Yes, and make things worse for themselves," said Benjamin. "If they act like that they may provoke even more drastic measures – we've seen it happen quite recently."

"People will always do anything to get out of being posted," observed the sister-in-law.

Simon's brother shrugged dejectedly. The fact that he'd withdrawn from the conversation enabled the argument to take a turn for the better. More happy endings were quoted, in which reason had prevailed and unhelpful administrators had been foiled.

"It's a well-known fact that lots of people manage all right. The ones who get it in the neck are poor dopes without any friends or influence," said Benjamin's wife, nodding her chin at her spouse. Then, to Simon: "You're the only one we can turn to."

A tense silence followed. Simon still sat motionless and pensive in a chair facing that of his sister-in-law. He was the one who had spoken least, not because he was an introvert by nature, but because as a civil servant himself he didn't want to get mixed up in recriminations against official regulations, however much he might disagree with the latter.

He was the most distinguished member of their comparatively modest family. It was him all the cousins came to with their problems: scholarships for their children, housing problems, jobs. He realized most of them exaggerated the importance of his post at the ministry, and he'd often been tempted to explain that he was merely a clerk and not some senior official. Had he done so, they would have been horribly disillusioned – if they'd believed him. More probably they'd have suspected him of trying to fob them off. The reason he hadn't chosen this way out of all the trouble his family's claims brought him was to spare them the truth. He preferred to be accused of indifference, caprice, uselessness and egoism rather than damage the fiction of his own importance.

And now, in the silence that followed his sister-in-law's "You're the only one we can turn to," he felt the moment they had all been waiting for had come, the moment for which all the rest had been but a prelude. He gazed thoughtfully at his wedding ring. His wife finally caught his eye.

"Why don't you do something, Simon?" she said. "I know it's not easy, but after all this does concern your brother."

Simon raised his eyebrows: the silence was so oppressive he was surprised those appendages didn't make a noise, like the hands of a rusty clock.

"I suppose I'll have to have a try," he said.

No one actually sighed, but the relief was almost tangible. For the first time, Simon's brother looked a little more cheerful.

"Perhaps you could speak to the minister who asked you to dinner," Simon's wife suggested. "A word from him would be enough . . ."

"Has he had dinner with a minister?" exclaimed the sister-in-law. "He didn't tell us!"

"And not just any old minister!" said Simon's wife, with a gesture that seemed to say, "If you only knew!"

As soon as Benjamin's wife had heard the word minister her jaw had dropped, but her husband looked depressed.

"Don't you want me to ask him, then?" Simon asked him.

"Yes, yes – I do," was the answer. "But I just don't know . . . Has he got enough influence . . . ?"

"What?" Simon's wife interrupted. "How can you say such a thing? A minister of his importance? I'd no idea you were so naive, Benjamin. What do you say, Simon?"

Everyone expected him to laugh or lose his temper at his brother's foolishness, but he didn't do either. His face clouded over.

"Did you want to say something?" he asked his brother, who sat with his head bowed, looking guilty.

"No," answered the other at last. "Perhaps what I've said already was stupid." He lowered his voice and leaned closer to Simon, as if he'd have liked the others not to hear. "They had some manoeuvres in our area not long ago, and there were some rumours about . . . I can't tell you exactly what was said, but I did hear something about some of the soldiers rebelling against that minister of yours . . . Of course there may not have been anything in it . . ."

"No, they must have been just rumours. What else?" said Simon. "I'm surprised you listened to them. You know it's not right to spread gossip . . ."

"Gossip? What gossip?" interrupted Simon's wife.

"Nothing," he answered. "Just foolishness."

This was the second time he'd heard hints about the minister, but he went on looking reprovingly at his brother as if to say, "Other people may take an interest in such things, but what possesses you to poke your nose in – haven't you got troubles enough already with this business of postings?"

A week earlier in the cafeteria, when Simon had overheard two people talking about the person he thought of as "his" minister, he'd nearly passed out. At first he hadn't realized who they were referring to. He'd just caught the words, "It doesn't matter if you're a minister or not, if you do a thing like that you've had it." But as he was standing beside the speakers in the coffee queue, he couldn't help hearing more, though he wasn't in the habit of eavesdropping. The other two kept on about the misdeed in question, expressing surprise that anyone in such a position as a minister could have been guilty of it. Simon concluded that at the worst the speakers' own minister must have committed some impropriety. But as the queue moved slowly forward and he heard the words "manoeuvres" and "order" mentioned, he realized with horror that they were talking not about their own minister but about "his" . . .

Although he tried later to reassure himself with the thought that, if there was any criticism in the press or in the government about a minister, rumours of this kind might easily get spread around, a niggling doubt still remained. And this had something to do with the somewhat odd behaviour of the vice-minister who had taken him to dinner with the distinguished personage in question, and who, the first time they met again afterwards, had not only pretended to have forgotten that memorable evening, but had also given Simon the impression that he wished to avoid any reference to it or to the minister himself. At first Simon had interpreted this as the kind of affectation practised by those who try to minimize things that are important in order to show that they themselves are above them. But after overhearing the conversation in the cafeteria, Simon saw it all differently. He remembered that the vice-minister hadn't phoned him for several days after the dinner party. He remembered the doubt that had seized him not only during the dinner itself, during Enver Hoxha's phone call, but also in the days beforehand, when he'd kept wondering why anyone as insignificant as himself had been invited. He'd asked his friend the vice-minister about it, quite straightforwardly and without any *arrière-pensée*, and accepted as quite plausible the reply that leaders sometimes need to make contact with the common people, with ordinary clerks from the ministries, and that this is often more useful to them than all the official reports. But after the conversation overheard in the cafeteria, and Simon's own reflections thereafter, this explanation seemed inadequate, not to say specious. He even recalled hearing it said that it is when they fall from favour that the mighty tend to be more gracious to the humble. He dismissed this line of thought by telling himself that if this were the case the minister could easily have found hundreds of subordinates to be gracious to. But the poison of doubt still lingered, and eventually grew all the stronger precisely because it lacked foundation.

Who knows how far Simon would have pursued his investigations if he hadn't seen his minister shown on the television news one Thursday, attending some official ceremony. He cursed the rumours for having frightened him for nothing. Then he cursed himself for a psychopath and a double-dyed idiot: why had he got so upset? It wasn't as though the minister was a relation or friend, someone on whose career his own future depended. Of course, Simon might be sorry if anything unpleasant happened to him, because that would mean the end of certain dreams arising out of the memorable dinner. But that was all. There was no point in exaggerating – as he had done by worrying for days on end – just on the strength of some tittle-tattle put about by fools.

However no sooner had his brother mentioned rumours about the minister than Simon relapsed into all his former anxiety. What he'd heard in the cafeteria wasn't just silly gossip: his own brother, out in the back of beyond, had heard about it. True, it was a godforsaken spot – but it *was* near the place where the manoeuvres were held, and where the deed was done that couldn't be overlooked . . . Only pride prevented Simon from asking his brother if he knew anything more.

"Do it, I beg you, Simon – do it for us," implored Benjamin's wife, interrupting her brother-in-law's reflections. "We know it's difficult, but think of the mess we're in! And you've only got one brother, haven't you?"

"All right, I'll see to it," said Simon, surprised by his own resolution.

And he meant what he said. If the minister had lost some of his influence, that would only make Simon's own task easier. Didn't those in disgrace tend to be kinder? But this reasoning soon lost its cogency. Wasn't seeking a favour from someone when he had worries of his own like asking for a light from a man whose beard has been set on fire? Not at all the thing to do. And yet . . . The worries of the great must be on an entirely different scale. Of course – it's obvious, he told himself ten minutes later: everything is relative in this world, and even if the minister's authority was temporarily diminished he could still solve by a mere phone call a problem that would require superhuman efforts on the part of minor functionaries. Simon recalled the words of an old protocol clerk on the subject of a department head who'd seen his position undermined twice, but who nevertheless remained one of the bosses: "A lion can tear you to pieces even if he's got only one tooth." So even if "his" lion had only one tooth left, why shouldn't Simon take advantage of it? After all, he'd never asked anything of him before, and after this favour would never ask anything of him again.

"I'll try to get in touch with him tomorrow," he said, breaking the silence. Then, to his wife: "I'll wear my blue suit."

"It's all ready," she said, beaming round at the others as if to say, "You see, he finally made up his mind. Simon will see to it – you needn't worry any more."

"Yes, the blue suit's ready," she repeated. "I took it to the cleaner's a week ago, as if I had a presentiment you'd be needing it."

"Good," said Simon, remembering he'd made a stain on the jacket during the famous dinner.

The little apartment had come to life again. The mention of the blue suit had made Simon's intervention seem more real. Made to measure from Polish cloth fifteen years before, that suit enabled them all to bask in the glory reflected from Simon himself. It made them think of official occasions, grand assemblies, stately halls where political meetings were held, examination results were read out, workers given medals. When Simon came home after such ceremonies, it was his suit as much as his face which brought back a reflection of the bright lights of the presidium or the exhibition, sometimes made brighter still by the presence of television cameras or important foreign delegates. This had become so well established that if Simon had worn his blue suit on an ordinary day, his wife and all the others around him would have said, "You've made a mistake, Simon – there's nothing special about today."

This episode came back to him in his office. It had happened only yesterday, but so painful was its effect on him he felt he'd been struggling with it for a week.

And now those infernal girls in the next room had noticed about his suit! But Simon was not to be deterred by that, or by overhearing them say he must be a bit deranged. His only concern at present was how to make his phone call. On the evening of the dinner party the minister had given him both his office and his home number, but while, yesterday afternoon after Simon had promised his brother to intervene, it had seemed best to call the minister at the office, this morning it had struck him as preferable to phone him at home. Then he realized he might spend the whole day shilly-shallying, and end up not talking to the minister at either place. But having then resolved to take the plunge at once, he learned from a colleague – not without some relief – that their phone wasn't working again. Simon would have given up at that point, but for the fact that all his people would be waiting eagerly back in the apartment to hear how he'd got on. He couldn't expect them to swallow the excuse that his office phone was out of order. Better at least appease his conscience by gritting his teeth and getting the chore over. After that, let 'em all come!

But in the next-door office, when he'd already started dialling the number, it struck him that it would be better for the two women not to hear, so he hung up. Quite rightly too, for those two wretches, so quick to notice his suit, would certainly have listened to every word he said, despite their assumed indifference. Yes, he'd been quite right not to phone from their office. But that was no reason for not phoning at all.

As the end of the working day got nearer, Simon began to panic, but he comforted himself with the thought that if he couldn't reach the minister at the ministry he could certainly reach him at his residence. And he had every right to call him at either place.

When two o'clock arrived he still hadn't made his call as he stood in the corridor watching the other employees go home. This was the most propitious moment, with everyone in a hurry to leave and the offices emptying. He could find a phone without attracting attention. Eh? What did he mean by "without attracting attention"? A few days ago he'd have been proud to call the minister in front of everyone, and now he was letting himself be intimidated like this! It was unpardonable! If others could read his thoughts he'd be exposed to public obloquy. "Look at him – obsessed by rumours and gossip, a spreader of doubt! There's no place for people like him in our society, the lousy petty-bourgeois!"

He saw Silva and Linda locking their office door behind them, and was about to call out, "Hey, could you hold on a moment while I make a phone call?" But not only did he not speak – he shrank into a recess so that they shouldn't see him. I really must be going off my head! he thought. All the offices were swiftly being shut up one after the other – his chances were lessening with every minute that passed. He kept telling himself it didn't matter, but his anxiety increased. But why? – there was a phone down in the porter's lodge that he could use whenever he liked – in a way, that was the best solution. It was a sort of public phone, anonymous, so that if . . . If what? Now what crazy ideas was he getting? How shameful! How had he sunk so low?

He was now at the top of the front steps, just by the porter's lodge. He pushed the glass door open with a firm gesture.

"You want to use the phone?" said the porter. "Help yourself!"

Simon Dersha picked up the phone and dialled the first digits. One of the porter's eyes looked rather odd: red-rimmed, but watchful. After he'd finished dialling, Simon let the dial revolve back into place. But before it had finished doing so he was struck by a thought: What if things really were going badly for the minister? And he, Simon, chose this moment to ring him up? And where? At home! Hardly had the ringing begun at the other end than Simon pressed down the springs on the receiver stand and replaced the phone.

"No answer?" said the porter. "Perhaps you should have let it ring a bit longer . . ."

"Sez you!" thought Simon, making off without more ado. The fresh air helped him see things more clearly. He wasn't really sorry he'd given up on the porter's lodge: it would have been better if he'd called the minister in his office – at home it was a different matter. And what about the porter's bloodshot eye? . . . Still, not a bad idea to ring from a phone that didn't belong to anyone in particular. He could ring from a public call-box – funny he hadn't thought of it before!

When he came to a call-box he took a deep breath. He felt at bay. Never mind, let 'em all come! He put his hand in his pocket and got out a coin. All his movements were strangely rigid. It wasn't until he heard a voice say "Hallo!" at the other end that he gave a start.

"Hallo – is that the residence of comrade –"

"Speaking," said the minister.

"I'm sorry to bother you, comrade minister," stammered Simon. "Especially at this hour . . ."

He let loose a flood of words he'd have been hard put to it to repeat afterwards. For a moment he felt he'd never manage to explain. But he must try to overcome the obstacles: first tell the minister who he was, and then . . .

But to Simon's surprise the minister knew who he was straight away.

"You came to dinner at my place with . . . Yes, yes, I remember very well . . . Yes, of course . . . So what did you want to talk to me about?"

His voice sounded different – sharper, thinner.

Simon started to answer, but when the minister repeated the question he realized he hadn't explained anything. He began again, but felt himself getting in a worse muddle still. Two girls had appeared from somewhere, outside the call-box. That takes the biscuit! fumed Simon. Can't even phone in peace from a public call-box now!

"Oh, you wanted to see me?" said the minister. "No problem, my dear fellow. Come whenever you like. Today if it suits you . . ."

"Today?" Simon wanted to exclaim, "What's the hurry?" But the voice at the other end insisted.

"No point in putting it off. It so happens I'm free this afternoon. I'll expect you at my place at six. All right?"

"I don't know how to thank you, but . . . what shall I say? Just like that? Perhaps . . ."

"No point in complicating things! So that's settled – I'll be expecting you at six. See you then."

Good Lord, thought Simon, hanging up. Anyone would think he's dying for someone to go and see him . . .

As he made his way slowly home he couldn't throw off the feeling that it might have been a mistake to phone. That thin voice, followed by the eagerness to see him ... It left a bitter taste. Of course, that's the state of mind you'd expect in someone who's being ostracized. Could that really be the case? Had things gone so far? He tried to recall their conversation, but couldn't. He kept thinking of the television programme the previous Thursday, but that didn't help either. Why the devil did I have to come across that call-box? he grumbled.

"Well, what's new?" said his wife as he came in. "But what's the matter? You look quite drawn."

"Nothing, nothing," he said. "I spoke to the minister and I'm seeing him at six o'clock."

"Really? But that's wonderful!"

"Is there anyone here?"

"Of course – Benjamin and his wife. Who did you expect?"

"Oh, them," he grunted.

"I don't know why you take that tone."

He gestured vaguely.

"At least don't let them see you're in a bad mood!" she whispered, "It isn't polite!"

He took off his raincoat and hung it up.

"Simon's spoken to the minister!" his wife announced when they'd gone into the room where the other two were waiting. "He's going to see him today."

"Really?" Benjamin and wife exclaimed in chorus.

Simon slumped down on the settee.

"He's expecting me at six o'clock," he said, not looking at anyone.

His brother and sister-in-law didn't know what to do to show their gratitude. Their eyes shone, they babbled incoherently. Simon went on scowling. The sister-in-law signalled to Benjamin and they both stood up.

"We'd better be going," she said. "I don't know how to thank you, Simon. We'll never forget what you've done for us."

"It's nothing, it's nothing," said Simon.

Simon's wife thought her brother-in-law looked worried.

"Don't go like that," she said. "Stay for lunch, if you don't mind taking pot luck."

"No, thank you," he answered faintly.

Simon's wife looked at her husband reproachfully.

"Yes, stay," he said. "We'll manage."

"We don't want to inconvenience you," stammered Benjamin's wife.

"You won't be inconveniencing us in the least," said the hostess. "Stay for lunch, and then we can all wait together for Simon to come back. All right?"

Benjamin and his wife turned to Simon.

"Yes, good idea," he said.

The sister-in-law whispered something to her husband. He nodded, then stood up and went out into the hall. They heard the front door open and shut.

"Where's Benjamin gone to?" asked Simon's wife.

"Just out . . . He'll be back in a minute."

The two women went into the kitchen to lay the table. A little while later Benjamin returned carrying some cans of beer.

"You're being very rude," his wife told Simon when she came to call him in to lunch. "Why are you glowering at them like that? Just because you're doing them a favour? Don't forget your brother's had your mother on his hands all these years!"

"You don't understand anything about it!" he muttered. But she didn't hear.

During lunch Simon made an effort to be more relaxed, and the meal turned out to be quite cheerful. But every now and then the guests would be overcome, not to say inarticulate, with emotion.

"How we racked our brains to find a solution!" said Benjamin's wife. "We never breathed a word to anyone else, but we can talk to you, especially now . . ."

"She thinks it's all settled," thought Simon.

"We did think of one way out," his sister-in-law went on. "A pretty far-fetched one, though I gather some people have resorted to it lately. The husband gets a divorce so as not to have to take his family with him, the wife stays on in their apartment in Tirana, and the husband comes to see her in secret, like a lover!" She laughed. "Have you ever heard of such a thing?"

"Someone did mention something like it," said Simon gloomily, "but I thought it must be some vaudeville sketch."

"Not at all!" said the sister-in-law. "People are driven to shifts like that out of necessity."

"And did you decide to do that?" asked Simon's wife.

"Why not?" came the reply. "What else could we do?"

Goodness, thought Simon. Sham divorces, and then clandestine meetings, like lovers and mistresses. What a splendid idea! And you get rid of the mother-in-law into the bargain, because she can't go on living with a divorced daughter-in-law! It sounded ideal.

"Yes," said Simon's wife. "People are at their wits' end."

The table fell silent again for a while.

"Coffee, everyone?" said the hostess, collecting up the empty beer cans.

"Not for me, thanks," said Simon.

"Perhaps Simon would like to have a little rest?" his sister-in-law suggested.

"Would you?" asked his wife.

"Don't bother about us!" chorused the guests.

"Especially as you've got this meeting later on." His wife again. "Go and have a lie-down, Simon."

"All right, just for a while," he said. "That beer's gone to my head a bit."

"Yes, you have a little nap," said his brother affectionately.

Simon went to his room, undressed and lay down. But despite the faint muzziness due to the beer, he knew he wouldn't be able to sleep. He ought to have had a coffee. Well, he could always have one when he got up. He could feel a weight on his stomach, and this grew heavier as scraps of the lunch-time conversation came back to him. So, he mused, that's what they've been thinking of: a fake divorce, then rendezvous à la Romeo and Juliet, and to crown all, bye-bye mother-in-law! He wondered where he and his wife were going to put his mother if the other couple did leave the capital for good: the prospect made him shudder. The current arrangement suited him perfectly: he paid a thousand old leks a month for his mother's keep (it was only five hundred to start with, but he'd had to double it when his brother was posted), and in return he was left in peace. And now all that family equilibrium was going to be destroyed. As his wife kept saying, to have one more person in the house, especially an old woman, was asking for trouble. Old ladies have special expenses, they like to have their cronies in to see them every day, it'll cost about a thousand leks a month to keep her in coffee, not to mention all the rest. It was obvious that before long there'd be friction between his wife and his mother, and heaven knows where that would lead! He must solve this problem at all costs. It had been stupid to regret phoning the minister. I was quite right to do it, he concluded, burying his face in the pillow in the faint hope of getting some sleep. Yes, I was quite right. But he still couldn't drop off.

At about half-past four he got up, dressed and went out into the hall. A pleasant aroma of coffee and the sound of whispered conversation came from the kitchen. They were probably waiting for him to wake up. When he appeared they all fidgeted on their chairs, eager to make a fuss of him.

"Did you manage to get some sleep?" asked his wife.

"Not much."

"Would you like a cup of coffee?"

"Yes, please – I would now."

Even though the minister would probably soon be offering him another.

The day was drawing to a close. The warmth of the room, the sound of the coffee grinder, the quiet, desultory conversation – made Simon feel sorry for his brother. He must have missed all this since he was posted to the provinces. I absolutely must get him out of that situation, he thought. I absolutely must.

Night had fallen by the time Simon left the house. The air was damp and it looked like rain. Come straight home, his wife had told him. Don't forget we'll be dying to hear.

As he went along he tried at first to concentrate on minor aspects of the affair. Sometimes he would polish up one of the phrases he'd prepared: "I have to think about my mother as well, comrade minister . . ." But then he set that aspect aside: it didn't really present any difficulty. No, the problem was . . . What was it? said an inner voice more and more insistently as he approached the district where the minister lived. But he tried not to answer. Pretty dreary around here, he thought. The windows looked darker than they did elsewhere, the damp air froze you to the marrow. There were fewer and fewer people about. At last he reached the minister's street. It was only a quarter to six, and he had to walk more slowly so as not to be too early. The street, lined on both sides with small villas, was feebly lit and almost deserted. Simon quailed. That thin voice, that eagerness to see him . . . He tried to dismiss his fears, but they kept swarming back. All he could do was swipe at them one at a time: his fear that this démarche was all a mistake; the rows there'd be if his mother came to live with them; the lion who could still bite even though he had only one tooth; coffee in the family kitchen; last Thursday's television news . . .

He was now within a stone's throw of the minister's residence. The sentry on duty outside, muffled up in a black rain-cape, stood still as a statue. The front of the house was dark; a faint light was to be seen at the side windows. Simon slowed down as he approached the gate. The sentry's rubber cape gleamed wetly.

Simon realized that the time for ordering his thoughts, however inefficiently, was over, and prepared to address the sentry, who seemed to be keeping an eye on him. But at the last moment he suddenly remembered the Chinese business . . . It was usually during this sort of crisis that the struggle inside the Party flared up . . . Why hadn't he thought of it before? He'd wasted his time on all sorts of nonsense, not excluding coffee grounds, and overlooked this blinding truth!

He found himself walking straight past the sentry. What was he doing? Running away? Don't worry, he told himself, if you want to turn back you can, there's nothing to stop you. There are still two minutes to go till six o'clock. He went along by the railings for another twenty yards or so, then retraced his steps. But the thought of China persisted. Worse still, the closer he got to the gate the larger the idea loomed, until it seemed to be radiating out from inside the villa. It's in situations like this . . . crises like this . . . that deviationists rear their ugly heads . . . like rats before an earthquake . . . He was now only a few feet from the sentry, but he still hadn't decided whether to go in and see the minister or not. He slowed down and turned to look past the railings at the front of the house, which looked gloomier than ever through the dripping trees. He could feel the sentry's eyes on him again. Then he heard the rustle of rubber and the sentry's low voice:

"Do you want to see the minister?"

Simon swung round in amazement. How did the man know? Could he possibly be aware of his intentions? Without answering, Simon started walking along by the railings again. After a while he slowed down again. But this time he didn't turn back.

He must have been someone else, thought the sentry, who'd been told to expect a visitor. And he watched the retreating figure vanish in the distance.

Inside the villa, from the window of the main drawing room on the ground floor, the minister watched Simon Dersha disappear. He's not coming, he observed. He'd been watching his to-ings and fro-ings through the slits in the shutters, and at one point had even reached out to ring a bell. Then he'd remembered the sentry had been warned to expect a visitor. When the figure outside finally walked away from the guard, the minister had almost exclaimed, "What's that idiot up to? Why didn't he let him in?" In other circumstances he'd have sent someone out at once to ask the man what had happened and why the visitor had gone away. But this evening he didn't feel like it ... In other circumstances ... The minister gave a hollow laugh. In other circumstances, he told himself, you wouldn't be lurking behind the shutters waiting for a wretched clerk whose name you can't even remember to make up his mind whether to come in or not ...

Meanwhile the figure had disappeared past the end of the railings. In other words, this wasn't a matter of chance. For it was no accident, either, that phone calls and visitors had grown scarcer and scarcer during the past fortnight. Dozens of times he'd tried to dismiss his suspicions, but dozens of other times those suspicions had returned to the charge.

He'd spent all the previous week in this state, apart from Thursday evening, after the TV news. But the reassurance this had brought didn't last long. It had been succeeded by more of those almost deaf and dumb days spent staring at all the telephones on his desk, at all those buttons and lights, at his secretary slinking in for instructions. He'd kept telling himself, "I'm still a minister, damn it!" Nothing had changed. The guards were still there in the ante-room, and then his aides, his assistants, and a whole lot of departmental heads all waiting to do his bidding, just as before ... But he knew very well that it wasn't really like that. Things were different ... There'd been a change ... He couldn't have said exactly what it was, but he had the feeling nothing was as it had been.

He'd wondered more than once if he was suffering from some psychological illness, but realized he wasn't being honest with himself. He'd have been only too glad if it *were* all the result of a disordered brain. Unfortunately he knew it wasn't.

He was looking rather drawn, but that could happen to anyone. What he didn't like was the sound of his voice -- it sounded strained, and he was afraid this might give the game away to others. He had tried to disguise the change, to deepen his voice when he spoke, but he couldn't keep it up for long. At the most it worked on the telephone. He really couldn't reconcile himself to the change in his voice – it was as if that were the source of all his woes. In his attempts to improve matters he'd done things he'd never have dreamed of before: for instance, he drunk water straight out of the refrigerator in the hope that it would make him hoarse. But to his intense irritation, it didn't work. His throat, once so sensitive to damp and cold, was unaffected.

His mood changed from frenzy to self-pity, then to a phase of comparative calm. He managed to convince himself nothing had happened, and even if it had, the trouble would soon be over. He'd been in this kind of mood when Simon Dersha rang up. He'd placed him at once, because he was connected with the evening of that other, that fateful phone call. The minister was ashamed of himself now – he even tried to hide from himself the fact that he, a member both of the government and of the Politbureau, had been glad to receive a phone call from so insignificant an individual. But he'd enjoyed his lunch, afterwards, more than he had for a long time.

"I'll make you a coffee," his wife had said when they'd finished.

Then he'd gone to his room to lie down, but he couldn't sleep. However, he couldn't help feeling slightly better -- though only slightly, and the improvement was tinged with bitterness. He'd been put out at the previous lack of phone calls, and this one gave some cause for satisfaction. The man who'd made it was neither a bumpkin nor one of his own entourage. He worked in a ministry, and it was a well-known fact that people like that were good at sniffing out . . . the minister wouldn't let himself think the word "changes". Yes, when it came to . . . that sort of thing, that sort of man was the first to know.

He gazed up at the bedroom ceiling. His thoughts were in confusion. He'd wondered several times why this humble clerk wanted to see him, but told himself that was of no importance. What mattered was that he should come to see him. When you're the victim of such . . . no one will come near you. It's as if you had the plague.

But what if he was worrying for nothing? he asked himself for the umpteenth time. Supposing all these black thoughts, all these torments, were unfounded? He turned over. Oh, if only that were so, he wouldn't mind all the anguish! He'd put it all behind him, if only it had been a mistake!

From then on he didn't try to hide his fears. What still wasn't clear to him was when it had all begun. But probably Enver Hoxha's phone call during that dinner party was the turning point, the watershed between before and after. Unless it all began before that, one cold evening on the dreary plain from which he was directing the grand manoeuvres, when he was informed that a group of tank officers had disregarded one of his orders. He had stood at the entrance to his tent staring at the liaison sergeant who'd brought the message – or rather at the square of anonymous face left uncovered by the hood of a raincoat: just the lower part of a forehead, eyes, mouth and two patches of cheek.

"The tank officers have disobeyed the order to encircle the town's Party committee," the man had said in a tired, expressionless voice. And the minister had suddenly felt hollow inside.

"What?" he'd cried. "They dare to disregard an order?"

And as the sergeant, still in the same faint voice, started on some sort of explanation, the minister had started to yell louder and louder, drowning the other's now baneful words. "Arrest them!" he bawled. But something of what the man was trying to say had sunk in . . . The officers . . . had said that in no circumstances . . . could the tanks . . . encircle a Party committee . . . .

"Arrest them!" he shouted, louder than ever. "Arrest them!"

When the courier had gone he stood at the entrance to his tent for some time, an icy void in his breast. Despite his subsequent efforts to hide it, his anxiety had probably started when he gave that order.

But had it begun even before that? – on an evening in Peking, after he'd come back from the theatre? It was a hot, damp night, and he was in a state of excitement. He wanted to stay up late, to talk to someone, to unburden himself. He'd never have dreamed a Chinese play could affect him like this. People were right when they said the Chinese party line emerged most forcefully in the theatre. The play he'd just seen was extraordinary. In the finale, a victorious crowd of good characters dragged the first secretary of a provincial Party across the stage by the hair.

"What did you think of the play?" Zhou Enlai had asked him afterwards, turning aside from escorting an African head of state towards the exit. He hadn't known what to say. Zhou had looked very ambiguous.

"Perhaps we'll meet again after supper," he said, "when I've seen our friend here home."

Driving back through the dark to the government guest house, the minister felt strangely troubled. He'd never experienced this mixture of pleasure and horror before. It had begun during that final scene at the theatre when the mob hauled the Party secretary across the stage – the thrill you feel at the destruction of something sacred. It seemed odd that the Chinese, with their reputation for dogmatism and inflexibility, should allow such a thing. He couldn't wait to hear what Zhou said about it. His eyes sparkled.

Zhou came straight after supper, as promised, and as soon as they'd shaken hands he asked again, "What did you think of the play?"

"Well . . . how shall I put it? Rather strange," said the minister.

Zhou Enlai gave him a piercing look.

"It was magnificent," he said.

The minister felt a shudder run through him again.

The two men then retired to a room in the guest house where they could talk alone. As he listened, the minister wondered why on earth Zhou Enlai was daring to speak like this to him. When you confided in someone you usually chose a person whose attitudes you could take for granted. Had the Chinese been bugging his, the minister's, conversations with one of his aides? Both of them, carried away with enthusiasm for what they'd seen happening in China, had let fall a few criticisms here and there about the situation in Albania. This didn't seem impossible, especially as their objections were mostly about the way the Party at home had its finger in every pie. In China, on the other hand, the position had become very different. Not only was it obvious that the Chinese Party was dominated by the army, but apparently other bodies were superior to it too. Of course, the minister and his aide weren't in favour of any such aberrations in their own country, but the time had come for Party control to be relaxed. People were fed up, to put it politely, with being called to account before the Central Committee for the least little thing. The Chinese had put a stop to that kind of nonsense: an officer in charge of a military region was his own master, and didn't take orders from either the regional committee or the Central Committee of the Party. And was China any the worse? Had China been weakened? On the contrary, China was stronger than ever.

That was more or less what the minister and his aide had said, and perhaps the Chinese had listened in. Perhaps that was even why they'd taken them to the theatre. As Zhou went on talking, the minister became convinced that such was the case.

"The revolution before everything!" Zhou was saying. "The revolution changed everything, and to it nothing is sacred, not even the Party!"

"Not even the Party?" stammered the minister, at once ecstatic and appalled.

"You need the same thing in your country," said Zhou.

"In our country, a thing like that could never —" began the minister.

"I know, I know," Zhou interrupted. "A lot of things aren't allowed in Albania, but that can't go on much longer. China's preparing to make changes that will alter the balance of the whole world. The question is, will you come with us or no? If you do, you will remain our friends. If you don't, we'll have to ditch you. For the moment we're putting it to you very nicely — or rather, *I'm* telling *you* in the strictest confidence . . . please don't tell anyone else. We're going to see upheavals and sudden storms all over the world, especially in the Balkans. And as an old Chinese poem has it, in bad weather it's up to everyone to take shelter. But it's something that has to be thought about now. Afterwards, it'll be too late. Glorification of the Party was meant to prevent change. That's why Mao has abolished the cult of the Party. And in your country too . . ."

Zhou Enlai went on and on. The conversation changed from one subject to another, but always came back to the Party. It was now openly identified as the main obstacle to progress. It was no accident that Mao Zedong had permitted two lines to coexist within it. If it hadn't been for that they would never have seen that play this evening. "But they'd never be allowed to put on a play like that in my country," sighed the minister. "I know that," said Zhou, "but there are lots of other things you could do. You've knocked down the churches and mosques, haven't you? In that case, why should you hesitate to tackle another kind of worship?" "Oh, not in our country – it would be practically impossible!" "One always thinks it's impossible to start with . . . But once you get started . . . !"

The minister suddenly got a grip on himself. This was getting a bit out of hand. How dared Zhou? . . . And so openly? What's more, he was talking to him as if he were a mere vassal . . . The time had come to let him understand there were limits! The minister drew himself up as he sat in his chair.

"I'm not sure I quite understand you, comrade Zhou Enlai," he said coldly, throwing his head back so as to seem as distant as possible. But his bravado didn't last. Zhou Enlai stared back at him unremittingly, his eyes seeming to converge and grip the minister as in a vice.

"You used to be more frank, once," he said quietly. "Our Yugoslav friends have told us – maybe they had it from the Soviets themselves – about a certain private conversation you had with them just before the row between Albania and the U.S.S.R. in 1960. You were much more open then!"

The minister felt his eyes glaze and his mouth go dry. He'd thought that story had long been forgotten. It had happened twenty years ago, and strangely enough the Soviets had said nothing about it. And now, when he least expected it, here in Peking of all places . . . He was completely thrown. As he had been in 1960, when the Soviets, to make him sit down and talk to them, had reminded him of a conversation he'd had once with the Yugoslavs: "We're well aware of what you said to the Yugoslavs in 1947 . . ." they'd said. When he'd started to get over the shock, the first thing he'd asked himself then was why the Yugoslavs had sold him down the river? and for how much? Perhaps in exchange for Krushchev's visit to Belgrade, when he went to apologize to Tito? Perhaps for something to do with Kosovo? Or had they simply sold him in instalments?

And now here he was, betrayed again. But by whom, and why? Because of a conversation. Oh, if only I'd held my tongue in 1960, or even in 1947! That wretched conversation – the years went by, but like a plague bacillus it refused to die! We know what you said to the Soviets in 1960 . . . We know what you said to the Turks in 1911 . . . And what you said before that, in 999, about the destruction of the socialist bloc . . . Not to mention what you said to Pontius Pilate that famous night in the year dot . . .

His mind was in a whirl. If you looked at it closely, it was only an ordinary conversation, but these people clung to it like limpets and wouldn't let it go . . . Yes, just an ordinary conversation – and what were they doing now, really, but just having a chat, man to man?

He'd never been in such a mess. And to crown all, Zhou's eyes were still riveted on him. But they were now slowly loosening their vice-like grip. The Chinaman's expression was softening, and what he was saying came back to the beginning, like a loop of recording tape. "That's how one always feels to start with. It seems impossible, but once you've taken the first step . . . For example, you could do something that looks quite modest but has a great symbolic value. Do you see what I mean?"

But he couldn't concentrate. His mind drifted back to the prologue to all this, that windy, rainy day in February 1947 when, biting his nails nervously, he'd listened to the Yugoslav, in his broken Albanian, filling him with bitterness.

"As if you weren't as capable as anyone else! You're cleverer than them, really, but . . ."

The Soviets had told him the same thing later, in 1960, and it had seemed to him that from now on he would always be haunted by those terrifying words. One day, returning home at mid-day, he'd frozen as he went into the drawing room: someone was saying them again. It took him some time to realize it was his son. He fell upon the boy, tore the book out of his hands, and started to yell like a madman. The boy didn't understand. "It's only my textbook on medieval Albanian literature, Father," he murmured . . .

"You see what I mean?" said Zhou Enlai.

But the minister didn't see anything at all.

"I'm sorry – would you mind saying it again? I'm sorry . . ."

"It doesn't matter – I understand," said Zhou, smiling affably. "I was saying you could do something symbolic. Such things have always been important in a country's history, and always will be. Things which look quite ordinary at first sight, but which take on a special meaning in their context – an alliance, a symbolic marriage, for example. To show you what I mean I'll tell you about an episode in my own life. As you know, my wife is the sister-in-law of our greatest enemy, Chiang Kai-shek. Have you ever considered the fact that, through all the changes and chances China has gone through, I have never ended my marriage? It wouldn't have been difficult for me to find another wife – most of our other leaders, Mao first and foremost, had remarried. And my rivals in the struggle for power might well have tried to exploit what they called a dis-honour. And try they did, but someone stood in their way every time: Mao himself. Leave Zhou's marriage alone, he'd say, and the matter was closed. But he didn't do it out of friendship for me, still less out of friendship for my wife! No, he did it because it was in the interests of us all."

Here Zhou paused for breath.

"Mao didn't do things like that for nothing. That marriage was and still is imprinted on the consciousness of the Chinese people. For it has a meaning. Behind my wife there was Chiang Kai-shek, and behind him the United States! Every time I heard Mao say 'Leave Zhou's marriage alone,' I realized that marriage would turn out to be useful one day. And now, it seems, that moment has almost come . . . But that's enough about me. I just wanted to illustrate the influence of symbolic acts. Now let's get back to you. Don't look at me like that! I know you're married —" he laughed. "You're not going to be asked to marry a woman from the old guard! You can do something else – something apparently unim-portant, but really very significant. For example, during manoeuvres you could encircle a Party committee with your troops, or better still your tanks. I don't say it has to be the Tirana Party committee – that would be premature – a district committee would do. As you probably know, in the course of our Cultural Revolution hun-dreds of Party committees were burned down. So surround a district Party committee with your tanks. It sounds simple. It *is* simple. But it could act as an important symbol, and the people are always influenced by symbols! It will travel by word of mouth in the form of rumours and conjectures, it will awaken ideas and hopes. We've initiated many great actions in China like that!"

As Zhou was speaking, the minister thought of the cynicism with which the Yugoslavs, Soviets and Chinese – an infernal triangle that seemed intent in keeping him in its clutches all his life – had passed that conversation to and fro. Once or twice he thanked his lucky stars that the Chinese weren't asking more of him. To hell with their symbolic act – he'd do it, if that would shut them up!

That cursed conversation! He'd never have dreamed a chat could cost so dear. Why on earth hadn't he owned up to it at the time, directly after the break with Yugoslavia, when all members of the Party were asked to report what they'd talked to the Yugoslavs about? "One day, comrades, I too, fool that I was, impelled by jealousy, that survival from the world of the bourgeoisie, told them how frustrated I felt when X was appointed instead of me to post Y . . ." That would have done it . . .

"You seem very thoughtful," said Zhou. "The play seems to have made a great impression on you. I see it's not only Shakespeare who can set your head in a whirl!"

And they'd gone on talking about surrounding a Party committee, about the Party in general, and about how urgently necessary it was to overhaul it.

Later on, when he was back home from his trip to China, what Zhou had said still remained on his mind – though he didn't know whether to call it a piece of advice, a suggestion or an order. He didn't have a word for it in Albanian. In his imagination it was like a snake coiled up inside him, which stirred whenever he got a phone call from the Central Committee, especially one that summoned him to a meeting. What did they think he was, a minister or a bus driver, ringing for him every time it suited them?

Even so, he would never have followed up his talk with Zhou, never have dared to do anything, symbolic or otherwise, if, some time later, the Chinese prime minister hadn't sent him greetings through a member of a government delegation.

Relations with China were not so warm as they had been. One evening, at an official dinner at the Brigades Palace, the Chinaman sitting next to him, and to whom he'd so far paid no attention, started to talk to him in broken Albanian.

"Comrade Zhou Enlai sends you his best wishes. Comrade Zhou Enlai still thinks of you. You went to the theatre, magnificent, wasn't it?" said the Chinaman, with a high-pitched laugh that had nothing to do with what he was saying. He went on, more and more openly, his words sounding now like a message and now more like a menace.

"The moment comrade Zhou Enlai spoke about is coming. The test, hee-hee! Everyone must do something, can't just wait for it to fall in lap, hee-hee! Difficult times ahead, hee-hee!"

The minister's fork was suspended in mid-air. He had lost his appetite. So nothing had been forgotten! The day of reckoning was apparently at hand, and they were explicitly letting him know what was expected of him. He looked round at the faces of the other guests, trying to guess which of them had been given a similar message. At one point he had the impression that all the tables were full of giggling Chinamen. I must act before it's too late, he thought – do something, even if it's only symbolic, to keep them quiet. A sort of consideration, the price of their silence about the Soviets and the Yugoslavs. Something symbolic: the Party secretary dragged across the stage, tanks surrounding a district Party committee . . . Afterwards, if there really was an upheaval, as Zhou Enlai had said . . . But for the moment, the symbolic act would do . . . They *were* on the eve of some manoeuvres . . .

"How is comrade Enver?" asked the Chinaman. "Not too well, eh?"

The minister's mouth was full of dust and ashes. If only the blasted dinner would end! But his anxiety lasted several more weeks, until the cold afternoon when he finally gave the order to encircle the Party committee.

All the rest of that afternoon he'd felt completely disorientated, pacing back and forth in his tent, peering out now and then and scanning the plain for a messenger. The messenger arrived at nightfall. The order hadn't been carried out. He didn't let anyone see how shocked he was, stepping back into the tent to conceal his dismay. He wouldn't listen to any explanations of this act of disobedience – he just pretended not to understand, and kept shouting, "Arrest them! Arrest them!" As he did so he told himself the best thing would be to settle the matter there and then so that no one would know about it, so that the fact that the order was given would be forgotten, today, tomorrow and until the end of time. But it was too late. All he could do now was simulate an anger he didn't feel, because fear left no room for wrath. So whenever anyone opened his mouth to try to offer some explanation of how the officers accounted for their behaviour, he cut them short, shouting, "I don't want to know! I don't want to know!"

And he didn't want to know, either. His only desire was for the matter to be buried in oblivion as fast as possible. That blasted suggestion of Zhou's! Why had he let him pour that poison in his ear? What he had done struck him sometimes as fatal, sometimes as merely premature. His days became full of chill terror. He realized the affair wasn't going to die of its own accord. The officers themselves had talked to various people. If they weren't punished they'd probably talk to some more. By some means or other they had to be silenced. One way of intimidating them was to have them expelled from the Party; and he managed that without any difficulty. But apparently, after they were expelled, they wrote a letter to Enver Hoxha. That was what the phone call had been about, the evening of the dinner. The minister hadn't slept a wink all that night. He was obviously going to have to explain himself to the Central Committee. But one of his staff convinced him that what the officers had said about him might easily be interpreted as subversion, as propaganda against authority. So in his report to the Committee he maintained that the officers' behaviour infringed the laws of the Republic. A fortnight later, at the Central Committee, when someone asked what measures were going to be taken against the officers, the reply was brief: "If they've broken the law, let the usual measures be taken." The minister rubbed his hands. So the Central Committee wouldn't get drawn into details about the officers' fate? Well, *he* knew very well what to do with them! He slept soundly that night, the first time for ages. Then he began to wonder: should he send the officers to prison, or leave them unpunished? To tell the truth, he would have swallowed his resentment and let the matter drop if he hadn't been afraid they'd start talking again. No, prison was safest. His aides agreed with him. One of them suggested it would be best if they were dismissed from the army first, so that their arrest would seem purely political.

The minister had imagined that after the tank officers were arrested his peace of mind would be restored once and for all. But on the contrary. It was then that he started to notice the long silences of the telephone and the lack of visitors. Sometimes he put all this down to the current cooling off of relations with China, which was a general preoccupation then. The very name of China sent a chill down his spine. Great changes were in the offing, though there was nothing definite yet. Perhaps it would start with economic retaliation?

The silences of the telephone seemed to get longer every day. What's going on? he wondered. I'm still a minister. No one has criticized me. What have I got to worry about? He dismissed the situation as absurd, grotesque. But after a while the clouds of uncertainty gathered again. Rumour spreads by word of mouth, Zhou Enlai had said: it was as influential in a country's affairs as the newspapers. If Zhou had encouraged the episode of the encirclement just in order to start such a rumour, it must be because he believed in it. And if he was right to do so, if rumour really was as strong as all that, the lack of phone calls and the absence of visitors was only too comprehensible. The rumour would have told how the minister had ordered the Party committee to be surrounded, how the tanks had refused to obey the order and been thrown in jail for insubordination – and would have ended by asking, Was the order justified? That was quite enough to make people shun him like the plague. No need to arrange for critical articles to appear in the papers, or to dismiss him from his post, and so on. Rumour – curse it! – was more powerful than all of these. He'd sent for the head of army intelligence and asked what he knew about the rumour. The answer took him aback. "We know nothing about anything of the kind, comrade minister." He'd started to laugh with relief, there and then, in front of the head of intelligence. Then his laughter changed to a grim smile at his own gullibility. No, what was causing his anxiety was not a rumour in the ordinary sense of the word, but something more subtle, nameless, and all the more pernicious because it was imperceptible. Something that seeped into everything, everywhere, like the air.

Where had it started? Whose mouths had uttered it first? And in what office, institution or mysterious ante-chamber? The most depressing possibilities occurred to him.

The minister had spent the last two months in this state. Meanwhile the Chinese had done nothing. Everything seemed to be paralysed. I did what I could, he explained in an imaginary conversation with Zhou Enlai. I tried to encircle a Party committee with tanks, but it turned out to be impossible. I was lucky to escape with my life. We don't go in for that sort of thing here, you know. We don't harm the Party even symbolically, as you suggested – so you can imagine how feasible it is in reality! They'd smash you to smithereens! Smithereens! Ask me to do the most horrible thing you can think of, but not that! Not that, ever!

The television news on Thursday had reassured him somewhat. It'll pass, he thought. The phones will ring again, the door-bell will be heard once more. That was what he was thinking when the phone actually rang. It was the clerk. No guest was ever awaited so eagerly. The minister had tried to take an afternoon nap, but he couldn't sleep. As soon as he got up, his wife asked him:

"Would you like a cup of coffee?"

At first he thought he'd wait and have one with the visitor, then he said yes please. If the visitor came, he could always have another with him . . . *If* the visitor came? How could he doubt it? It was unthinkable that he shouldn't turn up.

The doubt lingered until Simon Dersha appeared. But then Simon Dersha vanished again beyond the railings.

The minister stood at one of the drawing-room windows. The trees stood outside – massive, dark, indifferent. Once or twice he imagined himself hastily ringing for his bodyguard and his chauffeur, diving into his car as it emerged from the garage, and hurtling along the street after his quarry. The man would try to get away, but he would stop him, clutch him by the sleeve and say tearfully, "What came over you, going away like that? Why are you tormenting me too, as if all my other troubles weren't enough?"

That is what he imagined, staring out at the garden, with the drops of rain from this afternoon's downpour still hanging from the branches and reflecting some invisible source of light. Then he reached out and rang the bell, and did all the other things he'd imagined. But slowly.

As the car was driving out through the gate and the chauffeur asked where he was to go, the minister said:

"Just drive around."

They were soon in a main street where the pavements were crowded with people. To the minister they looked at once hostile and unpredictable. Who knew what was inside those heads? What thoughts did they emit? What terrifying rumours?

As he gazed at the anonymous faces he began to be afraid. They were probably thinking of China, and of him. What would become of him? What verdict would they pronounce?

Somewhere amongst them must be his guest. He wanted to find him and whisper, "Oh ghost, oh phantom, why did you disappear?"

He sighed and looked again at the passers-by. Some of them stared at his car with a grim expression that seemed to him tinged with irony. What if the Chinese had betrayed him? he thought suddenly. What if they'd sacrificed him to some temporary arrangement? But this thought was pushed aside by the crowds in the street: he felt somehow that they held his fate in their hands, and that if only the sound they made, the rumour they spread, were to stop, he would be saved. Otherwise it would gradually rise to the highest authorities, and that would be the end of him. So he was dependent on their silence. But was that asking too much? After all, what had he done wrong, for heaven's sake? He'd tried to organize some manoeuvres, a mock military operation . . . A surge of hatred for this merciless mob swept over him, together with the self-pity and resentment generated by humiliation. He felt like getting out of the car, kneeling down in front of the crowd, beating his breast and crying: "Don't be angry with me – I swear I wasn't trying to do anything real! It was just an exercise, pure make-believe! Don't soldiers themselves talk of the war game?"

At the same moment, Simon Dersha was walking along amid the crowds on the pavement. Now he'd left the district where the minister lived he felt calmer, though whenever he glimpsed a black limousine he dodged behind the nearest passers-by in case it had the minister inside, scanning the street to find him: "Hi, Simon – where are you off to? You're supposed to be coming to see me – you phoned up yourself! Jump in and I'll drive you home with me!"

When Simon reached his flat he found the family as he had left them. Waiting to see how he'd got on. They could tell at once that he'd failed.

"Well," said his wife, breaking the silence, "wasn't it any good? . . . What happened?"

He shrugged as if to say, That's the way it is. If only they didn't badger him for explanations . . .

"Oh God, what a mess we're in!" groaned his brother, burying his head in his hands.

Simon glanced at him. He felt like saying: You should talk – it was you who sowed this doubt in my mind!

"But what happened?" repeated his wife. "Didn't he listen to you at all? Isn't there any hope?"

Simon shook his head.

"I never heard of such a thing!" his wife exclaimed angrily. "Everybody gets their friends to put in a good word – one hears of cases all the time – but when *you* try to do it it doesn't work!"

"I couldn't help it . . . It didn't just depend on me!"

"It did depend partly on you! But you made a mess of it! You're an idiot!"

"What?"

"Yes, an idiot! You always have been."

"You have the nerve to say that –!"

Simon had turned pale.

"Stop squabbling!" said his brother. "It's bad enough without that . . ."

Simon had no desire to make things worse, and it took him only a few moments to forget the insult. It was all for the best, really. His wife's wrath had got him out of having to give explanations.

"Could I have a cup of coffee, please?" he said, to show he hadn't taken offence.

"Didn't he even offer you a coffee?" exploded his wife. But her brother-in-law gave her a reproachful look, and she got up and put the coffee on.

"We're sorry," said Benjamin. "We've got *you* into trouble now. But it isn't your fault – you can't help it."

"No, I can't," said Simon.

For a few minutes the room was silent, except for the sounds of coffee being prepared.

"So what are we going to do now?" sighed Benjamin's wife.

"What are we going to do?" said her husband. "We're going to try again."

The conversation that followed was much the same as the discussion the day before. To Simon if felt like a mere continuation, as if his failed attempt to see the minister had been only a dream.

They talked about the various subterfuges people resorted to in order to get out of being posted, and how, if they were, they took care not to lease an apartment in the provinces for fear of losing the one they had in Tirana.

"When were these rules introduced?" asked Benjamin. "They're so pernickety they might be Chinese . . ."

"Do you really think so?" said his wife.

"Don't you?"

"No . . . Posting has always been common practice."

"Not by rotation, like this."

"You ought to be glad if the rules are Chinese," said Simon's wife. "At least that means they might be abolished after the Chinese themselves go."

"I doubt it."

"Why?"

"Weeds aren't uprooted so easily."

"You think not?"

Simon sipped his coffee and watched them. He took no part in the conversation. Their voices seemed to reach him faintly, as from far away. They were talking about sham separations between husbands and wives, and in their attitude to these subterfuges there was no trace of disapproval. In their view these people had no choice, so they couldn't be called immoral. Anyhow, some of them got married to one another again, so what was all the fuss about? Even in the ordinary way, a lot of couples got divorced and then remarried – some of them three times! – and nobody threw up their hands. So why be more severe on people posted to the provinces? They were only human, just like everybody else. If there was a mother-in-law to complicate the situation, that didn't make any difference. In a way it made it better, because then the husband could come home without any concealment, on the pretext of visiting his mother.

Yes, all this applied to their present situation, thought Simon. And as he'd foreseen, it wasn't long till his brother and sister-in-law started talking about their own divorce. And to tell the truth, that wouldn't be an irreparable misfortune, as he'd thought to begin with. Naturally, it would upset their friends and relations, but that was nothing compared with the possibility of his mother coming to live *here*! Ugh! That was to be avoided at all costs! Their mother only had to go on occupying a room in what would then be her daughter-in-law's apartment, and, even if there were children, morals would be preserved. Apart from the fact that Benjamin would officially be separated from his wife, nothing would really have changed.

For the first time, Simon felt slightly relieved. But he was in no hurry to say he approved of this solution. The longer he put off doing so, the longer they'd remember that it wasn't his idea, and that he'd only accepted it because there was no alternative. He remained silent. They kept looking at him. Finally his wife could bear it no longer.

"Well, Simon, what do *you* think?"

He frowned, looked thoughtfully out of the window, and said to no one in particular:

"Well, we must do something . . . We'll have to see."

This was vague indeed, but it was enough to convey to the others that he wouldn't oppose their plan.

10

SUDDENLY THERE WERE SIGNS of an improvement in relations with China. These signs were cried up not only by those to whom this development was welcome, but also by those to whom it was not, but who wanted to see the situation cleared up one way or the other. To the satisfaction of the first group and the chagrin of the second, the signs turned out to be not without foundation. They reflected part of the truth, a truth increasingly clear to certain ministries: the Ministries of Construction, Telecommunications, Foreign Affairs and Planning, and above all the Admiralty, which received information about the movement of ships. It was said that after a long wait in Chinese ports, ships belonging to the Sino-Albanian company Chal had at last set sail for Albania. According to some they had already passed through the Straits of Gibraltar. Others said they were still near the Cape of Good Hope. But in any case it seemed certain that the ships in question had set out with their expected cargoes. No one was prepared to deny that.

When Gjergj came in he found Silva preparing the salad for lunch. He talked to her over the sound of the tap as she stood at the sink washing lettuce leaves. She kept laughing at what he said.

"You ought to find out how Victor Hila stands now," she said. "I think I've told you about him . . . He's our best guide to China's present attitude towards us."

Gjergj burst out laughing.

"And how's he getting on?" he asked.

"Not all that well, as far as I can make out. A few days ago he wanted to come and see me at the office. I believe he's been chucked out of the factory where he was working."

"Really? That's a definite sign that we're cosying up to China!" said Gjergj, laughing.

"I doubt it."

"So do I. I think it's out of the question."

The telephone rang in the hall. Gjergj went to answer it.

"Silva – it's for you!"

She hastily dried her hands and hurried out into the hall. It was Skënder Bermema.

"I'm sorry to bother you at lunch-time," he said, "but I absolutely must talk to you."

Silva felt her heart beat faster.

"Whenever you like," she said.

"It concerns the matter you came to see me about."

"Yes – I thought as much . . ."

"The trouble is that I leave for Peking this afternoon – unfortunately I couldn't ring you earlier . . ."

"How's that?"

"I was busy all morning . . . You do believe me?"

Silva felt herself blush, and tried to explain.

"I didn't mean that! I was wondering why you're going to China!"

"It *is* surprising! But in spite of all the talk, they notified us yesterday that our delegation had to be ready to take off without delay."

"And you leave this afternoon?"

"Yes – at a quarter past five. On the London–Shanghai flight of Pakistani Airlines. Listen, Silva – it's twenty past two now and I have to leave for the airport at four o'clock at the latest if I want to be there by half-past. Could you come to my place at half-past three?"

Silva thought for a moment.

"Half-past three? All right. No problem," she said.

"Good. I'll be waiting for you. So long!"

Silva hung up, then went slowly back into the kitchen.

"It was Skënder Bermema," she told Gjergj, who as usual was standing by the window. "He's got something to tell me about Arian."

"Is that so?"

Silva hadn't told Gjergj she'd been to Skënder's studio a few days before to get news of her brother.

"I gather he's just leaving for China?"

"Yes – this afternoon."

223

"Another sign . . ."

"I have to be at his place by three-thirty," said Silva.

Gjergj looked at his watch.

"You've got plenty of time. We can have a snack lunch. But where's Brikena?"

"Now you mention it, I have no idea."

Silva set about laying the table, but something prevented her from doing it as automatically as usual.

"So the exchanging of delegations has started up again," said Gjergj, still looking out of the window.

Silva was thinking of how awkward she'd feel, coming face to face with Skënder Bermema's wife again. For years they'd pretended not to see one another if they met in the street.

"Unless it's just the dying throes . . ."

"What are you talking about?"

Gjergj looked at her affectionately.

"The only thing you can think of is this business about your brother . . . But don't worry . . . I have a feeling it will all be sorted out."

"Do you really think so?" she said, looking at him but still busy around the table.

He nodded emphatically, and winked for good measure.

"That must be Brikena," she said, going to the front door.

Out in the hall, their daughter could be heard making breathless apologies for being late.

Gjergj turned away from the window and sat down to lunch.

The closer she got to the street where Skënder Bermema lived, the more doubtful Silva felt about going to see him so soon before his departure. True, she'd been there before, but his wife hadn't been at home then. It was unlikely that she'd be out today. If Silva hadn't been so worried about her brother she would probably have turned back. The most difficult moment would be meeting Skënder's wife. It wouldn't have been so embarrassing if they'd never met before, but unfortunately they'd known each other well in the past and then gradually drifted apart. I only hope she doesn't actually open the door! thought Silva as she went up the stairs. If she did, could Silva say she wouldn't come in as she knew they must be busy getting ready for Skënder's trip? Then she could hear what he had to say at the door, or if necessary just inside the hall.

She rang the bell, determined not to go in. It was exactly half-past three. Surely he would come to the door himself? – he must find the situation as awkward as she did herself.

But the footsteps approaching the door were too light for a man. For a second, Silva was tempted to rush back down the stairs. But it was too late: the door opened and Skënder's wife appeared. He might have had the tact to open the door himself, thought Silva briefly. Her hostess was standing with her back to the hall light, so Silva couldn't make out her expression.

"How are you?" Silva asked, flustered.

Should she introduce herself, as if they were strangers? That didn't seem right, though.

"How are you?" she said again. "I'm sorry to bother you at a time like this, but Skënder phoned me . . ."

"Yes, I know," said the other woman. "Unfortunately he had to go out."

Silva was taken aback.

"But come in," said the other woman affably. "He had an urgent call from the foreign ministry – they probably wanted to give him some last-minute instructions. We'll have seen everything by the time this delegation takes off!"

She smiled so naturally as she spoke that half Silva's embarrassment melted away.

"I do hope you'll forgive me," she said again. "It's not a very good day . . ."

"It doesn't matter in the least," said her hostess placidly, sitting down opposite Silva. "We can wait together. The children are away skiing near Mount Dajti – they don't even know Skënder's leaving today."

Silva covertly examined the other young woman's oval face, ash-blonde hair and bright eyes: her expression might be interpreted as either serenity or indifference, according to the attitude of the observer. So we're going to wait for him together, thought Silva. As if we were both at a concert. She suddenly felt she'd done the other woman an injury, and had an almost irresistible desire to apologize. But almost immediately she thought, Why should I? I never did her any harm . . . And yet, and yet . . . Not only had Besnik Struga ditched this woman's niece on account of Silva's own sister, but for a long time Skënder's name too had been linked to

225

Ana's. This must have had a profoundly disturbing effect on this other woman's life: she must have considered it an outrage, and it might well have given rise to painful domestic scenes.

Silva went on looking at her hostess with an expression unusual for her.

"Skënder said something to me about your brother, but he'll prefer to tell you himself."

"Is it serious?" asked Silva.

"No – just the opposite, as far as I can tell."

Silva felt like flinging her arms around the other woman and asking her forgiveness again – forgiveness for everything. But perhaps she'd forgiven everything already, now that Ana was dead. That was what her expression seemed to convey – her whole face, and the smooth curls that moved almost musically. That placid look seemed to be saying: "All those wild passions, all those problems and suspicions, for nothing! For the day must come when we have to quit the stage and leave it empty . . ."

Silva looked at her watch.

"He's late," she said.

There was a sound of tyres outside.

"That must be him," said Skënder's wife.

She was right.

"I knew I'd find you here!" exclaimed Skënder as soon as he saw Silva. "Sorry to keep you waiting, but they sent for me urgently. Last-minute instructions, as usual. There's no end to it. I hope you don't mind?"

"Not at all," said Silva. "It's I who should apologize – coming on a day like this . . ."

"I asked you to! It's no bother at all. The only thing is –" looking at his watch – "we ought to leave right away . . . I know, Silva – why don't you come with us to the airport? There's room in the car, and we'll have more time to talk there. Otherwise I'm afraid we might be late. What do you think?"

"I'm quite ready to come, but are you sure there really will be room? I don't want to –"

"Of course! Plenty of room!"

"Yes," agreed his wife. "And then we two can drive back together."

Again Silva felt like falling on her neck.

"You're both very kind," she murmured.

226

"Let's go, then!" said Skënder, grabbing his case and his overnight bag.

"Sure you've got everything?" said his wife as they were getting into the car. "Did you remember to pack the notes for your book?"

He nodded.

"Oh, are you writing another book?" said Silva.

"Mmm," he replied, his usual way of implying he didn't want to go into it.

"He hasn't actually started yet," said his wife. "I gather it's going to be a subtle kind of a novel. But I don't know why he's taking his notes with him. I shouldn't think he'll have much time for writing."

"Come on!" he cried. "We're late already. If the delegation's cancelled because of me, I don't like to think what the Chinese will say!"

"When they asked you to go to the ministry just now I thought the trip was going to be postponed again."

He laughed.

"I don't blame you. I've never heard of a mission being put off so many times."

"One can see why," said Silva.

"It hits you in the eye!" he agreed. "But since, as no doubt you've heard, there seems to a bit of an improvement in the relations between the two countries, the Chinese informed us that they were expecting us. But even so, it wasn't easy. They needed time to re-cast the invitation. And do you know in honour of what the delegation of Albanian writers is finally going to Peking? You'll never guess if you rack your brains for a hundred years! In honour of the Day of the Birds!"

Silva burst out laughing.

"You're joking!"

"Am I joking?" he said, turning to his wife.

"No, it's the truth," she told Silva. "I laughed when he told me."

Skënder started to explain how the man at the foreign ministry who was in charge of the delegation had also said "You must be joking!" when the Chinese cultural attaché handed him the invitation. But the attaché had replied that he was quite serious. When the vexed Albanian official observed that his country wasn't in the habit of sending delegations abroad on such topics as birds, he pointed out that the Day of the Birds was a perfectly serious occasion, which also figured in the Albanian calendar. He then produced one, pointing out the date in early spring when the day occurred.

"I don't suppose either of you knew that, did you?" said Skënder. "I'm sure I didn't."

He went on to describe how the Albanian official had asked why this was the occasion for which the delegation was to be invited, and the Chinese attaché explained that the Chinese Union of Writers, abolished under the Cultural Revolution, hadn't yet been revived. So they had to find another peg on which to hang the forthcoming visit, and the Day of the Birds was the best that could be found. He thought it was an excellent idea: the connection with airiness, the sky, inspiration . . . Very subtle, no?

Skënder's wife and Silva laughed again.

"You have to have dealt with them to believe it!" said Skënder. "It's enough to drive you crazy. And as a matter of fact, I can't look at a bird now without feeling a kind of affinity . . . What do they say about being as free as a bird?"

That set the other two off again.

"Who else is going?" asked Silva.

Skënder pulled a face.

"A chap I pointed out to you one day . . . C— V— . . ."

"Oh! Why him?"

"Apparently the Chinese like him. This is the second time he's been invited."

"It's not hard to see why," said Skënder's wife.

Soon after that they arrived at the airport, which seemed busier than usual. There were a number of Chinese in the departure hall and around the customs areas.

"You can tell there's been a change in our relations with China, can't you?" said Skënder as they made for the cafeteria. "You should hear what the foreign radio stations say about it! Some of them say Mao Zedong knew nothing about the cooling off, and that when he found out he flew into a rage, gave his aides a dressing down, and ordered Zhou Enlai to see to it personally that all the goods that had been held up should be dispatched right away."

"The sort of tale they usually spread!" commented his wife.

"Still, something has changed," said Skënder, with what looked like a rueful smile.

At the cafeteria, they bumped into C— V—.

"So here you are!" he exclaimed. "I was afraid you wouldn't get here in time."

"We'll go all right, don't worry!" said Skënder, not looking at him.

Silva frowned. It didn't look as if Skënder was going to have a chance to talk to her about her brother. Sometimes he seemed to have forgotten all about it.

She heaved a sigh of relief when C— V— went over to a group of relations who'd come to see him off.

"What would you like to drink?" Skënder asked the two women. "We can talk better here," he said, turning to Silva. "I preferred not to say anything in the car because of the driver."

"I understand," she said faintly.

He suddenly looked serious. Silva felt a chill run down her spine.

"It took me some time to discover what it's all about," he said, fiddling with his plane ticket, which was lying on the table. "It's a strange business – mysterious, you might say, in some ways. But what's certain is that your brother and some other tank officers were arrested for refusing to obey an order."

"I knew that," said Silva. "Arian told me . . ."

"Yes, but listen," Skënder went on, still toying with his ticket. "It was an order that I myself, and most other people, would have disobeyed."

"What?"

"And since we'd all have done the same as he did, and we're all free, he ought to be free too, even though they've put him in the nick for the moment."

Silva was about to say, "For the moment . . . ?", but he didn't give her time.

"Don't ask me anything more," he whispered. "I don't know any more myself. But what I *have* told you is absolutely true. For the present, the whole affair is shrouded in mystery . . . But there's no need for you to worry . . ."

It was gradually sinking in. At first what she'd heard had seemed very unremarkable, because she'd been expecting something more detailed, more precise. But now she realized there were some important bits of information buried in what Skënder had told her. In short, she told herself, Arian is innocent! Innocent!

"You do understand, don't you?" he said, putting his hand on hers. "There's no need for you to worry. Perhaps when I get back from China . . ."

"Thank you, Skënder," she faltered. "I'll never forget what you've done for me."

"And here's the cultural attaché!" he cried, smiling at a Chinese diplomat who was coming towards them, together with the foreign relations secretary of the Writers' Union. "How are you, comrade Hun? Well, I trust? Allow me to introduce you: my wife and a friend of ours . . ."

"Great pleasure," said the Chinaman. "Come to wish you bon voyage."

"Thank you, comrade Hun. So the birds are flying to Peking – tweet tweet tweet!"

The Chinese attaché laughed.

"Pretty little things, birds, eh?" he squeaked. "Good for inspiration! Where's the other comrade gone?"

Silva could feel her relief at the news about her brother slowly turning into euphoria. She wanted to laugh and shout. The whole place was full of the buzz of conversation. What a lot of people seemed to be going to Peking . . . Suddenly, among all the travellers hurrying to and fro, she noticed a Chinese with one foot in plaster. Victor Hila's Chinaman! It could only be he!

"Look at that Chinaman over there," she whispered to her friends.

"The one with his foot in plaster?"

She nodded.

"If he's the one I think he is, that foot is behind an absolutely fantastic story."

And to the accompaniment of giggles from Skënder's wife and guffaws from Skënder himself, she told them about the incident between Victor Hila and Ping, the Chinaman.

"Wonderful!" said Skënder. "Incredible! An X-ray of a Chinese foot mixed up with diplomatic notes!" Then, with a sigh: "To think of the country I'm about to be transported to through the air, like Nosferatu!"

His wife's face fell even before she stopped laughing, and Silva recalled the presentiment she herself had had sometimes when Gjergj was in China. I hope to God he never has to go there again! she thought.

230

There was an increased stir of activity in the hall.

"The plane has just got in," they heard someone say.

Outside, it was getting dark.

Over the public-address system a woman's voice asked all passengers travelling to Shanghai to be ready for embarkation.

The three of them stood up and went over to the glass door. Skënder's wife, stifling a sob, kissed him goodbye; Silva did the same. Then both women stood by the window, watching the stream of passengers make their way over to the huge aircraft. Some turned and waved. Perhaps because of the heavy bags they were carrying in either hand, they looked as if they were tottering rather than walking. Through the dusk, Silva made out the figure of C— V—, then that of Ping, hobbling as he brought up the rear. He and Skënder will be travelling together, she thought regretfully.

The passengers were beginning to disappear into the plane. Skënder turned at the top of the steps and waved to them, though probably he couldn't actually see them from all that distance.

"Look!" his wife suddenly exclaimed. "Look who's going up the steps to the plane!"

"Yes, I noticed him before," said Silva, trying to smile. The other woman looked terrified.

"I have a feeling he's a bad omen," she whispered.

Silva wanted to protest, but couldn't find any words.

"Why did they both have to go on the same plane?" asked Skënder's wife fearfully.

The two women stood with their faces pressed against the cold glass until the plane lifted off the runway and vanished into the night.

By the time they got back into the car it was quite dark. They sat for a long time in silence. Silva could see how upset her companion was, but what was there to say? She felt very tired herself. Something Skënder Bermema had said came back to her vaguely – "It looks as though there's something going on in the army" – mingled in her mind with the sound of aircraft engines and the sight of a lone Chinese hobbling after the rest of the passengers on to the plane.

"Well," she thought sleepily, "after all that fuss, all those diplomatic notes and radio messages, after having caused another man's misfortune – how are you really any better off?" She shuddered at the thought that Skënder Bermema might tread on the Chinaman's foot by mistake as they were finding their seats on the plane, and trigger off another scandal . . . "A subtle kind of a novel . . ." – that's how Skënder's wife had described his new book . . . She knew that if she'd been alone in the back of the car she'd have nodded off to sleep.

"Drop in and see me one of these days," said Skënder's wife as the car stopped and Silva prepared to get out. "We can keep each other company for a while."

"Thanks," said Silva. "I'd love to."

They said goodnight, and Silva hurried towards the front door of the apartment block where she lived. Only then did it occur to her that Gjergj must have been worried at her being away so long.

Rumours went on multiplying about an improvement in relations with China, though the press was silent on the subject, apart from a couple of articles in a literary review about the discovery near Peking of the tomb of an early emperor. None of the large freighters said to have set sail on the express orders of Mao Zedong had yet reached the port of Durrës. There wasn't even any news that they'd passed through the Straits of Gibraltar.

The matter of the freighters was the main subject of all conversations, and accounts of their long voyage were so many and various that people came to imagine a vast fleet of ghost ships wandering through the mist. Some observers maintained that it was all deliberately engineered by the Chinese to keep the Albanians in a state of doubt and anxiety.

Enver Hoxha referred to the matter in his speech closing the current plenum of the Central Committee. As he spoke his eyes ranged slowly over the side of the room occupied by members of the government responsible for economic affairs. Everyone else was so quiet you could almost hear their eyes turning towards the group Enver Hoxha was addressing.

Some members of the army were visibly relieved. So the others are in for it, thought Minister D—. Just so long as the thunderbolts don't fall on us!

"In order to modify their general line – in other words, to draw closer to American imperialism – the Chinese have had to prepare the ground and remove any obstacles to such a turnaround. One of the obstacles was the Party. So they made it a puppet of the army, subjected it to the terror of the Red Guards – so much so that they practically annihilated it . . ."

Here Enver Hoxha paused for a moment. His eyes seemed to be seeking out someone. Minister D— felt as if all the columns on the other side of the room were tilting towards him.

"Here too there are some people," Enver Hoxha went on, "not just anyone, but people who have risen to high places, who, perhaps in imitation of the Chinese, perhaps at their instigation – time will tell – have tried . . ."

He paused again. The group of soldiers he was now looking at directly shook in their shoes.

"To try to encircle a Party committee with tanks is tantamount to rehearsing for a military putsch . . ."

This is the end, groaned Minister D—. He'd never have dreamed it could all finish so suddenly. The columns that had hitherto seemed to be leaning towards him now appeared to be falling on top of him. Between the blows the voice of Enver Hoxha came to him, at once distant and deafening.

"I can't say for certain that it was done with evil intent. I'd prefer not to have to believe such a thing. But that's not the point . . . The point is that the order was not carried out, and such orders never will be carried out in Albania, no matter who issues them. And that's what's so marvellous, comrades! It is not through decrees and orders, but if necessary *against* them, that our great popular mechanism, acting of its own accord, without being commanded by anyone, defends our glorious Party!"

Popular mechanism! moaned Minister D—. Acting of its own accord . . . He couldn't imagine anything more frightful.

But could he himself escape its tentacles? Was all hope lost? "I can't say for certain that it was done with evil intention. I'd prefer not to have to believe such a thing . . ." He felt like yelling out, "That's right, comrade Enver! I didn't mean any harm!" But he was buried beneath all those columns, his mind was reeling, neither his breath nor his voice would obey him.

"The Chinese have recently shown signs of desiring a rapprochement," Enver Hoxha continued. "They've even expressed regret for some of their attitudes. For our part, we have no wish to add fuel to the flames. If anyone holds out the hand of friendship to us, we hold out our own hand in return. But time will tell if these gestures are sincere or not. At all events, *we* are prepared for anything, either way."

The plenum ended late in the afternoon. As the members of the Central Committee drifted out of the room in groups, Minister D— muttered to one of his pale-faced aides:

"Should we free the tank officers right away?"

"Isn't it a bit late for that?" said the other faintly.

"Let 'em out at once!" said the minister, through clenched teeth.

Ekrem Fortuzi stood on the edge of the pavement watching a convoy of cars drive up the central boulevard. He concluded there must have been a meeting of the highest importance somewhere. A plenum, perhaps, he thought, patting his briefcase as if to check how nice and full it was.

When the traffic thinned out he crossed over. They could have as many plenums and congresses as they liked, so long as his case had plenty in it! He stroked it as he might have stroked his stomach after a good meal.

He was in a very good humour. After a month and a half without any requests for translations from Chinese, he'd suddenly been given four different jobs at once – all urgent, too! He was hurrying home to give his wife the good news.

"Oo-ooh!" he called from the hall. But he could tell from the sound of running water that his wife was in the bathroom. "I've got good news for you, darling!"

She didn't hear, so after hanging up his coat and hat he went to the bathroom door. But before letting her know he was there, he bent down and had a look through the keyhole. H'mm, pretty well-stacked, especially from this angle . . . He waited until a chance movement showed him her pubic hair, looking darker and more bushy than it was in reality.

Then, as she emerged from the bathroom with a towel round her head:

"Good news!" he told her.

"Some translations?"

"Yes!"

"Good! That means they're patching things up?"

"It looks like it."

While she was plucking her eyebrows in front of the mirror, he paced up and down telling her about his successful tour of the various offices.

"Is the work you've got worth twenty thousand leks?" she asked.

"Well, I couldn't really say. I think . . ."

"Don't try to pull the wool over my eyes, Ekrem!"

"Pull the wool over your eyes! For heaven's sake!"

"I repeat – is it worth twenty thousand?"

"How should I know? Perhaps."

"My astrakhan coat is completely worn out."

"Hmph!"

"Never mind about 'hmph'! I'm sick of wearing that horrible old thing!"

"Just as you say, my dear."

"I don't want to look like one of those floozies at the National Theatre playing some aristocratic dame from the past . . . I want a nice new fur coat . . ."

"As you wish, my love. And in return, what about letting me have this little fleece, eh? The more you use it the sweeter it is . . ."

She was glad he'd said "The more you use it" rather than "The older it gets . . ." For some reason he couldn't explain, Ekrem found the word "use" arousing. As arousing as the image of her sex being penetrated by another had been a few years ago, when he'd been sure she was deceiving him.

He leaned over and whispered something in her ear, at the same time breathing in the perfume from her neck.

"All right, all right!" she said. "There's no need to grunt like a pig. God, when will you manage to be a bit more elegant?"

He prowled round her chair in delight.

"And don't whisper rude words in Chinese at the critical moment, either! I don't like it!"

"But Chinese works me up, my pet!"

She pulled a face.

"You've got a positive gift for sullying everything!"

He opened his satchel to take out the papers that had to be translated.

"Keep those horrible hieroglyphics out of my sight!" she shouted. "And don't go getting undressed – we're going to see the Kryekurts. We haven't congratulated them yet on Mark's engagement."

"Whatever you say, my own."

Half an hour later they were going through the Kryekurts' gate, bearing a large cake. As usual, Hava Fortuzi glanced at the outside staircase leading up to the first floor of the villa. The vines that twined all over it looked pretty lifeless at this time of year.

Inside the house, in addition to Hava Preza, Musabelli, and several other of the Kryekurts' usual guests come to offer their congratulations, there was an elderly couple the Fortuzis hadn't met before. The newcomers got the impression they were interrupting a very pleasant conversation.

"Forgive us for being so late," said Hava Fortuzi. "We couldn't help it. Ekrem's up to his eyes in work as usual, and I had a headache . . . Still, we're here now! All our best wishes to Mark! . . . But isn't he here?"

"Thank you, thank you!" said Emilie. "Mark's in the other room with his fiancée. He won't be a moment . . ."

"Don't disturb them on our account," laughed Hava Fortuzi, with a wink.

"He's teaching her French."

"Oh, French! I think I can speak that kind of French myself!" Hava Fortuzi gurgled. "Ekrem, do you remember the French lessons you used to give me when we were engaged?"

The elderly couple looked shocked. Emilie pursed her lips.

"And to think it's Chinese that you're trying to teach me now!" Hava Fortuzi's mirth had suddenly turned to tears.

"There, there, Hava, my dear . . ." whispered Ekrem, who knew his wife was subject to these mood swings.

It wasn't the first time she'd lost control of herself. But her host and hostess and their guests were taken aback. Only Musabelli wore his inevitable smile.

"Please forgive me!" said Hava Fortuzi, taking a handkerchief and pocket mirror out of her bag.

"It doesn't matter in the least, my dear," said Hava Preza. "It can happen to anyone."

"It's so sad to see how fast time flies."

"Yes, indeed."

"She's hypersensitive," Ekrem explained to the elderly couple. "She may react like this to anything, good or bad. She's always been like this."

Hava Fortuzi was peering into her compact and trying to repair the damage her tears had done to her mascara. When she had made herself presentable again, she cheered up.

"We're so glad about Mark's engagement," she said, shutting her compact with a snap. "Ekrem and I often wondered what he was waiting for . . ."

"His poor grandmother used to worry too, when she was alive . . ."

Ekrem looked at a large photograph hanging on the wall.

"Poor Nurihan, how happy she would have been if she were here today!"

Now it was Emilie's turn to burst into tears.

"And what about you? How's the work going?" asked Hava Preza, to change the subject. "From what Hava says, I gather you're very busy."

"Well . . . I did have a slack period, but now, yes, I am pretty occupied."

"In other words," said Hava Preza, "relations with China are set fair again. Let's hope we shall be the better for it! We were talking about it just before you came. And I thought to myself that you, Ekrem, were the person best placed to tell us what's what."

As soon as the conversation turned back to China, the elderly couple seemed to perk up. Gradually everyone joined in, including Musabelli, and all agreed on one point: the improvement in relations with China was welcome, and they only hoped nothing would happen to spoil it. Occasionally, as they spoke, they would turn to the portrait of old Nurihan, as if asking her for her opinion. She was made for this kind of debate! Each of them thought how surprised she would have been if she could have heard what they were saying! It had all been so different the last time, when Albania broke with the Soviets: for days on end they'd whispered together here in this room, hoping the crisis would get worse and the two governments scratch one another's eyes out as soon as possible, shaking with fright at the least sign of a rapprochement and breathing sighs of relief when such signs turned out to be wrong. Now it was quite the opposite: they trembled at the smallest hint of a rupture, and wished with all their hearts that Albania's friendship with China would last for ever.

As if to get old Nurihan on their side, but also to reassure themselves, they listed all the advantages they could expect to enjoy from such a relationship. How stupid they'd been to be so hostile to the Chinese at first! How sarcastic they'd been about the customs, dress and language of the Chinese, when in fact these same Chinese were really their salvation! It wasn't just a matter of their rapprochement with the Americans, which had come about only recently and served to open their eyes. Long before that there had been other, incredible scraps of information. At first they'd rejected them as absurd inventions, dreams or slanders. But after going into them further and seeking evidence from people who'd been there, they'd come to the conclusion that the Chinese were treating former capitalists very well: some had been made assistant heads of factories, and even, as a signal favour, given a percentage of the profits. This had produced many sighs among the old guard in Tirana: some former factory owners, their hands shaking with age or illness, even started to work out their possible future gains. But they soon had to yield to the facts: however delightful the effects of Sino-Albanian friendship, it was highly unlikely that such a state of affairs would exist here, at least for another couple of generations. After that, who could tell? Their morale then plunged to a very low ebb, until a fresh crop of rumours came to pep them up. Forget about your percentages and other such foolishness, they were told. All that's over and done with. Consider instead the real advantages we can get out of the Chinese. Haven't you heard what's going on there? A storm has been unleashed, sweeping all before it. And recently they've turned on the Party, and they're trampling it underfoot. Imagine, a communist country smashing its own Party! It's a miracle, and that's putting it mildly! That's what you want to watch in China, never mind about the rest. The Party's the key to everything. When you attack the Party you attack the very foundations. And after that, there's nothing left standing. All is disintegration and chaos. It's only people like us, in our little corner, who are left in peace. And you dare to complain? Hush! Keep quiet! Not a word! We're in the front seats, watching the show. In Shanghai and Peking the communists cut one another's throats. The class struggle, the war between the schools of thought and the party lines or whatever the hell they call them now – all this has been transposed to within the Party itself. Their hatred is directed against one another now. And who performed this miracle? The Chinese themselves! And you have the cheek to criticize them? You don't realize what it means to have the communists tearing one another to pieces? Perhaps you'd rather they turned against us? So stop ranting on about the Chinese – just bow your heads and say a prayer for them! They're a godsend to us, the instrument through which divine Providence has chosen to help us!

Such were the arguments that had been bandied about before and that they now adapted to the present situation. That was the truth, and time had confirmed it even beyond their expectations. But now, as then, enthusiasm was punctuated by doubt: would the Chinese continue in the same vein? Mightn't it be a false spring, one of those shows they're so good at? When they'd finished settling scores amongst themselves, mightn't they round more furiously than before on the ex-bourgeois? "You rejoiced too soon! You thought we'd forgotten you, did you? Well, now we're going to hit and club and decapitate any of you we can lay our hands on! . . ."

"I'll never forget when they launched the slogan, *Let a hundred flowers bloom, let a hundred schools compete among themselves,*" said Hava Preza. "That gave us all a flicker of hope again. At last they're loosening their grip a bit, we told ourselves. But what happened? It was only a monstrous trap, one of the most extraordinary ever. The unfortunate butterflies flocked to the meadow covered with daisies, but instead of nectar they found only poison."

"Alas!" sighed Musabelli.

"That was the whole object of the exercise," said Hava Preza. "To attract the butterflies to their doom."

"Alas!" sighed Musabelli again.

"And do you remember what happened next?" The hand holding Hava Preza's cup shook so much that a couple of drops of coffee splashed unnoticed on her dress. "Instead of having a meadow with a hundred flowers in front of us, we were confronted by the Gobi Desert, as poor Nurihan used to say."

"She wasn't often wrong," murmured Musabelli.

But for some time, without venturing actually to interrupt, Ekrem Fortuzi had been shaking his head to show he didn't agree with what Hava Preza was saying.

"Allow me to contradict you," he said finally, as Hava Preza stopped to take a sip of coffee. "It's quite natural that you should be sceptical: we've often been deceived, sometimes quite cruelly, as in the case of the break with the Soviets, on which we'd built such hopes. But this time, believe me, things are different."

"Ekrem's right," said one of the other visitors. "It's not the same this time. Who would ever have thought the Chinese would invite

239

the American president to go and see them? And yet that's what's happened."

"True enough," agreed the others.

"Maybe," Hava Preza conceded. "I only hope you're right! Don't you think I want the same thing as you do? I've wished a thousand times that it should be so!"

"Believe me!" said Ekrem Fortuzi again. He was now quite carried away. "There's no one in the whole of Albania, perhaps in the whole of Europe, who has studied the philosophy of Mao Zedong as thoroughly as I have. I have unravelled all his secrets, understood all his hints, worked out all the symbolical implications of his slogans in a way that is only possible if you study the original texts. While all of you were making fun of me for learning Chinese, that was what I was doing: trying to find the key to the enigma."

"As far as learning Chinese is concerned, you were right," said Hava Preza. "On that subject you were certainly wiser than the rest of us."

"Thanks very much!" said Ekrem. "But where was I?"

"The philosophy of Mao Zedong."

"The enigma."

"Oh yes! Well, after going deeper and deeper into Mao's doctrine I was convinced of one thing: it would be hard to find anyone this century who's done as much for us, the dispossessed bourgeois, as he has. I suppose that sounds paradoxical to you?"

"We're past finding anything paradoxical as far as the Chinese are concerned," said Musabelli.

"Mao is our only hope," Ekrem went on. "He's the one who'll save us from the cursed class struggle that hounds us like the Furies!"

"The class struggle!" said Hava Preza with a shudder. "To think of spending all our lives in the shadow of those three awful words!"

"And you see them everywhere!" cried Musabelli. "On walls, in shop windows, even in love songs sometimes! Sorry, Ekrem – if you ask me, if there's one thing we'll never get free of it's those words!"

"With the help of the Chinese I think we shall," Ekrem answered.

"I doubt it."

"It doesn't seem very likely to me either," said Hava Preza.

"You mark my words," Ekrem insisted. "Especially in the last few years, when they've undergone constant modification, Mao's thoughts have accorded less and less importance to the class struggle – in the end it's become as insubstantial as an opium smoker's dream. Believe me – Mao's philosophy now secretes a kind of drug that brings oblivion, where everything is reconciled with everything else as on the plains of Purgatory . . ."

"Religion deals in reconciliation too," said Hava Preza. "It's been talking about it for two thousand years. Not to mention hundreds of philosophers and poets. So there's nothing new about your Mao."

"There's nothing new about reconciliation itself, I know," Ekrem admitted, "but you can't deny that to hear a communist leader talking about it *is* a bit of a novelty! When religion and philosophy preach general harmony it doesn't help us a bit – on the contrary, the more they talk about it the worse things go for us! But when Mao Zedong talks about it, that changes everything!"

"Yes indeed!" chorused the elderly couple.

"Mao, pastor to a billion human beings, the great helmsman, the red sun of the peoples of the earth, the fourth or fifth great classic of communist doctrine, ha ha!"

"Ekrem is right!" Musabelli conceded.

"Absolutely," said the others.

"And take this challenge to the Party that we've talked about before . . . Don't forget the Party's the main thing, the foundation of everything else. And when the foundations start to crumble you can expect the rest to follow."

"Talking of which, I heard something about some manoeuvres here where some tanks, I think it was, encircled a Party committee . . ."

"What? What?"

"For heaven's sake don't pay any attention to that kind of thing! Tanks, Party committees . . . forget it!"

"Hava's right! Let's get back to the Chinese!"

"Mao!"

"Are we really going to owe our salvation to him? Did we have that treasure all this time without realizing its value?"

"People never appreciate things till they're on the point of losing them."

"No question of losing him!"

"Out of the question!"

"Relations are getting better."

"Things always get sorted out in the end."

"I thought I'd have a fit when I first heard the rumours about a cooling-off! Was the Lord going to abandon us again? Just as fate was smiling on us for once, God seemed to be turning his back on us."

"Ekrem has shown he's got more intuition and perspicacity than any of us."

"That didn't stop you making fun of me!"

"Forget all that now, and recite something to us in that wonderful new lingo of yours."

"By the way, where's Mark got to? He hasn't even put his head round the door!"

"Leave him alone – he's all right where he is! Come on, Ekrem – they tell me you're jolly good at Chinese!"

"Well . . ."

"Now then, Ekrem, don't be coy!"

They could tell that with a bit more persuasion he would perform.

All this could be dimly heard in the next room, by Mark and his fiancée.

"*Il fait froid*," she read from the textbook open in front of her. Then they both looked up and gazed into one another's eyes. Hers looked rather tearful and troubled. "*Il fait froid*," she said again faintly, looking at him as if she expected something from him.

As a matter of fact, soon after they first met and just before they first had physical relations, he had told her about his one previous affair, with a married neighbour whom he'd taught French some years ago. This adventure was closely linked with the words his fiancée had just spoken: when his *cliente* (the only word he could think of now to describe the young woman) had reached the phrase *Il fait froid*, they had abandoned the textbook and made love. The brief episode remained his most vivid memory.

To his astonishment he saw that any reference to this incident upset his fiancée, to whom also he'd started giving French lessons. Every so often she would ask him to tell her about it again: she wanted to know as much as possible about his former neighbour and about his life in general in those days. What is she doing now? she would murmur, imagining one of those lovely, enigmatic creatures who, having had some ups and downs in their love life, are not supposed to be excessively attached to their husbands. Mark told the little he knew, and promised to show the other girl to her when she came back to visit the house (she had grown up in an apartment on the first floor). And what about him – the husband? What did he do afterwards? Was that why they separated? Mark shrugged. He didn't know. He wouldn't have thought so. If it hadn't happened for that reason it might well have happened for another. They were both distant and elusive people, seeming to live in another world. As a matter of fact, perhaps it was all really like that then . . .

"What do you mean – 'it was all really like that'?" asked Mark's fiancée.

He tried to give her some idea of that unforgettable period when everyone lived in a state of wild hope and expectation . . . The atmosphere was incomparably more intense then than now, though of course things were the other way round. In those days they (he nodded towards the other room) longed for sudden change, whereas now they wanted things to stay as they were . . .

"The two periods seem to have quite a lot of things in common, though," mused Mark's fiancée.

He almost told her that the similarity between the two situations might have been the cause of their own engagement, but decided to put it off till later, when they knew one another better. But he himself was convinced that this more than anything else was what had made him want to get married.

"*Il fait froid*," she repeated softly, still with the same imploring expression. "Tell me some more about those days."

"What else is there to tell? As I said, it was like being in a fog . . ."

"Don't you remember some particular incident?" she asked, undressing so slowly she looked as if she might freeze like a statue. "*Il fait froid* – don't you think it's rather cold?"

"I suppose you think the world's turned upside down?"

"What do you mean?" She had been almost panting. Now she held her breath.

He'd thought he'd only said the words to himself.

"That's what she said," Mark answered.

"Why haven't you told me before? What does it mean?"

He tried to explain, but the harder he tried the harder it got.

"What she said applied to the situation in general: she thought

I wanted to see her people stripped of power after the break with the Soviet Union; but she thought it wouldn't happen like that; she thought that by having an affair with me she'd . . ."

". . . she thought she'd lowered herself?"

"Something like that, I believe . . . She was very proud by nature, the daughter of a veteran communist who was also a vice-minister . . . To her, it was sinking pretty low . . ."

"Tell me what else she said."

She brought her moist, imploring eyes closer. Perhaps he shouldn't have told her about all that, he thought. But the next moment it seemed to him his earlier affair probably made him more interesting to her.

After a while, when their breathing had slowed down somewhat, they could hear the old clock ticking, then the hum of the visitors' conversation in the next room.

"Muttering away just the same as before!" he said.

"Just the same as before," she murmured to herself.

He imagined the older people sitting in the same old row on the sofa, like waxworks in a museum.

"All life long the same eternal whisperings!" he exclaimed. "Don't they ever get tired of it?"

"Ssh! I'd like to hear what they're saying. I've never heard what the old guard say to each other before, when they're alone."

"Haven't you?" he smiled. "Well, you'll have plenty of opportunity now! It'll be coming out of your ears!"

"Be quiet!"

She strained to listen, then pulled a face because she couldn't hear properly.

"Put your ear to the wall," Mark suggested.

She got up from the couch and followed his advice. After a few moments she beckoned him to join her.

"Listen!" she breathed, looking surprised and a little bit scared.

He put his ear to the wall. A couple of seconds later:

"Good grief!" he whispered. "They're speaking Chinese! . . . This time they really are losing their marbles!"

Silva had made the necessary preparations for the next day's lunch and was curled up wearily on the living-room sofa when the doorbell rang. She got up with some annoyance, thinking it must be some unwelcome visitor. But when she saw it was her sister-in-law her face lit up.

"Sonia! I'm so glad to see you! Come in!"

As Sonia was taking off her coat, Silva noticed she'd had her hair done very becomingly. She was just going to tease her about making herself beautiful now her husband was back. But, hair-do apart, Sonia looked rather down.

"What's the matter, Sonia? You look upset."

Sonia chewed her lip, but didn't contradict.

"Well, I must say!" exclaimed Silva. "Aren't you two ever satisfied? Instead of being happy that things turned out all right, you still go around with faces like fiddles!"

"Don't you think I've told Arian so?" Sonia retorted. "But I might as well talk to a brick wall!"

"Why? What's wrong?"

"I don't know. But he spends all day moping. I hardly know him."

"Perhaps he's worrying about being expelled from the Party? But I expect they'll reinstate him, don't you?"

"That's what people say."

"But that doesn't cheer him up?"

Sonia shook her head.

"There's something more serious bothering him."

A surge of pity made Silva forget her momentary annoyance.

"I suppose it's understandable. You do your job properly and all of a sudden there's a bolt from the blue and you find yourself chucked out of the Party and into prison. It's horribly unfair – disgusting. But there's no point in letting it get you down . . ."

Sonia sighed.

"That's what I keep saying, but it doesn't stop him being depressed . . . And that isn't all. There's something else . . . and it frightens me . . ."

"What do you mean?" cried Silva, going cold.

"I'm half dead with fear," said Sonia. "One day, when he let himself go for once, he said something terrible . . . I can't get it out of my mind."

"What did he say?"

"We were just sitting talking, and for the umpteenth time I'd said more or less what you just said, and he interrupted me. 'Do you think I'm like this because of what happened to me? Well, it's something quite different that's bothering me! What I can't accept is that both sides, ours and theirs, come out of the business unscathed . . .'"

"What did he mean?" cried Silva.

"Let me finish telling you. 'One side or the other must be declared guilty,' he went on, 'otherwise it's all a lie and the world has been turned upside down.'"

"I don't understand. What other side was he talking about?"

"The people who had them arrested."

"Oh," said Silva, going pale. "But they say it was the minister himself who gave the order for their arrest . . ."

"That's who he means," answered Sonia. "And that's why I'm afraid."

They were both silent for a moment.

"You're right," said Silva. "It's enough to make your hair go white."

"If he goes around saying things like that he'll be back in jail before he knows where he is. And next time . . ."

"Shall I try to talk to him?" asked Silva. "What do you think?"

"I don't know what to say. I doubt if it'll be any use. But you can always try . . ."

Silva remembered Arian's almost untouched plate at Brikena's birthday party. It all seemed to have happened in another age. But now, as then, she felt a pang of anguish.

Minister D— put his name to the fourth document, then stared at his signature. It looked strange. What was happening to him? He picked the paper up and held it closer to his eyes, but it made no difference – his writing was smaller and more cramped, and his surname tailed away pitifully.

How can this be? he wondered. He'd thought a person's signature was always the same – witness the evidence of handwriting experts in court, and the model signatures kept in Swiss banks . . . Perhaps there was something wrong with his sight?

He reached out for the other documents he'd just signed. All the signatures looked alike – shrunken, as if withered by the cold. He remembered that he'd had cramp in his arm yesterday evening. His fingers were still numb. That must be the explanation.

He put the paper down and decided to think no more about the matter. But after a moment he found himself looking at the documents again. Could there be something wrong with his pen? Yes, of course, he admonished himself, shaking his head reprovingly. And he'd almost believed it was that wretched affair that was at the root of everything, altering his voice, his breathing, his taste and finally his signature!

He pressed a bell for his secretary.

"What use are these pens supposed to be? The nibs are as fine as needles – absolutely no use for signing things! Please get me some that are broader – twice as broad, as broad as possible!"

"Very well," said the secretary. He came back soon afterwards with a handful of other pens. "Try these," he said, putting them down carefully on the desk. "They should be all right."

The minister tried one of them on a scrap of paper, then signed his name several times with some of the others, examining each signature closely and trying to persuade himself it was the same as usual.

"What are you still here for?" he asked his secretary rudely, when he noticed him watching placidly. "That'll do – I don't need you any more!"

When he was alone again he put his head in his hands. It wasn't the signature. Something else was wrong. He knew very well why he was anxious, but he refused to think about it. Every morning he hoped the new day would deliver him from his anguish, but it wouldn't let him go. He tried everything. But no matter how many meetings he called, how loudly he pounded on the table and upset the flowers, how fierce the threats he uttered or how severe the punishments he handed out, it made no odds. Every word and gesture seemed somehow muted, the people he chastised seemed to be trying not to laugh. The sound he made when he banged the desk sounded so dull he'd looked under the red plush cover to see if the wood had changed into some other substance.

Was he or was he not still a minister? If other people were asking the question, they had only to dismiss him as soon as possible and put a stop to the whole affair. But who really had the power to do this? Those who were against him were his inferiors – some of them had never sacked anyone in their lives, not even a protocol clerk or a porter. So how could they get rid of him? Nevertheless he felt they'd cast a spell on him.

He vaguely remembered colleagues in other parts of the world –

not in Latin America, where a mere handful of colonels could con-
spire to terrorize a government, but in more serious countries, where
ministers of defence were held in respect, not to say fear. Whereas
he, far from inspiring fear in anyone else, was scared of everyone,
not only people he knew but also the humble civil servant whose
name he couldn't recall and the crowds in the streets who were all
the more terrifying because they were anonymous.

How had it all come about? Those manoeuvres, those tanks, had
been enough to loosen the mysterious screw on which his whole
life depended. What secret, irreversible mechanism had thus been
set off? Hadn't Enver Hoxha spoken of a formidable popular mechanism that started up of its own accord? Was the cause of his own
harassment real or subjective?

The tank officers had been released, but that hadn't helped either.
On the contrary, his anxiety had only increased. He'd expected
they'd write to him, and even calculated how long their letters
would take to write and then to reach him, allowing a margin of
error. But there was no sign of any letters. Perhaps they'd seen the
error of their ways? Again, instead of soothing his fears, his ingen-
uity only increased them. Why on earth didn't they write?

At this point, as if reading his thoughts, his aides suggested his
going on a tour of inspection that had been put off because of the
problems with China. He greeted the suggestion with open arms.
For the first days he was almost happy, sitting there in the back of
his limousine whizzing along the roads, escorted by his staff-cars
and bodyguards. He wondered why he hadn't thought of it before.

He hurried from one regiment or depot to another as if afraid to
slow down, one day visiting a fort on the coast, another dropping
in on a tank brigade, the next on a military airfield. Looking back
through the rear window at barracks, hangars and anti-aircraft
batteries disappearing on the horizon, he told himself he must have
been out of his mind to think other people had doubts about him.
He felt like laughing at the very idea now. How could anyone throw
the least suspicion on him, when he had all these guns and tanks
and planes at his disposal – a Latin-American colonel could overthrow any number of governments with only a tenth of them! He
himself had never used them except for manoeuvres, for a mere
game. Could he have set people against him just for that?

He almost choked with resentment. Instead of looking askance
at him they ought to be grateful! Anyone else in his position would

have been aggrieved. Like anyone falsely accused and tempted to get his own back by committing the very crime that had been wrongly attributed to him, he was almost ready to organize a putsch! They were almost forcing him into it, instead of thanking him for abstaining.

He gazed out at the bare winter landscape, ruminating. If he came to a decision, would he be capable of translating his ideas into reality? He didn't have to think twice about that!

But on the fourth day of his tour, he felt his confidence wane once more. He remembered the speech about a popular mechanism that triggered itself off like the system for restoring the current when the electricity breaks down. Again he found himself wondering where, in which offices, the levers of command were to be found.

By the roadside, at the crossroads, outside railway stations and at the entrance to almost every village, his eyes met with slogans: *Party-People-Unity . . . No power on earth can break the unity between Party and people . . .* Some were handwritten on walls, others on metal hoardings, but a few were picked out in stones, or cut out in the grass, on hillsides. He had the impression there were more of them now. Sometimes it occurred to him that invisible hands had put them there the day before, especially for him. Where did their orders come from . . . ?

The thought of that mechanism terrified him more every day. He imagined it in various different forms, but finally saw it as a mass of telephone wires, weather gauges, snares, hidden microphones and rusty old fox-traps, the whole lot stowed away on some distant stretch of wasteland. Perhaps its dilapidated appearance was only a camouflage . . . And it was all controlled from some unimaginable place – he wouldn't have been surprised to learn that the orders came from underground, from the kingdom of the dead. And so he couldn't consider it as a source of salvation.

Whoever attacks the Party devours himself! He looked back to check whether the slogan had been real or only an illusion. But the plain was shrouded in fog and he couldn't see anything. I'm seeing things, he thought. The slogan hadn't been in the usual style. He turned round again, rubbed his eyes, but the fog hid everything. He wouldn't have been all that surprised to find he was having hallucinations. He felt like shouting, Stop writing messages to me on the hills! Can't you see I can't do anything about them?

On the fourth afternoon of his tour he felt his voice going different again. And he noticed again a certain slackness in the soldiers' salutes, a certain lack of polish on their helmets and even on the barrels of heavy artillery pieces and anti-aircraft guns. He had a feeling that if he'd given the latter the order to fire, they'd only have produced silent flashes and blank projectiles, the sort you sometimes see in dreams.

What if it was all a nightmare? Anyhow, he couldn't give orders to the army now. He pleaded indisposition and interrupted the tour.

And there on his desk in the office there lay the long-awaited letter with its dozens of signatures. He sat and looked at them for a long while, as if to say, Now what am I going to do with you?

II

A FEW BIRDS CROSSED the vast north-west frontier. Some others took off from the jungle, accompanied by millions of insects, to over-fly the southern borders. Nothing and no one could cross the Himalayas, and the seaboard turned back any birds setting off from that direction. So the plane carrying Skënder Bermema and C— V—, his colleague, was one of the relatively rare winged objects to enter Chinese air-space that winter morning. The thought of their delegation being invited on the occasion of the Day of the Birds had given rise to all the inevitable pleasantries. But most of these had been exhausted before they left Albania, the last of them on the way to the airport, and now all that was left of the joke was a half-hearted smile or two. The great day was today or the day after, but they weren't likely, thought Skënder Bermema, to see any actual birds. His thoughts, already numbed by sleeplessness and the fatigues of the journey, were assaulted by the immense space that seemed to rise at him from below.

That's China down there, he kept telling himself, to drive home what was happening to him. But apart from the sight of three or four birds crossing the Mongolian frontier, his mind was a blank.

C— V— drowsed beside him, his head leaning on the back of his seat. His open mouth and heavy though not loud breathing made him look rather vulnerable, but didn't evoke any pity. Perhaps you're dreaming of a world without writers, thought Skënder. Well, you've got a country like that underneath you, the first in the history of the human race.

Almost before he'd completed the thought, Skënder himself fell asleep. The plane drilled on into the great continent. Below, half China was in the grip of winter. Men, animals and plants all struggled against the cold. Vast, dark, unexplored caves in the bowels of the earth, the kind that engender earthquakes, contained only silence. Another metastasis silently formed in the Chinese prime minister's right side. But this was only one of billions of phenomena to occur that winter's day.

The Hsinhua press agency didn't announce the delegation's arrival until forty-eight hours later. A brief communiqué ended with the words: "Our Albanian guests were met at Peking airport by the official in charge Chung." Next day there was another terse bulletin about the dinner held for the guests at the Peking Hotel, hosted by the same official in charge Chung.

"What's his job then, 'official in charge Chung'?" asked Skënder Bermema, examining the communiqué. "What's he in charge of? I've never seen anything so vague."

C— V— shrugged.

"The Writers' Union has been dissolved – someone had to meet us and invite us to dinner."

"That strikes you as normal, does it?" asked Skënder gloomily.

C— V— looked evasive and shrugged again, as if trying to avoid an argument.

"It's their business," he muttered.

The next day their programme took them off to south-east China. Every provincial paper gave its own muddled account of the event. One connected the visit with the Day of the Birds, another linked it to a campaign to exterminate sparrows, while a third talked of the inauguration of a large incubator. But if the provincial press was vague, that was nothing compared with the nebulousness of the reception the two writers received from their erstwhile Chinese colleagues, now squelching about in the paddy-fields. These unfortunates, far from thinking of writing anything about the visitors, were terrified of birds and anything else that might evoke their now despised art. They'd been under the impression that writers had been wiped off the face of the earth for ever, and now here were two of them roving all over China! Their reaction was a mixture of excitement, terror, confusion and curiosity (why had they come?). The total effect was one of aversion from themselves and anything that reminded them of what they used to be. They were particularly uneasy at night, perhaps because they then sensed the presence of the visitors somewhere up in the sky. They tossed and turned on their pallets, groaning in their sleep. Why had they done it?

The two Albanians flying overhead from province to province were unaware of all this. Only once, late in the evening, when their plane was coming in to land over some nameless town, Skënder Bermema, looking casually out through the window, thought he glimpsed something tragic through the moonlight glittering over the rice-fields. There must be writers there somewhere, he thought drowsily. He stared at the muddy waters as if looking for traces of human souls.

Peace be upon them, O Lord, he found himself murmuring. He was surprised at these words from his distant past. He was still more amazed to realize that his hand, slowly and clumsily, as if weighed down by the clay of the graveyard, had just made the sign of the cross.

As soon as he opened his eyes Skënder thought it must be Sunday. It seemed to be written on the silk curtains of his hotel room. Unable to pursue his thoughts further, he turned over and went to sleep again, muttering, "It's Sunday." He woke again, and went to sleep again, a little later, rejoicing in the fact. They'd been in China for three weeks and this was their first day of rest.

He was exhausted. At one point during the night it had seemed to him, for some reason, that this build-up of fatigue was due to the chain of Byzantium, the great rusty chain that had been lying on the bed of the Bosphorus since 1449, when it was put there to protect the city from the Turkish fleet. There it still lay, lonely and overgrown, unseen by human eye. The idea struck Skënder as so unbearable he heard himself groan in his sleep.

He woke and slept, woke and slept again. Time was like a mass of wool, not only because of the peaceful white light that filtered in through the curtains, but also because minutes and seconds tangled with one another to produce a vague sensation now of rest and now of weariness.

The alternation of sleep and waking grew faster: he felt a profound uneasiness. Fragments of dreams first crystallized, then faded . . .

He was at a meeting of the Writers' Union. It was unbearably hot, and someone had proposed that authors' royalties should be abolished. That didn't bother him – to hell with royalties, but if they were abolished the temperature would go up . . . He woke up, smiled, fell asleep again still smiling. After some other, incoherent dreams, he found himself back at the meeting, with someone else suggesting something else should be done away with. He asked the people on either side of him what was going on. Why were they there? What were they going to abolish now? But no one would say. Finally he made it out: they were going to forbid author's names to be put on their works. C— V— was addressing the meeting. "Comrades," he exhorted them all, "let us follow the example of the Chinese and stop putting our names on the covers of our books. The glory belongs to the masses rather than to us . . ." "Yes," said someone. "With a lousy name like yours you've got everything to gain! The sooner the better!" Uproar followed. Those with Muslim patronymics shouted the loudest.

When Skënder woke again, all he remembered was the room where the meetings were held. He hadn't been in Tirana when those famous proposals were put forward, but he'd heard so much about it he felt as if he'd attended all the meetings. They'd gone on for days, with the heat made even worse by the noisy breaks spent drinking bottles of orangeade. Not to mention the bright red hair of the Tirana Party secretary, well known for his pro-Chinese sympathies.

"I should like to inform the meeting that I have renounced the royalties of four thousand new leks due to me for my latest novel . . ."

This was greeted by shouts and interjections all over the room. It was hard to tell whether they were expressions of approval or disapproval, or merely sarcastic laughter. C— V— was in the seventh heaven. He was speaking for the third time running. They were still discussing the removal of author's names from literary works. Q—, the playwright, had just pronounced against it.

"I don't see what you can put in its place," he said. "A book is the work of someone, isn't it? What *are* you going to put on it? – the name of the place where he was born? the members of his executive committee? perhaps the local farm cooperative!"

Amidst the laughter, C— V— glared at the previous speaker and took the rostrum:

"I don't at all approve of the way the previous comrade approaches the problem. Nor of the laughter with which he was received. All that is the result of an unwholesome intellectualism which we ought to have thrown off by now. Some people think it's wrong to suppress authors' names – they're quite scandalized at the idea. But I'd like to ask those comrades: don't you think it's even more scandalous that thousands and thousand of ordinary people toil away on all the fronts of socialism without asking for their names to be advertised, without seeking any vain notoriety? Have those comrades ever reflected on the fact that our heroic miners, our worthy milkmaids, our noble cooperative farmers have never asked to have their names on coal trucks or milk churns or sacks of wheat? Why do they think it would be so terrible if their names no longer appeared on their books?"

The party secretary nodded his agreement. The Minister of Education and Culture, also at the meeting, did the same. But when a voice from the back of the room piped up, "What shall we put instead of the author's name? The name of a cornfield or of an irrigation canal?" it was greeted with more hoots of laughter. The secretary lowered his large head menacingly, and said loudly to C— V—, "Go on, comrade, even if what you say isn't to everyone's taste."

Skënder closed his eyes for one last doze, then lay for a while trying to make up his mind which was more disagreeable, returning to the world of sleep or plunging into the world of consciousness.

When he woke up for good his head felt heavy. Sunday still seemed to be written all over the curtains, but less clearly than before. The void inside him was so tangible it was as if there were another person beside him. What's the matter with me, he thought, thrashing about in the bed. But the void wouldn't go away. He lay still for a few minutes looking up at the chalky white ceiling and depressively projecting concentric circles on to it. He suddenly realized that the strange body inside him was none other than his own unborn novel.

He lay on motionless between the white sheets. For several days now he'd felt the book stirring, groaning, slowly asphyxiating. And now, this Sunday dawn, his novel had started to give up the ghost.

What could he do to keep it alive? Where could he go? To whom could he protest? He could feel the book growing cold inside him, like a corpse. I should never have agreed to come on this trip, he told himself. Wandering around in the midst of this dehumanized society had killed his novel. For days he'd been feeling it leave him, evaporating, drying up as if in the desert.

Well, it wasn't surprising. He should have expected it. Still lying there, he remembered what Gjergj Dibra had said about the aridity of human contacts in China. He'd laughed at the time, not suspecting he'd be experiencing it himself one day.

The death of human relationships, that was the cause of everything. Human relationships are at the root of everything, and here they'd managed to annihilate them. They'd stifled and dehydrated them until they turned into thorny cacti. "What wouldn't I have given for an ordinary conversation," Gjergj had told him. "A conversation between thieves sharing out the swag would have done, so long as it was the real thing!"

He rubbed his temples. Chance alone couldn't explain what had happened. It had all been orchestrated in accordance with some diabolical plan. In order to do away with literature and the arts, you have to start by atrophying human speech. For three thousand years it had been cultivated. Without this marvel, life would be mere primitive stammerings. And now Mao Zedong had come to strangle it.

Is such a thing conceivable? he wondered. He contemplated the white ceiling. No, it couldn't be true! He remembered the titles of some Chinese poems he'd read: *Conversation by Moonlight, Conversation with My Friend Van on Mount Tian Kun in Late Autumn, Conversation with Lu Fu on the Day of the First Snow* . . .

Carried away by the memory, he threw off the bedclothes and stood up. When he looked in the mirror on the wall his face looked rather pale, and if they hadn't been his own eyes he'd have said they were cold as ice. Sleep with a blind man and you wake up cross-eyed. Where had he heard that saying?

He looked at the wall between his room and C— V—'s. We may be in the same hotel, thought Skënder, but I'm as far away from him as ever. And leagues away, light-years away from this Chinese Milky Way. So you may think, said a voice inside him. But your novel's dead, just the same.

He began pacing frantically round the room, not only his expressions and gestures but everything about him reflecting his exasperation. He felt as if the death of his novel had completely destroyed his equilibrium. People talked about lack of vitamins and shortage of red or white corpuscles, but how did you feel when a work you'd been carrying for months in your body and mind was removed?

He was still flinging about when there was a knock at the door. It was C— V—.

"So you're up, are you?" he asked, poking his head into the room. "Coming down to breakfast?"

Skënder looked at him as if he were a murderer.

"I don't want any breakfast," he said.

"Suit yourself," said C— V—, shutting the door.

Skënder growled. The room felt too small for his pacings. This trip, he thought. Before they'd left, the secretary of the Writers' Union had said, "There may be some friction between you, but I'm sure all that will be forgotten. I hope the trip will bring you together."

Skënder growled again. This cursed trip.

Every day the relations between the two of them grew colder. The offer of a cigarette or a lighter, some word exchanged in the car, might seem to ease things for a bit, but by the evening, when they went to their separate rooms, the tension would be worse than ever.

I should never have come, he told himself again. Or at least not with him. He'd thought he'd be able to put up with him. For years he'd despised him, but that was all. In China his feelings had started to intensify. He'd thought that despite their different views about things, the fact of being thrown together into that great ocean of Chinamen would bring them together. But precisely the opposite had happened.

It had become obvious with Skënder's first attempts to talk to C— V— about the silly things they came up against everywhere they went. He'd known C— V— had a soft spot for anything Chinese, but he'd never have thought his admiration was such that he wouldn't listen to a joke about the crass stupidities even the Chinese themselves must be ashamed of. That was Skënder's last attempt to get closer to his travelling companion. It's ridiculous! he grumbled, going back to his room at nine in the evening when he'd have liked to talk with someone till dawn in this strange hotel thousands of miles from home. He couldn't forgive C— V— for being so unapproachable. It would be easier to communicate with an ape! Then he calmed down, reflecting that it was only natural. Given that C— V— was so fascinated by everything Chinese, he was bound to be against any kind of dialogue. And perhaps after all it was better so. Heaven only knew what construction he might have put on what Skënder said to him, and he might well send in a report about it to the Party committee when they got back to Albania. Skënder thought of the day when he'd glanced through the open door of C— V—'s room and seen a lot of papers on his desk. "What are you writing?" he'd asked. "The same as you," C— V— had answered spitefully.

The same as me, thought Skënder now, standing by his own desk. It too was strewn with papers. Well, one thing is certain, he told himself – we're definitely not writing the same thing!

He picked up one of the pages, read a couple of lines, then put it down and looked at another. He hadn't re-read any of this since he'd started writing it: it was a kind of travel journal, or rather "nocturnal", since it was during the night that he'd jotted down these impressions, reflections and notes of ideas for future works.

Perhaps this was what had made him abandon his novel? What a depressing thought! He shoved the papers aside. His eye lighted on his suitcase, standing in a corner. He went over to it, slowly and cautiously, as if afraid to break some spell. The draft of his novel was inside the case, right at the bottom.

Good Lord, even the handwriting looked wrong! It seemed to have grown dull and shrivelled from being shut up like that.

He leafed clumsily through the exercise book to which he'd con-signed his work. There were all kinds of notes and sketches: parts of chapters, descriptions of characters, different versions of the same scene. Every so often there were scraps of verse, accounts of dreams, chapter headings, odd episodes that might or might nor be incorpor-ated into the novel: such as one passage, for example, called *The Soliloquy of the Sphinx*. Other scraps: "Three in the afternoon, the time of day he always dreaded . . ." "Men's beauty contest, Doomed Heights 1927."

The bits of poetry were so ethereal they looked as if the slightest breath might harm them, turn them solid. The psychological notes were incredibly subtle, with streaks of unorthodoxy that made them all the more compelling.

"Snow in Tirana, 18 January 1967, the morning after the inaug-uration of the equestrian statue of Skanderbeg. The prince waking up under the snow. His cloak and his horse all white. Inhabitants of the capital crowding round. A voice says: 'The snow's a good sign, a good omen . . .'"

He skipped a few pages.

"The beach at Durrës in the 30s. The fashions in bathing costumes. Loulou the courtesan's sunshade. The king's afternoon coffee time. The whole history of the monarchy is there: alliances, factions, rivalries, sexual perversions. And the sand, the sand . . ."

Some pages further on there were observations about winter. "Hail falling outside. The windowpanes rattle, the shutters bang against the walls. But harsh and stinging as it may be, hail has something feminine about it that seems to pervade the rest of the day. The morsels of ice come down as if there were furious women up in the sky, tearing the beads from their pretty necks and hurling them to the ground. And if one listened properly one would hear their angry voices saying, through the rattling windowpanes, 'I'll never take you back again – never!'"

Streets and parks were described turning white. It might have been only a dream, but the page on which it was written had a date: 17 March. Under the date was a hasty note: "11.30, urgent meeting at the vice-minister's."

Skënder went on leafing through the notebook. The handwriting seemed to get more and more careless.

He tended to pause at the poetry, perhaps because it was comparatively rare. "How often have I ignored your tears . . ." "I loved you and knew it not . . ."

> One morning when I woke
> The world without you seemed empty.
> I realized what I'd lost,
> And knew what I had gained.
>
> My sorrow shone like an emerald,
> My joy glowed like a sunset.
> Which was the brighter of the two
> My heart could not decide.

To whom were those lines addressed? He couldn't remember. He'd never told anyone about this phenomenon in case it was seen as the affectation of a philanderer, though he cared as little about that sort of criticism as about the more facile kinds of praise. As a matter of fact, in most cases he genuinely had forgotten the origins of his poems. Even when one seemed to refer to a real-life episode, the nature and dimensions of that episode would somehow change, would merge with other episodes. And the same applied to the person originally involved: his or her own eyes might well, in Skënder's verses, come to shed the tears of another. As time went by these modifications, these individual landslips, built up into something like a shoal of shifting sands, and Skënder, coming upon a set of initials in the title of a poem, would pause in surprise, having remembered the lines as dedicated to someone else.

"Happiness and to spare. Viola . . ."

He smiled.

Had she really been called Viola, or had that name stayed in his memory because she was studying the violin? He could remember quite clearly the night of their chance meeting, one May; the hours they'd spent dancing together; then her hair spread out on the pillow. As he gazed at those tresses – and looking at the hair of a sleeping woman always seemed to him like watching a projection of his dreams – he tried to understand why she was toying so lightly with her own happiness, heedlessly drawing him with her to the brink of hell. She was beautiful, and he'd thought to himself she had happiness and to spare, like a pond brimming over in spring. Perhaps her happiness too needed to be drained, to avoid some fatal excess . . .

As he read on, first his fingers and then his whole body grew deathly cold.

". . . The sound of music wafted in through the north-facing windows; from those facing south came the strains of another song . . ."

". . . Inside his studio, all was golden silence. His wife, still beautiful, but pale from her recent abortion, sat on the couch reading a magazine. It seemed to him the walls of the room had pulled back to contain these treasures, garnered not from gain but from loss . . . He reached out and touched her pale cheek . . ."

". . . Evenings at the Strazimirs'. I used to enjoy these gatherings. There was always something more than met the eye – a hidden sweetness that even shone out of the stones in the women's rings. Sometimes it seemed to me these jewels lit up before the eyes of their owners' did. While the women themselves still held back, their diamonds and rubies would sparkle at each other in anticipation . . ."

Enough! Skënder pushed the book aside. He was well aware that, next time he opened it, these loops and scrawls would have finally disintegrated there in their coffin; would probably be quite illegible. As often happens in such circumstances, the colder, harder side of his nature now got the upper hand.

"That's that!" he exclaimed harshly, slamming the book shut. He felt it was the existence of its contents that had made him feel so on edge.

The notes he'd written since he'd been in China were lying nearby. Perhaps, to even things up, he ought to crumple them up too – ought to curse them and chuck them away. But he couldn't bring himself to do it.

Instead he drew up a chair, pulled the lamp nearer, and started to read.

. . . Yesterday, at a commune called "Sino-Albanian Friendship", we were introduced to a *trifshatars*. It took me hours to find a way of translating those blasted ideograms into some sort of equivalent in Albanian. Literally it's something like "man-triple-peasant", but it might be clearer to render it as "3 x peasant". But even that doesn't fully convey the essence of the person we met yesterday – a sample of a new race of men, the natural product of a climate dominated by the philosophy of Mao Zedong, a unique human type with an exceptionally high rusticity ratio. There he stood on the edge of his rice-field, as difficult to describe in ordinary language as to paint in ordinary colours. According to our Chinese escorts, he was a new type of peasant, from whom all individualism had evaporated like moisture from a well-fired pot – devoid of any vestige of intellectualism, free of all traces of urban mentality and all that goes with it.

He'd been elected to represent the commune at the great Peasant Congress soon to be held in Peking, no doubt in the presence of Mao Zedong himself.

"I suppose the Congress will celebrate the birth of this new Chinese peasant," I said.

"Not necessarily," said one of our guides. "China's a big country, and it wouldn't be surprising if the popular masses produced even more advanced models."

"You mean 4 x and even 5 x peasants?" I asked. "What do you suppose *they* would be like?"

My tone implied, "Who needs monsters like that!" My guide had got the message and looked at me askance. I turned to C— V— for support. But he was scowling at me with disapproval too.

THE COMMITTEE FOR THE BEGETTING OF LEI FEN –
SYNOPSIS FOR A SHORT STORY.

The committee had been pregnant with its offspring for some time. While everyone knows the gestation period for a woman is about nine months, no one knows how long it lasted in the case of the Virgin Mary, from the time she was impregnated by the Holy Ghost to the time she gave birth to the Infant Jesus. This being so, the length of the committee's gestation period would hardly have mattered if there hadn't been a phone call, a week before, from the General Bureau, insisting on an immediate delivery.

The committee members didn't know what to do. There'd been rumours going around Peking lately, suggesting that theirs wasn't the only committee established for this purpose: there were others in the capital equally pregnant with the thoughts of Mao Zedong. As a matter of fact, the man who'd rung up from the General Bureau (or *Zhongnanhai*, as they called it) had not only given the order very curtly, but he hadn't bothered to disguise the threat that hung over them if they were late: their offspring would simply be rejected. Let their committee make no mistake: it wasn't the only one from whom the State had ordered a child.

So it was now clear that in Peking, and perhaps in other Chinese cities, there were scores, perhaps hundreds of committees all endeavouring to perform the same task.

"Good Lord!" exclaimed the committee chairman as he replaced the receiver. "They've turned this country into one vast maternity hospital!" And within the week all the committees would bring their offspring to the General Bureau, which would choose just one from amongst the numerous candidates.

"Just one," said the chairman, mopping his fevered brow. And then what? What was going to happen after that? No problem about the rejected infants – they'd be got rid of in the same way as all aborted babies were got rid of. "But what about us? What will happen to us?" They'd probably be sent to some godforsaken commune in the back of beyond, to toil in the rice-fields under a sweltering sun. But not before they'd been made to go through hours and hours of compulsory autocritique, in which they had to own up to any remaining vestiges of bourgeois mentality – individualism, intellectualism, contempt for the people, and so on. Or might they just be given another chance, and tried out on a different task?

For a while the chairman of the committee was completely knocked out. The only thing he could think of was that no expectant mother had ever gone through what his committee was suffering. He cursed their situation up hill and down dale. Then suddenly his mood changed. He looked at his watch, then started ringing up the members of the committee one after the other. They all sounded as if they'd just had their throats cut.

All that week the committee met in practically permanent session. Sometimes they sat until after midnight. The *Zhongnanhai*'s order had been categorical: the file had to be in by Saturday at the latest. It was rumoured that Mao Zedong was taking a personal interest in the matter. He was eager to see the various models submitted by the different committees, and to select from among them one that could be held up as an example to the whole Chinese people. The entire propaganda machine – the press, publishing houses, artists, schoolteachers, universities, television and radio – would be set in motion to popularize the chosen prototype, the *homo sinicus* to which all the Chinese, and even all the Maoists in the world, would be expected to conform.

The members of the committee turned up to every meeting puffy-eyed with fatigue and lack of sleep. The file on the man to come went on expanding like the belly of an expectant mother. Many things about him had already been decided, but others still awaited a solution. Hours were spent discussing each one. For example, though they'd thought it would be quite easy to fix how tall he should be, they soon found they were wrong. At first they reckoned he should be quite tall, but then one section of the committee denounced this as bourgeois individualism, since exceptional stature might be linked with a desire to be different from other people. This section now won majority support with the suggestion that the ideal man should be short, though some thought this might be regarded as a defect. The former advocates of tallness put up a last-ditch struggle for medium height, but this was dismissed as an unsatisfactory compromise. The qualities so far agreed upon for the ideal man were rehearsed – simplicity, modesty, desire to be only a humble cog in the wheel of Maoist thought, and, above all, determination never to distinguish himself by any kind of originality (in other words, to be as ordinary as possible in the most ordinary of possible worlds). The majority concluded that shortness went best with all these characteristics; and so the vote for it was carried.

When this was noted on the file, the chairman still had plenty on his plate. There were a number of points outstanding, and the Saturday deadline was approaching fast.

On the Wednesday and Thursday the committee sat almost non-stop. Age, profession and family status were all dealt with fairly easily: the model man was to be twenty-five years old, a soldier, and a bachelor, without any sentimental attachments but love of his mother. But what about behaviour in everyday life, ideological training, and judgment? These questions took up most of the remaining time. Despite the members' weariness, the committee's discussions became more lively. Although it was agreed that our hero – as one to whom pride, individualism and love of material comforts were all alien – was capable of collecting old toothpaste tubes and selling them for the benefit of the State, one committee member was afraid this might make him resemble negative and miserly characters like Pliushkin in Gogol's *Dead Souls*. This objection was soon swept aside, but it had raised an issue that made the whole committee frown. Our man would have no interest whatsoever in the miserable rags known as novels, they said. They consoled themselves with the thought that future generations wouldn't even have heard of their existence. Not for nothing was the great Mao working to wipe every form of literature off the face of the earth.

There followed some embroidery on the theme of our hero's modesty. His extreme self-effacement might make some people in Europe regard him as degenerate, subhuman. But Mao had taught them to take no notice of what the Europeans thought, or the wicked Americans either. Yes, the committee's creation would be content just to be a tiny, anonymous cog in a wheel. And it would be a good idea if he copied this slogan out in his journal.

The committee had already decided that the future hero should write down not only his thoughts but also his acts. They had discussed at length whether these records should take the form of letters, articles, or reports made during political training sessions. Other possibilities were denunciations to the Party committee or the relevant ministry. But in the end a kind of personal log-book was judged to be most appropriate. A sub-committee of two was working on a mock-up of this log-book, containing individual examples of thoughts and actions already agreed on in principle.

Thursday's session lasted till three the next morning, when the chairman suggested they take a break before tackling the last item on the agenda. The members, preparing to take an uncomfortable snooze where they sat, were pleasantly surprised when the chairman said they might go home briefly and get some proper rest. No such concession had been allowed so far that week, and they couldn't believe their ears until the chairman repeated what he'd said. The remaining point concerned the hero's death, and the chairman apparently thought the arms of Morpheus an appropriate preparation for deciding it.

It had been established earlier that the hero must eventually die, for only thus could his words and deeds carry their full weight. Moreover, this would enable them to conceal him if necessary from the curiosity of his contemporaries, especially that of the foreign journalists who were sure to do all they could to obtain an interview with the model man of the new China.

All Friday – the last day before the deadline – was spent deciding on how the model man should die. No one had foreseen that this would be one of the most difficult parts of their task. On the contrary, they'd looked forward to it as a piece of cake, a foregone conclusion.

But Friday morning went by, and so did Friday afternoon, and even when dusk was falling they still hadn't made any progress. In fact, the later it got, the more hopeless it seemed. "My God," groaned the chairman, "now we're really in a mess!"

There was no shortage of suggestions from all quarters, but the meeting kept coming back to where it had started. They felt as if they were shrouded in a thick fog which no one knew how to break through. No sooner would they start debating whether their man should die from natural causes or by accident than an argument would start up as to the kind of final illness that would be most suitable. It mustn't be one of the spectacular, far-fetched maladies that bourgeois intellectuals deemed appropriate for the heroes of their novels: they didn't want any heart attacks, brain haemorrhages or any other maladies indirectly glorifying intellectual labour; nor would they hear of diabetes or leukemia. What they wanted was something nice and ordinary, as simple as the rest of the hero's characteristics and as much a target for the intelligentsia's mockery: a stomach ache, or one of those diseases you get from working in the country or from contact with beasts of burden. Then someone pointed out that a lot of precious time had been wasted on medical talk, when it still hadn't been settled whether death was to be caused by illness or accident. So there they were back again, trying to choose between chance and necessity, fatal accident or mortal illness. This was accompanied by endless quotations from Mao, and these contradicted one another so often, and thus gave rise to such complicated debates, that everyone lost the thread of the argument. They then strayed off to a consideration of the different kinds of accidents, in case this option should be adopted. Was it to be an ordinary accident or an extraordinary one? – a choice even more ticklish than that between ordinary and extraordinary illness. For if the hero was to be run over by a train, fall off a horse, die in a fire or drown in a river, the considerations such happenings aroused might eventually conflict with the general Party line, or affect the struggle between the two factions within the leadership, or, worst of all, add to speculation (it gave you goose-flesh to think of it!) about who was to succeed Chairman Mao.

For hours the committee was buried in these considerations. They ruled out letting the hero be trampled to death by a horse: such an image might provide ammunition for the reactionaries who claimed that the peasantry hampered the progress of the revolution. They were about to consent to his being run over by a train when someone pointed out that this conflicted with Mao's notion that the country should encircle the town: for in this scenario the train (the town) could be said to triumph over the hero (the country). So then they had another think about falling off a horse, until it occurred to two or three members of the committee that the two solutions might be combined, and the hero might perish trying to save a horse from being run over by a train. At first this was greeted as a marvellous idea, but its drawbacks soon became evident. In the course of discussion the permutations and combinations of man, horse and train became so involved that the committee abandoned the tangle in despair. Fire and water then came under review, but they too proved unsatisfactory. For one thing, weren't fire and flames symbols of the revolutionary movement? And as for water, didn't Mao have a special feeling for rivers – witness the many references to them in his Thoughts, and his famous swim in the Yang-Tse, after which millions of Chinese had flung themselves into the sea, into rivers, canals, lakes and ponds and even into cisterns. It would be positively indecent to have the hero drown in a river! – almost tantamount to suggesting that Mao himself had lured him to his fate!

It was half-past three in the morning, and the committee was still discussing the last point on the agenda. Everyone's lucidity was fading fast. All minds would soon be blank, or worse. If we don't finish soon, groaned the chairman inwardly, we'll all go round the bend! At half-past four they were still going on about rivers and ponds and trains trying to run horses over, but by now it was all mere babble. As dawn was breaking, one member of the committee suddenly shouted, as if he'd just woken up: "What, isn't he dead yet? Strangle him, then, for the love of God! Bash him on the head! Anything you like, so long as you put a stop to *our* agony too!"

This outburst at least had the virtue of bringing the chairman to his senses. Mustering such strength as still remained to him, he declared: "I suggest we just say he dies by accident, trying to save a comrade. That's the best I can do. It's all too much for me."

The others all nodded agreement. Their heads were all so heavy the chairman was surprised their necks could support them.

The secretary noted the form of death agreed on, and the chairman was about to close the file when a voice cried: "What about the name? We've forgotten to give him a name!"

The baptism didn't take long. They gave their man the first name that came into their heads. Lei Fen. And the file was closed.

The sun was rising as they straggled, silent as ghosts, out of the chairman's office. The chairman himself sat on for a while at his desk. The file lay in front of him. Then he got up, went over to the window, and watched his colleagues walking away along the empty road. They were as unsteady on their feet as if they'd just given birth! . . .

And then his dazed mind realized what he and his committee really had done: they'd just given birth to a dead man.

Morning found the chairman still there, sitting alone with his file. He gave it to the first messenger who arrived, to deliver to the *Zhongnanhai*. Then, while the man went down the stairs, he went back to the window. He waited to see the messenger emerge and go off down the road with the file under his arm. Then he had to restrain himself from running after him, shouting out to the passers-by, "Stop him! Bring back the monster before it's too late! Kill him as if he were a bastard! Choke this anti-man, this sub-man, this new-born non-man!" Then he himself would catch up with the messenger, snatch the file away from him and tear it to shreds in full view of everyone. As he imagined the scene he clenched his trembling hands, driving his fingernails into his palms as if he were wresting from the file the flesh and bones of the man he and his committee had borne and then killed with such pain.

"Monster!" he croaked, trying to make out the figure of the messenger, now vanishing in the distance. "Monster in the file, spreader of plague – there's nothing to stop you now from infecting the whole of China!"

... Yesterday, meeting with Guo Moruo. He made a very adverse impression on me. He kept saying, "Do you know what I am, compared with Mao Zedong, on the score of intelligence? A three-month-old baby." Then he told us he was worried because the enemies of the régime didn't speak badly enough of him. It kept him awake at night.

"I'm still an intellectual," he said several times. "I'm going to wallow in the mud, then go and purify myself in the river."

I thought about the *trifshatars* ...

THE HOUR OF THE RIGHT – SYNOPSIS

"Listen – this time you can be sure I'm right: the hour of the right has come!"

"I don't believe you ... Don't look at me like that! I just don't believe you, that's all. And if you want to know what I really think, I'll tell you without mincing my words: I don't want to hear any more about it. I've had it up to here! I don't care whose hour has come – the hour of the right, or of the left, or of the half-left, or of the quarter-right! I don't want to know, and that's that! I just want to live the few days left to me normally – I can't bear to listen to all that stuff any longer. I'm tired of it, exhausted by it, I can't take any more!"

"If you want to stop up your ears that's your business. Perhaps you don't want to be committed any more? Perhaps you've grown immune to poison?"

"Stop, Lin Hen – that's enough!" said the other, burying his head in his hands.

They were both sitting in an old tavern where tea was served in tin cups and soon got cold.

"Don't take what I say too hard, Lin Hen. I can't help it either. My nerves are in shreds."

"Do you think mine are any better?"

"Perhaps not . . . But still . . ." – one hand was unbuttoning his shirt – ". . . you haven't got marks like these on your body. Do you see these scars?" He was almost shouting now. "I've had them since the days when 'a hundred flowers were blooming,' when like a fool I thought the hour of the right had come. And do you see this other mark, under my breast? That's a souvenir of the next hour that came, the hour of the left, when in order to wipe out the memory of the hour of the right I tried to be more to the left than necessary, and went to a meeting and stuck a picture of Mao into my own chest."

He drank a few sips of tea, then went on more slowly and thoughtfully.

"I got blood-poisoning, and barely escaped with my life. Because the infection itself was nothing compared to the suffering I had to endure in hospital. My wound became a bone of contention. The staff was divided in two, one group maintaining my wound was an ordinary injury that required normal treatment, their opponents claiming that Mao's picture could be a source of infection, and that I'd injured myself deliberately so as to discredit him. These arguments took place across my bed, where they kept putting on and taking off my bandages according to which party was in charge, and needless to say the debaters soon came to blows. The hospital became a battlefield. I had a raging fever and long periods of delirium, but what I saw in my lucid intervals was even worse than the scenes in my nightmares. Each of the two competing sides got the upper hand alternately. When the right were in the ascendant, the barefoot doctors were beaten to a jelly and their popular remedies trampled underfoot or thrown out of the window. But not for long. When everyone least expected it, the tide of battle would turn and the left be on top again. Then – I still shudder at the thought of it – they would tear off my bandages and call a meeting to examine the prescriptions of their predecessors for detecting implications hostile to Chairman Mao. The following week there would be another reversal, and the doctors of the right, whom their opponents, after giving them a suitable thrashing, had set to cleaning the toilets, emerged once more in their white coats. And so on . . . And all the time I was getting worse . . . I shall never forget it as long as I live! That's why even now my hair stands on end whenever I hear the words 'left' and 'right'. You see, Lin Hen, I have seen hell with my own eyes, and that's why I don't, why I won't . . . !"

His friend looked at him sympathetically, but with eyes still cool and severe.

"I understand all that. Nevertheless, the hour of the right has come, Vun Fu. In fact, the things you've just told me about are so many warning signs."

"How can you still believe that?" said the other, buttoning his shirt up slowly, as if wanting his scars to be seen one last time.

"They're going to allow private shops and reopen the churches," said the other.

Autumn in Peking

A flock of wild geese rises into the sky.
  The last golds of autumn are dimmed for ever.
  Winter approaches bearing cold and frost,
Its dreary greys, and a plenum to liven it up . . .

The *datsibaos* in Peking on a rainy day. The long wall covered with dozens of posters fluttering in the wind. Dreariness by the mile. Bits of rain-soaked paper full of thousands, millions of horrible insults. Genuine anti-autumn!

❊   ❊   ❊

AND YET . . . I have to write this in capital letters. And not just once, but over and over, three, three hundred times. And yet. And yet. And yet . . .

And yet, yes, they're a great people, and it would be small-minded not to bear witness to that in these notes. Though they make up only a quarter of the human race, the Chinese have probably endured half of all its sufferings. If anyone ever wrote a *History of Hunger*, the Chinese would be the main characters. The immense poverty, the immense hunger, the immense backwardness of an old world. The strength that could change all that must have been immense too.

The Chinese have had that strength. You'd have to be insane or reactionary not to admit it. They demolished that old world, and the dust from its ruins now floats over their country. On the one hand are the ravings of the Cultural Revolution, on the other the ancient ghosts. In what immemorial archives did they find the model for their current relations with us? From what imperial chancelleries did they derive these factional struggles for power, the icy guides and officials who separate us like a wall from the ordinary people?

And yet. And yet. And yet . . . Strange – I think I'm going to miss this country.

12

SKËNDER BERMEMA PUSHED his notes aside and rubbed his aching forehead. He found it hard to turn away from one last manuscript, though. Should he read it or not?

He'd dashed it off in three nights in a dreary hotel in Chang Ha, on the basis of an incident he'd been told about. Now he was as curious to see what he'd made of the story as if someone else had written it.

And his eyes had started to read it without waiting for him to make up his mind:

SPIRITUALIST SESSION IN THE TOWN OF N—.
SYNOPSIS FOR STORY.

1

The little boat dropped anchor in the river port at N—, just to unload a few crates marked "Insecticide" in black letters. It was late on a cold September afternoon, and by the time the boat had plunged back into the mist, the crates, together with the two men who seemed to be guarding them, were on a Xin Fu truck driving hell-for-leather towards the town centre. Later, when a lot of people claimed they could dimly remember that distant afternoon, they found it difficult to specify any details. As a matter of fact, apart from the man in charge of the little port and his two clerks, no one had witnessed the unloading of the crates from the boat or their swift loading on to the lorry. And not even the men in the port had been in a position to notice the strange fact that the Xin Fu truck, instead of pulling up outside some farm commune or municipal office or depot for hotel supplies, had disappeared into the yard at the back of the Department of Public Safety.

It seemed to be expected. No sooner had they seen the door of the truck fly open than Tchan, the director, and his assistants rushed over. From the way they all bowed, it was clear that the men guarding the crates were extremely important.

"We would have come to the port to meet you, but we were instructed . . . by wire . . ."

"I know," interrupted one of the new arrivals coldly. "Is everyone here who ought to be here?"

"Yes, indeed."

"Let's get them all together, then," said the other, leading the way to the entrance. "I have a few words to say."

Sitting round the table in the director's office, the local officials gazed at the stern-faced envoys from the capital with a mixture of respect, uncertainty and terror.

"As you may imagine, we've been sent here by the *Zhongnanhai*, the General Bureau – in other words, directly by Chairman Mao."

"As you may know," said the other envoy, "the *Zhongnanhai*, despite its unpretentious name, occupies a special place: outside the Party, outside the state, outside the army, and outside yourselves. And in this context, 'outside' means 'above'. The *Zhongnanhai* is above everyone because it's the instrument of Chairman Mao, an extension of his hand and mind."

He paused for a moment, half-closing his eyes, as if not wanting anyone to meet his gaze and distract his thoughts.

"More than once," he went on gravely, "our enemies have tried to infiltrate the Bureau in order to encourage hostile tendencies. They've tried to draw our people into foreign plots, they've slandered us, asked for the *Zhongnanhai* to be abolished, but the Chairman has always defended us. He has defended us because we are blood of his blood, flesh of his flesh."

He suddenly banged his fist on the table, making the others jump.

"Now Chairman Mao, our great helmsman, wishes to have at his disposal direct and accurate information from all over our great country, unmodified by any intermediary. And that's why, from today on, he's going to sow, to distribute these . . ."

He gestured at the crates, which he'd had deposited at their feet.

"These microphones, which we've brought here today in those crates, are his ears . . ."

There was a pause.

"Do you see?" he went on. "So long as these ears hear properly,

China will have nothing to fear. But if they get stopped up, China will be lost. That is the message we are bringing you today."

The others were still stunned by what they'd just heard. Ever since they'd been told that mysterious envoys from the capital would be coming to see them, bringing crates containing secret equipment, they'd imagined this would be something very out-of-the-way, and they were dying to know what it was. Though the crates were marked "Insecticide", they'd expected them to contain special weapons – explosives, new kinds of hand-guns, tear-gas or electric truncheons. The idea of microphones had never entered their heads.

"*Qietingqi, qietingqi*," they muttered to themselves, as if repeating the name of the things would make them seem more real. Now they understood why some electrical engineers had been told to come here today too. Up till a few minutes ago they'd been looking down their noses at these eggheads. Now they began to treat them more affably.

So the boxes were full of mikes. The ears of Chairman Mao. Hundreds of thousands of them. God alone knew how many, installed all over China ... They felt the first faint stirrings of delight.

The other envoy then described the workings of these devices, and how they were to be installed. He spoke very quietly, as if through one of the microphones he'd been working with so long.

As he spoke, the two electrical engineers made notes. The visitor first told them the crates contained various kinds of microphones: fixed ones, portable ones, and very small ones for attaching secretly to a suspect's clothes. Then he instructed them in the various ways of setting them all up, in connecting and disconnecting them (the envoy used the words "sowing" and "harvesting"), in remote control, in the treatment and editing of tapes.

While the engineers scribbled feverishly, Tchan and the others listened open-mouthed. No one noticed that, outside, night had fallen long ago. A dismal night, wet and windy.

2

The same night, Van Mey, a citizen of N—, hobbled along the Street of the Red East on the way to see some friends. The street lanterns were few and far between, and blowing about in the wind and rain. But if he was worried it wasn't only because of the weather, or because, in the mist, the light from the lamps was dimmer and gloomier than usual. The same thought kept going round and round in his head: it was incredible that on this night in late September, in the town of N—, in the People's Socialist Republic of China, in the middle of the Cultural Revolution, he, citizen Van Mey, chemist in the laboratory at Factory No.4, member of the unions, praised for his zeal in studying the thoughts of Chairman Mao and his speeches at meetings held to denounce Liu Shaoshi, the liberalism of Deng Xiaoping, the idealism of Confucius, the four mysticisms, the seven demons of the country, and so on – that he of all people should have left home and gone out in order to take part in a spiritualist séance.

And on a night like this into the bargain! It might have been specially ordered!

A week or so ago a couple of his friends had given him a great surprise. For years they'd all been moaning and groaning about the boring life they led – a life without one heart-warming element, without restaurants, without traditional customs, without even the chance to flirt with a pretty woman; a life of chaff without wheat, insipid as canteen rice without salt or garnish; a life in which even fear was ugly, and anguish dry and calculated, nothing like the good old terror that used to be inspired by ghosts and spirits . . . Well, a couple of weeks ago these two pals of his had told him they'd organized a spiritualist séance.

Were they making fun of him? Could such a relic really still be found on Chinese soil? Even when they swore it was true, and said the medium they'd managed to find was only waiting to be told when they wanted to meet, Van Mey still couldn't bring himself to believe them. Were they sure this man was to be trusted? That he wasn't an *agent provocateur*, trying to lure them into disaster? Heavens, no, said Van Mey's friends. Safe as houses.

And now here he was on his way to throw down the biggest possible challenge to that existence made up of meetings, slogans, quotations, empty phrases, hate and sterility. He was ready to swap the whole lot for a twinge of genuine old-fashioned terror.

He was drenched by the time he got to his friend's house. He knocked at the door and went in. Both his pals were waiting for him. As was the medium. He was pasty-faced, with a flaccid skin, hair plastered down on his skull, and big bags under his eyes. Well, he doesn't look like an *agent provocateur*, thought Van Mey. He's the old China all over.

The room was small and sparsely furnished: a plain wooden table, a few glasses, a thermos flask, and the inevitable anthology of quotations from Mao. The medium's eyes seemed to be looking inward, not seeing anything in the external world. Nobody said much. The host poured tea from the thermos flask into the glasses.

"Well, Tchaï Chang," he said, smiling rather guiltily at the medium, "we've arranged this gathering . . . and we're eternally grateful to you for making such a thing possible in this day and age . . ."

The medium listened impassively. Perhaps he had his doubts too: might *they* be *provocateurs*, trying to lure *him* into a trap?

"I've got some candles – you said we'd need them," said the host. "I don't know if you want anything else . . ."

The medium glanced at the uncurtained windows.

"Oh, I get you . . . someone might see . . . And we'd need some reason for using candles instead of electric light. I thought about that. We'll take the fuses out of the box, so that even if someone comes and knocks on the door . . . But I shouldn't think they will. It's late, and in this weather . . ."

"No, there's no danger," said Van Mey's other friend. "Even if some nosey parker did look in, he'd only see four people talking in the light of a couple of candles because there's been a power failure."

"And the windows are streaming with rain," added their host. "It would be practically impossible to see in . . . What should we do now, Tchaï Chang? You only have to say. We're at your service."

The medium nodded towards the naked light bulb hanging from the ceiling, and spoke for the first time.

"Take out the fuses, as you said."

His voice was normal, and less mysterious than Van Mey had expected.

Their host got two candles from the sideboard, lit them, and went out into the hall. A few seconds later the whole apartment went black, until people's eyes got used to the candlelight.

As they all looked at one another, Van Mey felt as if the flickering of the candle flames was communicating itself to his whole being.

"You are going to concentrate, concentrate very hard, and think about the person whose spirit you want to summon here tonight," said the medium, looking round at them all. "I can only make him come back with your help."

"What?" said the host. "We hadn't actually thought of anybody in particular . . ."

"You mean you haven't chosen the dead person you want to speak to?"

They looked at one another.

"Well, I suppose . . . I suppose we could choose someone now . . . Sorry, Tchaï Chang – we were so excited we didn't think about details . . . Does it matter if we decide now? Is it allowed?"

"Yes. It's quite possible," said the medium.

"No problem then. There are several dead people whose voice we'd like to hear. But the one we'd probably all choose first is Qan Shen, our dear Qan Shen, whose death caused us such sorrow and left such a void. What do you think, Van Mey?"

Van Mey had nodded in agreement even while their host was still speaking. Who else should it be but Qan Shen, with whom they'd had so many quiet chats until his sudden death the previous year? Van Mey's grief was still quite evident.

"Especially as he died . . . in such suspicious circumstances . . ."

Van Mey wondered if they'd be able to question Qan Shen about his death. Brr – a chill ran down his spine at the mere thought.

"And he'll really come, and we'll be able to communicate with him?"

"I think so," replied the medium. "It depends on you. And on me too, of course."

"Forgive our ignorance, Tchaï Chang," said the host, "but may I ask you if it's true, as I've heard, that sometimes one can not only hear the dead person's voice but also see something of them? Excuse me if that's a silly question."

"Yes, it is possible to see the dead person," the medium answered. "But not usually at the very first séance, and of course not completely. What you might see is a sort of ghost of his hand or face or some other part of his body – a vague image, rather like an X-ray photograph . . ."

"Of course," said the host in a quavering voice. "Of course . . . That's a great deal, anyway . . . And what are we going to do now?"

"We're going to begin," said the medium.

277

What happened next Van Mey could never remember as a whole, but only in fragments that didn't seem to belong in the same space and time. Perhaps this was due to the flickering light of the candles, or the rain streaming down outside, or the silence into which they poured their unspoken appeal to the dead man. "Qan Shen, it's we, your bereaved friends, who are calling you from the depths of our grief. We can't forget you . . ." Perhaps it was all those things together that blurred the outlines of everything so much at the time that Van Mey's memory couldn't join them together later.

His eyes were riveted on the medium's face: the life seemed to drain out of it, leaving a mere mask. But as his face froze, his chest rose and fell in ever greater agitation until his breath came in one long groan, punctuated every now and then by a sort of stifled death rattle. He had entered into a trance. You could tell that all his strength was being bent to the task of summoning the spirit. It obviously wasn't easy. Heaven knew what heights and depths his call had to travel through, not to mention the dark and the wind.

"Qan Shen, we're waiting for you," Van Mey silently implored. "Please do come down amongst us, who miss you so." His two friends were no doubt sending out the same supplication.

Finally, after what seemed a very long time, the medium's breathing changed. In something resembling a silence, you could feel a presence.

"Are you there, Qan Shen?" muttered the medium. "You can speak to him now."

But their lips seemed sealed. Neither then nor later did they know whether they actually managed to speak to Qan Shen or if they only thought the words: "Qan Shen, please forgive us for disturbing you on a night like this . . ."

"Don't ask me questions!" said the medium curtly, transmitting the words of the dead man. "Don't ask me questions about that day! It's better for you not to know . . . It's always too late . . ."

And those were the only words they heard. No matter how often they addressed the dead man again, they got no answer.

"He wasn't here long," said the medium, when he was himself again. "Perhaps he'll stay longer the next time."

The others stared in wonder as the medium's ashen mask gradually changed back into its normal form and texture.

It was almost midnight when they all emerged from the apartment and set off for their various homes. The wind was still blowing, the rain was still falling, and the wan streetlights still swung back and forth overhead.

3

Four days later there was another meeting in director Tchan's office. This time it included all those who were going to be involved in supervising the installation of microphones in the town of N—. The two representatives of the *Zhongnanhai* were there too.

After he had given a brief account of how the first technical teams were to be trained, director Tchan handed over to the man from the *Zhongnanhai*, who was going to talk about how the project was to be supervised.

The envoy from Peking gave a supercilious look at his audience, and opened his address with a question.

"No doubt, during all the time you've been studying this matter, you've wondered where the microphones are to be placed, and who is to be bugged, and according to what considerations? The *Zhongnanhai*'s answer is quite plain: the *qietingqis* are to be placed everywhere. Is that clear? Right, now let's go on. I expect there are some among you who think "everywhere" doesn't apply to the Party, i.e. to party officials. The *Zhongnanhai*'s answer to this question is equally clear: if any suspicion arises, microphones will be installed anywhere, from the office of the first secretary of the Party committee to the premises of the humblest individual. No need to say more on this point. But before I conclude I should like to emphasize three things: first, the *Zhongnanhai* is subject to no restriction; second, nothing must escape the ears of Chairman Mao; and third, you must keep this operation secret, or pay for it with your lives."

His audience assiduously wrote down what he said, their heads bowed over their notebooks. Although his message was so daunting, they felt the joy they'd anticipated at the previous meeting beginning to burgeon. They would soon be performing the magical process of listening to what people thought was quite private: outbursts of resentment against the state, gossip, confidences, things people said in their sleep, secret baseness, the things people said when they were making love.

Already the prospect made some of those present feel faint and parched and short of breath. Others thought of the possibilities concerning men they hated or envied, and women they hadn't been able to attract and so dismissed as frigid or over-sexed. Others again dreamed of unmasking plots, winning medals, and having brilliant careers.

When the meeting was over, director Tchan stayed on alone in his office, staring at the ashtray. The thrill he, like the others, had experienced hadn't lasted. It had been nipped in the bud by an as yet unspecified fear. Not fear of responsibility, or of uncertainty, or of the jealousy of other officials: no, something more vague than any of those, but which nonetheless made him shudder with apprehension . . .

He was going to listen to all that was going on in space, to plumb all secrets, go down into the utmost depths of the human heart. But good heavens! – that was like descending into hell, where no one else had ever gone! And if he was going into a forbidden realm, he was probably going to be punished for doing so.

4

The first mikes were put in place at the end of the week. The work started with those that were easiest to install: those destined for some rooms in the town's main hotel, for certain offices, for the guest-house where foreign delegations were accommodated, and for two or three apartments whose occupants were away on missions.

It was normal to begin like that, without undue pressure, while the workmen involved acquired the necessary experience. But they knew it couldn't continue indefinitely: they knew they wouldn't always be able to take down a chandelier or unpick the upholstery of a settee at leisure, and introduce a microphone while a colleague kept watch at the door. They'd soon have to operate in more difficult circumstances, perhaps even in the presence of their victims, who would think they were repairing a switch or a tap.

In fact, by the following week, the number of mikes to be installed had quadrupled. (The operation, like everything else, was being carried out according to a plan.) The technicians, disguised as plumbers, painters or sweeps (what could be easier than to block someone's chimney if you wanted to plant a bug on him?), embarked on a mass campaign. On two occasions they narrowly avoided disaster. The workers in question were almost caught red-handed, but fortunately, remembering their instructions, they pretended to be ordinary criminals and were taken, much to their relief, to the nearest police station.

At the same time as the permanent microphones were being installed, a series of tests was carried out with others operated by remote control. But the placing of four small bugging devices counted as the triumph of that week's achievement. There were very few of them, and the workers had been told to handle them with particular care (they trembled at the mere mention of them). Bugs were as difficult to remove as to plant. If they were to accompany the suspect wherever he went, they had to be attached to his clothes. The state had spent a colossal amount of money on miniaturizing them for this purpose, said one of the envoys from the *Zhongnanhai*. However, unlike a kitchen cabinet, a bed or a W.C., which could be fitted with a mike in their owner's absence, a person's clothes were something he carried about with him. The only solution seemed to be to slip the bug into one of his pockets. But then, no matter how absent-minded or easy-going he might be, wasn't he bound to notice you doing it? And even if you did manage to slip it in somehow, wouldn't he find it the next time he put his hand in his pocket? And then, even if he was the type who never did put his hands in his pockets, how were you ever going to get the mike back again? (For they did have to be got back again once they'd performed their allotted tasks: first, because the Chinese state would never break the sacred rule of thrift and merely write them off; and second, because they were top-secret equipment, and as such mustn't be allowed to fall into the wrong hands.)

Oh no, said the envoy, pockets were definitely out. He passed on to the possibilities offered by linings. For this you had to be able to unpick a seam and sew it up again, or else make a small and as near as possible invisible opening in the material. But you couldn't do this when your man was actually wearing his clothes. So you had to get into his house when he wasn't there, under the pretext of mending a tap, etc. Your problem was then solved, if the victim owned a spare suit. But most of them didn't. Then what? You might put the mike in another garment that was just hanging in the wardrobe, waiting for the appropriate season. But that involved the problem of having to keep someone intended as a winter victim under surveillance the previous summer, and vice versa, which would make intelligence gathering impossibly complicated. There was only one solution, said the envoy from the capital, and that was to wait for, and take advantage of, the moment when the suspect took off some garment in a public place. This might be during a morning session of physical exercises, in a theatre or office cloakroom, while he was taking part in the mass cross-country run in spring, or in some private sport or other. You might have to follow him for months before you got a chance to slip him his *qietingqi*. As for getting it back again, you didn't wait for him to go to the public baths or for the next spring marathon: you just watched till he went home one night, and then faked a burglary, during which you managed for a few moments to get hold of his jacket or trousers or whatever.

But your troubles weren't over even then, or if – ideally – you got access to the garment in a cloakroom. (By the way, a padded anorak was best for concealing things in.) Not to mention the fact that its owner might leave the meeting or office or factory before you expected him to (there were ways of avoiding this), you needed both skill and sangfroid to remember precisely where you'd placed the bug and extract it neatly without damaging the garment it was in. (This was referred to as "gathering in the fruit".)

And all the aforementioned precautions had to be multiplied a hundredfold in the case of the rare and costly independent mini-mikes. These had their own recording spool, and were so expensive they'd only been produced in very small numbers so far. Their advocates argued the advantages of a device which could function independently of the listening centre, wherever the suspect happened to go, and which worked continuously day and night until its battery ran out. It was of course especially necessary to recover this type of microphone when its work was done.

Director Tchan knew all these dangers and difficulties, and more, so when the technicians came and announced that they'd placed five bugs and two independent mini-mikes in the anoraks of the relevant suspects, he rubbed his hands with glee.

"But don't forget," he reminded his men, "that you've only done half the job so far. The other half may well be much harder!"

Despite strict and repeated exhortations to secrecy, a rumour grew up, vague and fearful at first, and then increasingly distinct, though still concealed: they were installing bugging devices, people said, in the town of N—.

Director Tchan tried in vain to trace the leak. His aides were equally unsuccessful, though they resorted to threat and even actual arrests. What worried Tchan most was that the representatives of the *Zhongnanhai* were still in town. If the rumour came to their ears there'd be the devil to pay. He cherished a faint hope that they might leave before they suspected anything: after all, who were they going to find out from except *him*? But one day the sourer of the two envoys said curtly: "There's a lot of talk in the town about microphones. How do you explain it?" Tchan quaked and tried to babble something. He couldn't believe his eyes when the envoy smiled.

"Quite natural," he said. "It usually happens."

Tchan still didn't see what he meant.

"Isn't it disastrous? Won't it sabotage . . . ?" he began.

Now I've put my foot in it, he thought. Why did I have to go and meet trouble halfway? But to his amazement:

"Oh no!" said the man from the *Zhongnanhai*. "It has advantages as well as disadvantages. The best thing is that it makes everything into a kind of myth. People invent so many fantastic stories about the microphones that in the end the rumour, which makes everyone vigilant to begin with, gradually lulls them into a kind of lethargy. And that's when the hour of the *qietingqis* has come!"

Tchan was so relieved he lit a cigarette. He couldn't wait to get the first results of this new intelligence technique. Meanwhile he went on receiving information through the earlier network – that is, via the human ear. His own spies, probably the first people to learn of the advent of the microphones, were sure to be annoyed, and afraid these newfangled devices would put them out of a job. Director Tchan had been told of murmurs to this effect, and eventually their resentment reached such a pitch he decided to summon his crack spies to a meeting. They were the fine flower of their profession, and their deeds would go down to posterity. Hun Hu had spent three days and three nights lying like a corpse in the morgue: he suspected his victim wasn't quite dead, and hoped to extract one last word from him before he finally gave up the ghost. Xin Fung had been decorated by Chairman Mao himself for keeping a factory under surveillance for a hundred hours, while standing near a giant cutting machine. He was completely deaf ever after. Others had made other sacrifices in the service of their profession: some had deserted wives and children, others had renounced marriage altogether. Chan Vung was perhaps the star of N—'s spying fraternity: he had gouged his own eyes out in order to improve his hearing.

In view of all this, Tchan spoke to them with special warmth and consideration, invoking the glorious, three-thousand-year-old tradition of surveillance which in China had been put at the service of the people. No technique, however advanced, could take the place of the ear, for the human factor was always the most important – only a technocrat or a revisionist could think otherwise. Then Tchan turned to the possibility of using listening devices. These were special appliances designed for special cases, above all those involving foreigners: they had nothing to do with their own great domestic surveillance. Just as agriculture used modern technology as well as beasts of burden; just as medicine relied both on highly trained specialists and on barefoot doctors; so intelligence too would employ not only microphones but also the human ear, which would still play the most important part in surveillance. Carried away by his own eloquence, Tchan embroidered on this theme, maintaining that a microphone was only a pale imitation of the human ear. This ear, reared on the quotations of Mao Zedong, was irreplaceable. And, he implied in conclusion, so were they, his audience.

The spies, reassured, dispersed, and in the next few days sent in a mass of information unprecedented in both quantity and quality. As he looked through the weighty file on the desk in front of him, Tchan meditated on two possible reasons for this influx. Either the spies themselves were working with extra zeal to show they were far from being mere has-beens. Or the ordinary people, confronted with a future in which rumour would be superseded because of the microphones, were taking advantage of what time remained to have a good gossip.

Tchan rubbed his tired eyes. Either of those two reasons would account for that fat file. Probably both.

The spies seemed to have taken particular care to report popular resentment against the *qietingqis*, Tchan noticed, smiling sardonically. Perhaps they cherished a lingering hope that this might help get rid of the horrible things.

Tchan studied the various comments that had been made about the new device: it was an invention of the white foreign devil, and would bring nothing but trouble; it was a new dimension, but a bad one, and what use was that to humanity? it was the gateway to hell . . . Aeroplanes were prefigured by the flying carpets of legend, television by magic mirrors. But where were the precursors of the micro-spies? They were to be found in the voices of ghosts and vampires, in occultism, black magic, spiritualist séances and all kinds of other vestiges of the old world . . .

Yeah, said Tchan to himself, looking up from the file.

6

As he came out of the factory he heard someone calling him from the pavement.

"Van Mey!"

He turned round, and was glad to see his two friends. They hadn't met again since the famous night.

"How are you, Van? It's been a long time."

"And you two – how are things?"

"Fine, fine. We were thinking of dropping in on you to say hallo . . ."

"Good, good! I've been very busy in the evening lately . . ."

Why, after that evening, had they all avoided one another, rather than meeting the very next day to exchange their impressions? What had come between them because of the spirit they'd raised?

"I see you've bought yourself a new anorak!"

"Yes," said Van Mey. "The old one was falling to pieces. So I counted up all the money I'd saved last summer . . ."

"Quite right. Winter's early this year."

They walked along for a while without speaking, but they all knew they were thinking about the same thing.

"I can't get that night out of my mind," one of them admitted at last.

"Neither can I," said Van Mey, quite relieved now the subject had been broached at last.

"What do you think – should we have another meeting?"

Van Mey looked at the other two.

"What do you think? And what about the medium . . . ?"

"The medium said the spirit might stay longer next time . . ."

"I didn't mean that – I meant can you get hold of the medium again?"

"Of course!" they said. "We wouldn't have mentioned it otherwise."

"I'm willing," said Van Mey, with a shudder.

"What do they say about the micro-spies?" said one of the others, to change the subject.

"What don't they say!" exclaimed Van Mey.

They told one another all they'd heard.

"I don't mind betting things are going to get difficult," said one. "Those *qietingqis* bode no good."

"I expect you're right," answered Van Mey absently.

In his mind's eye he could already see the little flames of the candles at the next séance, and their own anguish as they waited for the spirit to come.

7

Director Tchan had imagined it quite differently, the fateful day when the mikes would reproduce the very first voices, when his spies of flesh and blood would be joined by an army of soulless instruments. But nearly a fortnight had gone by since the first microphones were installed, and no great day had arrived. On the contrary, the first time he'd listened in live to microphones installed in people's homes he'd found it tedious and wearisome, as well as unproductive. The mikes in question weren't those that had been placed in the villa reserved for foreign visitors: the villa was empty at present, and the mikes there silent. The ones Tchan listened in to were in the main hotel, but these transmitted snores more often than words, and if there was a conversation it was usually trivial and devoid of interest. The mikes in government offices conveyed nothing but endless discussions, and Tchan soon gave up listening: he had enough boring meetings himself in his own office!

Disappointed by listening in direct, he waited eagerly for the first "harvest" from the temporary mikes, the ones placed in private houses and bedrooms, and above all those fixed to people's clothes. There were seven of these, almost the number prescribed in the bi-monthly plan. Tchan was sure that what was recorded on these tapes would prove to be the most important part of their work.

Everyone was waiting for them and trying to conceal the gleam of anticipation in his eyes.

One morning when he walked into the building where he worked he sensed that they had arrived. He couldn't have said where he felt it first: by the box where the sentry stood; as he passed some of his colleagues on the stairs; or in the characteristic silence of the corridors. Anyhow, when his assistant came into his office, Tchan knew already what he was going to say:

"Comrade Tchan – the first tape . . . !"

"It's come, has it? Bring it in at once."

"I've got it here."

Tchan had given orders that no one was to listen to it before he did. He was very excited. He locked the door, lit a cigarette, and asked his assistant to start.

After an hour's listening he was even more disappointed than he had been by the permanent mikes. His assistant tried to catch something of interest by rewinding the tape several times, but it consisted mainly of silences with crowd and traffic noises in the background. There was an occasional hoot from a taxi, or a car door banging; the few odd scraps of speech were of no significance whatsoever. But what could be more natural? Tchan tried to reassure himself. He ought never to have listened to this tape just as it was, even before his closest assistants. It was like a great mass of mud and stones which would have to be carefully sifted if it was to yield the least particle of gold.

"The sound quality's very good, isn't it?" said his colleague.

Tchan nodded wearily. What more could you expect from a soulless piece of apparatus? He remembered his speech about the human ear. If he could have talked to his old spies now he'd have treated them with even more deference.

But his disillusion didn't last long. Three days later his assistant received the first serious results, selected from tapes on mini-mikes that had just been recovered.

Tchan shut his eyes so as to concentrate better. The recording contained complaints about the state, the Cultural Revolution, the unprecedented shortages and the universal chaos. Some people objected to the banning of ancient customs, others to anything that undermined the authority of the Party. Then came some very dubious remarks made by the first secretary of the Party in N— to some dinner guests of his: he was being malicious and sarcastic at the expense of the central government. Tee-hee, Tchan chuckled. His relations with the first secretary had cooled since he'd summoned Tchan to ask him for a report about the installation of the *qietingqis*. Tchan had refused to tell him anything, and the first secretary had flown off the handle. After they'd exchanged a couple of quotations from Mao Zedong, Tchan, realizing the first secretary had the advantage of him on that score, decided to tell him straight: "I'm not accountable to anyone but the *Zhongnanhai*!" At the mere sound of that dread name the first secretary started to stammer so much that Tchan almost felt sorry for him. "I'm not even accountable to my minister," he'd said to soothe him down a bit. And now here the fellow was, making fun of him to his guests: "He's not a bad sort, old Tchan, but he really is as thick as two planks!"

Laugh away, thought Tchan grimly. His face showed no expression. His assistant stopped the tape and glanced at him to see if he wanted to go on listening.

"Perhaps more out of curiosity than for the actual content . . . ?" suggested the aide. "It's only a private matter . . . intimate, really . . . very intimate . . . Though perhaps one might detect something that's . . . Well, the way the couple try to imitate the West, even in their physical relationship . . . a certain excess in their love-making . . . In short, they adopt capitalist ways of doing it, like . . . like . . ."

This last, unfinished phrase made Tchan's mind up for him, and he signed to his assistant to start the tape again. They both listened in silence, as before. Not a muscle moved in the director's face.

From the loudspeaker there came first the panting of the man, then that of the woman, quieter. She was almost sobbing as she implored him not to do something which she apparently at the same time desired: "No, not like that . . . No, please, not like that . . . It's wrong . . . Don't you think it's wrong? . . . Ah . . ."

"Well, at last we've got something really important," said the assistant when the couple's moans had ceased . . .

From the very first words, director Tchan had known why his aide had kept the next bit till last. He knitted his brow. This was what he called results! Just what he'd been waiting for all this time.

Words hostile to Jiang Qing. He started to break into a cold sweat. This wasn't the first time he'd heard people insult her . . . So why was he so worked up? . . . The black-souled Empress Vu was an angel of light compared with this one . . . The old dodderer must have gone soft in the head to put up with such a viper . . . Director Tchan had heard all this before, or rather read it in his spies' reports, but it was another matter altogether to hear the words spoken by human voices and accompanied by malicious laughter . . .

It wasn't until his aide had left the room that Tchan began to feel a little calmer. He lit a cigarette, though there was another, still unfinished, resting on the ashtray. The material supplied by these mikes was clearly quite a different kettle of fish from the work of his spies. They merely reported things orally or in writing, relying on their memories, and the value of their evidence depended not only of the acuteness of their hearing but also on their training, talent, culture, and state of mind at the time. However reliable and devoted they were, there was always an element of uncertainty about their reports, which might exaggerate things or play them down, distort them wholly or in part, or even invent them altogether. It depended on the individual spy's ambition, his recent successes or failures, and his personal relations with the suspect, if he happened to know him. The spies looked down on *agents provocateurs* and ordinary informers as underhand, unreliable, and often corrupt. "*We* don't skulk around deceiving people," they boasted. "*Our* work is clean and straightforward: we put our ear to the wall or the ceiling and report truthfully. We heard this or that, or we didn't hear anything at all. Whereas informers and *agents provocateurs* – ugh! they make things up, they slander people, they settle personal scores . . ." Nevertheless, the spies themselves weren't always entirely objective, whereas this new equipment was honesty itself, and reported everything exactly as it was, fully and impartially. Now Director Tchan really could pride himself on doing his job properly.

Now he really could listen in. The implications were dizzying. The whole chaos and tumult of humanity would now be wafted up to him. This morning's work opened up vistas of light and darkness, ecstasy and horror. He thought of the mysterious power exercized by the demons of old. What could they do that he himself couldn't do now?

8

Van Mey met his friends at the end of the week. They swapped the latest news as usual; as usual it was awful, and could only get worse. A fierce power struggle was said to be going on among the factions in Peking. The winter would only bring new waves of terror. Apparently Mao wasn't well.

"An Albanian delegation came to the factory yesterday," said Van Mey, "and I had to take them round."

"What were they like? What did they say?"

"Hard to say, really. I took them to the shop floor, as we usually do with foreigners, but they just looked and smiled. You couldn't tell what they were thinking."

"How can they like what they see? And they don't know half the horrors we have to live with . . ."

"All they see is just window-dressing," said Van Mey.

"But it's not very difficult to see past it."

"Perhaps they do see past it, but they pretend not to," said Van Mey. "In Albania, apparently, people go to concerts to listen to Beethoven – the women wear lipstick and jewellery. The delegation *must* have noticed how barren and monotonous our lives are here."

"But they pretend not to notice. Partly for political reasons, partly because they think this sort of life is quite good enough for the Chinese."

"Do you think so? Well, *I* think their own lives will gradually become just as arid as ours. Then they'll understand how awful it is, but by then it'll be too late."

"All the time I was taking them round I wanted to say to them: 'Are you blind? How can you possibly not see what's going on here?'"

"That would have been sheer madness!"

"Maybe, but if I'd had the chance I'd have whispered a message to them in the few words of French I know. I'd have told them, 'Don't believe anything you see – everything is going to the dogs!' But it was quite impossible! I only had about half a minute alone with one of them, and as soon as I opened my mouth the other guide showed up. But I think that Albanian guessed something."

"Are you sure?"

"Almost certain."

They went on trudging along the muddy road, amid the ruts left by the wheels of heavy lorries. It was cold.

"We'll probably be able to meet next week for you know what ... The medium is going to get in touch. So on Thursday or Friday . . ."

"I'll be there," said Van Mey. "Without fail!"

9

Every morning now when he got to his office, Tchan, instead of looking at the papers, or any urgent reports, or his timetable for the day, sat straight down and listened to the tapes that had been recovered during the previous night.

After which, he usually looked very down in the mouth, and was in a bad temper for most of the morning. His assistants had noticed all this, and had tried to think of a way of getting him to listen to the tapes at the end of the day instead of at the beginning. But all their efforts were vain. And to think this was only the start! What would it be like when the weather got really cold and people got even more discontented? The *qietingqis*' tapes would overflow with complaints.

They were full enough now, in the middle of autumn. It was hard to see how they could hold more, or more sinister, grumbles. Everyone and everything was castigated, no one and nothing was spared. Insults were directed as much against members of the Party as against yesterday's men. Supporters of Zhou Enlai bad-mouthed supporters of Lin Biao and Jiang Qing to the top of their bent, while the latter did the same to Deng Xiaoping, and all of them joined together to criticize Mao. Tchan couldn't believe his ears. He wound the tape back. But there it was – he hadn't been imagining things. What a diabolical racket!

On many a morning Tchan found himself burying his head in his hands, or clenching his jaw so hard he could scarcely feel it. What was all this clamour? According to the proverb, water must go murky before it can start to clear. Was this the explanation? He shrank from this hypothesis. But Chairman Mao couldn't have made a mistake. It must be the Chinese themselves: they had been getting more wicked lately.

Tchan felt his own attitude hardening daily. He had sent one

291

report to the *Zhongnanhai* via the two envoys, who had just left N—, and he was now preparing another. When instructions came from the capital, he would strike. And he would strike without mercy, so that the citizens of N— would remember it for generations.

Later on, at the end of the day's work, he put his report in an envelope, sealed it, and sent it, together with two tapes, to the villa in Peking where foreign delegations were put up. The covering note read as follows: "As none of our staff speaks Albanian, we are sending you, for decoding, some tapes concerning the Albanian delegation which has just left N—." Tchan was exhausted. He locked up his office and went out to the waiting car,
"Home," he told the driver.

The car had to stop in the Street of the People's Communes. A crowd was blocking the road.

"Now what's the matter?" growled Tchan.

The driver got out to see. He was soon back.

"A pedestrian's been crushed by a bulldozer," he said, starting up the car again. "A man called Van Mey."

"Van Mey?"

It seemed to Tchan he'd heard that name before. But by the time the car had left the crowd behind, he'd forgotten it.

10

And so the winter went by, one of the worst director Tchan had ever known, full of work and worry. Far away in Peking the power struggle apparently still went on, though no one could say which of the two sides was getting the upper hand. Now one and now the other was borne upwards. Only the *Zhongnanhai* remained unmoved and unassailable, above the mêlée. Tchan felt his own star was hitched to it from now on.

He'd had to deal with plenty of problems during the winter. Once or twice he'd come quite close to disaster, but in the end chance had been on his side. The microphones were an additional complication. They had become the main cause of tension between him and the other local officials, giving rise to rivalries, intrigues and reversals of alliances. Sometimes Tchan felt he would never struggle free of this imbroglio.

Meanwhile the installation of microphones went on, with the inevitable ups and downs, pleasant and unpleasant surprises. But Tchan was more used to it now; he'd gradually become immunized, as to a poison, by his daily dose. The same thing seemed to be true of the population in general: the rumours about the mikes had died down, as the envoys from the *Zhongnanhai* had said they would.

But time, though it sometimes hung heavy, was passing by, and Tchan was amazed when, at the first meeting held to exchange information about the *qietingqis*, one of his subordinates started his speech with the words:

"It was just a year ago that in accordance with direct instructions from Chairman Mao, our town began installing listening devices . . ."

The meeting was attended by two representatives of the *Zhongnanhai*, different ones this time, who took down copious notes about everything. The speakers dealt with every aspect of microsurveillance, exchanging experience, drawing conclusions, and calling attention to successes and shortcomings.

The conference lasted two days, and after it had ended and the *Zhongnanhai* envoys had left, Tchan realized that everything was going to continue just as before. His attention had been caught by one out of the many speeches he had heard at the meeting. It had been delivered by a young technician, who had entitled his paper, "On some changes brought about in the way people speak by the introduction of *qietingqis*." Tchan had noticed this phenomenon himself some time before, but it was like a revelation to hear it spoken of and see it written down in black and white. As a matter of fact the young man had only touched on the subject and not gone into it deeply. His main point was that the task of those whose job it was to transcribe the tapes was getting more and more difficult, for many of the conversations recorded now required decoding if they were to mean anything.

Tchan had already devoted some thought to this phenomenon, and he now paid it special attention. This was the people's riposte in their duel with him: they were changing the way they talked so that he couldn't understand it. It was no accident that the spies themselves had been complaining lately: "Our ears are perfectly all right – we've just had them tested. But we can't make out a word of some of these conversations. Is this some new kind of Chinese that people are talking?"

Tchan paced back and forth in his office, which was heavy with tobacco smoke. This was more serious than he'd thought. By way of opposition to him, people were gradually inventing a new language, an anti-language. A growing proportion of the tapes was becoming unintelligible. Where would it end? What would happen?

Perhaps nothing would happen, thought Tchan after a while. If you looked at the matter calmly, it wasn't so much a case of covert language changing, as of covert language coming to resemble overt language.

Was he going senile, inventing such ideas? But he couldn't get it out of his head. Hadn't the overt language been gradually filled with and eventually almost taken over by slogans and empty phrases? While the covert language, the one people spoke among themselves, had escaped that process and remained clear and precise. So what was really happening now was that the overt language was gradually infiltrating the covert one. The two were becoming one, and all because of micro-surveillance.

I'm raving, thought Tchan. If I go on like this much longer I'll end up in the madhouse or in jail. I shan't listen to the blasted tapes any more. I'll have a couple of months' peace.

But he knew very well he couldn't do without them for a single day. He was as addicted to them as he was to tobacco, and he'd never succeeded in giving up smoking.

And so winter went by, the second after the coming of the *qietingqis*, and then it was spring again. Director Tchan didn't go crazy, and didn't end up in jail. He was so busy he didn't even notice the arrival of summer, and neither he nor his aides took any leave. One morning some dead leaves were blown against the window, followed by a gust of rain. He looked up from his desk for a moment. It was autumn.

In the same week as the first frost an urgent order came from the *Zhongnanhai*: in the new situation arising out of the cooling off of relations between China and Albania, top priority was to be given to collecting information about alleged acts of provocation committed by Albanian citizens in China, whether students, embassy staff or members of delegations.

11

An hour later, Tchan summoned his aides to his office to tell them about the new instructions.

"Here in N—," he said wearily, "there aren't any students or foreign embassies. That makes our task easier. As for the only Albanian delegation that ever set foot here as far as I know, I believe we sent the tapes recording their conversations to Peking for decoding, because we didn't have anyone who knew the language?"

"That's right," said his aide.

"Regarding their contacts with people here, I think we have some reports on the subject. Is there anything in them that's relevant to what this order asks? Some provocative phrase or other?"

"No," answered his aide, but not very convincingly.

Tchan thought he looked rather uncertain too.

"What?" he said. "It looks to me as if certain things went on that I wasn't told about."

"No, no," said the aide nervously. "There isn't anything in the reports. I was thinking of something else."

Tchan looked him straight in the eye. He squirmed.

"What *were* you thinking of, exactly?"

The aide gave up.

"Perhaps you remember that two years ago we lost a mike," he stammered. "One of those special mini-mikes . . ."

"What's that got to do with the present question?"

"There is a connection. Perhaps you also remember that the man whose clothes it was attached to was killed. Van Mey, his name was . . ."

"Van Mey," Tchan murmured.

Yes, he did remember. That had been the only mike they lost, and Van Mey's name had been mentioned . . . Yes, it was all coming back to him. They worried themselves sick about that lost *qietingqi*. The instructions about looking after them had been very strict, especially for the mini-mikes, and they'd had great trouble hushing the matter up.

"So what, then?" said Tchan. "What's it got to do with this?" – pointing to the order.

His aide swallowed.

"The only person to act as guide to the Albanian delegation and exchange a few words with them was Van Mey," he said. "If that mike hadn't disappeared we'd have a tape of what he and the Albanians said to one another."

"Really?" said Tchan.

Even after two years he could still remember their agitation about the loss, but he couldn't remember the details. Had they written a report? he asked.

"Of course," said the other. "Shall I go and get it?"

Tchan nodded.

When the aide came back and started to read out the report, Tchan remembered quite clearly the day he'd been told one of the independent mikes was missing because the person wearing it had been killed a fortnight ago. They hadn't been able to recover the device from his anorak, for the simple reason that the anorak had disappeared. After searching the victim's flat and finding out he'd had neither family nor close friends in N—, they tried the crematorium. Unfortunately, it hadn't been functioning at the time of Van Mey's death because of a fuel shortage: they'd had to bury the body in the old town cemetery. "To hell with him and his mike!" Tchan had cried. "Write a report and bring it to me to sign!" . . . And so the case had been closed.

"It was my fault," he admitted now. "But how was I to know that our relations with Albania would sink so low, and that that cursed mike . . ."

"Of course," said one of his assistants. "How could you have known?"

"What's done is done," said another. "No point in talking about it now."

"Wrong!" roared Tchan. "I'll raise that mike from the dead if I have to!"

And he gave the gruesome order.

12

That very evening two lorries stopped outside the old cemetery, now used only for bodies that couldn't be dealt with by the crematorium because of fuel shortages. Tchan and his two assistants got out of one truck, and a few municipal workers out of the other. The sexton was waiting for them at the gate, a lantern in his hand and his face dark with terror.

"Lead the way!" commanded Tchan.

They set off in silence along a path, the man with the lantern leading and the others occasionally shining their torches.

"Here it is," said the sexton, pointing to a mound of earth.

The torches gathered round and then were switched off, leaving only the faint light of the lantern on the grave.

"Switch on the headlights of the lorries," ordered Tchan, drawing back a pace or two. "Then get cracking!"

They proceeded almost in silence. The headlamps came on quite suddenly, casting a white light tinged with mauve. The workmen spread a tarpaulin by the side of the grave.

Tchan watched the picks and shovels at work, while the sexton leaned over from time to time, presumably to tell the workers when to stop piling the earth at the side of the grave and start putting it on the tarpaulin. They'd decided to sift the earth that might contain, among the dead man's bones and what remained of his clothes, the lost mike.

Tchan was so obsessed his head was splitting, though he had high hopes of getting his hands on the precious device. He'd show the *Zhongnanhai* what he was made of! Maybe Mao himself would come to hear about it. Tchan looked up from time to time: he hoped it wasn't going to rain! Spadefuls of earth were starting to fall on the tarpaulin. Any one of them might hold the treasure. The sexton couldn't remember Van Mey's funeral now, but he did tell them that when someone died instantly in an accident and didn't go into hospital (the bulldozer had practically cut Van Mey in two), they were usually buried in the clothes they were wearing at the time.

"Careful," someone called. "You've reached the skeleton."

The heap of earth on the tarpaulin went on growing. They were going to sift as much soil as possible to be on the safe side. Heaven knows how long this would have gone on if Tchan hadn't suddenly called a halt.

"That'll do," he said. "No point in digging up the whole cemetery."

The first drops of rain began to fall, and they hurried to remove the tarpaulin before it got any heavier. As it was it took six of them to lift it on to the lorry.

"Lucky we got away before the storm!" said Tchan as the lorries drew away.

It was raining hard by the time they got back to headquarters. There were lights in the windows of the lab, and the lab assistants were waiting in silence, wearing sinister long rubber gloves. Again it took six men to carry the load upstairs. Then they set about crumbling up the soil.

Tchan stood watching with folded arms. Bits of skeleton and stone were put on one side to be looked at again later if nothing was found in the earth. The skull seemed to be grinding its teeth at them. "Gnash away as much as you like," Tchan muttered. "You won't stop me finding your voice!"

Every so often a chill ran down his spine, either with unnamed apprehension or because it had been so cold and damp in the cemetery.

It wasn't yet midnight when one of the lab assistants came on a button belonging to the anorak. That lifted their spirits. Twenty minutes later they found the mike itself. Only then did they notice that they and everything around them, including the floor and the tables, were covered with mud.

13

Was it really on the same night, or did people's memories run the two horrifying and unforgettable events together and make them coincide? But even if the second spiritualist séance did take place a few days before or a few days after the finding of the mike, it wasn't surprising if people thought of the two things as happening together.

Be that as it may, Van Mey's two friends, together with the medium, had met for another séance to commemorate Van's death and summon up his spirit. The meeting they'd all planned, at which they were to have invoked Qan Shen, had of course not taken place.

They'd been sitting round the table for some time. The candle flames flickered more lugubriously than ever, and the medium's face looked more pallid. He'd been in a trance for a long while, but his painful breathing, broken by occasional rattles, suggested that something was preventing him from making contact with the dead man.

According to later evidence it must have been at exactly this moment that, in the lab not far away at Public Safety headquarters, Tchan and his assistants had started to play the tape taken from

Van Mey's *qietingqi*. Their faces were ashen as they listened to the voice from beyond the grave. It sounded slow and hollow, like a disc being played at the wrong speed. And like a ghost.

"The tape must be damp," said Tchan, bending over the machine.

"Not surprising after being in the ground all that time," said one of his aides.

The voice was scarcely audible, and interspersed with dull thuds. Tchan wound the tape backwards and forwards to eliminate the blanks. Suddenly they all started. In the midst of the other noises there arose a shriek, abruptly cut off.

"The accident," said Tchan.

He must have been right, for the sinister cry was followed by a hubbub that might well have been made by a crowd gathering round the dead man. Further on in the tape, thought Tchan, there must be a recording of the corpse being taken from the crematorium to the cemetery – perhaps even of the burial. He wound the tape forward, and thought he heard the sound of spadefuls of earth falling on the body. After that there was an ever-deepening hush. My God, thought Tchan: that's what they mean by silent as the grave . . .

He listened transfixed until the end of the tape. He must be the first person in the world to possess a sample of the silence of death. Now he could say he had gone down among the shades.

He was roused from his reverie by the click as the machine switched itself off. He wound the tape back again to find Van Mey's voice, slimy-sounding and decayed after spending so long in the earth. It must have been after midnight now – according to later evidence, the same time as that at which, in a cold room a few hundred yards away, the medium, trying in vain to bring the voice of the dead man back to his two friends, gasped out, "I can't, he doesn't want to come – something's preventing him . . ."

Skënder Bermema stared at the last few lines as if he'd have liked them to go on of their own accord. It seemed to him this last part was written rather carelessly and didn't fully exploit the possibilities of the subject.

It took him some time to remember what had happened next in that town in central China.

After he'd heard the evidence, Tchan had no difficulty finding out about the séances and the names of the people who'd attended them. Nothing was known about their arrest, but it probably took place without delay. It wasn't certain whether Tchan had had them nabbed without more ado, or if he'd waited to catch them in the act during a séance. If the latter, he probably did make the macabre speech often attributed to him: after the door was smashed in and the conspirators were captured as they sat around the candles waiting in vain to communicate with the dead, Tchan is supposed to have said mockingly, "Were you waiting for his voice?" Then he burst out laughing. "Well, I'm afraid he's stood you up, gentlemen! I've got both his voice and his soul – in here!" And he showed them the little bugging device.

It was the Albanian ambassador in Peking, an old acquaintance of his, who first told Skënder about the dreaded *Zhongnanhai*. And when he heard about the business of the microphones he was sure the General Bureau must have been mixed up in it. The same day he asked an embassy official who spoke the language what the ultra-secret mini-mikes were called in Chinese. "*Qietingqi*" was the word, he was told – pronounced "tchietintchi".

"Are you going to write something about it?" the ambassador asked Bermema when he spoke to him about the séance. "China is still haunted by ghosts and spirits, despite all the denunciations of the old days."

Skënder sat down on the bed and gazed at the white curtains as he revolved all these memories. Various other incidents were now coming back to him . . . He lay down . . . A lunch near Tirana with some friends, after a rehearsal of one of his plays, and the maunderings of someone at a nearby table who'd had too much to drink: "In the third millennium, Albania will become Christian again, and if you want to survive you'd better change your name from Skënder to Alexander" . . . Going into hospital a year ago, the syringe in the nurse's hand, and his own sudden doubt about it – a doubt that was somehow like the confusion he'd recently felt going into the Hôtel Helmhaus in Zurich, because in Albanian the word "*helm*" meant "fish" . . . The women he'd loved, a tune, a balcony overlooking the sea, manuscripts and more manuscripts . . . An ashtray in a café, full of cigarette stubs of which only one had lipstick on it, symbolizing the disproportion between the emotion felt by the unknown man and that felt by the unknown woman . . .

He thought he must have drowsed off for a moment. And it was in a state between sleeping and waking that he imagined Ana lying in her grave. Or rather not her but a gold necklace which he'd given her once, and of which he'd caught a sudden glimpse as they closed the coffin.

He moved his head on the pillow to drive away the thought. But on the other, cooler part of the pillow Lin Biao's question, *"Where are we going?"*, seemed to be waiting for him, together with Lin Biao's plot to kill Mao – strangely like Mao's plot to kill Lin Biao.

But Skënder had had enough of these ruminations. His thoughts turned to the children's skis in the hall of the apartment at home, and how his wife did her hair, sitting at the dressing-table, and a letter from a woman reader who was a bit cracked . . . And, for some reason or other, a poem he'd written long ago:

> Like a Jewess exchanging her old religion for a new one,
> There was a sudden shower of hail.
>
> Every time winter taps on the windowpanes
> You will be back, even if you're not here.
>
> Even if you were changed into music, or mourning, or
>   a cross
> I would recognize you and fly to you.
>
> And like someone extracting a pearl from its shell,
> I would pluck you from music, the cross or death.

Alexander Bermema, he said to himself, trying out the new name the man in the restaurant had suggested. And again there went through his mind, like beads on a string, the coming of the third millennium, the ringing of bells, Ana's tears, and the Place Vendôme in Paris on an afternoon so cold it intensified the shiver the prices of the diamonds in the shop-windows sent down his spine . . .

That was how Skënder spent the rest of the morning, sometimes lying down and sometimes pacing back and forth in his room. Every time he thought of his dead novel his hand went instinctively to his ribs, for it seemed to him something had been removed from his side.

At midday C— V— came and knocked at the door to tell him

it was time for lunch. They went down together to the almost empty dining room, and hardly spoke to one another at all throughout the meal.

Back in his room, Skënder felt this Sunday would never end. For want of anything better to do he rang the bell, and when the Chinese floor waiter put his head round the door he ordered a beer.

At three in the afternoon there was another knock, and this time it wasn't C— V—. But before Skënder identified his visitor he noticed he was holding out a card with red ideograms inscribed on it: clearly an invitation. Skënder wasn't sure whether it was by chance that he'd concentrated exclusively on the card, or if the messenger had trained himself to disappear as if by magic behind the proffered invitation.

As Skënder held out his hand for it he raised his eyebrows inquiringly.

"A concert," the man told him, smiling.

Skënder scrutinized the card. The Chinese characters made no sense to him, but he managed to pick out the figures 19.30, which was presumably the time the concert started.

Well, a concert would be a welcome distraction amid this sea of boredom. It wasn't four o'clock yet, but he was so glad to have something to do he opened the wardrobe and started looking for a suitable shirt.

13

IN ANOTHER HOUR (by which time Skënder Bermema had shaved again and chosen a shirt and tie, while in a nearby room C— V—, with whom he hadn't been in touch, had done the same), all eleven hundred invitations to the official concert had been delivered to various addresses in Peking, and most of the recipients were in their rooms getting ready for the evening.

Some of them – mostly women – were still lying luxuriously in the bath, the shapes of their bodies blurred by the warm water, while in the distance their husbands were on the phone, asking other diplomats what they knew about this impromptu concert to which everyone was invited at scarcely three hours' notice. Was it just the way the Chinese did these things, or did it have some special significance? It was very odd . . . Was it a concert being brought forward from a later date, and if so why? It had been rumoured for some time that Mao was ill . . . Or was it Zhou Enlai? Who could say? Anyhow, the concert was not to be missed. It would provide all kinds of hints as to what was going on: what you had to watch out for was the order in which the Chinese leaders arrived, who was seated with whom in the boxes, whether Jiang Qing was there or not . . .

Skënder looked in the mirror and put the finishing touch to his tie, then felt the little cut he'd made on his right cheek while shaving. At that moment each of the eleven hundred guests was doing something connected with the concert: putting something on or taking something off, adjusting a collar or combing his hair. Ambassadors kept hurrying from their mirrors to their phones, which rang more and more often, while their wives got out of their baths at last, the gurgle of the water going down the drain – half a sob and half a cry of pleasure – carrying with it a hundred little mysteries the ladies couldn't have explained even if they'd wanted to. Warm and naked still, they selected their jewels for the evening, while out in

303

the hall their husbands were still on the phone, discussing the same theories as before: "Do you think it's something to do with Mao? Or with Zhou Enlai? It's not impossible, now we know that he's ill too . . ."

Unusually for him, Zhou Enlai was also looking at himself in the glass. His swarthy face looked greenish and chill. He tried to imagine what he'd look like when he appeared in his box. The men who for years had been hoping to take his place, men like Wang Hongwen, Zhang Chunqiao and Hua Guofeng, would probably heave a sigh of relief. All things come to him who waits. Zhou Enlai smiled bitterly. He couldn't do anything now to deprive them of their satisfaction: as soon as he appeared in public everyone would think the same thing – he was attending his last concert. And it was true.

He wanted to turn away from the mirror, but he couldn't. He felt his face slowly with his hand, as if it were a mask.

Every time he had to go to a political meeting, an official gathering, a session of the Politbureau or a government reception, he glanced briefly in the mirror before he left home, to make sure he hadn't forgotten to assume the necessary mask. The idea of a mask had been suggested to him either by the descriptions of his face in the foreign press, or else by the rumours about all the top leaders that the *Zhongnanhai* picked up all over the country. Zhou couldn't remember which. But it didn't matter. He was now so familiar with the idea that he wouldn't have been surprised if, as they were going out, Dan Yingchao, his wife, had asked, "Zhou, are you wearing your mask?", just as you might ask someone if they'd remembered to take their gloves or their handbag.

People had been talking about this for a long time, but Zhou took no notice. He had three masks: the mask of a leader, the mask of one who obeys, and the mask as cold as ice. The first two he usually wore to government and Politbureau meetings or committees. The third he kept for occasions when he had to appear in public.

The clock on the wall behind him struck six. This was the first time he had gone out without one of his three masks. They were all out of date now. Instead he now wore a fourth. A death mask.

On the chest of drawers below the mirror lay the envelope containing his will, which he intended to send to Mao that evening. How many people would have given anything to know its contents! Especially those who were waiting to step into his shoes. But it was not what they expected. It set out only a few general observations, followed by a request that his ashes be scattered in the sky over China.

A handful of dust, he thought – that's how everything will end. Other people would have liked his will to contain a list of names suggesting his successor, together with accusations and settlings of old scores. But he had left all that far behind. He had no connection with the world any more. All he had to do was go to the concert, and wait for the curtain to fall. Then nothingness.

The invitation card lay just beside the will. Perhaps I've already ceased to exist, he thought. Perhaps it's only my ghost that's going to the concert . . .

Yes, perhaps so. The concert was other people's affair – he was merely a visitor, a visitant, half living and half dead. It was his first and last concert. The last of his life, the first of his after-life.

He would scarcely be any more present at tonight's event than at future ones that might be attended by his ghost. There, that's where he used to sit, people would say afterwards, looking at his empty box. (Would it really be empty?) Actually, he rather relished his present detachment. He would listen to this concert as if from a box in the beyond, set free at last from the passions and rivalries of the power struggle.

The clock struck again. Sometimes the ghost, sometimes the real man seemed to prevail within him. Why don't I go for one last walk round Peking before the concert, he thought, before dismissing the idea. He felt as if he could do anything he liked. As if he had only to wish himself in his box and he would be there without any need for a car or a journey or an escort.

It was natural enough. A ghost had no use for such things. But still, he thought at last, I'd better get there somehow or other, or someone else might go and sit in my box. *The box is occupied . . .* Where had he heard that before?

Juan Maria Krams took out his invitation again to check that he hadn't made a mistake about the time of the concert. No, he still had plenty of time, he thought, settling back in his chair by the window. But he didn't stay there long. He suddenly realized he hadn't noticed any other figures but 19.30 on the card. He checked. Yes, it didn't say the number of the seat, and as far as he could tell, with his meagre knowledge of Chinese, it didn't say whether it was in a box or in the stalls. This seemed very odd, for an official concert.

Juan Maria hurried out of the room and ran downstairs. As usual, one of his guides was waiting for him in the lounge on the ground floor of the villa. Juan Maria showed him the invitation and pointed out that the seat number wasn't specified. To his surprise, the guide didn't react.

"Don't worry, comrade Juan," he said with a smile. "I know the numbers of the seats."

"You mean . . . ?"

"Yes, everything's as it should be."

Krams went upstairs again, more slowly. It seemed very strange. His guide, though he hadn't stopped smiling, had nevertheless refrained from telling him the number of his seat. This was obviously something to do with the security measures taken for an event at which top leaders were to be present, but still Krams was rather offended. Why were they showing so little confidence in him, Chairman Mao's "European godson", as friends and enemies alike called him, half-joking, half-serious? He'd learned to forgive the Chinese their little unpleasant surprises, but this time he thought they were going too far. But then, he reflected, this mystification probably applies to everyone. And in the present tense situation, extreme precautions might really be necessary.

Yes, that would be it. He mustn't be too touchy. There were much more serious things than the number of his seat to worry about in connection with the concert. It gave him an opportunity to guess which of the two factions in the struggle for power had the best chance of getting the upper hand – which, for the moment, enjoyed to however small an extent the favour of Mao. It was upon the outcome of this confrontation that his attitude to China depended, together with that of his group.

The Chinese guests were also getting ready to go to the concert. There were about seven hundred of them, all official figures – senior civil servants for the most part, ministers, members of the Central

Committee, representatives of different nationalities, veterans of the Long March, members of the mysterious *Zhongnanhai* or General Bureau, and so on.

The member of the Politbureau who always wore a towel wound round his head like a turban looked at his invitation, and sighed. His seat was in box number 7. He wondered where his rival would be sitting – "Double-Barrel" as he was called, the man who claimed to live on two barrels of chick-peas. It was some comfort to know that as all the top leaders took their places in the concert hall, dozens of others would be straining their eyes to find out the answer to this question.

But it was only one preoccupation, and a small one at that, among the many that would be engaging the guests. The pulses of the Chinese would be beating fast over much more serious mysteries as they entered the hall. As most of them belonged to one or other of the various rival factions, secret or otherwise, such questions were a matter of life and death. They knew that all those rows of heads rising above the red plush seats were seething with plots, coups, putsches and massacres. All these projects depended on different eventualities: the death of Mao, the death of Zhou Enlai, or both, a seizure of power by Deng Xiaoping, or by Jiang Qing and her gang. Three deaths together, a single night of slaughter, or a blood-bath lasting for years? ... There were other factors, too, that might trigger off a plot or coup – developments at home or abroad, natural phenomena. These categories might include provocative acts on the part of the United States or the U.S.S.R., a reversal of the situation in Vietnam, a famine decimating the population of India, a drought in northern China, floods, earthquakes, epidemics of cholera or smallpox, a plague of rats or locusts ...

Many of the guests at the concert would be seeking signs that evening as to how they should take advantage of such events. They would look for symbols in the movements and gestures of the dancers, the dark red of the prima ballerina's cloak, the white of the cloak worn by the dancer next in seniority, the undulations of the dragon's tail, the antics of the little monkey, the horses sweeping through the dreadful desert and finally exiting covered in gore.

But these signs wouldn't be at all easy to decipher. You might easily get it wrong.

*   *   *

All the lights were on in the guest-houses for important foreign visitors built in the western part of a large park. Two kings, four sheikhs, a sick imam, two regents living in exile and a widowed queen were all getting ready for the concert, together with their guides and bodyguards and concubines. Powerful whiffs of perfume floated out towards the cars that waited outside with their engines already turning over.

In the last and most modest of the villas, set slightly apart from the others, Pol Pot, the master of Cambodia, was poring over a hefty volume about symbols, leafing through the pages impatiently. In the course of the last few days he'd been secretly thinking up a new massacre, greater in scope than anything that had gone before, not only in his own country but also in the whole of Asia, if not the world itself. He hadn't told anyone about the scale of this project; this evening, at the concert, he would try to make out if the time was ripe for it. He'd started consulting this venerable tome as soon as he received his invitation, but there wasn't much time, and the subject was extremely complex. He had a feeling that the answer to his question was to be found in the movements made and the colours worn by the second woman dancer, as these related to the figure of the ancient serpent; but he wasn't quite sure. And if his interpretation was wrong it might cost him dear a few days later when he asked for Chinese backing for his plan.

It wasn't easy, it wasn't at all easy, he thought, his fingers trembling nervously. His eyes hurt, he was tired, and felt rather sorry for himself. Instead of being able to look forward to the concert in peace, like everyone else, he had to go on working right up to the last minute.

Behind the scenes in the theatre where the concert was to be held, there was the usual bustle before the show. People ran to and fro. Male and female dancers vanished into the make-up rooms, dressed as magicians, princesses, eunuchs, or priests preparing for human sacrifice. Not to mention those merely swathed in long strips of silk, who were to represent parts of the serpent or of the dragon's tail. Former stars of the company, directors and the various technicians appeared and disappeared, looking worried. Some of their anxiety transmitted itself to the faces of their colleagues, even those of the dancers, which were covered with such thick layers of cosmetics you wouldn't have thought they could reflect any expression but those that had been painted on them.

It wasn't surprising if they were worried. Like all official concerts this was a great event: in theory all the top executives of Party and state were coming, and so was the diplomatic corps. Moreover, rehearsals had been punctuated by visits from mysterious officials not usually seen in artistic circles. Some people said they were there on the orders of Jiang Qing, and even that she herself might come to the dress rehearsal. Others suggested that the visitors were from the *Zhongnanhai*, and this really scared everyone. But no one had been able to find out for sure who the visitors were. What was certain was that changes had been made right up to the last minute – even at the dress rehearsal the night before – changes affecting certain scenes, the lighting, the movements of the principal dancers and the colours of their costumes. Most of the company had been told something of the significance of these changes; in any case, they already knew how important a part symbols played in the theatre, especially on an occasion like this. But they didn't really understand much, and if the organizers themselves were somewhat better informed, even their notions on what was going on were very hazy. Not that there had been any shortage of rumours on this subject in recent years! Some anti-Party theatre companies, such as the Three Villages group, were said to have used their productions to exchange messages about sinister possibilities like the overthrow of Mao, or events like Peng Dehuai's plea for mercy from his judges. But even after the plot had been unmasked and many of the company's artists and administrators arrested, no one ever found out exactly how their messages were sent.

And now it was being whispered that at the end of the first scene, and somewhere around the middle of the second, and also at the yellow stork's exit just before the interval, something of the highest importance was concealed in the movements of the second woman dancer and in the lilac tints of her costume. It might have something to do ("Not so loud! Put your mouth closer to my ear!") – it might have something to do with Mao's approaching death and the question of who was to succeed him. Just to hear such things made your blood run cold. What was more, there might be world-wide repercussions; the messages might have to do with terrorism in general, or with massacres in various parts of the globe, or with heaven knew what! It was more like a calamity than a concert!

The second woman dancer leaned against a pillar in the wings, gazing at the agitation all around her. Because of her heavy make-up, her face looked as if were set in plaster. The only sign of life was the worried expression in her eyes, all the more striking because of her impassive mask.

She looks terribly anxious, thought one of the make-up men as he went by. Perhaps she'd found out the meaning of the symbol she was being made to convey. The make-up man himself didn't know much about it. He watched her surreptitiously, wondering what feature of her performance would act as a signal for the massacre of the intelligentsia that some people were predicting, always supposing it wasn't a delusion.

"Are you worried?" one of the oldest dancers in the company asked her younger colleague. "There's no need. You've nothing to reproach yourself with . . . A few years ago I myself was accused of driving two ministers to commit suicide, but it wasn't my fault at all . . . I know it's different in your case – people are talking about wholesale massacres – but that's no reason why you should fret. It's not your fault, is it?"

"I don't know what you're talking about," the girl replied. "You're the second person who's spoken to me like that, and I still don't understand what it's all about."

"I thought you were worrying about . . ."

"Not at all! I was thinking of something quite different. Do you know what? . . . If I tell you, Lin Min, you must promise not to breathe a word to anyone else."

"You can count on me!"

The girl looked at her for a moment, hesitating, then made up her mind.

"I don't even want to know what you were talking about, Lin Min. I don't understand such things. All I can think of is when the show is over and the foreign members of the audience come up on the stage to congratulate us . . . Perhaps I'll be lucky and one of them will kiss me . . . You see, Lin Min, at the last concert, in October, there was a fair-haired man who smelled so delicious . . . I shall never forget him . . ."

As the young ballerina was speaking, her colleague looked at her with an expression that might have been either envy or pity.

Then the older woman went away, and the young dancer was alone again. She tiptoed over to the heavy velvet curtain, pulled it aside a little, and looked through the gap into the auditorium, where the seats all looked weighed down under the same red plush. The audience weren't there yet. An oppressive silence seemed to rise up from the great empty space. The girl sighed and let the curtain fall back into place.

To Hua Guofeng the chiming of the clock on the wall sounded different from usual. For some reason he paused with the comb and scissors in his hand, waiting for the seventh stroke. I've only got fifteen minutes left, he thought. As he lifted the comb and scissors to his head again he noticed that his hands were trembling. He was nervous – he should have started getting ready sooner. It wasn't his fault though . . . The idea that his resemblance to Mao might be increased had suddenly occurred to him that afternoon. The notion excited him, though he was sorry he hadn't thought of it sooner. The fact that he looked like Chairman Mao hadn't gone unnoticed among his friends, who sometimes made rather risqué jokes about it, but it hadn't occurred to anyone that the likeness could be improved, cultivated like a species of fruit. The thought had taken a long while to come to the surface in Hua Guofeng's own mind, wandering first along devious and mysterious ways, as most ideas do. He'd wondered for some time about Mao's possible successors, and had occasionally thought of the *Kagemushas*, the doubles whom medieval Japanese war-lords used to send to replace them in battles and at celebrations. If I were just a little bit more like him, he reflected, I could be Mao's *Kagemusha*. Then, as it became more and more difficult for Mao to preside over ceremonies and receive distinguished foreign visitors, and especially when the Politbureau first deliberated over whether he ought to give up appearing in public, Hua thought about the *Kagemusha* more and more. But it wasn't until the meeting of the Politbureau this afternoon that everything around him seemed to freeze, and the idea of the double suddenly emerged from the depths of his brain, hitting him like a cosmic ray. The meeting had ostensibly been discussing something quite different, but, as usual lately, it was clear everyone was thinking about the succession. The problems involved were well-known: Zhou ill with cancer; Jiang Qing, Mao's wife; her band of supporters; the Deng Xiaoping faction . . . People said Zhou would soon be sending Mao his will . . . Everyone let his thoughts run riot. And it was then that an inner voice cried out to Hua: "Why not you? Why do you stand modestly aside? The others are no closer to him than you are. You have a definite advantage in your face and physical appearance. As for the soul, no one can see that." Then a host of chaotic thoughts crowded into his mind: a case of mass psychosis, a people yearning for its lost leader, their longing to see his face on the rostrum again . . .

"This very evening!" shrieked the inner voice. "Appear as him this evening, and you will triumph!"

Back home again, he had wandered around the rooms aimlessly until he realized what it was he was looking for. A mirror. He stood for a long time gazing at his own reflection. He couldn't send for a hairdresser or a make-up man from the theatre – no one must be let into the secret. Everyone had been suspicious and on the alert lately. He'd manage by himself.

As if afraid of being overheard, he tiptoed over to a cupboard and got out a comb and a pair of scissors. Why were his hands shaking? Other people had used poison or a dagger . . .

That thought calmed him a little. But when the first tuft of hair fell down beside the mirror, he was almost surprised it wasn't spattered with blood. It was half-past five when he started on his task; at seven o'clock he still hadn't finished. As he plied comb and scissors alternately, his thoughts wandered to the still empty theatre, the envelope containing Zhou Enlai's will, and other more trivial things. His hands went on shaking. Sometimes he thought the resemblance was increasing, sometimes it seemed to have disappeared altogether. Once he suddenly turned and looked at the portrait of Mao up on the wall: he appeared to be looking back at him sardonically. The scissors in Hua's hand flashed as if with menace.

At a quarter past seven there was a knock at the door. It must be one of his bodyguards. The time has come, he thought, and tiptoed back to the cupboard, put the comb and scissors back in their drawer and covered them up with a towel. Then he walked towards the door. But just as he was reaching out for the door-knob, he remembered in time and went back to the mirror and the tufts of hair still lying around it. He gathered them up in his handkerchief; rubbed the top of the dressing-table to make sure there was no trace left behind; then he went over and opened the door.

* * *

The car taking Skënder Bermema and C— V— to the concert drew up outside the theatre. As they alighted they saw other groups of guests, Chinese and foreign, making for the lighted entrance as their limousines glided quietly away like empty shells.

As he entered the auditorium, Skënder was dazzled by the bright red velvet. The stalls were starting to fill up, but there was practically no one in the boxes yet.

Skënder and C— V— followed their guide as he located the seats assigned to them. They settled down. The theatre was quieter than Skënder had expected, but when he looked around he saw that the stalls were now almost full, except for a few latecomers picking their way to their places. The boxes too were filling up, and Skënder noticed that the people round him were looking at them as he was, but without actually turning their heads. It was twenty-five past seven. Skënder, like all the rest, went on watching the highest dignitaries arrive. He saw the Albanian ambassador and almost waved to him; but of course the other wouldn't have noticed. Then he spotted the Politbureau member with the turban: he was in the same box as "Double-Barrel", whom he recognized from seeing him on television. But this wasn't the moment for laughter.

At seven-twenty-eight Jiang Qing and Wang Hongwen took their places in their boxes. There were only two boxes vacant now. At first glance it was as if the whole power of the state was embodied in those present, and the two empty boxes didn't count. But a few seconds later, by some mysterious process, the opposite came to be true: for the thought of those who were absent sent a chill down everyone's spine. They might make their appearance at any moment, with their pallid faces and the mocking smiles that seemed to say, "You rejoiced too soon at our not being here!"

There wasn't a murmur. On the contrary, the silence deepened, and only a mute kind of stir ran through the theatre when Hua Guofeng appeared in one of the last two empty boxes. "What's this? What's this?" hundreds of people silently chorused. Skënder watched their guide's profile: his pale face had gone red, as if it were bathed in a sulphurous light; he wore an expression of mingled terror and hope, like someone pleading for mercy. "Hua Guofeng's face!" Skënder exclaimed inwardly. "What's happened to it?" But he didn't expect to get an answer here, in this place inhabited by ghosts. His own mind, that mechanism so apt to produce the strangest associations of ideas, soon supplied him with a number of possibilities. Hua Guofeng's face was the spitting image of Mao's. He might have taken the skin off Mao's face and stuck it on his own. Many others must have been revolving the same horrible thoughts as Skënder, for the whole theatre seemed to have suffered an electric shock.

It was exactly seven-thirty when the house-lights began to fade. And it was at that precise moment, between the house-lights going out and the foot-lights coming on, that Zhou Enlai appeared in the one remaining empty box.

So now the boxes are full, thought Skënder Bermema.

Zhou Enlai seemed to hover between being a human being and a phantom. The curtain slowly rose. "God!" exclaimed Bermema, astonished to find himself using a word that had been obsolete for so long.

The concert had been going on for an hour, and it was evident there wasn't going to be an interval. Hundreds of motionless heads gazed at what was going on on the stage. Although everything seemed so cold and stiff, one was instinctively conscious of something, some thrill of apprehension, passing from the stage to the auditorium and vice versa. When the second woman dancer, rustling her lilac-coloured skirts, went over and almost brushed against the yellow stork, the whole audience held its breath. Pooh, thought Skënder, what has it got to do with me? But try as he might he couldn't help sharing in the general feeling of dread.

The second woman dancer twirled more and more slowly near the stork. The audience was mesmerized. Suddenly, as if by mistake, a red spotlight swept briefly over the boxes, so that their velvet walls seemed to be streaming with blood. Skënder thought he saw a pair of eyes rolling in ecstasy. What face was this that he thought he recognized? He'd seen it somewhere before, in a book or perhaps in a newspaper article about Cambodia. Again he told himself all this was nothing to do with him, but the more he said it the more involved he became, as the music went on throbbing through the theatre. He thought he was going to faint. Once or twice he almost stood up and shouted: "Stop these celebrations! I've got a novel that's dying!"

He glanced at C— V—, whose profile showed he was watching the show with a mixture of interest and exasperation. Skënder leaned closer and whispered in his ear, so quietly he couldn't hear himself: "My novel's giving up the ghost."

The other didn't react, but Skënder thought he saw a brief grin show briefly on C— V—'s lips. "I certainly chose the right person to confide in!" thought Skënder angrily. But was his colleague's smug smile caused by what he himself had just whispered, or by something that was happening on the stage?

A gong sounded, the audience started, a light suddenly illuminated the second woman dancer's face. At the sight of that livid mask, Skënder was filled with horror: it expressed at once distress, accusation and an icy, unearthly anger. If only this nightmare would end, he thought. God, let it end soon!

A few minutes before the show finished, a vague stir in the auditorium – perhaps a member of the public had happened to turn his head – made Skënder look up at the boxes. What he saw took him aback. Some of the boxes were already emptying. Not until a few moments later did the whole audience seem to register the no doubt unprecedented fact that part of the political leadership, the most important figures in the government, were leaving before the curtain had come down.

"What does it mean? What does it mean?" everyone seemed to be shouting as if through the most powerful loudspeakers, though no one actually uttered the words. Had they disliked the show? Had the symbols they'd seen triggered off anticipation of some disaster? For a moment Skënder imagined carnage must already be raging outside . . .

At last the curtain fell and the lights revived as if after a long swoon. As the spectators stood up to leave, they now looked openly at the empty boxes. Jiang Qing, Wang Hongwen and Zhou Enlai had vanished. And though most of the leaders had chosen to stay, they seemed colourless and uninteresting compared to those baleful absences.

"What does it mean? What's going on?" Skënder asked the Albanian ambassador when he finally found him on the way out.

The diplomat's expression was surprisingly enigmatic. If Skënder thought he caught a gleam of some kind, it came from the ambassador's spectacles rather than from his eyes.

"I don't know what to tell you," he said. "Perhaps Mao . . . As you know, he took to his bed a long time ago . . ."

"Yes. But I got the impression it was something else."

"Your theory could be right."

"How do you know what it is?"

"Oh, it's easy enough to guess," said the ambassador, smiling.

They said goodnight and went in search of their cars. Only then did Skënder remember C— V—, who was some way off, trying to attract his attention.

They drove back to their hotel without exchanging a single word. Their guides sat scowling too.

As he got out of the car, Skënder could feel almost physically the pain in his side, in the place from which he imagined his novel had been removed. He was afraid he mightn't be able to walk. The guides said goodnight to them in the hall.

Back in his room, he knew he wouldn't be able to sleep. After walking up and down for some time, he went and stood by the window. Through the cold panes he could see a part of the street, with some neon ideograms that looked as though they were suspended in the darkness. "Just look what the Chinese language has come to," he thought. "In the past people wrote magnificent works of literature and science in it, but now those characters are used only for insults, incitement to hatred, empty phrases, all the things that C— V— delights in." He glanced at the wall that separated their rooms. That was how C— V— regarded language . . . as a vehicle for poison! Such people were plague-carrying microbes. It was they who had killed his novel! Skënder seethed with rage. He must have a talk with his travelling companion – tell him exactly what he thought of him!

"A talk!" he said to himself, grimacing. "I'll show you what I'm made of! How would you like to have a little discussion?" He still wasn't sure how he was going to handle it, but thoughts of something rather more violent than mere debate were flashing through his mind.

He was still grinning when he went out into the corridor. After glancing to left and right he went and knocked on C— V—'s door. "Who is it?" asked the other, after a pause.

"It's me!" Skënder imagined himself saying softly. "Let me in!" But he didn't really say anything. He was imagining, as he stood there, the scene that might follow . . .

In his mind's eye he saw himself pushing the door open. However much he tried he couldn't restrain himself. C— V—, in pyjamas and bedroom slippers, seemed to recoil. Perhaps because of Skënder's sudden irruption, perhaps because of his increasingly menacing smile, C— V— took a step or two back. His expression seemed to say, "What is all this? Have you gone mad?"

He had come to a standstill in the middle of the room, waiting to hear what the intruder had to say, when Skënder, instead of saying anything, clenched his fist and punched him on the nose, like a character in a silent film.

C— V— staggered and caught hold of the bed-post to stop himself from falling.

"What's got into you? You must be out of your mind!" he cried incredulously. Skënder himself was even more amazed at what he'd done, but that didn't stop him raising his fist again.

C— V— managed to dodge the second blow. He even attempted to fend Skënder off, but seeing that his visitor was too furious to desist, he launched a few blows of his own. But either because he'd been taken by surprise, or for want of experience, his arms only flailed about in an ineffective and effeminate manner.

"Rat! Vermin! Not C— V— . . . W.C!" roared Skënder.

He hit him again, but the blow glanced off the other man's jaw. This, together with the allusion to water closets – it wasn't the first time he'd heard this pleasantry – finally got to C— V—.

"Swine!" he bawled. "Savage!" And kicked Skënder right in the groin.

Bermema let out a howl of pain. The pain was atrocious – if C— V— had been wearing shoes instead of slippers, he would probably have been writhing on the floor. He turned pale, his mind went blank for a second, then started to race again. He vaguely associated the attack on his genitals with C— V—'s jealousy about his love-life, with reviews by C— V— criticizing the plots of his novels, with the women he, Skënder, had known, and even with the memory of Ana Krasniqi and her marble belly, now consigned to the shades . . .

"So that's how it is, is it?" Skënder growled through clenched teeth, hurling himself on his adversary once more. "Is it?" he repeated, trying to drive the other into a corner.

Blind with rage, he rained blows on his opponent, who was caught between the window and the radiator.

"Take this for the two truths . . . and this for the four errors . . . and this for the three demons of the city . . ."

Then he heard himself mocking: "Here we are in the midst of a battle of ideograms – when are they going to come to your aid?"

But the other man didn't answer. Their hoarse breathing was all there was to be heard. Outside, because of their own exertions, the ideograms were jigging about as if they had St Vitus' dance.

"It's just what you deserve – to be beaten up in the middle of China, with your billion Chinese comrades unable to come to the rescue!"

. . .But Skënder Bermema was really still out in the corridor, leaning his head against C— V—'s door. He'd imagined the previous scene so vividly that his fists hurt from being clenched so tightly. But no, he mustn't act so disgracefully here in China. He mustn't sink so low.

"Who is it?" said the voice from inside the room again.

Skënder felt like answering, "It's shame!"

How shameful it would have been. Everyone would have known they'd gone for one another like two fighting cocks while on an official visit to China. A visit that coincided with the Day of the Birds!

Skënder turned away from the door and began to wander up and down the still-empty corridor. He glanced both ways: not a soul. He concluded that no one could have heard them: the scene he'd imagined was still so clear in his mind that he wouldn't have been surprised to see someone rush up to see what the noise was all about. He hesitated for a moment at his own door, uncertain whether to go in or not. At the end of the corridor, sitting in a little glass box, there ought to be an attendant, a combination of guard and floor-waiter, who saw everything. He'd certainly have noticed Skënder's comings and goings. Skënder tiptoed towards the glass cage. Yes, the man was there. Skënder thought he should make sure he was wearing the necessary smile, but when he caught sight of his reflection in the glass of the cage he saw that his expression, such as it was, would do: after all the man was a Chinese, and Skënder didn't know him from Adam. The man looked back at him vacantly: he obviously hadn't noticed anything.

Skënder nodded affably. Unusually, the man didn't return his smile.

"*Ho*," said Skënder, using the only word of Chinese he knew. "Everything all right?"

"*Ho*," replied the other, still not smiling.

Hell! thought Skënder. He must have noticed something.

"Quiet, isn't it?" he said.

The Chinese leaned nearer to the glass, and spoke. He was probably saying, "What?"

Skënder tried scraps of all the languages he knew in order to try to communicate, but it was no good. Then he remembered that these attendants had to pretend they didn't know any foreign languages, even if it wasn't true. He waved to the man by way of goodnight, then turned and began to walk away. He was amazed to hear a voice behind him call out in English:

"Comrade!"

The Chinese had stepped out of his cage and was obviously trying to tell him something. He's seen my comings and goings in the corridor, thought Bermema, and the scoundrel means to concoct some slanderous report about me. He started to go towards him: after all, if the man was prepared to talk to him, perhaps he wasn't going to write a report, merely give him a friendly warning.

"Eh?" said Skënder. Then, in English: "Do you speak English?"

The Chinese nodded, rather guiltily. Skënder smiled, and told himself to keep cool.

"Can't you sleep?" said the Chinese. "I can't, either."

Skënder's jaw dropped. A Chinaman talking about sleep like an ordinary human being? Their usual way of referring to the subject of repose was: "Imperialists and revisionists sleep with one eye open," or "Revolutionaries mustn't rest on their laurels."

"Why not?" asked Skënder, though it was rather a ridiculous question: the man was on duty – he was supposed to stay awake.

"The Chairman in dying," said the Chinaman.

Skënder leaned nearer. His breath misted the glass of the cage and made a sort of screen between him and the other.

"Mao dying?" he repeated. It was hard to believe a Chinese could bring himself to say such a thing.

The man nodded. His eyes were red and mournful.

"I'm sorry," said Skënder, nonplussed.

Through the mist on the glass the man looked grief-stricken.

Skënder muttered some words of sympathy, and found he couldn't just walk away. As the Chinaman's almond eyes looked blankly back at him, it struck Skënder that these people's slanting orbs were made to express suffering. Why hadn't he noticed it before?

He'd have liked to offer the man some consolation, to show sincere fellow-feeling. It seemed barbaric just to leave him alone in his cage with his sorrow.

What's happening to me? Skënder wondered. Why was he feeling so overcome with pity when he least expected it? Was it just a passing reaction, due to the fact that the word "dying" evoked for him the phrase "giving up the ghost", and thence an image of the soul? Or was it some other association, deriving from the thought of that placid round face, which seemed a million miles away from hatred; of his words, now those of a rather senile old man – "I am only a wandering monk with holes in my umbrella;" of the children he had lost, the wife who had died too, and the poem he'd written for her – "Perhaps we'll meet again amongst the stars;" and of how he now lived in a cave like a kind of deranged hermit. But the important thing was that whether you liked it or not, he was the creator of the new China . . .

But think of all his misdeeds too! Skënder reminded himself. It's true that he made modern China, but then, after that, his disturbed mind led him to create a frightful chaos, unprecedented in the annals of mankind. He mowed down the intelligentsia ruthlessly; he had the fate of Cambodia on his conscience . . . No, how could one feel any sorrow for him? It was other people who ought to be pitied!

Still, when a billion human beings grieved, you couldn't help being affected, just as on a damp autumn evening you feel something of the chill of the sea.

Yet what was strange about it was not so much the thing itself as the process by which it came about – the mysterious paths along which the contagion of pity moved. Pity, and repentance, and remorse.

But all this was unimportant compared with what he was about to witness: probably the greatest grief there had ever been.

The man in the cage was sobbing now. Apparently the consternation he'd seen on the foreigner's face had unleashed his tears. Skënder tapped on the glass to wish him goodnight. But the man stood up and came out into the corridor.

"My sincere condolences," said Skënder, holding out his hand.

The other stretched out both of his, bending forward stiffly like someone unused to demonstrations of feeling.

Skënder, embracing him, felt his tears on his own cheek.

"May he rest in peace!" he murmured. It seemed to him this venerable expression was the phrase best suited to the occasion, existing as it did on a plane above truth and untruth, above all human passions.

He walked slowly back to his room. Before going to bed he went over to the window again and looked out at the ideograms shining here and there in the darkness. "The Chairman is dying," he repeated. There were no doubt plenty of signs out there that meant "chairman", but probably none that meant "death". But tomorrow, he thought, or the next day, or in a week at the latest, it will be there.

He put his hand to his face, where there must still have been traces of the Chinaman's tears. How strange: he hadn't embraced any Chinese when it would have been natural to do so; but he had embraced one now, unexpectedly and at the moment of parting. Was it an omen? If so, of what?

He paced up and down for a while as if to clear his head of his swirling thoughts before trying to sleep. It was the moment of parting from evil, certainly. The omens foretold a farewell to suffering. The pain which history had inflicted on Albania at the end of the present millennium was about to end.

He felt like shouting for joy.

"Let the bells ring out!" he cried aloud. "There has been a sign from heaven, and we have come to the parting of the ways!"

He looked in the mirror at his cheek, at the place where Asia had bestowed a final kiss.

Outside, the unintelligible ideograms hung in the sky like words in a dream. He turned away from them and went to bed, but before he fell asleep they crept back into his mind, a vast galaxy in which, somewhere, an invisible hand prepared to switch on another, paler light: the ideogram of death.

14

MAO ZEDONG WAS STILL on the point of death. For hours his closest relations and colleagues had been in his bedroom watching him die, and many others were waiting in nearby rooms. Some were still in the clothes they'd been wearing at the concert, when the news came that the Chairman was dying. Every so often, in his lucid intervals, he would look round at them as if to say, "So you went to the concert, did you?" And then they wished they could slip away and change into mourning. But they were all kept rooted to the spot by the knowledge that if they were away for a moment they'd find the door barred to them when they got back.

Mao moved in and out of a state of coma, but even when he emerged from it he was usually still delirious. At one point he saw the world, shrivelled to the size of a pitiful little globe, flying through infinite space, surrounded by cosmic dust and carrying his own coffin. It was tied down with ropes which would later serve to lower it into the grave. (Lord, where was it all happening? On the forty-second or the forty-third parallel, or at some unknown latitude?)

The faces of those around him merged with other visions. Zhou Enlai must be dead by now, he thought in a lucid moment, otherwise they wouldn't have been able to keep him away from my coffin. But, in a kind of painful whirlwind, the word "coffin" kept changing into "power", and then changing back again, endlessly. As for the other people, they all vied with one another to hang on to the bronze handles of the coffin. If he could have spoken, he'd have shouted to them not to buffet him about like that!

That was the picture they conjured up, so obvious was their hatred of one another. Only the prime minister was missing. His will, his request that his ashes be scattered over China ... It was when he, Mao, heard of Zhou's last wishes that he himself had been struck down. God alone knew how many days had gone by since then. Zhou must be dead and buried a long time ago. Otherwise he'd be here, hanging on to the coffin handles with the rest. "Careful!" he called out inwardly. "Can't you let me spend my last hour in peace?"

His dimming eyes scanned their expressionless faces. His mind conjured up, only to destroy them, one scenario after another for what would happen after his death. The uncertainty was unbearable. The various possibilities whirled around in his head like a ghostly ballet. Hua Guofeng put up against a wall to be shot. Jiang Qing made empress, her crown ornamented with Deng Xiaoping's gold teeth. Yao Wenuan married to Jiang Qing after her triumph, then murdered by her in his sleep. Then both of them superseded by Deng Xiaoping. Then Deng, a lame man, in power, as in the days of Tamburlaine. (Deng-lang, perhaps they would call him.) Jiang Qing mouldering in prison, her hair hanging loose in despair. An empty plane flying in search of people, alive or dead, to take to Mongolia, but no one would go on board – Hua Guofeng rose out of his grave to tell Mao, with a diabolical grin, that *he* wasn't so stupid as to do so! "What have you done with your scissors and comb?" Mao asked him. "I hear you fancy yourself as a hairdresser lately!" "Who told you that?" gasped Hua Guofeng. "Jiang Qing – it was the last denunciation of hers I was able to read, just after the concert you all rushed headlong to . . ."

The others stood round the coffin, silent.

"I oughtn't to have left them so divided," thought Mao with a groan, trying to turn over. The nurse hurried forward to help him. His eyes were half closed, but he could still see Zhou Enlai strolling through a field leading a crab on a string. "Why aren't you attending to affairs of state?" Mao asked him. Zhou smiled and pointed to the crab. "I have to look after this now," he said. "It's my cancer, and I'm trying to tame it." "You've got it on a lead like a dog!" said Mao. "Of course, you've always been attracted by English customs." Zhou didn't answer. He started to walk away. "Are you dead?" Mao called after him. "It's a long time since I read the papers or listened to the radio . . ." But by now Zhou was too far away to hear.

Lin Biao appeared instead. He was strapped into a plane seat, and the words "No smoking" kept blinking on and off over his head. Where were they flying to – the Kingdom of the Blue Monkey? "You plotted the coup – you ought to know what happened!" said the marshal. "As the victim, you had a ring-side seat!" Mao retorted. "All the accounts were doctored, both on earth and in heaven!" said the other. Both on earth and in heaven? Mao was taken aback. He felt like asking Lin what *had* become of him. As a matter of fact, Mao *had* wondered at the time whether something hadn't gone wrong . . . But he decided not to pursue the matter at present.

Then he saw Lin Biao again, but in the distance this time, wearing a raincoat and standing on a grassy plain. It was raining, and people were collecting up the débris from a burned-out plane. Mao nearly said, "You're clutching your coat around you as if you were burnt to a crisp." The other only drew his coat closer with his yellow fingers.

"The fool – does he really think he boarded that plane alive?" thought Mao.

Lin smiled coldly. "I know everything," he said. "But I'm looking for the person who burned in my stead. I'm trying to find his upper left canine. When you chose the poor wretch to take my place you forgot that *my* upper left canine is gold . . ." He laughed. "All great criminals get caught in the end because of some small oversight!"

As he laughed he made sure to show the gold crown in question. "It's this little toossie-peg that gave you away!"

"All ghosts like bragging," Mao answered. "Do you think I'm so foolish as to have put someone else in your place? It was you all right in that plane, you wretch! Have a good look at the débris and you'll recognise yourself."

Lin tried to feign indifference, but it was clear that he was astonished.

"But you yourself admitted you had me killed in a car!"

"Yes . . . But afterwards, during the night . . ."

"What? What happened during the night?"

So you don't know as much as you'd like everyone to think, thought Mao. As for how the plane was brought down, neither you nor anyone else will ever know.

> All but the grasses will seek in vain
> To find the truth of the Mongol plain . . .

How could he make sure this couplet would survive him?

Mao groaned. The nurse helped him turn on to his other side.

*   *   *

It looks as if he's going to die tonight, thought the observer at the North Pole, easing off his headset.

The satellites and teletype machines were going great guns . . . He remembered a very cold night when he'd slept at his maternal grandfather's for the first time. The dogs barked a lot, but that wasn't what had frightened him. Even now, after all these years, he couldn't forget how one of them had bayed and bayed, and how his grandfather had said, "Someone in the village is going to die tonight."

Someone is going to die tonight on this planet, he thought with a shudder. The obituary notices were ready. The ravens were waiting for the signal to take flight.

He put his headset back on again and adjusted it. Mao Zedong was still in a coma. The rumbles he could hear were in his own stomach. No matter how much he twiddled the knobs, all he could hear were death rattles . . .

Ekrem Fortuzi huddled over the radio, his brow furrowed in concentration, trying out various wavelengths. He still cherished a faint hope that some station, somewhere, would be more optimistic about the state of Mao Zedong's health. But they all seemed conspiring to say he was slowly dying.

"Ekrem," his wife called from her pillow. "Are you coming to bed or not? – this is the third time I've asked you!"

"Just coming!"

"I shan't call you again. Mind you don't wake me up!"

"I'm coming now, my dear."

He stood up, looked first at the radio and then at the bed, then bent down and switched the set off.

"About time," said his wife, making room for him. "You drive me mad with your Chinks!"

"Your talcum powder does smell nice," he whispered.

"All I ask is that you don't speak Chinese at the psychological moment," she said. "I'd rather you spoke Italian."

"Because that reminds you of Luigi, I suppose?"

"Of course not! What are you getting at?"

"I know it does remind you of him!"

"It doesn't, I tell you! It's just that I can't bear the sound of Chinese any more!"

"Admit it does remind you of him, and I'll do whatever you want."

She didn't answer.

"Go on, admit it!"

"Well, it does remind me of something. But it was all so long ago . . ."

"Right, I'll speak Italian then . . . But remember – no Chinese, no Italian! Do you see what I mean?"

"No – what?"

"I told you before: no Chinese, no hope of Italian either. But that's enough philosophy. Or rather, let's philosophise down here . . . like this . . . *Amore mio* . . ."

Their grunts and groans gradually died down. Then in a clear voice, not at all breathless, she said.

"You spoke Chinese again!"

"Did I? I didn't notice."

"You're hopeless!"

He didn't answer. He didn't need to get round her any more. She was well aware of it, so she turned over and went to sleep.

He lay still on his side of the bed until she had dropped off, then he got up and tiptoed over to the radio. He switched it on, very low, and put his ear to the loudspeaker. He stayed like that for a long time, and might have remained there in a kind of lethargy till dawn, if at a certain point his wife hadn't heard him let out a sob.

"Ekrem!" she cried, in a fright. "What's the matter?"

He couldn't bring out any words. She stared at him wide-eyed, and was about to jump out of bed and come over to him when he managed to stammer:

"Mao is dead."

She looked over at him with pursed lips.

"Idiot!" she said.

But he wasn't listening. He went on weeping, sobbing out every so often:

"My Mao, my own little Mao, you've gone . . . you've gone . . ."

"He's round the bend," she thought. "He's gone completely bonkers!"

He went on talking to himself, mostly in Chinese, but reverting to Albanian for the affectionate diminutives he knew only in his own language.

"My own little Mao – and to think that while you were giving up the ghost I was making love like a pig!"

I'll have to take him to see a psychiatrist, she thought. Tomorrow!

Her first impulse was to make fun of him, insult him, but suddenly, seeing him so forlorn, she couldn't help feeling sorry for him. He must be the only person in Europe who was carrying on like that. She got out of bed, threw a cardigan round her shoulders, and went over to him.

"Ekrem," she whispered. "What's wrong? Come to bed, or you'll catch your death of cold."

Though she was still quite angry, she'd made an effort to speak gently. But he went on weeping buckets, perhaps even worse than before.

"He had to die some time!" she said soothingly. "He was very old – everyone said he was decrepit! What did you expect? Everyone knew he was at his last gasp. Come to bed, dear."

"I can't! Leave me alone!"

He's nuts, she thought again. My God, what's going to become of him?

"I can't, you see," he went on. "I feel all hollow inside. I studied his works very seriously – I was the only person in the world who understood all the nuances of his philosophy. I've compared the original texts with the English and French translations – they're not at all accurate . . . I fell in love with him, we understood one another so well . . . He was so good . . . he didn't believe in the horrible class struggle!"

"All right, all right," she said, "you've told me all that before. Now come to bed before you get bronchitis, like last winter!"

"I kept telling you, but you only made fun of me. He was our only hope, our star . . ."

Here we go, she thought.

". . . and now it's gone out, our star has disappeared. We've all had it now. We're finished. And you don't even realize."

"It might be just the opposite," she suggested, trying to reassure him. "Perhaps they'll find a reason now for getting closer to China again. It's always like that – people wait for a death in order to fix something that wasn't working properly. They'll say he and his obstinacy were the cause of all our differences . . ."

"But he was so good, so gentle, soft as velvet. And his face . . . his face was so smooth too . . ."

"Be that as it may, I'm sure it'll work out as I say. They'll blame him for the cooling off in our relationship, and we'll patch things up. Then everything will be all right."

"Do you really think so? I don't believe it for a minute."

"Of course! It can only make things better."

"And what if they go wrong again? He was a poet and a philosopher – a natural peacemaker. Where are they going to find another like him?"

"Others will be more liberal – you can be sure of that. The Chinese are fed up to the teeth with the Long March or whatever you call it . . ."

"*Zhang Jeng*," he said.

"Well, they've had it up to here with the *Zhang Jeng*! What they want now is peace, comfort and women . . . Don't they say that at the Hôtel Peking there's a room where the Chinese leaders spend their evenings with ballet dancers?"

"If only things *could* turn out like that!" he sighed.

"We'll know more about it tomorrow. We'll go and call on a few friends and find out what's going on. And now come to bed."

"It's a good thing you're here to cheer me up," he said, straightening up a little.

He had a restless night. Twice he made to get up to listen to the radio again, but his wife stopped him. The third time she spoke to him severely.

"What more do you expect to find out? It's happened, and there's nothing to be done about it."

He just looked sheepish.

"No, but I'd like to know what you're hoping for," she said, more gently.

"I'm hoping they might deny it!"

She laughed.

"You really are . . . !"

"No, why? It wouldn't be the first time. There have been false reports of his death before. Several! Don't you remember?" He was getting close to tears again. "As if they couldn't wait for him to die!"

"Now that's enough!" she said decisively. "Let's get some sleep . . ."

It was a grey, reluctant-looking dawn. That morning it was she who made the coffee and brought him a cup in bed.

"Do you think they'll embalm him?" he asked.

She gave him a sidelong look.

"Will you please give it a rest? We'll go out and see some people – then we'll find out something."

"Which people?"

"Anyone you like. We could go to the Kryekurts'. They usually know what's really going on."

"You're right. Let's get dressed and go."

"Don't be ridiculous! It's far too early. If we don't watch out, people will be suspicious."

"Yes, I suppose so. We don't want to attract attention."

They didn't start out for the Kryekurts' place until after ten o'clock, but when they got there they saw they needn't have worried about being too early. Apart from frequent visitors like Hava Preza and Musabelli, they found Lucas Alarupi, Mark and his fiancée already there. Alarupi was the former owner of what was once a little soap factory; it had now expanded to produce washing machines, shampoo and tooth-paste. Mark had the day off, as the concert that evening had been cancelled.

"Cancelled?" said Ekrem, as if to check he'd heard aright.

"Yes," said Hava Preza. "No need to ask why."

"It's a good sign, I suppose," said Hava Fortuzi.

"On the way here I saw a lot of official cars going towards the Chinese embassy, no doubt to offer condolences," said one of the others.

"I told you so," whispered Hava Fortuzi to her husband. "The concert's cancelled, the officials are going to register their condolences at the embassy . . . It's going to be all right!"

Ekrem tossed his head and gazed at the shiny, sallow face of Lucas Alarupi. He'd heard a lot about him, and wondered why he was out visiting on a day like this. He must be a mine of information.

"Do you often come here?" Ekrem asked him, while the others went on with the general conversation. "I've been wanting to meet you for a long time."

"I don't go out very much," answered the other. "We're swamped with work, especially now, when we're just coming up to the end of the quarter. And as well as production there are the committee meetings at Party headquarters, and socialist endeavour, and cultural activities, and all sorts of other things which may seem less important but which need a lot of attention. Running a factory involves a lot of problems, especially now, after the decisions taken at the last plenum of the Central Committee."

Ekrem's wife goggled, then looked round at the others as if to say, "Just listen to him!" She felt like shouting, "What's all this about Party meetings and socialist endeavour? You're just a yesterday's man like the rest of us! They don't let you anywhere near your old factory, let alone consult you about their problems!" But Hava Preza gave her a look, and Ekrem nudged her, so she didn't say anything.

"Well," said Hava Preza to break the silence. "So you've got plenty to do and plenty of worries?"

"Of course," said Alarupi tonelessly. "As I said, carrying out the plan is only one of our problems. We also have to meet people with new ideas, evaluate pilot experiments, and so on. It sounds easy, but it takes a lot of doing."

"He may be crazy himself," Ekrem's wife whispered to him, "but I don't understand how the rest of you put up with his maunderings."

"Ssh," he said.

"But he's in the same boat as we are, isn't he? If not worse! No job, downgraded socially. So what's all this about endeavour and committees?"

"I know, I know," Ekrem answered. "But he believes, and wants to make other people believe, that things are back to what they were before . . ."

"But how . . . ?"

The fact was, Alarupi had started to entertain this delusion when he heard that in China former factory owners had been made assistant managers of what had been their own firms, and were even allowed a share in the profits.

"I've always said that's the most fantastic thing that ever happened, even in China," said Ekrem's wife.

"When it was announced he became a new man. It knocked him completely off-balance, and he started to spend all his time hanging round the factory. It's his whole life. His briefcase is full of press cuttings about it, and graphs about the progress of the plan. At home he's got a whole collection of wall newspapers, citations for workers' awards, and so on. When things at the factory go badly he's quite ill. If the Party criticizes it, he can't sleep. In short, it's the only thing he lives for."

"Poor man!"

"Of course, he never forgets to calculate his share of the profits."

"There you are!"

"Of course! What did you think?"

Hava Fortuzi could scarcely keep from laughing.

"Even so, he must be completely ga-ga."

"Perhaps. I'd say he's typical of our age – just an extreme example. Perhaps the most extreme in all . . ."

"In all Europe?" she interrupted.

"Maybe . . . What are you looking at me like that for?"

How else? Hadn't she told herself only a few hours ago that her husband must be the only person in Europe to weep for Mao Zedong? And now here was another, hardly less extravagant oddity. What an age we live in, she thought. Ever since she'd left her youth behind, she'd always thought the world was going to the dogs. But she hadn't expected it to go as fast as this!

"He's a hybrid," said Ekrem, continuing his whispered conversation with his wife. "A capitalist-communist hermaphrodite."

"A loony, anyhow," she answered. "I'd like to throw a bucket of water over him to bring him to his senses."

"But why? He's probably quite happy as he is."

"Yes, dreaming! But we're awake! Why should we have to suffer his nonsense, and without an anaesthetic!"

"It's not his fault," said Ekrem. "And anyway, perhaps it's not just a dream. Perhaps it's an omen, a sign of things to come!"

"No chance! It's too late now for wool-gathering!"

At that she caught Hava Preza's eye, which had been fixed on her reproachfully for some time because of the Fortuzis' lengthy private parleyings.

Lucas Alarupi hadn't noticed anything. He was still droning on.

"A fortnight ago we had a very good meeting with the star workers about exchanging jobs. We haven't done so well with socialist endeavour, though, I'm sorry to say. The Party's going to have something to say about that. Still, we can only do our best . . ."

People were surreptitiously shaking their heads. It was incredible to hear such talk in this room of all places. I wouldn't have come if I'd known, thought Ekrem's wife.

"But what do you say about what's happened now?" Ekrem asked the former factory owner, trying to stem the flow. "Will Mao's death change anything?"

The other man shrugged.

"Difficult to say," he answered. "It all depends on the struggle between the two factions that all the radio stations are talking about. We'll have to see which side wins."

"I wasn't talking about China," said Ekrem. "I wonder what's going to happen here."

"Precisely . . ." Alarupi began.

"There's no telling," Hava Preza interrupted. "Some people say Mao did all he could to prevent relations between China and Albania deteriorating. Some say he did his best to undermine them."

"What? I'll never believe such a thing!" protested Ekrem.

"Time will tell."

While they were exchanging theories about this, they heard the sound of a car drawing up outside.

"It's the man upstairs," said Emilie, pointing to the ceiling.

"They're worried. He looks very down to me," said Hava Preza, who'd been peering out of the window.

"Let's hope nothing awful's going to happen."

Then they heard footsteps going down the stairs, and the sound of the car driving off.

Mark and his fiancée listened lethargically to the rest of them as they went on with their discussion. The girl's grey eyes grew darker.

"*Il fait froid*," she whispered to Mark, looking him straight in the eye.

He was anxious to go into the other room, too. From there these debates and reminiscences sounded like an echo from another world, forming a mere background to their amorous exchanges.

"In a moment," he whispered. "Wait just a bit longer."

Emilie served coffee, and they all sipped solemnly, still talking about Mao's death. Every so often their eyes would turn to where the portrait of old Nurihan looked down at them from the wall.

"*Il fait froid*," murmured the girl again.

Then without a word she and Mark both stood up, not looking at anything in particular. When they were in the other room she was silent for a while, then flung herself into his arms, shivering not from cold but from a feeling of emptiness and some other, indefinable sensation.

"God, is it always going to be like this?" she sighed.

It was not a sigh of despair, or of joy; nor did it signify any expectation either of better or worse. It was more like a question containing something of all those feelings. Would she always have to make love like this, amid whisperings about some foreign country (this was usually the subject of the conversations they could hear through the wall), and echoes of another woman saying "*Il fait froid*" during another winter?

"Perhaps," he answered faintly. Neither of them could decide whether they liked things as they were, or if they dreamed of a better world together.

Silva was late getting to the office, and when she did arrive she asked if she could leave early to go with Gjergj to the airport.

"Is he going away again?" asked her boss. "Where to?"

"Where do you think?" said Silva. "China."

"I presume it's got to do with Mao's death?"

"I suppose so."

Linda was following all this with bated breath.

"You spend your life at the airport," she said to Silva when the boss had gone out of the room.

"Do you know who I saw there the last time? I forgot to tell you at the time. I saw Victor Hila's Chinaman, with his foot in plaster!"

"Really?"

Linda felt herself blushing, and didn't know how to hide it. As for Silva, she was troubled too, at the thought that her friend might ask her what she'd been doing at the airport.

But at that point the boss came back and their conversation was interrupted.

At eleven o'clock Silva said goodbye to both her colleagues and left the office. When she got home, Gjergj wasn't yet back from the foreign ministry, and after wandering around for a bit she sat down on the settee in the sitting room, her hands clasped in her lap. Then she remembered how her mother used to say it brought bad luck to sit with your hands like that, and she hastily unclasped them. She wished Gjergj weren't going on this trip. For two, perhaps three weeks the apartment would seem silent and empty without him, and the life she and Brikena led there alone would seem very dreary.

333

Then she told herself she was being unfair: the separation would be much worse for him than for them.

There was a ring at the bell, and she hurried to open the door. It was Gjergj.

"How did it go?" she asked.

He gave her a look that seemed to say, "What a question!" She noticed he was carrying his briefcase, and realised that her secret hope that the trip might be cancelled at the last minute had been in vain.

"Let's go," he said. "I'm a bit late."

They hardly spoke on the way to the airport. Silva gazed at the wet road and the heaps of rotting leaves on either side. What awful weather to die in, she thought.

The airport was full of Chinese with their eyes full of tears. She saw Skënder Bermema's wife waving at her from a little way off.

"What are you doing here?" Silva asked, going over.

"I'm waiting for Skënder. He's coming home today. What about you?"

"Just the opposite," said Silva, looking to see if her husband had got through the customs yet. "Gjergj is leaving."

"Really? He'll probably fly out on the plane Skënder flies in on."

"Perhaps. Frankly, I'm not very keen on this trip!"

Skënder's wife didn't know what to say to that. They looked at one another for a moment, their smiles fading, though their sympathy did not.

Gjergj reappeared, and they all chatted quite cheerfully for a bit about the coincidence, but Silva couldn't quite conceal her uneasiness.

"You shouldn't harbour such thoughts," Gjergj teased. "I know it's because the trip's connected with a death, but the coffin isn't going to be on our plane, you know!"

"Thank goodness for that at least!" Silva exclaimed.

"The plane's late," said Skënder Bermema's wife, looking at her watch. "It ought to have landed some time ago."

She was looking less animated now, as if she'd suddenly realized that while the other two were joking about anxiety, it was she who now had the right to be feeling worried.

"It's a beastly night," said Gjergj. "No wonder the plane's late. Why don't we have a coffee or something?"

They found a table and ordered coffee. A female voice announced that the plane had been delayed by bad weather, but would be arriving in ten minutes. The whole place began to stir. Some people got up from their tables and went over to the window to watch the plane land.

In due course the plane emerged heavily from the clouds. The interval between the time when the wheels touched down on the landing strip and the moment the aircraft came to a halt outside the terminal seemed endless. The passengers started coming down the gangway. Most of them were Chinese, and as they came nearer you could see their eyes were red with weeping. They must have heard about Mao's death during the flight.

"Look, there he is!" cried Skënder's wife, waving, though he was still a long way off.

"Yes!" said Silva. "He's with the other chap . . ."

Skënder Bermema kissed his wife several times. The tenderest kisses are those of husbands returning from China, thought Silva. Through the noisy crowd that had come to greet the travellers, she saw that C— V— had a bruise on his cheek. It seemed to puzzle his friends, who were evidently asking him how he came by it. She was tempted to ask the same question. But a second or two later she had forgotten all about it.

Silva got home at about three o'clock. Brikena had put the lunch on, and was waiting.

"Did Father get off all right?" she asked.

"Yes."

Brikena was clearly disappointed that they hadn't taken her with them to the airport. After a moment she said:

"Uncle Arian phoned."

"Did he? What for?"

Brikena shrugged.

"Did he sound all right?"

"I think so. He wanted to speak to Father. Perhaps to wish him bon voyage."

"I expect so," said Silva, feeling relieved.

They ate almost in silence. The apartment seemed unnaturally quiet. While Brikena did the washing up, Silva wandered round the rooms, not knowing what to do with herself. Usually, when Gjergj went away on a mission, she and Brikena embarked on some kind of work in the house that couldn't easily be done except when he wasn't there, such as washing the curtains or remaking the mattresses. But this time Silva didn't feel like doing anything like that. She wasn't even tempted by the big trunk in which she kept family possessions that had been passed down from generation to generation. Often, when Gjergj was away, she and her daughter would spend hours poring over bits of embroidery, the white dress and tiara which three generations of Krasniqi brides had been married in, and innumerable other mementos.

Silva went out on the balcony; walked along between the clotheslines, with their multi-coloured plastic pegs waiting for the sheets to be hung out to dry; and had a look at the lemon tree. But she couldn't take any interest in the lemon tree either. She realized that the date for spraying it with insecticide was long past. She sighed. All the tedious things one was supposed to bother with . . .

She went back inside. Brikena was crouching down by the bookcase in the living room. She felt a day like this called for some unusual occupation, and as her mother hadn't said anything about the trunk or the mattresses, she'd decided to look at some of the family albums. Silva sat down quietly beside her and watched. Brikena's fingers looked more slender than usual, perhaps because of the care with which she was turning the pages. Silva thought of all the things they might be doing: seeing to the curtains or the mattresses, admiring ancient embroidery. But a voice inside her told her to leave the afternoon as it was: empty. Perhaps it would find some way of filling itself.

15

EVERY EVENING SINCE Gjergj had gone away, Silva waited impatiently for the television news to see what was happening in China. But it was all very confused. They usually began with various speculations about what was going to be done with Mao's remains. Some people said the body was going to be embalmed, others disagreed, and the commentators tried to link what was going to happen to the corpse with whether or not the Maoist line was still going to be followed in China. But it was obvious that all these generalities represented merely a transition to less important items of news, so when Silva heard the presenter talk of a "confused situation" and a "state of uncertainty", she stopped listening for a while and used the interval to ask Brikena:

"Did anyone call from the foreign ministry?"

"No," said her daughter.

Never had any of Gjergj's absences seemed so long. Reason told Silva not to worry. As a foreigner he wouldn't be involved, whatever might be happening in China. But Silva couldn't help remembering his description of the charred walls of the British embassy in Peking, just opposite the Albanian embassy.

After they'd discussed every possible theory about developments in China, the television pundits would come back to the less ephemeral subject of the embalming.

In everyday life, conversation tended to concentrate on much the same topics. People started referring to ancient Egyptian mummies, even citing names like Ramses II and Tutankhamen, though in the past the dates of the Pharaohs had made them fail their history tests. The talk would then move on to schoolboy japes and anecdotes about examinations, and this would lead them back to Mao's corpse again. There was always some worshipper of the past to maintain that the skills of our distant ancestors had never been surpassed in certain fields, and that there certainly wasn't anyone today to rival them in the art of embalming.

"All this talk about a body!" said Arian Krasniqi, Silva's brother, one evening. "They'd do better to tell us what they're going to do with his soul!"

Since Gjergj had been away he'd come to see his sister more often, and Silva was glad to see him joining in the conversation again.

"You're right," she told him. "Even if you have to talk about the body in these circumstances, it's the soul that matters."

"What?" said Brikena. "And supposing the soul doesn't exist?"

Silva and Sonia burst out laughing.

"We were only talking about his ideas!"

Sonia stroked her niece's cheek. Brikena had blushed after she'd spoken.

"My clever little girl," Sonia whispered to her.

"Skënder Bermema got back from China a fortnight ago, and the day before yesterday he read us a poem about the embalming of Mao," said Silva. "Wait, I think I've got it in my bag." She went over to the sideboard. "Yes, here it is. Would you like to hear it?"

"Yes, yes!" cried Arian.

Silva unfolded the piece of paper, and even though she had heard the poem before she frowned as she saw it again, as if remembering she'd been shocked by it.

"It's called 'The Old Embalmers'."

> The old embalmers from the province of Kung Lin
> started out on their way and are still on it.
> On they march to Peking in the biting cold,
> For there it's said the Chairman is dead.
>
> Among embalmers they have no equal.
> Peerless are they in their time.
> One guts the body, the second empties the brain,
> The third excels at preparing balms and spices.
>
> They go gladly along the roads
> knowing that the mortal remains
> of the aged and illustrious departed
> have been consigned to their zeal.

All three were so sad before
At never being summoned to Peking.
And now "The day of the immortals is over!" –
they sigh dejectedly.

Lin Biao was dead, Zhou Enlai too.
The bones of the first charred under a foreign sky.
The ashes of the second scattered in the wind.
And no one had thought of the three little old men.

"It looks as if we shall die without embalming anyone
   any more,"
They sighed as night enfolded them.
Then one day they saw someone coming:
A messenger from the distant capital.

So they set out, driven mad by the good news.
Summer and winter they marched, year after year.
One guts the body, the second empties the brain.
The third excels at preparing balms and spices.

Silva looked up.

"Strange, isn't it?" she said.

"It's more than strange!" exclaimed Arian. "If I'm not mistaken it says at the end that the embalmers have gone mad."

Silva checked.

"Yes. Here's the line: 'So they set out, driven mad by the good news.'"

She was just going to say something else when they heard the phone ring. It seemed to ring more loudly than usual. Silva and Brikena both got up together.

"Arian – it's for you," Silva called from the hall.

"Who is it?" he asked as he came towards her.

But she just shrugged as she handed him the receiver.

As he was speaking, everyone left in the room fell silent. When the women looked outside they could see it was dark. It was as if the ringing of the telephone had suddenly made night fall.

Arian was on the phone for a very long time. When he came back into the room his face looked drawn.

"What was it?" asked Sonia.

"Nothing. Just a notification to go somewhere."

"Where?"

He looked round at all of them, and perhaps he would have told them what it was all about if he hadn't seen how anxious they were to know.

"Somewhere," he said, going back into the hall for his coat.

"What's going on?" asked Sonia, looking at Silva. "Can it be as urgent as all that?"

Silva got up to see her brother to the door. She looked at him imploringly.

"Arian, why . . . Can't you just . . . ?"

He stared back at her.

"I can't understand you all," he said. "You're all acting so strangely. I'm not a baby! I don't need to be wrapped in cotton-wool!"

"It's not that . . . But you might . . ."

"You want to know where I'm going? All right, I'll tell you. I'm going to see my ex-minister!"

"Going to see your ex-minister?" faltered Silva, not trying to hide her bewilderment.

What did he mean by "ex-minister"? The man was a minister still. If he'd been sacked they'd have heard about it. In any case, it was too ridiculous . . . A sacked minister didn't summon people like that . . . The words must mean something else . . . But of course! Why hadn't she thought of it before? As Arian wasn't under the orders of the minister any more, he could refer to him as his "former" minister . . . Still, all that was of no importance. What mattered was that he'd been summoned.

"I expect it's some good news," she said. For a moment she imagined him being reinstated in the army and the Party, and the party they'd give to celebrate. "But what's the matter – you don't look very pleased?"

He smiled sardonically.

"Arian, you're keeping something from me! Such an urgent summons, at this time of day . . ."

He laughed aloud.

"I swear I'm not keeping anything from you at all! I haven't the faintest idea myself what he wants to see me for. I know as much about it as you do. Only I'm not very hopeful . . ."

Silva would have liked to ask how anyone knew he was at her

place, who it was that had phoned, and so on. But he already had his coat on, and his massive frame seemed already on its way. As she opened the door for him she just had time to say:

"Anyhow, don't forget that he's still a minister . . ."

As he ran down the stairs she called after him:

"And come back here as soon as it's over! Do you hear, Arian? We'll be waiting for you!"

Strangely enough, the question of why he'd been sent for was not uppermost in Arian Krasniqi's mind as he strode towards Government Square. Stranger still, what did often occur to him were bits of Skënder Bermema's poem about the embalmers who went mad. The more he tried to dismiss them, the more obstinately they echoed, more or less accurately, through his brain: "All three were so sad at never being summoned by the minister . . ."

Hell, he exclaimed inwardly. He didn't really expect anything from this interview, which he regarded merely as a chore. As for the poem, it was just crazy, like the person who'd written it, and his own sister, who took such pleasure in reciting it. Like himself too, if it came to that, for not being able to get the wretched thing out of his head. But after a moment he felt he'd been unfair to all concerned. After all, there was something about the lines, with their memorable rhythms, rhythms that reminded you of walking, of a journey on foot, even of a long march. And most important of all, the poem had mysterious undertones that hinted at the confused and inexplicable series of events he himself had lived through here in the last few months, against a background of even more enigmatic events in China. But perhaps he'd better forget about all that now and concentrate on why he'd been summoned. As he came to that decision he found he'd arrived at the entrance to the ministry. The large baroque building was almost entirely in darkness. Only a few windows overlooking the inner courtyard had lights in them.

Arian followed an orderly along an endless corridor where it was obvious the radiators had been turned off long ago. The first thing he noticed on entering the minister's office was the minister's face. It had got thin, but not in the way that's associated with illness. The minister's throat seemed to have wasted away around the Adam's apple, where it sagged more than before yet at the same time looked tense with anxiety.

341

"Dear me," said the minister almost jovially, getting up from his desk to greet the visitor, "whom have we here? If it isn't the rebel, the offender against military discipline! But I'm only joking – come in and shake hands!"

I'd have done better not to send for him, thought the minister, gazing at the door for some time after it closed behind the former tank officer. He had wanted to see with his own eyes and hear with his own ears one of the men who'd been making his life such a misery. Even if it didn't get him anywhere much, he had hoped to get his visitor to admit that when he and his fellow tank officers refused to obey his order they hadn't been able to explain the reasons for their insubordination, or at least hadn't been able to explain it clearly.

But the other had denied him this relief. On the contrary, he had stubbornly maintained that while they had indeed taken no notice of his order, they had given a clear explanation of their motives.

The spacious office seemed to echo with scraps of their conversation – mostly, with the minister's own words, for the visitor had spoken very little. The phrases that now came back to the minister ranged from the solemn to the familiar, the flippant to the philosophical, but he had the feeling that despite all his efforts not only had he got nothing useful out of his interlocutor but he'd also given himself away.

After his opening words, the minister had gone on:

"It's officers like you the Party needs! And that's my attitude too, even though I admit you make things difficult for me at times! But that's precisely why I like you – not only because you make life difficult for me when you think it necessary, but also because you criticize me, and criticize me severely sometimes, if I make a mistake, as in this business with the tanks . . . It was you, comrades, who were right, and I who, even though unwittingly, was wrong. But the stuff we communists are made of is something special, isn't it? We don't mind acknowledging our errors. It can happen that we get caught up in routine, rules and regulations and the arts of war, so that we forget that above all there is the Party, and that the greatest art of all consists in being a good communist! That's why we call ourselves comrades – because we want to help one another, correct one another, prevent one another from persisting in error. You, for example, were quite right not to carry out an order that wasn't justified . . . But, to be realistic, you might have been clearer about it . . . more what shall I say? . . . a little more trusting. When you refused – quite rightly, quite rightly – to obey the order, you might have supplied a little explanation, don't you think? I don't mean you ought to have made a speech about the primacy of the Party or dialectical materialism or whatever, but you might have given me just a tiny, weeny little explanation of your refusal . . ."

At which point the other had interrupted.

"We did explain our refusal, and we did so quite clearly."

This reply seemed even colder and more momentous now than it had done at the time. The minister felt his innards going taut. He'd summoned this man to get him to admit that while he and his colleagues had seen the minister's order as subordinating the Party to the army – something which was wrong under any régime, but even more so under a socialist one – they hadn't actually formulated their opinion. And the extent to which the minister was wrong to punish them depended on whether or not he knew the reason for their disobedience. If he did know it, he could be held responsible, because then the order to encircle the Party committee ceased to be a chance decision – "If it had ever occurred to me to see the order from that point of view, I'd never have issued it" – and became a premeditated act. If he didn't know it, his guilt was less and his anger more excusable, for there isn't a military man in the world who doesn't go off the deep end when an order of his is challenged, especially if that military man happens to be a minister.

He'd hoped the interview would establish the fact that the officers hadn't explained their insubordination. But they weren't even conceding that much!

The ex-officer just sat there, expressionless. The minister made another desperate effort. Could it have been, by any chance, that as the officers themselves saw the question quite clearly, they took it for granted that no explanation was called for, since they had great confidence in their leaders – too much confidence perhaps, for people forget that leaders in general, and a minister in particular, may have weaknesses, may get angry, may be arrogant and brutal, may fail to study properly the documents issued by the Party and the classics of Marxism . . . er, where was he? Oh yes, had the tank officers, and Arian Krasniqi himself, considered it unnecessary to

343

provide long explanations, and thought it quite enough to say, "It just isn't done to encircle a Party committee"?

Even before the minister had finished speaking, the officer had started shaking his head. No, not at all. They had explained the reasons for their disobedience briefly but quite clearly. If the comrade minister wanted more details, he could supply them. As soon as he received the order he had asked: "Encircle the Party committee? But why?" The order had then been repeated. Then he and two other officers he'd got in touch with had asked: "Is there an enemy commando about, or the threat of some commando raid?" The answer they got was curt: "It's nothing to do with you! Just obey orders!" The officers had repeated their question, and this time the reply was: "No, there is no enemy commando. Obey the order!" It was then that they'd said: "The order is unacceptable. Tanks cannot encircle a Party committee, or any other legally constituted body – if they do so, it's tantamount to trying to establish a dictatorship . . ." There had been some more terse exchanges, during which the tank officers had repeated that if there was no enemy commando involved, the surrounding of the Party committee couldn't be justified. When one of the signals people let out an oath, Arian Krasniqi had shouted, "We're not living in Shanghai, are we?"

The minister flinched at this. Then he went on:

"That was all quite right and in the spirit of the Party, and I'm sure that's what you said. But the point is, did the others hear you properly? Perhaps not, because of bad weather or technical conditions. If I remember rightly, it was very stormy at the time, with lots of thunder and lightning . . ."

The officer just repeated what he'd said before.

"We explained quite clearly why we were disobeying orders."

"Ah . . . I didn't know that. In that case . . . That alters everything. Of course you and your colleagues are not guilty. But perhaps the signals people were responsible for all this business, or members of my own staff left things out of their reports. Unless they're not to blame either: there's no denying that the weather was awful, and there was a lot of thunder and lightning . . ."

But he realized that whatever he said it would be in vain. He began to falter. All he wanted now was for the fellow to go. He'd have told him, "All right – that's enough! The interview is over!" if he hadn't been afraid of putting his back up even further. I ought never to have sent for him, thought the minister as he went on protesting about how glad he was to see him, and how much he appreciated people who stood up to him . . .

In the end he didn't really know what he was saying, and when the officer turned and left he heaved a sigh of relief.

The confrontation had exhausted him. And he hadn't even got anything out of it. On the contrary, his visitor had almost certainly guessed how worried he was. And if so, he had only himself to blame for making things worse! All he needed now was for everyone to know his real state of mind.

The minister stared at the notes he'd scribbled in preparation for his autocritique.

He was going to have to confront the plenum of the Central Committee, and there was no doubt he would be expected to carry out a thorough autocritique. Day after day he'd scribbled, crossed out and scribbled again, without ever arriving at a satisfactory result. Go deeper! – the words with which he'd tormented so many other people at other meetings were now terrifying the minister himself. He'd noticed that every time the phrase was addressed to someone performing an autocritique, the victim literally seemed to sink into the ground. Now he was going to be on the receiving end.

He tried to push the thought away. He looked round his desk, at the array of telephones and red and green buttons marked "Alarm No.1", "Alarm No.2", "Army Headquarters", "Admiralty", "Air Force" . . . He kept thinking how any Latin American colonel, with only half all these means at his disposal, could . . . But, like a drug to which a patient has grown accustomed, the thought no longer did him any good. "That's no consolation!" he exclaimed. For it was plain that no one gave him any credit for doing right when he had at his fingertips so much power for doing wrong.

His hands went on toying instinctively with the draft of his autocritique. That's right, he told himself, forget about those buttons. Your fate depends on these notes.

He already had a wad of them, but he knew he'd have to write more. He scrabbled for the passage that referred vaguely to the tanks. Since Enver Hoxha had mentioned the business specifically, he would have to explain it in full to the plenum. He skimmed quickly through what he'd written. It was too flimsy. He'd dealt

345

with the aftermath of the affair and his anger against the tank officers (which he'd presented as unjustified, the result of his own presumptuousness and lack of contact with the masses), but he hadn't yet said anything about the beginnings of the episode – the mental processes that had led him to give such an order, his underlying motives. He could already hear a voice calling out to him: "The causes! – go deeper into the causes!"

No, he would never go that far! He'd never tell this plenum, or the next one, or the hundredth or the thousandth plenum after that, about that cursed dinner with Zhou Enlai! He'd take the knowledge with him to the grave. They could yell at him to "go deeper" until they were blue in the face, but he would never dig all that up again. Zhou Enlai was no longer of this world, so *he* wouldn't care one way or the other . . . But somehow or other he, the minister, was going to have to justify himself.

He absolutely must find something to say. It wasn't enough just to explain what he'd done as due to lack of political foresight on the part of a technocrat who hadn't gone into Marxism-Leninism properly. If he wanted to be credible he would have to make a greater sacrifice than that. Perhaps the best thing would be to admit a bit, just a tiny little bit, of the truth? People always said the most plausible lies were those that contained something of the truth. For example, he could say that the idea of encircling a Party committee had probably been suggested by the events of the Cultural Revolution in China – an incorrect interpretation of the struggle against Party bureaucracy or the anarchist slogans of Mao. Also, admittedly, by his own imperfect acquaintance with the classics of Marxism-Leninism. All this would be exposing himself to criticism, but he had to take some risks to avoid complete disaster. Let them think what they liked of him. Let them call him a Sinophile, a half-wit. Let the Party mete out some punishment or other. He was prepared to put up with anything so long as the real truth never came out.

At least he didn't have to worry about Zhou Enlai. He was as dead as a doornail – and he didn't even have a grave! Sometimes the minister felt a surge of resentment: if all Zhou wanted to do was end up as a handful of ashes scattered into the sky, why had he bothered to get him, the minister, into such a scrape? But on the whole Zhou's death could be regarded as a blessing.

Perhaps after all the situation wasn't as bad as he'd thought.

He'd certainly have to go before the plenum of the Central Committee, but the meeting was supposed to be chiefly concerned with the economic situation. And everyone knew the economy was in a bad way. Moreover, he wasn't the only person who was in trouble, and when old colleagues found themselves all in the same boat they could always be counted on to help one another. They did it instinctively, without being asked, like a pack of wolves each looking chiefly to his own interests.

Yes, the economic situation would probably distract attention from his case. When the economy goes wrong people forget everything else. Material concerns soon bring everyone to their senses. They take everyone by the sleeve and say, Just look at these statistics – never mind about the encircling of Party committees, and all that other symbolic carry-on . . .

And after all, leaving aside the evidence of the man he'd just interviewed, the fact that the tank officers had explained their disobedience couldn't be laid directly at his door. The signals people had come into it long before he did, and they could be held responsible. And then there were his own aides, and the bad weather, the wind, the thunder and lightning! Oh, they weren't going to get him as easily as that!

He turned his head. Something had banged against a windowpane. Probably a dead leaf. The wind was howling outside. The minister returned to his meditations, still concentrating on those that were most reassuring . . .

Mao's death and the troubles that had broken out in Peking would come in useful . . . He looked at his watch. Time for the television news. There was alarming news from China every day, and that could only help to distract attention from him.

He stood up, stuffed his autocritique into his pocket, and went out of the office. Outside, the wind had almost emptied the streets. His car seemed to waft him home more swiftly than usual. As he alighted, a column of black dust appeared before him, and he let out a shriek of terror.

Arian Krasniqi wrapped his scarf round the lower part of his face to keep out the dust. He regretted having stopped off at a bar for a cup of coffee after coming out of the ministry, instead of going straight back to Silva's place. He hadn't expected such a nasty wind

347

to spring up. It made him feel depressed and light-headed.

But, going into the building where his sister lived, he breathed more easily and felt better.

"Well?" said Silva, opening the door. "How did it go?"

He smiled noncommittally.

"Is Sonia still here?"

"Of course – we've been waiting for you. What happened?"

"Nothing," he said, taking his coat off.

The voice of the television newscaster could be heard in the living room.

"Don't worry about me," said Arian, smiling again.

Silva felt as if a load had been lifted off her shoulders: he looked quite serene.

"Have you heard what's happened?" she said. "Great upheavals in Peking!"

"Really?"

"Yes – Mao's wife and some of her cronies have been arrested. They've just announced it on the news."

"How strange," he murmured, looking at the TV screen, though the images no longer had anything to do with China.

Like Silva a few minutes ago, Sonia now looked at Arian's placid face and heaved a sigh of relief.

"Incredible, isn't it?" said Silva.

"What? Jiang Qing's arrest?"

"Of course. I can hardly believe it."

"It doesn't surprise me," said Arian.

"Why not?"

But Silva couldn't catch his eye.

She'd have liked to ask him why nothing surprised him any more. She was more worried by his present indifference than she had been by his previous agitation.

"I'm worried about Gjergj," she said. "What bad luck to be over there just now!"

"Father ought to have been back the day before yesterday," said Brikena, who had slipped into the room unnoticed.

"Yes – all the plane timetables have been upset because of what's going on."

Silva went over to the television and changed the channel. The Italian TV was showing the same thing: the arrest of Mao's widow. Then came shots of the Cultural Revolution – meetings, chanting crowds, people running in all directions. Commentators put forward various theories about what was going to happen next. Silva was getting nervous.

"Don't go," she said when her brother and his wife got up to leave. "Stay a bit longer – please!"

They exchanged glances. Silva made no attempt to conceal her anxiety.

"You've no need to worry," Arian told her, still looking at archive shots of the British embassy burning.

"Father says our embassy is only a few yards away," said Brikena.

Arian tried to say something to distract them from what was going on on the screen, but they were mesmerized.

"Hell!" he murmured.

"What?" said Silva.

"Nothing . . . What a business!" he improvised, pointing at the screen.

He's all right for the moment, thought Silva, but he nearly got it in the neck before because of China. Hadn't his reference to Shanghai made things worse for him? She couldn't help feeling that her nearest and dearest were still in danger.

The longer she thought about it the more impossible it seemed that her brother's fate could have anything to do with what was happening now. But she couldn't make out whether this was a good thing or not.

"Do stay," she pleaded. She didn't want herself and Brikena to have to spend the evening alone.

So the visitors took their coats off and sat down again. They tried to talk about other things, but kept coming back to the events they'd just seen depicted on the screen, and the interpretations put on them by the various commentators.

The phone rang. It was Skënder Bermema. "Is Gjergj back?" he asked. "No," said Silva. "When's he arriving?" "I don't know – why do you ask?" "Eh?" "I meant, what made you suddenly think of him?" "Oh, I see." "I suppose you watched the news?" "Of course." "So you *didn't* just phone by chance . . ."

They could all hear him laughing at the other end.

"Why don't you come round for a coffee?"

"What, now?"

"Yes!"

A moment's silence.

349

"All right. I'm on my way."

Silva came back into the room, delighted. She obviously wanted to be surrounded by as many people as possible.

"It was Skënder Bermema . . . I think I introduced you to one another, Arian . . ."

"Yes. But he probably doesn't remember me."

There was an unmistakeable note of reluctance in his voice.

When Skënder came in about twenty minutes later Silva noticed that her brother still looked rather put out. He wouldn't scowl like that, she thought, if he knew the trouble Skënder went to on his behalf when he was in jail. But she soon forgave him: what brother *would* be at ease in the presence of a man whose alleged affair with his sister had been the talk of the town?

"Were you worried because I asked if Gjergj was back?" the newcomer asked Silva, laughing. "I soon guessed why! But though it *was* the latest news that made me think of him, it wasn't for any sinister reason. I just wanted to see him. Do you know the first thing that came into my head when I heard that Jiang Qing had been arrested? I thought, well, as in the case of Lin Biao's death, Gjergj will bring us back at least a dozen different versions of what happened!"

They all laughed, including Arian.

"Are his versions useful, then?" asked Silva.

"I should think so! And I can prove it!"

He reached for his briefcase and got out a large envelope.

"Here's something based on what he told me. I'll leave it for you to give to him when he gets back. You can read it yourself if you like, and if you have time."

"I certainly shall!" she said.

"'Twelve Versions of the Arrest of Jiang Qing!,'" someone quipped.

But Skënder Bermema wasn't so cheerful now. A hidden preoccupation of his had risen to the surface again. He'd do better to concentrate on the different versions of his own death, he told himself. Three days before he'd received an anonymous letter full of threats. The second in a month.

"What would you like to drink?" Silva asked him.

"Anything!"

They talked for a while about the mysteries of China in general, then discussed what was going to happen to Jiang Qing and the likely repercussions of current events on relations between China and Albania. Silva said she couldn't believe Mao's widow was in prison; Skënder said *he* couldn't believe she was still alive.

"You always go to extremes!" Silva told him.

"Gjergj will satisfy our curiosity when he gets back," said Sonia.

"I don't think anyone could satisfy my curiosity about China," said Skënder, looking at his watch. "Don't let's miss the late-night news. There's bound to be something new."

But though Silva tried all the channels, none of them was showing any news.

Arian Krasniqi woke with a start, as if someone had shaken him. For a moment or so he didn't know where he was. Then he heard his wife breathing in and out beside him. It must have struck midnight long ago. He had the feeling that something he couldn't identify had been weighing down on him in his sleep, something he'd tried to thrust away, only to find his hands pinned down by it. They were still quite stiff and cramped. He even had difficulty separating them from one another. It was as if he'd emerged from the horrible sensation of being handcuffed.

It wasn't the first time he'd had this sensation while he was asleep. The shrill whistle of a train was fading away in the distance. It must have been that which suggested the feeling of handcuffs: he'd heard the whistle of a train when he'd first had to wear them, the night after his arrest.

He turned over in bed, but he couldn't get back to sleep. Fragmentary memories of the past evening kept coming back to him. Dinner at Silva's; people talking about the arrest of Jiang Qing . . . Sonia had asked bluntly if these new developments could mean more trouble for her husband. If her question hadn't been addressed to Skënder Bermema, Arian would have insisted on changing the subject. He didn't want to hear any more about China. If my life is going to depend on what happens there, he thought, then God help me!

As a matter of fact it did sometimes seem to him, especially at night, that his fate depended on the vagaries of a political mechanism that now affected more than a single country – a terrifying international juggernaut! Chained to those chariot wheels, how could you tell which direction misfortune would strike from? The chains you were bound with might come from as far away as the forges of Normandy – or from even further: from those of the Golden Horde. "Will you sleep with me, floozie? – you won't get even a walk-on part unless you do!" These words, spoken backstage in some theatre in Shanghai, far away in time and space, might one day influence his own destiny. For didn't people say that it was the memory of some such ancient insult that had made Jiang Qing pursue the Cultural Revolution so ferociously, especially in Shanghai?

"Do you think we're living in Shanghai?" The weary eyes of the examining magistrate bored into his. Why had he shouted such a thing on the telephone, during the famous manoeuvres? What had Shanghai got to do with it? Why had he been thinking about Shanghai?

Arian turned over again in bed, and again he felt the weight of handcuffs. They felt so real that once more he flung his arms about to try to throw them off.

The telegram announcing Gjergj's return reached Silva the next day, just before people left their offices. It left her in some confusion, as it didn't give the number of the flight or the time of arrival. She phoned the foreign ministry, but the people who should have been able to give her the information she needed were not available. The airport was not much better: they weren't expecting any direct flights from China today – so the passenger she was interested in might come either via Belgrade or on the flight from East Berlin.

Fearing Gjergj might arrive just as she was wasting time on the phone, she got her boss's permission to leave early and rushed downstairs and out through the rain to the taxi rank in front of the State Bank. She was lucky: there was a taxi free.

"To the airport," she told the driver. "As fast as you can, please!"

On the way, she scanned the telegram to make sure she hadn't missed anything. But no. Gjergj couldn't have known himself what plane he was coming by.

The airport building was half empty. There was practically no heating in the arrivals hall. The sound of the rain streaming down the windows added to the sense of desolation.

The plane from Yugoslavia had landed some time ago; no one knew when the flight from East Berlin would arrive. Why? Because of the bad weather? Silva asked. Perhaps, said a woman at the information desk.

Silva sat in a corner and ordered a coffee. The rain went on pouring down. She clasped her arms round her knees and sat there thinking, staring at the windows. She was cold. Her thoughts were growing numb, and as they did so her impatience and alarm also faded. Was this because of the monotonous patter of the rain on the windows, or because she herself was so tired? It occurred to her that, to anyone outside looking in, she must look as vague and inaccessible as the landscape looked to her, inside looking out. It was an apt image for her, sitting here alone on this dreary day in this draughty airport, scanning the sky as she waited for a plane to emerge from the clouds, bringing back her husband by an unknown route from a far-off country racked by plots and shrouded in mystery.

She didn't know how long she sat there. At one point she came out of her reverie and saw that her coffee was cold and untouched. She hadn't noticed the waiter bringing it.

She went home very demoralized. The plane from East Germany had been cancelled, and no one knew if it would be coming the next day or the day after.

She wandered round the kitchen for a while, but hadn't the heart to do anything. As she was sitting down on the settee, she suddenly remembered the envelope Skënder Bermema had given her, and got up again to fetch it. She'd left it on Gjergj's bedside table, for a surprise when he got home.

As soon as she'd read the first few lines, she realized these notes might have been written specially for such a day as this.

Peking . . . Winter's day. Some international airlines have suspended their flights because of Mao's death. I'll have to wait a week, perhaps a fortnight, for them to start up again. You can imagine how fed up I am. Shut up in my hotel. Alone. Surrounded by people in mourning.

I looked again at the notes for my novel, half hoping that it would come to life again. But no . . . my hope was still-born.

Notes written in a state of boredom . . . I don't know where I

353

read that. The author was probably some Japanese monk who lived in the early Middle Ages.

I spent all day, in spite of myself, thinking about the death of Lin Biao. Probably because of the new rumour going around about the circumstances of his death.

I went over and over what Gj— D— told me about it. It's quite interesting to compare what was said then with what is being said now. According to what we've heard so far, it's generally admitted, both in China and abroad, that Lin Biao really did foment a plot aimed at assassinating Mao. So in a way Mao's riposte was quite justified. What we don't know is whether the marshal's plot to kill Mao was the same as Mao's plot to kill the marshal.

If Mao knew about the existence of Lin Biao's plot, he may also have found out how it was to operate, and being thus in possession of a ready-made scenario, he may have turned it back on its originator. But why? Did he do so to save himself trouble; for the unique delight, the excitement tinged with irony, of having his victim entirely in his power; out of sadism; or out of a superstitious sense of poetic justice? No one knows that, either.

I was dying to get back so that I could tell you all about it, Gj— D— said to me on his return from China. And now I feel the same. I've noticed that when one is abroad, and especially when one's alone, one enjoys imagining that kind of conversation.

"Do you know the real truth about Lin Biao's death? It's finally been brought to light. In some ways it resembles and in other ways it differs from the versions you brought back to us. Today everyone knows Lin Biao wasn't shot, or stabbed, or poisoned. He was shot down by a rocket."

"A rocket? But that was the theory everyone agreed to exclude from the outset!"

"So it was. Nevertheless, he was eliminated by the method that seemed the most unlikely . . ."

That's how I imagined the beginning of the conversation between myself and Gj— D— in the Café Riviera.

"He wasn't killed in the sky over China, nor in the Mongolian desert, nor at home, nor in a hangar at the disused airport. He was killed at a dinner party, or rather after it . . ."

As soon as I started thinking of the circumstances of the murder, I found myself so fascinated by that dinner party of Mao's that I soon forgot all about the Café Riviera. The old, already time-worn

354

story itself, with its faded, sometimes almost illegible characters, appealed much more strongly to my imagination, perhaps because its origins reached back so far into the past.

It was all to happen, then, at a banquet, as in a play by Shakespeare (Lin Biao and Mao Zedong had both been passionate advocates of the banning of Shakespeare's works – was it because they were both hatching a plot based on treachery at a banquet?).

In other words, both Mao and his marshal based their plots on the plot of *Macbeth*. The only thing was, in this case, Macbeth wasn't able to commit his crime because Duncan stole a march on him.

THE TRUTH ABOUT THE DEATH OF LIN BIAO.
SYNOPSIS.

A

Lin Biao was liquidated in a way that both corresponds with and differs from the theories put forward on the subject. In a nutshell, one might say he was killed by all those methods put together but by none of them in particular.

Many factors were involved in his murder: the sky, the earth, the words "Let him go," the launching of a rocket, the burning of the bodies, the plane, the crash in the middle of the desert, the words "Welcome to the banquet," the words "And now I'll wait for you at my place," and the after-thought, "Perhaps we'll meet again in a world where invitation cards have other things written on them . . ."

It was ten o'clock in the evening when Mao, his wife, and Zhou Enlai saw their guests to the door. "Goodnight, see you soon," "We hope you'll come and see *us* one evening!" "Certainly, certainly!"

The marshal's bullet-proof car glided away along the dark street. The little group at the door stood there for a while, watching their guests disappear. No one said anything until the sound of an explosion was heard in the distance.

Mao heaved a deep sigh. He turned to his wife and Zhou Enlai. "*You* see to the details," he told them. Then he led the way back into the house.

He knew he would sleep deeply. Just as his brain had recently

355

reflected the anxiety of the living Lin Biao, so now, he knew, he would learn something from the mortal slumbers of his dead enemy.

B

On the main road, at the bend near kilometre 19, the soldiers who had just fired the rocket came out of their look-out post.

After the blinding explosion everything seemed darker and quieter than it really was. On legs still cramped with waiting (they had been lurking there for a good two hours), they walked over to the remains of the car. They'd only seen it, or rather its headlights, for a second, as it slowed down to take the bend. It had looked large and black then. Now there was nothing in the débris to suggest any shape at all. It would be difficult, too, to identify the corpses in this mass of shattered metal.

They didn't know who they'd hit. They didn't know what they were supposed to do now. Fire at the car and then wait, they'd been told.

After a quarter of an hour they saw another set of headlights approaching. They were astounded when the car stopped and they saw Zhou Enlai and the head of Mao's personal bodyguard get out. The dead man must be very important for the prime minister himself to take an interest in him.

The new arrivals went over and began to inspect the débris by the light of an electric torch. No doubt they were looking for the corpses. The prime minister's face was very pale.

The soldiers heard someone behind them calling out, "Quick! Quick!" but they were still so numbed they didn't understand what it meant. Anyhow, now that their work was done, haste seemed irrelevant. Unless there was some damage to the road that needed to be repaired? Or it could just be pointless – some officers had got into the habit of shouting "Quick!" at the mere sight of a few ordinary soldiers.

C

So he was killed by a rocket. But grotesquely, in a car – not in the sky, aboard a plane, as you might expect.

Those responsible did their best to suppress all knowledge of the car's existence. After that they tried to suppress all reference to the rocket itself, but when that proved impossible they branded the propagators of any such rumours as traitors.

And then there was the treason perpetrated by one of the marshal's children – by his daughter and future son-in-law, to be precise. Though they were unaware of what they were doing.

The bugging devices apparently proved their worth. On the strength of a recorded conversation between the girl and her fiancé, Zhou had them detained separately and then questioned them himself.

It had been a long day. The marshal didn't know what was going on. He was just due back after a vacation.

Zhou Enlai had no difficulty in getting at the truth. The girl and her fiancé had been summoned urgently that morning. A black official car was waiting outside: "Comrade Zhou Enlai would be glad . . ." The two young people complied apprehensively. As they were driven along they probably wondered why they'd been sent for. Perhaps they whispered, "Could it be for that?" Even if they didn't, even if they only exchanged glances and gestures, everything was recorded by a microphone installed inside the black limousine.

When they reached the Forbidden City they were left to cool their heels for an hour or two, then separated and sent to different rooms. The reason was obvious: when Zhou Enlai interrogated them one at a time, he could tell each that the other had confessed, so what was the point of denials?

Mao had had his suspicions for some time. All he needed was final confirmation before giving orders for the axe to fall.

Meanwhile Lin Biao himself was on his way back to Peking. The closer the train got to the capital the more his apprehension increased. What had happened while he was away? His wife couldn't hide the fact that she was worried too. She and their son were the only members of Lin's family who knew about his plot, but he suspected that his son had told his daughter. Lin Biao had always been very touched by the closeness between the two, but now it had its drawbacks. He consoled himself with the thought that daughters are usually more attached to their parents than sons are, and he could be sure she wouldn't do anything to harm him.

When he got home he found Mao's invitation to dinner awaiting him. They usually did meet like that after either of them had been away on holiday. The marshal heaved a sigh of relief. Everything

357

was the same as before. In his euphoria he forgot to ask where his daughter was. Someone had said something about her – she would be late home, she was out somewhere with her fiancé . . . But he'd been too preoccupied with the invitation to take much notice . . .

D

So there *was* an invitation. But not to Peking. Merely to dinner.

And the words "Where are we going?" *were* uttered, but not by the marshal, and not in his car. They were spoken first in a small van, then on a plane, by someone whose name remained unknown. But that was later.

Meanwhile the bullet-proof car drove on in silence towards Mao's house. Night was falling. It was still only early autumn, but the turning leaves had already lost some of their brightness. In a way that made the landscape more beautiful.

The marshal looked out at it as they went along. This part of the outskirts of the capital was particularly appealing at this time of year. Probably that was why Mao had invited him out here, rather than, as he usually did, to his house in Peking.

The lamps by the entrance to the villa came into view. It wasn't quite dark yet, and the light they shed looked chilly.

E

Ten hours later, at dawn, the plane comes into the story.

Where from? Was it a hoax, a figment of the imagination?

That was what people thought at first when they heard the truth, i.e. the current version of the marshal's death. When it was given out that he had been struck down on the ground, in his car, at kilometre 19 on the road to Mao's house, it followed automatically that the story about his – or his corpse's – attempted escape by air, together with the details about his being in a hurry, the shots, the suggestion that the plane be brought down by means of a rocket, the words "Let him go," the charred corpses in Mongolia, and so on, were only inventions designed to camouflage the truth.

But if that was the first reaction, the voice of reason whispered, "But a plane really did crash in Mongolia! Here, inside China, we can dress things up in any way we like, but when they happen on the other side of the frontier they're beyond our control."

So a plane really did go up in flames. Shot down on Mongolian territory. With Chinese corpses on board. Was it a mere coincidence, exploited to make people think this was the plane on which Lin Biao had tried to flee? This didn't seem very likely, as even the most inexperienced investigator would have had no difficulty in seeing that the charred bodies weren't those of the marshal and his wife.

So the business of the plane couldn't have been accidental. It really did have something to do with Lin Biao, whether in reality or in some fictional account of it. Was the plane necessary as the only way of proving that Lin Biao had tried to escape to the Soviet Union? That would have been rather expensive. A more plausible explanation was that the plane journey was part of some previous plot that for some reason was abandoned. But rather than waste it – after all, this was in the middle of an economy drive, when everything possible was being recycled – the people concerned pressed it into service as a smokescreen.

The discarded scenario was probably also the source of the rocket, the invitation, and Mao's "Let him go." But such details were modified to fit into the new plan: the urgent invitation to Peking became an invitation to dinner, and the rocket was fired at a car instead of a plane. As for the words, "Let him go," they seem really to have been spoken, but in different circumstances. Something like this? One of Mao's personal bodyguards suggested, "Let me kill him after dinner, in the hall," but Mao said, "Let him go," knowing there was a nice big rocket waiting for him at kilometre 19.

Thus the rocket and the words "Let him go" figured together both in the reality and in the rumour, though in a different order.

And the plane still had its place in the story. Whether as an empty shell or a delusion, it was still too early to say. For a good billion Chinese it carried Lin Biao, still alive but pale with terror, on his attempted escape. For the inner circle around Mao, it carried only his corpse.

"It was Zhou who saw to the details of this business," Mao had said the following morning, drinking tea while the plane was still in Chinese airspace. "We shall all be called on some time to say what happened, but I don't think there's any cause for alarm. I have good reason to believe 'he' is dead by now."

The others didn't dare ask questions, especially as Mao told them bluntly he himself didn't know the ins and outs. They just sipped their tea, imagining what had happened. They all saw it differently except for one thing: a bloody corpse in a seat on a plane, with someone trying to fasten the seat-belt to keep it from slipping about.

But was that what really happened?

Silence. As they went on drinking tea, each one in his mind's eye went up the aluminium steps to the plane, stepped inside, and then drew back . . .

F

In the First Rumour about the death of Lin Biao there was always a reference to a drawing back. The marshal felt a sudden chill run down his spine before he stepped into the plane, and then drew back.

It was never explained. Some said Lin Biao was so frightened he scarcely had the strength to climb up to the door of the plane and had to be practically dragged inside. Later, when it was suggested that the murderers might already have been on board, Lin Biao's drawing back was explained as a recoil from the sight of those unknown faces. In any case, it was too late. The plane door closed upon him.

When, in due course, the theory that the killers were already on board the plane collapsed, like so many others, the idea that Lin Biao drew back became absurd. Even so, people still referred to it, whether as some kind of clue or as a sign that the marshal had a mysterious presentiment.

But the whole thing was incongruous, and those who studied the question could easily guess that it wasn't the victim who had shrunk back, but the people concerned with his fate, who projected their own reaction on to him. First, thinking he had been alive when on the plane, they'd been shocked at the image of his corpse. Then they'd received a second shock on contemplating the body itself. And then they attributed their recoil to Lin Biao himself, lending him their eyes and making him look at his own image and draw back from that.

As in all nightmares, these imaginings involved inversions in time and space, and other unnatural concatenations.

So Lin Biao hurries over to the plane on which he is to escape (in accordance with his own plans, or someone else's, or merely in somebody's dream?). Once on board he finds his own bloody corpse sitting there. He recoils in terror; turns away in the hope that it's only a hallucination; and then sees his own corpse again, in a different form . . .

G

To understand what really happened you have to go back to kilometre 19 on the main road, just after the car was hit by the rocket.

A voice went on calling "Quick! Quick!" and it didn't take the soldiers long to realize that these were no empty words. But they weren't being asked to mend the road. Nor to repair the kilometre-marker, which had been so battered and singed that the "19" was hardly legible any more. The soldiers weren't being exhorted to clear away the débris, either. No, it was the charred bodies they were to do something about. Someone pointed first at the corpses, then at a small van that had driven up unobserved.

"Quick, quick – remove the bodies!"

Zhou Enlai and the chief bodyguard stood at a distance, watching what was going on.

The soldiers approached the blackened heap, which was still giving off a smell of ashes and burning rubber. A couple of headlights lit up the scene. The remains of the car were all tangled up with bits of the missile and with the arms and legs of the dead. Some of the metal was charred, some – perhaps parts of the rocket – was still shiny. At first sight the heap of débris could have been the remains of a traffic accident or of a plane crash.

The soldiers extricated the corpses and carried them over to the van. The smell, combined with that of the burnt tyres, was revolting.

"And now get in the van yourselves!"

Inside the van the smell was even worse.

"Where are we going?" asked one of the soldiers.

No one answered. At their feet lay two formless black masses. Who were these unfortunate wretches?

The van drove on and on until it came to a lonely landing strip.

361

Dawn was just breaking. In the distance you could just make out the shape of an aircraft.

"Quick! Quick!" said a voice again.

The soldiers dragged the bodies – they left black trails behind them – on to the landing strip. Then on to the plane. Not into the hold. Into the cabin, where they were placed on a couple of seats.

"Now get on yourselves."

The two soldiers climbed on board. The door closed.

"Where are we going?" one of them asked as the plane rose above the clouds.

As before, there was no answer.

The soldiers, who had been up all night, occasionally drowsed off. Their hands and faces bore black traces from where they had handled the corpses, but they were so worried they didn't notice.

"Where are we?"

Down below there was a flat expanse that looked like the Mongolian desert.

. . . The plane was found soon after it crashed, about midday. The Soviet frontier guards examined the débris and the charred bodies with interest. No one, however expert, could have told the difference between one and another. Except for two of them. They had been burned to a cinder twice.

H

The likeness between the remains of the car destroyed the previous day and those of the crashed plane was probably the source of the subsequent duplication.

The plane appeared to have come into being during the night, after everyone had gone to bed. One might say that Mao, Zhou and the burned-out car all created it in their sleep.

It was as if, after the group of watchers had melted away in the silence of the night near kilometre 19, the blackened mass of metal, rising up like a Balkan ghost from the grave, re-assembled itself in a shape that suggested an aircraft.

Perhaps that is how the story will be told two hundred years from now, three hundred, a thousand. If it's remembered at all.

After the nightmare, then, the débris awakened. Silent and black as ever, but now thousands of kilometres away.

That was how the dream mechanism worked, with all its disconti-
nuities, illogicalities and inversions of time and space.

Much later on, simplified by time, the sad story of the marshal
will probably be told as follows: Lin Biao was invited by the Chairman to a dinner at which he was murdered. That night his corpse
rose up and went away, far away to the Mongolian desert.

I

But what about the bullets in the charred body? And the firing of
shots in the plane?

Oh well, it's impossible to get to the whole truth in this business.
You'd have to be inside the heads of each of the two protagonists,
Mao and the marshal – preferably both at once – to find out what
really happened. And even then . . .

MACBETH'S LAST WINTER. SYNOPSIS FOR ANOTHER
VERSION OF THE TRAGEDY

It's not true that I killed Duncan for his throne. The murder I'm
accused of is a typical case of an act the law condones as being
committed in self-defence.

Unfortunately people have got the story all wrong. I don't deny
that those (if there still are any) who think Duncan was killed by
his own guards are completely mistaken. But anyone who thinks I
myself killed the king because I was greedy for power are even
farther from the mark.

Fifteen years have gone by since it happened. And rumour about
Duncan's death has grown more and more rife all the time, until
this winter it has reached epidemic proportions.

I myself am responsible for the confusion. It would probably
have been better if I'd explained at the outset exactly how it happened, instead of kidding myself I could conceal at least half of the
truth. No doubt I should have said from the very beginning that
Duncan dug his own grave (tyrants often do), and I merely toppled
him in.

As a matter of fact, having known the ins and outs of the horrible business all along, I was sure I was telling the truth when I said Duncan had been killed by himself – in other words, by his own servants.

But my own certainty wasn't enough to exonerate me. Not that common talk and gossip in streets and taverns were to blame for that, still less the ham actor, Billy Hampston, who wrote a play based on such rumours (and had his manuscript confiscated by my secret police for his pains).

No, it was someone else's fault, and that someone was, surprising as it may seem, none other than Duncan himself.

This is how it happened.

For a long time he had looked on me with suspicion. This was the result of the mania which most rulers suffer from, and which makes them doubt anyone on the basis of mere slander or calumny. Or perhaps he cultivated the suspicion himself, in order to justify his hatred of me and the hostile schemes that followed from it. It's not unusual for people to hide from themselves, as too shameful, their real reason for disliking someone, and to try to justify their aversion by explanations even they themselves don't really believe in.

I had observed some time before how jealous Duncan was of me, though in fact it was my wife who had noticed it first. To begin with she'd detected it not in him but in *his* wife. "I can see something malevolent in her eye," she would say, as we were coming home from some court reception. I used to contradict her: "I don't get that impression at all! The queen seems very friendly to both of us . . ." But she persisted, and in the end she convinced me. This didn't in the least affect my esteem for Duncan himself. Too bad if the queen's like that, I thought. What matters is what he thinks himself.

But my wife, my beautiful and intelligent lady, would listen angrily and say, "If a wife is jealous, sooner or later the husband will be jealous too."

And that's what happened. Duncan's looks grew cold, and then grew colder. Gradually other people began to notice it. For my wife and me, this was the beginning of days of anxiety. I did all I could, regardless of expense, to win over some member of the king's entourage, so as not to be taken unawares.

When Duncan told me he was coming to stay for three days as a guest in my castle, most of the people who had detected a coolness between us thought this visit would bring it to an end. Needless to say, my enemies were appalled and my friends were delighted.

"Why do you both look so gloomy?" the latter asked us. "Aren't you glad that difficult situation will soon be a thing of the past?"

We pretended to cheer up at this, but our hearts were still heavy. For we knew what all the rest did not: namely, that Duncan was coming not to end our falling-out but to bring about my destruction.

His plan (which I learned of through my spy) was both diabolical and extremely simple: during the third night of his visit there was to be a noisy incident outside his bedroom door which would wake him up. Then he and his suite would rush from the castle, and before the sun had risen the rumour would have spread everywhere that Macbeth had tried to murder his guest, the king, in his sleep.

For my wife and me the days and nights leading up to the visit were agonizing. We kept asking ourselves what misfortune it really was that was hanging over us. And then again, if Duncan had decided to destroy me, why had he chosen this way of doing it? There were many other questions, but what they all came down to was, what were we going to do?

It wasn't too difficult to find the reason for the king's deviousness. His position had become somewhat uncertain lately, and I had a lot of influence over the country noblemen, especially those whose seats were on the borders. A direct and unprepared attack on me might have been very dangerous for him. So it seemed to him – rightly, alas – that it would be best to damage my reputation before attacking me. It wasn't the first time he had used this method. He had done the same thing, details of implementation apart, to the thanes of Cawdor and Glamis.

But our main preoccupation was what to do. Every hour that went by made the question more urgent. How were we to meet the approaching calamity? Just give in and resign ourselves to our fate? Hope the tyrant might change his mind? Run away?

As time went by our mood changed from agitation to apathy. I often found my wife scanning the horizon anxiously from the part of the terrace that overlooked the road. I could tell she too was hoping to see a messenger coming to cancel the king's visit.

That messenger never came. On the contrary, four days before the fateful date, part of the king's bodyguard appeared, riding towards the castle. Were they the ones who were supposed to provoke the incident?

My wife was the first to see them. She called me.

"Come and look!"

We stood together on the terrace and watched them approach. It was cold. My wife's face was white as chalk. My earlier hesitations came back to me: should we yield to fate, try to escape, or hope for clemency?

No, none of those. I was going to choose another way; I myself would adopt Duncan's wicked scheme. He had planned to put on a charade in my castle. Then he should die there himself, also as in a play.

Even before the approaching horsemen had ridden through the first gate, I had told my wife of my decision.

She didn't answer. Only went paler still. Her shoulders started to shake convulsively. "I'm wicked," she kept repeating. "I'm a sinner . . ."

"Neither of us has the soul of a murderer," I told her. "But if that's what's worrying you, I thought of it first."

"No," she answered faintly. "I did!"

I insisted that, even if I hadn't spoken of it straight away, I had been brooding over the idea for days. It was quite true.

But instead of consoling her, this only made her smile sadly.

"You have been thinking of it for days. I've been thinking of it for weeks. Ever since . . ."

I hastily interrupted to assure her that the thought of murdering the tyrant had occurred to me then too, and even before that.

But it was no good, and we vied with one another in a macabre attempt to go further and further back in time to claim the honour of being the first to conceive the crime.

It was at the banquet given by Lady K . . . The reception held by the Scandinavian ambassadors . . . The day it first snowed . . .

We propelled ourselves blindly backward, not noticing how close we were getting to the limiting point – the day when I was told about Duncan's plan to destroy me. If we went back any further we'd be unable to plead self-defence. On the contrary, we'd reveal ourselves as having always harboured the idea of killing him. My wife realized the danger just in time.

"Stop!" she cried. "If we go on like this we'll go mad!"

I leaned my head on her shoulder.

"You're right," I said. "We're not murderers. It's he who started this terrible thing. This murderous fever began in his brain, and he infected us ... But enough of all that. As you say, if we go on talking about it we really shall go crazy. Let's turn our minds to something else – to preparing for the 'incident'."

Until the deed was done, and even afterwards, we always referred to it as the "incident". I suppose it was a way of trying to convince our consciences that we were only carrying out something that had been initiated by someone else. We were actors in a play written by another. Only, on our stage, the bloodshed, the wounds, the groans and death itself would be real.

This parallel so stuck in my mind that I actually suspected some of the king's escort of being not guards but actors hired for the occasion. I could have sworn they had even rehearsed their scene before they came; perhaps Duncan himself had taken part in the rehearsal.

I was so taken up with preparations for the royal visit that I had no time to be nervous, and by the time Duncan arrived I was perfectly composed.

As usual he wore the humble and penitent expression that, more than his army, his prisons, his money and his secret police, had helped him confound his enemies. It was this appearance of his that always divided conspirators, or made them hesitate and weaken at the critical moment. It was the most difficult thing imaginable to attack so crafty a tyrant.

"Are there any ghosts in this castle?" he asked, laughing, as he mounted the stairs into the great hall.

Fortunately, my wife was talking to the queen, and didn't hear Duncan's question. It raised some general hilarity, and when this died down she asked, and was told, what the king had said. But hearing it like that was less of a shock than hearing it directly. I myself was able to go on guffawing like the rest without batting an eyelid, but I did wonder what Duncan was driving at. Was his question premeditated, the sort of things rulers say in such circumstances to impress people? Had he had a sudden premonition? Or was it an omen, one of those messages from on high which men usually fail to read correctly?

"What was all that talk about ghosts?" my wife asked late that night, when we were in bed.

"Just nonsense."

"It made me think of . . ."

"Go to sleep."

But I doubted if I myself would be able to sleep. I lay there turning the details of my plan over and over in my head. There were still a few points I hadn't settled. The chief of these was when to act. Should I stick to Duncan's scenario and wait till the third night? Or would it be better to take the initiative and go into action sooner, before he took it into his head to make some change in his plan that might undo my own?

Then there was the question of the guards. Did they already know of the part they were supposed to play, or would they be incited to it at the last minute by force, or guile, or wine and wassail? And, most important of all, what was to become of them afterwards? Did Duncan mean them to be slain there and then outside his door, or spared to give evidence against me?

Duncan must have pondered over their fate just as deeply as I myself was pondering now. I couldn't make up my mind. Should I have them slain outside my guest's door as irrefutable proof of their guilt, or let them live and get them to say what I told them to say when the matter came to trial?

What would I not have given to know what Duncan had decided to do! I was fascinated by his plan, and if I'd had it in my hand I would have followed it to the letter. The most idiotic ideas occur to you when you're under great strain: I found myself wondering whether to get up in the middle of the night, go and knock on Duncan's door, and say: "Your Majesty, just let me have a look at your plan and you'll see how good I am at carrying it out . . . The only difference will be that you're the victim!"

Dawn duly broke, and the second day took its course towards evening. I was still a prey to various uncertainties. Of these the chief was the one that had tormented me from the start: should I act tonight, or wait until the third night? I was ready to bet that Duncan too was tempted to change his timetable. Then there was the question of the guards, the intended provocateurs. What did the king mean to do with them after the "incident"? What was I going to do with them? Moreover, I had to decide how to deal with my own servants, those who were going to help me do the deed. Should I reward them, as I had promised? H'mm . . . Keep them in reserve in case there was some sort of trial? Or just kill them outright?

Duncan had probably chosen the last option for *his* accomplices – murderers always talk in the end. So there was no point in my going out of my way to be original. In any case, I couldn't have departed from his plan even if I'd wanted to. I was hypnotized by it. Sometimes I even felt his mind giving me orders, as it had done all my life.

During dinner on that second evening he invited me to visit him at his castle a couple of months later. This took me aback. Had he changed his mind, abandoned his plan, decided it would be easier to slaughter me like a lamb under his own roof? Or was his invitation just a trick designed to lull my suspicions?

My mind reeled. Try as I might, I couldn't cope with the swirling images his suggestion had suddenly conjured up. Myself, at night, in Duncan's castle, as his guest. Duncan performing my rôle. What would he do with the murderers . . . ?

"Perhaps he's decided not to commit the crime?" my wife said that night in bed.

"Don't you believe it!"

She sighed.

"Well . . . If you're going to act, do it tonight. Something tells me tomorrow will be too late."

And so the deed was done. On the stroke of two in the morning, in accordance with Duncan's (and my) plan. The only difference was that at the last moment, when I saw his body covered with blood (who would have thought the old man to have had so much blood in him?), I felt faint, and ordered one of my men to remove the corpse from the castle.

"Where to?" he asked.

I remembered a swift-flowing irrigation canal with peat-lined banks, a few miles away.

In the small hours it took some of the weight off my mind to think the body was out of the castle, with the blood being washed off it by the current.

Then something happened which gave rise to a lot of chat in the taverns, and which that fool of a Billy Hampston stuck in his play. In the morning, even though the corpse wasn't there, the news of the murder spread like wildfire. (Strange that the lack of a body didn't suggest to anyone that the king might still be alive, skulking in some corner.) Everyone hung round the bloodstained sheets, gaping in horror. It struck me that a missing body terrified people even more than a murdered corpse . . .

The finding of the body in the canal late that afternoon didn't change anything. And there had I been, pinning such hopes to my disposal of the remains! Fifteen years have gone by since then, but I can still remember every hour, every minute of what happened: the arrival of the cart carrying the king's body, dripping with water and mud; the shrieks of the guards under torture; the candles casting shadows on the walls.

I kept out of the way, gnawing my fingers with anxiety. I'd been right to send the body away, but I should have sent it further. A hundred, a thousand, two thousand miles ... But how? There wasn't a desert in Scotland, curse it.

My lady and I still hoped the moving of the body by night would help to conceal the truth. But we didn't breathe a word about it.

Later on, we often talked about what happened, she and I, on cold afternoons, sitting by a fire that warmed us less and less. And now she is no more I go over it all on my own, scarcely bothering whether or not the servants hear me.

Ever since my wife passed on my life has been very lonely, and this last year I have missed her worse than ever: my beautiful, intelligent lady, whom that ne'er-do-well Billy Hampston put in a play, depicting her as chief instigator of the murder. Is there no limit to the lies of these vile poetasters?

But now I wish I hadn't, in my rage, torn the wretched play to pieces with my own hands. I'd have liked to read it again, especially for some of the strangest passages ... And I oughtn't to have had the author of it executed. If I'd been satisfied with putting him in prison I could have gone down one night to his cell and told him to re-write his horrible play.

Some parts of it really were strange, but I can't remember them very clearly. Partly because it's so many years since the manuscript was confiscated; partly because I read it at one go, without a pause, almost blind with fury.

I remember one scene in which the ghost of Banquo appeared to me. It's true that at two or three official banquets I did suffer from hallucinations of that kind – but I never told anyone about them, not even my wife. How could that charlatan Billy Hampston have got to know about something which I virtually concealed from myself?

"You shouldn't judge him so harshly," my wife said sometimes. She was always noble and generous. She might easily have hated the man for defaming her so. "You shouldn't speak ill of him – his play is quite sympathetic to you, throughout."

"Do you think so?"

"I'm sure of it. That was my main reason for telling you not to tear up the manuscript, much less have its author's head cut off. But you were so furious when you'd read it you wouldn't listen to reason."

And so on through all those long autumn afternoons. More and more often we would find ourselves – she more than I – discussing passages from the no longer existent tragedy. One of the scenes that astonished us most was that which depicts the witches. Billy Hampston must have been out of his mind to entertain such visions. We had never seen anything so terrifying in any theatre. How could he have imagined such a nightmare, and what did it mean? I conjured them up in my memory one by one, time after time, but could never decide whether their sinister predictions lessened the weight on my conscience or added to it.

One day we were talking about it when I suddenly struck myself on the forehead.

"Of course!" I cried. "There we were racking our brains, and all the time it's quite plain . . . Those witches in rags and tatters . . . Didn't John Tendler, my spy at Duncan's court, send me a messenger disguised as a beggar woman two or three times?"

"Did he? You never told me . . ."

"It was of no importance . . . And the news he brought me was so worrying I paid no attention to anything else . . ."

As she listened, she looked at me with her piercing gaze as if she knew there was more to come.

"John Tendler's messenger . . ." I went on. "Disguised as a beggar woman dressed in rags . . . I can even remember where we met . . . It was a deserted field, beyond the old priest's house . . . That's where I heard for the first time about the plot Duncan was hatching against me . . . All that's as clear as day . . . What I don't understand is how Billy Hampston got hold of it . . . I always kept it a secret . . . You can bear me out on that, can't you?"

"Perhaps John Tendler or his agent confessed . . ."

"Do you think so?"

"They must have done. It can only have been one of them."

"I suppose so. Admittedly, I didn't follow what happened very closely after the fuss died down . . . But anyhow, it was Duncan who was chiefly implicated, while he was still alive ... Whereas now ... If John Tendler were still alive today, I wouldn't mind if he did talk ... It might even be to my advantage if he told what he knew ... But of course, he is no longer with us!"

"Perhaps his messenger is still alive?"

"The one he sent disguised as a beggar woman? But who can say who he was? John Tendler was the only one who knew ... And that messenger was so horribly disguised I wouldn't be able to recognize him myself ..."

"I see ..."

After that, I noticed that whenever the subject of the witches cropped up she looked very sad. One day she asked me gently, almost tenderly:

"Michael, are you sure the man you met on that heath really was John Tendler's agent?"

"What do you mean?"

She stroked my hand before she went on.

"Did it really happen, or might it have been a vision?"

As she told me later, I suddenly went pale. I could hardly speak.

"It was as real as can be," I managed to answer, through clenched teeth. "And if you don't believe me, your Majesty, come with me and I'll show you the very field."

"No, no – I believe you."

"Let's go at once!"

"Michael, please!"

"You've got to come, do you hear? You and all the others who still have doubts. Let them all get ready – guards, courtiers, and priests!"

"Don't shout so loud – the servants will hear."

"Let them! Let everyone know Macbeth's wife no longer trusts him!"

She began to weep silently.

Even now, after all these years, it hurts me to think of it. I don't know why, but ever since she died, of all the things we used to talk about it's the witches I think of most often.

One day (cold and gloomy, like today), I mounted my horse and rode out in the direction of the heath. As we drew near I told my guards to come no further. The heath where I had met John Tendler's tattered messenger looked more derelict than ever. A chilly drizzle fell on the stony scrub. I stood for a long while looking at the place where the woman in rags had appeared to me. I felt expectant, somehow. At one point I even thought I heard footsteps behind me. I swung round. But apparently it was only the sound of a bird dropping a twig.

Standing there in the rain, I remembered my lady's words. "Might it have been just a vision?" And for the first time I found myself wondering if I really had met John Tendler's emissary in this fallow field, or if it had all been a figment of my imagination.

God Almighty, I cried, deliver me from these ridiculous doubts! Over there were the two bushes growing together. And there was the third, a little way off. There was the splinter of rock, sticking into the ground at a slant. And to the right of it, the dead tree-trunk. I remembered it all quite plainly.

I intended all this to reassure me, but a voice inside me said, yes, you've been here before, not once but several times, but what does that prove? The question is, did John Tendler's messenger ask you to meet him here, and if so, did he really say those things to you. Or . . . ?

If Tendler had still been alive, I'd have gone and found him straight away, to gather from his own lips the proofs of Duncan's perfidy. Unfortunately I was reduced to going over and over everything in my own weary mind.

Back home I tried to recall my meetings with John Tendler. Or rather my one meeting, because after that, for security reasons, I avoided any further direct contacts.

"Duncan obviously dislikes you."

"Why?"

"Oh, it's easy to understand. As with all tyrants, his ruling passion is jealousy. Suspicion only comes afterwards, to justify the crime . . . What should you do? Keep your eyes open, my lord. That's the only advice I can give you now. I'll warn you if anything looks like happening. One of my men will come to see you disguised as an old beggar woman, muttering verses or some other mumbo-jumbo . . ."

Just before Duncan's visit John Tendler managed to send me a message: "My lord – beware of your guest. Another warning follows."

For days I waited anxiously for his messenger, longing to find out what Duncan intended to do while he was staying with me. I was haunted by the most terrifying possibilities. As if deliberately to reduce my nerves to shreds, the emissary still didn't come. My wife was as anxious as I was, if not more so. I didn't want to add to her anxiety, so I didn't tell her I'd decided to ride out to the old priest's house where all the rogues and vagabonds gathered on Sundays . . . I certainly heard plenty of mumbo-jumbo there . . . I spoke to one of the beggar women, but try as I might I couldn't make head or tail of what she said . . . Nor was I very lucid myself, after so much worry and so many sleepless nights . . . I took the old woman aside and whispered to her, twice: "Now we're alone, speak clearly!" But she only started raving worse than before . . . Apparently that was what she'd been instructed to do . . . She talked about a black cauldron, boiling something . . . It was very difficult to make her out, but she seemed to be going on about some imminent trick, some trap, someone being murdered in his sleep, an act of treachery . . . In the hope that she might then speak more clearly, I arranged to meet her again two days later on a patch of waste land behind the priest's house . . . And there, distraught, I waited for her for hours, on a day just like this . . .

"That's enough!" I shouted at last to my astonished guards, and set my horse off at a gallop. "I don't want to think about it any more. To hell with the shades of the past!"

Age was bringing me close to the kingdom of the shades myself, and I had no reason to fear it. Soon it would be I who frightened others, not as a king but as a ghost. Strangely enough, I found this thought soothing. There was no reason why I should cudgel my brains about something that had happened fifteen years ago. The only thing that mattered was that Duncan had plotted my death, and I had circumvented him. That was the heart of the matter. The rest was insignificant detail.

Feeling better, I went out on to the terrace and started to look through the regular report on the day's main events, and the account from the secret police on the rumours circulating among the people. I'd always taken a particular interest in the latter, especially in recent years, since gossip about the murder of D— had risen to the surface again. Noticing my interest, the chief of police was always adding extra material – whole conversations recorded by his spies, intercepted letters, prisoners' confessions, anonymous denunciations, and so on.

The strange thing was that some of the rumours coincided with what Billy Hampston had written in his play. All the gossip, from that which could be traced back to the Duchess of M— or the Bridge Tavern to the maunderings of the drunken Cheavor, mentioned Duncan's ghost. But there was frequent mention, too, of the bloodstains my late wife was supposed to have seen on her hands. I remember that was mentioned in Hampston's play too – I can even remember the first reference:

> 1: Take the body to the canal at Berverhill!
> SHE: Will the waters of the canal wash away the blood?

And in a later scene (one of the most melancholy, I recall: when my beloved lady read it she went terribly pale), she was shown trying to wash her hands, thinking she could see those cursed stains on them.

All the rumours more or less agreed on that point: during a meal, or a dance, or while she was busy at her embroidery, my wife suddenly saw her hands grow covered with bloodstains that no soap could ever remove.

Ugh! How deep can man's morbid imagination sink? The truth is that a year before her death she developed a skin disease on her hands. Her doctor tried every possible remedy, but couldn't cure her. My heart bled at the sight of those beautiful hands covered with ointments and bandages. In the course of a reception the shrewish Duchess of M— stared at my wife's arms and asked, "How are your hands, your Majesty? I'm told there's something wrong with them . . ."

My wife was dumbstruck. That night – or perhaps it was another night – trying to console her for her suffering, I started to kiss her bandages and to move them aside a little to kiss the skin beneath. But she pushed me away roughly, and in a toneless voice I'd never heard before, said:

"Perhaps you think it's Duncan's blood, too!"

My poor lady . . . It was apparently from then on that the rumours started about stains of Duncan's blood. Perhaps she confided her anguish to some trusted woman friend, thus becoming the source of her own misfortune?

How often have I asked myself, in vain, if those rumours really did start then, and if Billy Hampston, more skilful than my secret police, managed to hear of them and put them in his play. Or was it his play itself that exploded into a thousand rumours? Learned men say that it's like that, by means of particles coming into being, disappearing, and coming into being again in an endless cycle, that the celestial bodies are created.

I was sure there must be a copy somewhere of that wretched play, but though I did my best to get my hands on it, my efforts were in vain. My spies went through every nook and cranny with a fine-tooth comb, searched secret drawers, inspected cellars and the remotest priests' houses, to no avail. What didn't they find in the course of their researches? The most lurid manuscripts, descriptions of disgusting orgies, vile letters revealing the existence of immoral liaisons and abject vices, not to mention other aberrations too horrible to mention. Some of these were frankly ridiculous, others excruciatingly boring. But none of them remotely resembled Billy Hampston's play.

But I can't get rid of the idea that it's lurking somewhere, waiting for a more propitious moment to reappear. Or if not it, some variation of it, or else some other source for that damned rumour that will not die away. If so, I'd have to be mad not to admit that it's beyond my power to stand in its way. If the rumour of all mankind insists on turning me into a tragic character, no power on earth, let alone my own, can ever stop it. The only thing left for me to do is pray that if the play in question is ever produced, the posters announcing it will replace the name of the playwright, whatever that may be, with the name of Duncan, because he is its real author.

16

THE SUDDEN INFLUX of students back from China changed the look of the capital. The first to return were those concerned with the human sciences, and they were followed by the natural scientists and the various kinds of student teacher. They all began to fill the streets, cafés and restaurants of Tirana with an unwonted atmosphere of good humour. The fact that they'd been sent back at the express request of the Chinese government, in a note which gave as the main reason for their expulsion their allegedly improper behaviour towards Chinese girls, conferred on the newcomers a certain aura. People saw them as a seductive combination of Don Juan and Don Quixote, the heroes of countless adventures as mysterious as they were fantastic.

Stories of their exploits, preposterous enough without the inevitable exaggerations and accretions due to distance, circulated by word of mouth. Every day a new star emerged, each one a possible instigator of the famous note. Some, with a wink or similar gesture addressed to some Chinese damsel, had caused the Albanian ambassador to be summoned to the Chinese foreign ministry. The names of others were said to have figured on a list of complaints delivered by Zhou Enlai to an Albanian government delegation on an official visit to Peking. Not to mention the interesting condition in which some Chinese young women found themselves and of which some Albanian young men were already aware, though luckily it wouldn't come to the knowledge of the Peking authorities until four or five months later, when relations with China would certainly have deteriorated completely . . .

People listened to these tales with a smile. Especially those who had been students in the sixties in the Soviet Union or other countries then in the socialist bloc, and who had had to interrupt their studies because of the break between Albania and the various host

377

countries. "It wasn't like that in my day!" these would comment pensively. Of course, even then there had been plenty of comical incidents. One Albanian student in Sofia had chucked his lectures and managed to get himself made vice-chairman of a cooperative in a little Bulgarian town, while his family fondly believed he was still at the university and the ambassador had search parties out after him. But on the whole the stories dating from this period were rather sad – dull and lacklustre as an old pewter jug. As those who'd been students in the sixties started, with a certain modest pride, to recount their own memories, those just back from China waited impatiently for their stories to come up with something amusing. "But don't you see?" said their elders, "there wasn't anything funny about *our* experiences. We didn't feel at all like laughing when we had to part from our pretty Russian girls." The younger ones, the "Chinese" as they were called, couldn't understand how the others could have been wretched in such circumstances: they couldn't help bringing out the entertaining aspects of their own tribulations. At all events, the students of both these generations regaled everyone else with so many stories that a few old show-offs who'd studied in Europe half a century ago started to bring forth their own reminiscences – mostly insipid, old-fashioned romances with prim little, dim little *fraüleins* tinkling away at sheet music on hired pianos.

The new arrivals split their sides with laughter. They themselves had been delighted to break off their deadly boring studies. In the general euphoria, some of them got engaged within a fortnight of their return to girls they used to know before, but who seemed prettier and more desirable after their own stay in China. Others took up with Albanian girls who were so fascinated by these new-style Lotharios that they promptly ditched their previous boy-friends.

These goings-on lent a humorous touch to a situation mainly determined by the deterioration of Sino-Albanian relations after Mao's death and the arrest of his widow. But this time the Albanians bade an old friendship farewell with a smile, as one foreign correspondent noted, with an allusion to Marx. But he who laughs last laughs longest, he added. And who was going to have the last laugh here?

*   *   *

Silva opened her eyes for a few seconds, but, reassured by the sight of her husband's head on the pillow next to her, went back to sleep again. It had been light for some time, but she went on waking up and dozing off again as if to savour the joy of Gjergj's return as often as possible.

I think I'll lie in for a bit, she thought when she finally awoke properly. She tried to remember a dream: it was about some frozen snakes emerging from the snow ... But no, it wasn't part of a nightmare – it arose from something Gjergj had said in the pauses between their caresses. The frozen snakes had come to the surface just before the big earthquake. And now all China hinted that the tremor was a harbinger of Mao's death, and Jiang Qing's arrest in the middle of the night.

Silva looked at Gjergj's brow: she thought it showed signs of fatigue. As a child she had believed people's thoughts were concentrated there. She kissed him on the forehead – lightly, so as not to wake him – then got out of bed.

Their daughter had already gone to school. Silva made tea for the two of them, but as Gjergj was still asleep she decided not to disturb him. She left him a note: "Tea on the stove. See you at lunch-time. Love."

It was eleven o'clock by the time she left the house. Her boss had told her not to come in that day until she felt like it, but she didn't dawdle. All the government offices were working overtime because of the problems caused by the Chinese.

She thought of Gjergj's hair on the pillow and of how glad she'd be to find him there again at lunch-time. And she was filled with happiness.

When she got to the office, Linda and the boss looked unusually serious. She'd have preferred even the teasing they subjected her to the last time she saw them, about Gjergj's homecoming.

She soon learned the reason for their glumness. A meeting was due to be held in the minister's office at any moment, and as usual the boss, resenting it, was taking his annoyance out on Linda.

He came back after about half an hour, looking downcast. It was at short meetings like this that the severest criticisms were usually meted out. But today's gathering had been different.

"Well," he said, sitting down at his desk, "you already suspected

379

that the economic situation was very serious. But it's much worse than you thought."

In a low, weary voice he told them what the minister had said. When all the data were taken into account, it emerged that the defection of the Chinese had done much more damage than expected. It was no passing misunderstanding, causing only minor problems, as some officials and economists had thought, but a coldly premeditated rupture, calculated to do as much harm as possible. Whole sectors of activity that were dependent on one another were grinding irrevocably to a halt, in a chain reaction that eventually affected institutions which appeared to have no connection with China – for example, the State Bank. There was no end to the complications. Because the big dam in the north was near the frontier, and the Chinese had warned that it might burst if there was an earthquake, Yugoslavia was showing signs of alarm. And it was no accident that acts of sabotage had been perpetrated in the oil-fields. According to a report received by the Politbureau, some wells looked as if they had been bombed. Dozens of them had been abandoned, with machinery and pipelines left lying around to rust in the middle of the muddy plain.

"They're sending teams out to all the places where the Chinese have been or still are working," the boss went on. "The minister himself is leaving at any moment." Then, turning to Silva: "I know you haven't had much time with your husband since he got back, but I'm afraid there's nothing to be done – you and I both have to go to the steel complex."

Silva shrugged, as if to agree that there was nothing they could do about it.

"When?" she said faintly.

"Tomorrow. We might be able to put it off till the day after tomorrow at the latest. Linda – you'll have to hold the fort while we're away."

The two women exchanged a wan smile. Silva was thinking already about what she'd have to do this afternoon so that Gjergj and Brikena weren't too much put out by her absence. She must go and collect a suit of Gjergj's from the cleaner's. She must call in to collect a coat for herself and a dress for Brikena from the dressmaker. Oh, but that meant getting four hundred new leks out of the savings bank to pay the dressmaker what she still owed her for work done over the last few months. Perhaps she was spending too much money on clothes? This worry was soon replaced by another: what should she cook for Gjergj and Brikena that would last them for a couple of days? The best solution would be for them to eat out while she was away. It was more expensive, but as Gjergj was no good in the kitchen and Brikena had her homework to do . . . Silva still had no end of other things to do, but by now she realized that thinking about them was almost as tiring as doing them, so she tried to dismiss them from her mind . . . Oh yes, and she mustn't forget to remind Gjergj about the texts Skënder Bermema had left for him. There couldn't be a more appropriate moment than now for him to read them.

Her second cup of coffee in the workers' canteen did nothing to relieve the hollow she felt inside her. It had something to do with the dull day, and the way the smoke from the blast furnace seemed to pervade the whole complex. The same tension spread from one person to another by a kind of osmosis. Apparently the furnace had become partially blocked with slag almost as soon as it first came on stream. There were even more ominous rumours, though no one knew who had started them, or why. Some people said there was a danger that the furnace might go out altogether, and all the molten metal solidify. If that happened, the whole plant, built with such effort and expense, would be virtually useless. The only thing to do then would be to blow it up. Trying to melt its contents down again would be like trying to resuscitate a corpse. The fire of the furnace is its soul, said one of the workers. If it goes out, all you can do is go into mourning.

"The Chinese," said the boss to Silva, nodding towards the window in some awe. "Apparently they're getting ready to go."

She followed his glance. A group of Chinamen were picking their way across the clinker-strewn yard. They looked different from usual. Distant as ever, but with the peculiar self-satisfaction of those who, if they are leaving, are taking a valuable secret with them.

As a matter of fact it was widely said that they knew very well how the furnace could be unblocked, but they refused to reveal the method. But, to her own surprise, Silva felt no resentment against them. Perhaps because she couldn't help feeling grateful to them for going. They'd seemed fated to stay for ever. So long as they really do go, she thought, everything will sort itself out . . .

Coming out of the canteen she ran into Victor Hila.

"Victor!" she cried. "I've inquired after you several times. How are you?"

"Quite well," he said.

But his eyes were red with fatigue.

"I saw your famous Chinaman one day at the airport. He was catching a plane."

"Really?" he answered indifferently. Silva realized that he didn't feel like laughing any more about the business of the squashed foot. Nor did she, for that matter, even though it was she who'd broached the subject.

"What are you working on?" she asked.

"I'm in a mixed team trying to unblock the furnace."

"Is it true it might go out?"

Victor smiled.

"That's what everyone asks. They all talk about the accumulation of slag and the furnace going out as if one had to follow from the other. But never mind that. The fact is that the furnace really is in a bad way."

Silva noted his sunken eyes.

"Anyhow," he said, "we're going to do all we can to get it unblocked. Even if . . ."

Even if what? she wanted to ask. But he was already holding out his hand.

"I must go, Silva. See you soon."

"So long, Victor."

Hurrying to catch up with her colleagues, Silva noticed that the hollow feeling which had haunted her for the last few days was suddenly worse now she'd met Victor Hila. She soon realized why. Neither of them had laughed when the subject of the Chinaman with the squashed foot had come up. And this was connected with what was going on, and going wrong, in the world at large.

The hollow feeling was still there when Silva got back to her hotel room late that afternoon. She sat for some time with her hands clasped in her lap. Her thoughts moved slowly. Then it struck her that Gjergj's hotel bedroom in China must have been much like this one. Ugh! In her present mood, anything to do with China depressed her. What was she doing here? What were the Chinese to her, or she to them? . . . And suddenly, as if she'd been on the other side of the world instead of just a short journey away, a wave of homesickness swept over her, for her apartment, for the street she walked along every day, and even for her office at the ministry.

The first morning Linda entered the office after Silva and the boss went away, she shivered. She went over and felt the radiator, but it was quite warm. And she herself felt even colder as the morning wore on, as well as distinctly agitated inside. As soon as the phone started to ring her heart missed a beat, and she realized she was all worked up. Her state of mind was reflected in her voice: "Hallo . . . No, the boss isn't here . . . Yes, away on a mission. He'll be back in a few days' time."

She couldn't wait to get rid of the caller, and when she'd put the receiver down she checked that she'd done so properly. That was what she always did, she reflected, when she was expecting a call. Stop it! she told herself. She was behaving like a little girl, expecting "him" to telephone. Even if he did, what difference would it make?

Linda hadn't seen Besnik Struga again since Silva had introduced her to him. She hadn't even spoken to him, except once or twice, briefly, when he'd rung up and asked to speak to Silva. But she couldn't hide it from herself that she liked him; she liked him very much. So she hadn't been surprised to find herself thinking about him; her thoughts were only light and fleeting, easily conjured up and easily dismissed. She'd told herself everything would remain as airy as a watercolour, tranquilly pleasing as a fantasy of happiness. They lived in the same city – they were bound to meet again some time . . . And that was as far as her thoughts went, drifting back and forth without casting anchor. Still free.

But now, one fine morning, when she opened the door on an empty office, things had changed.

She'd had a premonition the day before, when she realized she was going to be alone in the office while her colleagues were away. That evening she'd imagined herself pulling the legs of people who rang up to speak to the boss: "Comrade Defrin? Yes, I'm comrade De-freeze . . . What can I do for you?" and so on. Yes, the phone would ring – but what if were "him", asking for Silva? So what? she'd thought, trying to kid herself. But in vain.

And now, this morning, she thought she actually heard the phone ring. And even though she soon had to conclude that it was a trick of her imagination, the shock was enough to turn dream into potential reality. Her feminine intuition told her he liked her. If he rang to talk to Silva and was told she was away, mightn't he go on talking to Linda herself? Mightn't he even ask, in passing, what she did with herself in the afternoon?

She shivered again. Now she realized it was because "he" hadn't rung up.

She went over to the window, and looked out at Government Square, humming sadly and tunelessly to herself.

It was still too soon to talk of suffering in connection with this new mood of hers. The feeling wasn't yet fully formed. It was still malleable, like the bones of an infant. But before long it would find its permanent shape.

There was a knock at the door. Linda didn't need to look round: she knew it was Simon Dersha.

"Telephone still not working?" she said, with her back still to him.

He looked at her for a while without answering. He was still wearing his navy-blue suit, and normally Linda would have teased him about it. Perhaps because she hadn't done so, Simon, as she now saw, went on gazing at her. She suddenly realized how worried he looked. Why hadn't she noticed before?

"What's wrong, Simon?" she asked guiltily.

He shook his head wearily, as if he'd been waiting for her to ask that.

"I'm not at all well," he mumbled.

Linda moved away from the window and came towards him.

"What is it? What's the matter?" She was about to add, "Do tell me if there's anything I can do for you," but as if trying to anticipate and avoid her question, he shook his head twice and went out, closing the door behind him.

How odd, Linda thought. She felt ashamed of using the word suffering, even in thought, about her own frame of mind, which she was now inclined to put down to caprice. She walked briskly back to her desk, her lethargy gone, and got down to work at once, so as not to relapse. At the same moment Simon Dersha was sitting down at his desk in the next room, muttering, "Oh, what a mess I'm in, what an awful mess!" Then he bent over a mass of pages covered with his slanting scrawl.

For the last week he'd been writing his own autocritique. No one had asked him to, and he hadn't even asked himself where and to whom he was going to read it. Was he going to deliver it in court, or send it through the post? He hadn't bothered with any of that. The main thing for him was to write it. Whether he would read it to the minister, the union, in court, at a fair, or anywhere else, was neither here nor there.

That was why the style in which it was written kept changing. One part was very academic, with digressions on general, ideological and sociological problems; another took the form of a psychological analysis; yet another section was in dialogue form, with questions and answers as in a police interrogation. He had also peppered his text with quotations, especially in a kind of profession of faith where he described his origins and social status: here he quoted twice on one page from Engels's *Origins of the Family, Private Property and the State*. Further on, in a passage describing how he came to meet the vice-minister responsible for all his woes (every time he re-read this section he wondered what woes he meant – but he didn't know the answer), the autocritique became a kind of detailed narrative, relating all their conversations and telephone calls, and dwelling particularly on the invitation to the fateful dinner. But even this section strayed into digressions on general principles: in one he considered the significance of banquets and dinners, relating them to tradition and popular philosophy . . . And so on.

The evening at Minister D—'s was described in exhaustive detail, starting with his meeting with the vice-minister who was to take him there, and who turned up five minutes late, going on to their walk to the minister's residence, and thence to the dinner itself. The guests were described, together with their conversation, which was much less weighty and interesting than he had expected. Then, in the middle of the evening, came the phone call from the leader of the Party, and the perturbation he thought he saw on the minister's face after he had hung up.

And what about the rest of you? And you yourself – weren't you at all affected?

Well . . . Yes, to start with. *He* was, certainly. He had Enver Hoxha at the other end of the line. That was no joke! We all ought to have been thrilled.

Ought to have been? Weren't you all really thrilled?

That's what I was just going to explain. As I said, the minister himself, despite all his efforts to disguise it, was terribly downcast.

It was only natural that his anxiety should communicate itself to us. Everything suddenly wilted away, and everybody, beginning with our host himself, wanted the dinner to come to an end as soon as possible.

Oh, so you wanted the dinner to end as soon as possible, just after a phone call that would have added life and zest to any other gathering? But you lot . . . ! Delve into your conscience, Simon Dersha, and dig out the real reason for your anxiety. Well? Or is your mind full of foreign propaganda, and the calumnies our enemies perpetrate against our leader? While all of you were banqueting, he was going without sleep to work for the people. And instead of being happy to hear his voice, you were all terrified. I suppose you all told yourselves: "He's going to put me in jail, liquidate me." Isn't that the truth?

I don't know what to say. Yes, I'm a miserable wretch.

Did you discuss it amongst yourselves?

No.

Not even when you first started hearing rumours about minister D—?

No, not then either. I tried to get in touch with the vice-minister, but I couldn't reach him on the telephone . . .

In spite of its exhaustiveness, this part of the autocritique was shorter than that devoted to Simon's second visit to the minister, or rather his abortive attempt to go and see him about his brother's posting. Like the previous section, this one digressed: there were remarks on the principles of postings in general, based on quotations from the decisions handed down by two plenums; this led to consideration of a popular misconception on the matter – a misconception apparently shared by his brother and sister-in-law, and by himself. Before giving a detailed account of his route to the minister's villa (not forgetting the coldness of the weather and the emptiness of the streets), he spent a few lines expatiating on his own petty-bourgeois psychology, his bourgeois-revisionist views on personal happiness, and other old-fashioned survivals due to his lack of contact with social reality.

When I got to the entrance to the minister's house my conscience started to reproach me, and I felt a sort of compunction about what I was intending to do.

Compunction? Or fear?

Well, both, I suppose. Yes, it must have been both.

But which predominated?

Fear, I suppose.

Perhaps fear was really the *only* thing you felt?

Yes, I expect you're right.

"I don't feel well, I don't feel well at all," Simon Dersha kept muttering as he re-read his autocritique. He felt caught between the pages, as if he were in the jaws of a trap. It didn't cross his mind that it was a trap of his own making, and that, to break free, all he had to do was screw the whole thing up into a ball and burn it, or throw it in the wastepaper basket. But even if it had occurred to him, he wouldn't really have been able to do it. For days these pages had been the reflection of his entire existence – his image, his identity card, his medical record, everything that made up the truth about him.

What sort of thing did you hear people say about Minister D—?

Delicate things. Very . . . tricky.

Are you sure you heard them? Couldn't they have been figments of your guilty conscience?

I don't know . . . It could have been both.

Both, eh? Of course it was you and your brother, your whole typically petty-bourgeois family, who made them all up. All very well for them, but you – an official in a government office – how could you indulge in such vile slander? But let's get down to the rumours themselves. You say they were about delicate matters. What sort of delicate matters?

Well . . . Some complicated affair about tanks. They were supposed to encircle some kind of committee . . .

A Party committee?

That's right!

Was there anything about the Chinese?

In connection with the minister? No, never.

Delve into your memory. Dig deeper.

What?

Despite her self-reproaches after Simon Dersha's departure, Linda soon found herself staring round at the empty room and the silent telephone, and beginning to fall back into her former state. She would have relapsed completely but for the fact that it was nearly the end of the working day, and there wasn't time for her to sink into what she now didn't scruple to think of as pain.

At half-past two, partly with relief, partly with regret at the end of another of the few bitter-sweet days when she would be alone with the telephone, she locked up the office and made her way slowly down the broad staircase.

All that afternoon and evening she kept herself busy with trivial things, so that she almost forget the agitations of the morning. If she did think of them, she put them down to a passing weakness induced by spending so much time all alone in the office. But as soon as she got in to work the next day, she was overcome by exactly the same feelings as before. Could one really be affected like this, all of a sudden, without even being able to see the object of one's obsession? Was this love? If so, what kind of love? Her second, or the first real one in her life? In any case, how *could* it come out of nowhere?

But the more she thought of it the more she realized that it had been coming on for a long time, slowly, invisibly, like a stream flowing secretly under snow. Everything remotely to do with him had become engraved on her mind – not only all Silva had told her, but all aspects of public events, past and present, that he was connected with. Anything relating to the Soviets or the Chinese had become associated for her with something about his looks or words or gestures. Even before she met him she had longed to know the mystery man whose life had included both Moscow and Ana Krasniqi. And after she'd met him, she longed more and more to meet him again. Whenever the television news showed an international conference, or she read something in a book or paper about the Moscow Congress, she thought of him: he became a kind of myth. The person she had actually met was merely one facet, a superficial, everyday aspect of an infinitely complex and inaccessible personality. He'd become so closely identified with the age he lived in that she'd failed to notice that she herself belonged to another era. Only now did she realize that there was something rather cold and artificial in her feeling for him so far.

She had made inquiries about his former fiancée: the reason why he had broken off the engagement – like many other things about him – had never been clear. Linda had heard that a month ago, at some engagement party where the conversation turned to the break with China, Besnik's ex-fiancée had stopped her ears and shouted almost hysterically, practically in tears, "Stop it! I can't bear to hear any more about it! Please, please, stop!" The person who told Linda about this incident treated it as a mere anecdote, but Linda guessed at once what lay behind it. The mention of the Chinese must have reminded the young woman of the break with the Soviets, and the days when her hoped-for happiness had been destroyed.

Now that, as she thought, she was seeing things more clearly, Linda decided to let matters take their course. He was bound to ring up one of these days. She imagined some variations on the ensuing conversation. "Hallo – is that you, Silva?" "No, it's her colleague, Linda." "Oh yes – haven't we met?" "Yes." "How are you? . . . Is Silva there?" "I'm afraid not." – Linda pulled a face at her own hypocrisy – "She's away on a mission." "Oh." This was the critical moment. The pause that seemed to cut the world in two. "Can *I* be of any use?" "Well . . . I wanted to speak to her . . . I don't know if . . ." "I'm at your service!" "Well, could I see you, then?"

Oh no! That wasn't it at all! Far too banal. Neither of them could be so tedious as that. They *mustn't* be! And that awful, coy "At your service!" Absolutely not!

As if winding back a tape recorder, she made a fresh start. "Silva's away on a mission." "Oh." A pause. Fragile; precarious; they could hear one another's breathing. "So how are you managing, all alone in the office?" "Oh, working as best I can. Getting bored." Yes, that was much better. "And what do you get up to in the afternoon?" "What?" "I asked what you did in the afternoon." "I heard what you said, but I don't quite know how to answer."

Linda's imagination then leaped forward a few hours, and saw them sitting opposite one another having tea in the Café Flora. "To tell you the truth, I'd been wanting to meet you for a long time. I thought you were so interesting . . ." Ugh! That wouldn't do at all! Much too direct. It might be better to talk about Silva to begin with. "Silva told me about you – we've been working in the same office for a long time, Silva and I . . ." No – that sounded as if she was one of those timid souls who dragged her friend along to a date to give her courage. "Whenever the break with China comes up, Silva and I talk about you . . ." That wasn't too bad, either. It gave him a chance to say something interesting about current events, like a character in a modern novel.

Suddenly it occurred to Linda that the phone hadn't rung all the morning. Perhaps it was out of order! She flew over and picked up the receiver. No, it was all right – she could hear the dialling tone. She didn't know whether to be glad or sorry.

Four days went by like this. The team that had gone to the steel complex might be back at any moment. Linda felt she would look back with regret on all these lonely, fruitless but in a way thrilling hours. On the fifth day, just before two o'clock, when she had already given up hope, the phone rang. Superstitiously, she let it ring three times, thinking that would turn any call into a call from "him". When she picked up the receiver she was almost sure of it. Yet strangely enough her hand was quite steady, and her face showed no emotion even after she recognized his voice. But the phone felt as if it weighed a ton, and everything else in the world seemed grey and monotonous.

They exchanged a few words: Silva . . . I remember meeting you . . . afternoon . . . Nothing of what she'd imagined.

She put down the phone as calmly as she had picked it up, then stood there for a while by the empty desk. It looked preternaturally bare, like something on the eve of great changes.

The hotel lift was out of order, and Silva, late already, ran down the stairs. Her colleagues were waiting for her by the minibus. They looked glum.

"Good morning," said Silva. "Anything new?"

"The Chinese have gone," said Illyrian.

The rest of them just went on smoking. From their expressions they might have been at a funeral.

"When?" Silva asked.

"Perhaps during the night. Perhaps just before dawn. We'll soon know," said the boss, climbing into the bus.

As it drove along, Silva looked out at the frozen plain. A few sombre-coloured birds swooped low over the landscape. In the distance she was somewhat reassured to see smoke still pouring from the furnaces. But one of these days it won't be there any more, she thought. It'll be like when someone holds a mirror to a dead man's lips.

The comings and going at the complex seemed different today, but perhaps that was just because everyone knew what had happened. The Chinese had vanished without warning, like ghosts. Albanian technicians had already taken their places. Everyone seemed to have gone deaf and dumb. But all eyes asked the same question: What are we going to do now? In the head office, a group of engineers gazed blankly at shelves full of files containing the complex's production plans. They were all in Chinese. The shriek of a passing locomotive expressed the engineers' anguish better than any human voice could have done.

A vice-minister had just arrived from Tirana: the minister for heavy industry would have come himself, but he was said to be ill. Rumour had it he'd been dismissed.

The panting of the furnace could be heard everywhere. Or perhaps everyone *thought* they could hear it, because they knew it was ailing. Whenever Silva heard someone say, "The furnace is going out," she remembered Gjergj's frozen snakes in the snow.

Back at the hotel, her room seemed more desolate than ever. She felt like writing to Gjergj, and even got her pen and writing pad out of her briefcase, but instead of starting a letter she found herself tracing the words, "winter's day". She remembered the snakes again, and realized she was falling into the same trap as Gjergj and Skënder Bermema in their hotel rooms in Peking. Nevertheless her hand still continued with, "It's not true I killed Duncan for his throne." She laughed and crossed it all out. Then sat for some time, pen poised, wondering whether to follow "Dear Gjergj" with "I miss you" or "What a pity we didn't have more time together . . ."

Forty-eight hours after the Chinese left, the situation was still the same – simultaneously paralysed and nervous.

Concern about the furnace had gradually distracted attention from everything else in the complex, though the other units had their problems too. Even in the town there was only one subject on everybody's lips: how were they going to get rid of the slag? Would the furnace go out?

A batch of reporters had come from Tirana, followed by a horde of young poets. Red-eyed with lack of sleep, they all roamed round the bars and workshops, showing one another their verses and articles. They often compared the furnace to the medieval citadel in the town, claiming that the "new fortress of steel" was even more impregnable than the old one. Others composed odes entitled "The flames will never go out," or "We will throw our hearts into the furnace," or "To Fire . . ." In the last, the flames of the furnace were a positive symbol, but in "Back, clinkers!", slag was used to represent revisionists and every other influence inimical to socialism, including decadent art.

Meanwhile, as it was absolutely necessary to consult the production plans in the original Chinese, a group of students just back from China was sent for from Tirana. As they tumbled noisily off the train they told all and sundry they were sure they'd be equal to the task: they'd eaten dishes made up of sharks' ears and cobras' innards, among other abominations, and they were familiar with all the tricks of the Chinks and the snares of their language. Some gave themselves nicknames like The Three Scourges of the Country or Look before you Purge.

But after a few hours in head office, the students had to admit they were flummoxed. One was said to have asked his friend, The Seven Demons of the City, "Can you make head or tail of these hieroglyphics?" By way of reply, The Seven Demons swore horribly in both languages. And that was the end of their reputation as translators. The authorities were for sending all the students back, but some of them had already joined up with the young poets, and they all roved round the bars together. Two got engaged to a couple of lab assistants, and so that they shouldn't be sent away, someone had the bright idea of co-opting them into the workers' amateur theatricals. The students were cast as Chinese baddies in their current show.

Silva and her colleagues went to see it, and as they came out afterwards, still laughing, she heard someone calling her name. But when she turned round, she didn't recognize the two youths who had hailed her. Or they might have been men, for their faces were quite black.

"Don't you know who I am?" said one of them. "Of course, like this, it's not surprising . . . I look more like Othello!"

"Ben!" cried Silva, surprised to find it was Besnik Struga's brother. "No, I really didn't recognize you! How long have you been here?"

"Several weeks. Let me introduce my friend – Max Bermema. We work together."

The other young man's face was even blacker.

"Are you related to Skënder Bermema?" asked Silva.

"I'm his cousin."

She was going to ask why their faces were so black, but Ben spoke first.

"Max and I work in the blast furnace – that's why we look like delegates from the Third World!"

They all laughed, but Silva was embarrassed that the two young men had met her coming out of such a low form of entertainment.

"Does an engineer called Victor Hila work with you?" she asked.

"Yes, we're all on the same shift."

"And how are you going to deal with the furnace?"

"We've put forward a suggestion. Let's hope it'll be accepted."

"So you're going to unblock it?"

"Yes. With an explosion. We've been up several nights working out the figures."

Silva looked from one to the other.

"Isn't it dangerous?"

They smiled, but their black faces made their smiles so weird that Silva was quite taken aback. She looked round at them after they'd gone, to reassure herself, but it was too late. Their faces had already vanished into the dark.

Silva walked on and caught up with her colleagues. But for some time she couldn't get those shadowy smiles out of her mind.

17

UNDER THE SHOWER, Silva decided she wouldn't tell Gjergj the news she'd brought back with her in the order in which she'd gone over it in her mind on the journey back.

She had arrived home suddenly by the last train, to her own and her daughter's delight. As she turned off the shower, she knew that Gjergj, back in their room, would be imagining the water pounding on her skin. She wiped the mist off the bathroom mirror, and saw the reflection of the joy that filled her own body.

This time she was the one back from a journey. She was even bringing as many stories about China as if she'd been to a miniature version of that country itself.

She said as much to Gjergj when she went back into their bedroom and bent over him.

"Did you miss me? Really? Very much?"

She went on murmuring sweet but earthy nothings into his ear until laughs and whispers changed into choking gasps, in accordance with the great paradox of nature that expresses the height of human pleasure by the sounds of suffering.

Only afterwards did Silva get round to telling her husband the other half of her news. Then:

"And what about here?" she said. "Anything new?"

He told her what had been happening while she was away – in particular, about the sacking of high-ranking officials. More dismissals were expected, even some punishments. Although the last plenum of the Central Committee had taken place quite recently, another was likely to be held quite soon, and the signs were that its decisions would be more severe. Silva was about to ask about the fate of the minister in charge of her own department when Gjergj mentioned the word "plot".

"What?" she exclaimed. "What do you mean?"

"People say they've uncovered a plot, but for the moment it's top secret."

For some reason, Silva thought of her brother, but she didn't say so. If anything had happened concerning Arian, Gjergj would have told her.

"They're holding meetings all over the place," he said drowsily. Then, before he dropped off again:

"I'm so glad you're back."

That was what she usually said to him.

The meetings went on well into the evening, especially in government offices. Those who had to write their own autocritiques stayed up later still, sometimes even till dawn. Meanwhile venerable scholars and academicians slept, as did writers, even those who went in for novels and other lengthy genres, and lecturers who'd had to prepare their lectures for the next day, not to mention translators from ancient Greek, lexicographers, graphologists, writers of anonymous letters, people who wanted divorces, and even writers of love letters, though they usually lay awake for a couple of hours at least after putting the last touches to their billets-doux. In short, everyone whose work, feelings or circumstances made them use pen and paper eventually slept, except the people who had to write their autocritiques.

For some it was the first time they'd gone through this ordeal, and their sufferings were particularly horrible. But even the veterans had a hard time. They were used to the traumatic experience of the self-examination itself, but it no longer brought them the relief the novices experienced. They knew how terribly depressing it was to read out a confession you were sure would have moved your audience deeply, only to meet with looks of complete incomprehension, usually followed by the question, "Is that all, comrade X? You don't think you might have left something out? Dig deeper, dig deeper!" The novices knew nothing of this. They themselves were so moved by their own outpourings they expected their judges to be equally affected, and already saw in their mind's eye the sympathy and pity that would no doubt earn them clemency and forgiveness. The mere thought of this made some of them actually shed tears in anticipation, weeping over their autocritiques as slighted suitors might weep over their love letters.

A window that still had a light in it after midnight seemed to radiate an aura of guilt. Some people who had never been criticized or rebuked for anything whatsoever woke up in the night, rummaged blearily for pencil and paper, and started to write an autocritique that had never even been asked for!

As the meetings went on and all sorts of people made their confessions, a great similarity began to emerge in the autocritiques, even though their authors' circumstances, professions and offences had nothing in common. So much so that rumour had it that, for a modest sum, certain hacks were ready to churn out autocritiques to order. No one could prove it, but humorists and song-writers found it a very fruitful subject for satire.

In such a context the unfortunates still poring over their own confessions felt more isolated than ever.

As time went by there came to pass what they had striven above all to avoid: they became more and more cut off from ordinary people, and were drawn closer and closer to the world of the guilty. Even when, as was usually the case, they didn't know one another, their names were more and more frequently quoted together in accounts of what was going on. They started to exist in a universe apart where they drifted about together in groups, like ghosts. And it was when they were in this misty, twilight world that memories painfully recurred, or seemed to recur, to them: an official reception at which a Chinaman had reminded them of a conversation they'd had together in China, in the Hôtel Peking; a party at the house of an unnamed Albanian minister; a conversation about the abandoning of former oil-fields or the encircling of a Party committee. And so on.

The vagueness and solitude of the realm they inhabited caused their autocritiques, even when written in a perfectly normal style, to be full of confusion and irrelevance, with answers to anticipated questions, admissions of deeds they'd resolved never to reveal, the most fearsome hypotheses, together with countless suspicions, anxieties, hopes and outbursts of anger. And at the actual meetings, even though they still hoped to be able to keep something back, their interrogators always came quite close to at least part of what they were trying to suppress. Moreover, in their reports to the Central Committee, the people appraising their cases would sometimes add their own comments, even their suppositions about what the speaker was allegedly trying to hide; and while some of these hypotheses were correct, others were not.

Notes designed to supplement the Central Committee records, by a delegate to meetings of various Party organizations in the Army. The question at issue: what is known as AN UNSUCCESSFUL ATTEMPT TO HAVE THE PARTY COMMITTEE OF THE TOWN OF X— SURROUNDED BY DETACHMENT N— OF THE TANKS. *Follow-up to previous analyses, which arrived at no definite conclusions.*

N.B. *These notes are not set out here in their final order. For further information see accounts of the meetings themselves.*

Extracts from the autocritique of staff signals officer S—: I am guilty, absolutely guilty, even though it might be said that I am only a vehicle, a cog in the machinery of command. That's what it says in army regulations, though I personally think they should be reviewed. In our army, no one can be happy to be a robot. That's what distinguishes it from the armies of bourgeois and revisionist countries. When I was given an order that harmed the Party, I ought, though I'm only a simple soldier, to have blocked the order, sent it back to where it came from, said to the person who sent it: I will not send it, for this, that or the other reason. But, comrades, I didn't do that. Like a mindless robot, not thinking that I was unwittingly helping to strike a blow at the Party, I transmitted the order to the tanks. My lack of ideological maturity, my merely superficial study of Marxism-Leninism, and so on . . .

Second signals officer (P—): I have nothing to add. I am guilty. We're both guilty.

Questioner: You claim you didn't know you were doing anything wrong. But did you regard the order as wrong in itself?

S—: Wrong? I don't know . . . A bit strange, yes, but not wrong. It came from above, so I thought it couldn't be wrong. But of course, in the Party there's neither high nor low . . . so that's true of the army too – that's what makes it different from bourgeois-revisionist armies . . .

397

Q: Right, that'll do. Another question. It was a long way from operation headquarters to the tanks, wasn't it? Nearly an hour on a motorcycle combination.

S—: Yes, almost an hour. Because of the weather.

Q: And during all that time you and your colleague didn't say anything to one another?

S—: No. The weather was very bad and the road was almost impassable. Even if we'd wanted to talk we couldn't have made ourselves heard.

Q: But the bad weather didn't stop you from thinking! What did you think as you were driving along?

S—: Nothing. I was concentrating on driving. There was a lot of mud and the bike might have skidded at any moment.

Q: And what about you, the other one? You were tucked away inside the sidecar, wrapped up in your raincoat – you had plenty of time to think, didn't you?

P—: Yes. As far as I remember I thought about a whole lot of things, but they hadn't got anything to do with the order we were supposed to be delivering. As a matter of fact . . . I don't know if . . .

Q: Speak out! You're not supposed to hide anything from the Party.

P—: That's right . . . Well, I was thinking about a girl I intend to get engaged to . . . About certain suspicions her behaviour had inspired in me lately . . . In short, I was afraid she was deceiving me . . .

Q: Well, here's a fine member of the People's Army! A fine communist, I must say! He can't think of anything but his own happiness, he's obsessed by the thought of being deceived by his fiancée, and meanwhile what does he care if he betrays the Party, even unwittingly! And then what happened?

S—: We delivered the order. To an officer whose first name was Arian, if I remember rightly. That's right – Arian Krasniqi. He listened to the order, asked me to repeat it, then he frowned. He was going to say something, but changed his mind. He just growled, "Very well, you can go back where you came from – we'll sort things out with H.Q. over the radio" . . . That's all.

Q: And then?

S—: We went back through the rain.

Q: Since, as you remember so clearly and so often, it was raining, why didn't it occur to you that you didn't have to deliver the order verbally? – that you could have sent it by radio?

S—: I didn't think of it. But even if I had I'd still have told myself the order came from H.Q. and . . .

Q: And you didn't think about anything on the way back, either?

S—: I told you – the road was very bad.

Q: And you, the other one – I suppose you were still thinking about your fiancée, and wondering if she was cheating on you?

P—: Yes.

Extracts from the autocritique of radio operator Dh—: I have nothing to say in my own defence. It was an offence, a grave offence on my part. I can't think of a worse one. There's only one thing I'd like to say: you can't imagine what it's like in that sort of situation. The confusion, comrades! You think you're going mad. Your head's ringing, but everyone wants to be put in touch with everyone else as fast as possible. They're all huffing and puffing, and you're in the middle of it all, the one who's supposed to answer everyone. The buzzing in your ears makes you think you must be in hell! Not to mention that you haven't had a wink of sleep for three days and nights. And as if that isn't enough, the weather's unspeakable, with flashes of lightning all the time. You've no idea of the effect lightning has when you're trying to use the radio – maddening! And then you hear some bloke telling you he's not going to carry out an order you've never even heard of! That's what it was like that day. A tank officer said he wasn't going to carry out an order, and proceeded to explain why not. But was I in any position to pass on all the details of his justifications to headquarters? Of course it was wrong of me, of course it was a serious offence on my part, but at the time I didn't realize it. I just started to transmit the essence of what he'd said to H.Q. But H.Q. interrupted me and said: No need for explanations – just see the order's carried out! I sent that message back, but the officer at the other end kept on arguing the toss with H.Q. So I lost my temper, too. If he could shout, so could I . . . Yes, I committed an offence, a very serious offence, when I started shouting and bawling into the mike. I admit it, comrades – I shouted all kinds of wild insults. I told him, "You can stick Shanghai up your mother's . . ." I admit I'm guilty, but at that moment I didn't know what I was doing.

My head was already splitting, and this blessed tank officer starts to talk to me about Shanghai! I ask you! In the middle of all that was going on, all I needed was the Chinese! So that's how I came to say it. "You can stick Shanghai up your mother's . . ." I'm in the wrong, I know. Seriously at fault . . .

The staff officer at H.Q., in *his* autocritique, admitted that he gave the couriers the verbal order to take to the tank group, and it was also he who heard the tank officer refuse, over the radio, to comply with it. In both cases he reported to the chief of staff, who in the first case told him the order had come directly from the minister, and in the second – the tank officer's refusal to obey – told him to report to him, i.e. the minister. [*Marginal note by delegate*: Are we sure what this "him" really means?!]

When asked if the motives for the refusal were clear, or rather, if he'd managed to explain to the minister why the tanks had refused to obey the order ("It's not done to encircle a Party committee," "This isn't Shanghai," etc.), the staff officer (M—) answered that he wasn't sure: in the first place because what he'd heard over the radio was intermittent, because of the bad weather (there was a lot of lightning that day); and in the second place – and this is very important – because the minister hadn't let him explain himself properly.

Why not?

Because he was shouting at the top of his voice. As soon as I opened my mouth to say the tanks had refused to obey, he started bellowing. He wouldn't listen to any explanations.

Why not?

It was only natural. He felt outraged. Such a thing had never happened to him before. His own dignity . . .

And so you didn't manage to explain to him why the order had been disobeyed?

No. I did get to say something, but I'm not sure he took it in, he was so furious. And on top of that our conversation took place in the open, outside his tent, and the weather was awful. The wind was blowing great guns.

So that you couldn't hear yourselves speak?

Not as bad as that, but it made conversation difficult. Especially since, as I said, he was practically foaming at the mouth.

How do you explain that?

I don't know ... He's a minister, a member of the government ... What's more, he isn't at this meeting ... But this is a Party meeting, where everyone is equal, and since you ask me I'll tell you frankly what I think. If you ask me, I think his anger was a sign of morbid pride.

There's another question on which we'd like to have your personal opinion, M—: why, when you had radio transmitters at your disposal, was the order to encircle the Party committee sent to be delivered orally?

M— didn't answer the question directly. He merely said there were certain orders which by their nature were better delivered orally rather than by radio.

M— didn't give a clear answer to the last question of all, either – namely, if in the course of this whole business there had been any mention of commandos. He said he had a feeling they had been referred to during his conversation over the radio, but neither at the time, still less now, was he able to say in what connection. At this point he started talking about the bad weather and the lightning again ...

Extracts from the explanations provided by Z—, leader of the commando group acting as the enemy during the manoeuvres: If you want me to say what I really think, well, as far as I'm concerned, I can't make head or tail of this business. According to the plan – approved in detail by staff H.Q. – the parachutists were to be dropped over Zone 04VS. But late on the Tuesday evening, the 11th, I was expressly ordered to send in my commandos straight away, not only before the agreed time but also over another zone, i.e. Zone 71T [where the Party committee was – *note by delegate*]. Try as I might to find out what the hurry was, I couldn't get any satisfaction. The fact is, radio conditions were very bad because of the weather, especially the lightning. [It was this same evening that the tanks received the order to encircle the Party committee – *note by delegate*]. I was therefore obliged to go ahead, carry out the order, and parachute my men in. I need hardly say the operation was not successful. Apart from the weather, the terrain itself was unsuitable, and hadn't been reconnoitred. Some of my men got lost, communications got into a horrible muddle, and, as you probably know, three soldiers were drowned. What else could you expect, asking people to grope their way about in the dark?

Didn't anyone try to find out afterwards why all this happened? Isn't there anything about it in the records of your unit?

No. The records just say the order was incorrect and the incident was regarded as closed. There was a rumour later on that a group of tank officers were at the root of it all.

What does that mean? Can you explain it more clearly?

It isn't clear to me either. The tank officers were eventually arrested, which made people think they'd deliberately caused the incident. But that was only a guess, and, as you know, the officers were soon set free again. After that no one has bothered about the affair . . .

Extracts from the autocritique of the head of personnel, motorized division: As regards the inquiries into the backgrounds of the tank officers, they were ordered by higher authorities, and I wish to make it plain from the start that although the instructions were issued by my superiors, much of the responsibility in this matter is mine. I don't deserve to be forgiven: I acted spinelessly, and my weakness made possible a deliberate mystification. I suspected from the outset (what head of personnel wouldn't have smelled a rat?) that the request to investigate the backgrounds of the tank officers was not based on genuine suspicion but on anger and resentment. I realized that the object was not to discover the origins of an offence, but to find a pretext – class origin, for example – for finding the officers guilty. In short, although the request to examine their backgrounds with a microscope was festooned in a lot of revolutionary phraseology (they'd even taken the trouble to include a couple of quotations from the classic texts of Marxism-Leninism), it was obvious that the real motive was revenge. I admit I never had a moment's doubt about that. Nevertheless, though I knew I was collaborating indirectly in a procedure inconsistent with communist morality, instead of opposing my superiors and fearlessly expressing my opinion as a good communist should, I not only turned a blind eye to the falsification of the truth, but I knowingly helped to make it more plausible. So I agreed to delve into the officers' pasts, and even though I didn't find anything of any moment, the mere fact of having done it in aid of personal vindictiveness is reprehensible

... Especially as ... Especially as I went so far as to interfere in certain aspects of people's private lives, aspects I'm ashamed to mention here ...

Consider yourself authorized to do so.

Well, for example, as regards the officer called Arian Krasniqi, I tried to cast aspersions on him because of rumours that circulated once about one of his sisters and her relationship with Skënder Bermema, the writer. I meant to show that Krasniqi's whole circle was morally "liberal", obviously in the negative sense in which we usually use the term. I also exploited the fact that Skënder Bermema took an interest in Krasniqi's case when he was arrested. I tried to cast grave suspicions on Krasniqi. I even ... I even ... I'm sorry, but I'm very upset ...

Go on.

I even went so far in my search for compromising facts that I bought a prose text by Bermema called *Forgetting a Woman*. It's said to have been dedicated to one of Krasniqi's sisters. So, as there wasn't much else to go on, I tried to make use of the book in this sordid affair.

How?

I sent it to a well-known critic – I can even tell you his name ... it was C— V—. I asked him to vet it for ideological errors, and he slammed it so energetically I must admit I could hardly believe my eyes.

Why did you choose C— V—?

He has a brother who works for us, and the brother had asked to be transferred to Tirana ... But I'd like to point out that C— V— agreed to denounce Krasniqi without asking for anything in return. That's why I was so surprised ...

Anything else?

Eh? No, nothing ... No, comrade, except that I don't deserve to be a member of the Party, and I hope you'll inflict the harshest possible punishment on me. But if the leadership will give me one last chance of coming back to life again, and do me the honour of letting me be a candidate for readmittance, I promise faithfully to do my utmost to deserve to be allowed back into the Party as one completely regenerated. That's all I had to say.

Are you sure the officers were sent to jail simply out of personal revenge?

Yes. No principles were involved at all. Only the desire for vengeance.

Extracts from the autocritique of the head of military intelligence: I admit my guilt. Although I knew perfectly well, because I had access to all personal records, that there was no real reason for placing the tank officers under surveillance – they were under no genuine suspicion, the only motive was revenge, as the previous witness said – I agreed to get mixed up in this nasty affair. Why? Out of servility, that wretched survival of bourgeois society! I knew what my superiors wanted, so I did what was necessary to please them. Nothing easier than to dig up a few things the tank men had said about staff in moments of anger, and present them as evidence of rebellion against army leadership, if not against authority in general.

Is that all?

It's the main thing. The rest is secondary. I'm ready to accept any punishment you care to impose.

Since you organized the surveillance of the officers, as if they really were suspected of treason, presumably you were in a unique position to find out what their real intentions were, and consequently to say whether they were innocent or not?

That is so.

And the bad weather, and the lightning, which have so often been mentioned recently, didn't prevent *you* from hearing quite clearly what they said?

No.

So what did you conclude from what they said?

That they had absolutely nothing to reproach themselves with.

Is that all?

Yes. What else could I have concluded? The purity of their intentions was as plain as could be. Their motives were clear as crystal. And to think I agreed to cover them with obloquy! I haven't been able to sleep for months!

Is that all?

I don't know what else you want of me.

Notes by delegate: Neither the head of personnel nor the head of military intelligence is being sincere. They're both hiding something.

I think the head of personnel is prevaricating when he says he thought that when his superiors asked him to investigate the tank officers' backgrounds they were acting out of a desire for revenge. I think he knew they were motivated first and foremost by fear. As for the head of military intelligence, he's lying even more outrageously, because he knew, even better than the head of personnel, about the fears to which the tank officers' attitude had given rise. The officers under surveillance had very probably often used such phrases as "It's not done to encircle a Party committee . . ." "We've explained it to them, but they wouldn't listen . . ." "We're not living in China!" . . . "If we want to prove it, we can ask the Central Committee . . ."

If neither of these two witnesses has mentioned fear, it's because that explanation would make them conscious accomplices in the wrongdoing in question.

As regards the bringing forward of the parachute landing, that was obviously motivated by a desire to justify the encircling of the Party committee by the tanks. They could say afterwards that they hadn't ordered the Party committee to be encircled; they'd ordered it to be defended. But apparently this was rejected as too crude. Moreover, the commando leader's protestations about the bringing forward of the jump, and especially about the failure of the operation, prevented it from being used as justification for the encircling of the Party committee: that might have run the risk of exposing the whole machination. The most superficial inquiry would have revealed that the order for the parachute jump was given *an hour after* the tank officers refused to encircle the Party committee.

Supplementary note by the delegate: For information, we append a copy of the text entitled *Forgetting a Woman*, by Skënder Bermema. This is an exact copy of the manuscript deposited in the safe in the office of the head of personnel, motorized units.

FORGETTING A WOMAN

And what am I going to do now? I thought, looking at the closed shutters, warped by the rain; at the carpet; at the door by which she'd gone out a few moments ago; at the china ashtray with "Tourist Hotel" written round the edge.

I wandered round the room until my pacings brought me close to the door. I stood on the exact spot where she'd kissed me goodbye, a gesture that neither emphasized our parting nor held out any promise. Such a farewell, at the end of a stormy afternoon, is usually seen as a gesture of affection, of regret for angry exchanges; the meeting of lips often leads to the meeting of minds again, to complete forgiveness and reconciliation. But it wasn't like that at all. I had kept my hands in my pockets – I'd even thrust them in deeper. I stood stiff as a ramrod as I felt her brush her lips against my neck and run her hand through my hair. I felt just the faintest impulse to put my arms round her in the age-old ritual for ending a quarrel, but I seemed somehow to have turned to stone, and couldn't move.

And now I didn't feel any remorse. I just felt tired.

The ashtray was full of cigarette ends, like corpses on a battlefield (hers wore red round their heads to show what side they had fought on). This array bore witness to the sequence of events this afternoon: the outburst of anger, the painful explanations, the mutual accusations, her unquenchable tears. If a museum of sadness existed, I'd have taken the ashtray and offered it to the curator.

I was exhausted. I had a bitter taste in my mouth. All I wanted to do was rest, sleep. I looked doubtfully at the bed – the blanket, the pillow. Did I really think I was going to be able to sleep? I felt like laughing, the idea was so ridiculous.

The soothing sound of rain wafted in from outside. I absolutely must forget this woman, root her out of my life. But above all I had to repossess this evening – that was my most urgent necessity.

I had to do all this because the pleasure she gave me was always less than the pain.

I found myself walking over every square metre of the room we'd both paced round in the course of that senseless afternoon. The overflowing ashtray brought me to a halt. I emptied the cigarette butts into the palm of my hand. They were quite cold now. And such a short time ago they had been so warm, so close to us – to our words, our sighs, our regrets, our sobs.

I went over to the window, half-opened the shutters and threw the cigarette ends out into the darkness. Like scattering someone's ashes, I thought. I *must* forget her. Use all my mental resources to denigrate her, so that when I was finally able to let her image go, it would vanish completely into oblivion. Destroyed.

I couldn't help feeling a twinge of regret at this prospect, but I was sure it was the only way. I would soon lie down – I'd noticed my most destructive thoughts came to me in that position – and then I'd begin . . . Would she hear the sound of the bulldozers, lying in *her* bed?

Suddenly I had an idea. What if I put all this on paper? Perhaps, written down, this evening would be expelled from my life more easily? I would give it form in order to kill it more easily.

Yes, that's what I'd do.

The thought of writing soothed me, as it always did, strangely enough, in such circumstances. Like a pilot flying his plane out of a storm, it bore me out of my turbulence into more tranquil skies.

The charm worked more quickly than I expected. I was soon fast asleep . . .

. . . I recognized the South Pole from a long way off. (It was slightly flattened, as I'd learned in my geography lessons in primary school.) I could hear the dull thud of hammering. As I got nearer I could see the noise was being produced by three squat little men trying to correct the earth's axis. To adjust the speed at which it revolved, apparently. Henceforward, days would last thirty-eight hours, nights twenty-two. After much research and many surveys, it had been decided this would be a great improvement. I seemed to have read something to this effect in a paper or magazine.

I wanted to ask them when the new calendar began, but for some reason I asked quite a different question: "Seeing you're experts at this sort of thing, I suppose you could remove bits of time?"

Of course they could, they replied. Child's play!

Good Lord! So what had seemed so impossible to me – getting rid of all that sadness – was really quite easy!

I tried to explain to them that I wanted to lose a day, or rather a particularly painful evening.

They started to roar with laughter.

"An evening? But we only do things wholesale! Half-centuries, decades, years at the very least. But still," – they looked at their tools – "perhaps if we used our most delicate equipment we might be able to manage days too . . ."

"Where is it?" asked one of them.

"What?"

"The day you want to get rid of, if I understand you correctly. You want to remove it, and then close up the gap, is that right?"

"Yes, that's it."

"So where is it?"

My God, I couldn't remember anything! I was drenched in sweat and my head was in a whirl.

"Maybe you can remember the year, or the decade?"

But I couldn't. I only knew the day itself was sad, mortally sad . . .

"What happened in the world that day? What empire was overturned? Was there an earthquake?"

As I didn't reply, they looked at one another. Then they cast their weary eyes around, to where in the distance a maelstrom of fallen empires slowly revolved, together with plinths brought down by earthquakes, the skeletons of the ages. They all whirled around in the darkness, lit up by cold flashes of lightning.

I still couldn't remember anything. All that remained was the bitter taste in my mouth. Nothing could remove or lessen that.

Then I suddenly thought I could see something that reminded me of a dress, floating sadly in the wind.

"A woman," I told them. "A woman was there that day . . .".

They laughed, but coldly. Then looked at their equipment again.

"In that case it's impossible. These instruments aren't any good for that kind of work."

"Please! Please deliver me from that evening, and from that woman!" I started to howl . . .

. . . And woke myself up.

It was the sound of the rain that told me where I was.

The hotel. Outside, the fallen leaves and the little cigarette corpses, one army distinguished from the other by their red headbands . . .

She was there, only a few yards away. She'd be feeling uneasy, because somehow or other she must have sensed that I was trying to bury her.

*   *   *

Meeting followed meeting. What had been written or thought during the night was said there, sometimes so changed that, as he sat down, the person who'd read it out was amazed and told himself: "Good heavens, I thought I'd said something quite different!"

Minister D—'s autocritique was due to be heard at a meeting at

408

the ministry of defence. The tank officers, whose case was now the talk of the town, were also asked to be there.

"I suppose you're going to speak," said an officer – his badges showed him to be a sapper – who was sitting next to Arian Krasniqi. He seemed to have recognized Arian, and was gazing at him with admiration. "Dash it all, if anyone ought to speak, it's you. Don't miss the chance of making these scoundrels shake in their shoes! I only wish *I* were you!"

Arian smiled mechanically. And what would you do if you *were* me? he asked the other inwardly. Wave a flag and win another stripe?

Other people had indirectly given him the same advice. They were openly disappointed to find him so reserved. They were no doubt saying to themselves, "What a drip! He's not up to the situation!"

These others were in a state of permanent euphoria. They were firmly expecting to take the places of those about to be ousted, and could scarcely conceal their delight when they saw that the latter included some enemy with whom they had a score to settle, whether because of personal rivalry, or a grudge, or – this was very frequent – some trouble over a woman.

Despite their efforts to mask it with slogans or other empty phrases, their hostility was so obvious that at one meeting the person delivering his autocritique, taken aback by his interrogator's spite and well aware of the real reason for it, ignored his questions and shouted wildly: "It wasn't my fault at all! It was hers, Margarita's, because she told me she loved me!"

"What do you mean – Margarita?" the other yelled back. "We're talking about matters of importance here, matters of principle! And you go picking petals off a daisy! . . ."

"Could I help it if she wouldn't marry you? . . ."

The chairman of the meeting then intervened to say that either the man in the dock had gone out of his mind, or else, as people in his position often did, he was pretending to have done so to try to avoid receiving his just deserts.

Sometimes, at other meetings, still more embarrassing and unanswerable questions were asked, such as, "Why did you trample underfoot the blood of the martyrs?"

Arian found all this utterly pathetic. Once or twice he felt like playing the hero, but he easily resisted the temptation. "You don't look in a very good temper," someone said to him one day. "Have you got something on your mind?" "Do you think I like what's going on?" he answered. "What do you mean: the exposing of all these dirty tricks?" "That and all the rest." "It all depends on the way you look at things."

This was on the day Arian found out that Ana's name had been mentioned at one of the meetings. He could have borne any accusation against himself better than an aspersion on his dead sister. He was almost blind with fury. But his anger was followed by bitterness. Would these people stop at nothing, digging up that name, bringing it back from the void to scatter it over the pages of their sordid confessions?

The mere thought of it filled him with disgust. Those responsible were probably here in this very room, perhaps they'd just delivered their autocritiques, perhaps they were going to take the stand again. If he'd wanted to, he could quite easily have found out their names, but he refused to do so. He knew that if he did, and then came up against one of them, it would be difficult to remain impartial. And at a meeting like this, where people's fates were at stake, and heads were in danger of rolling, he simply must remain unprejudiced.

The silence in the room grew deeper and deeper as minister D—'s autocritique proceeded. By the time it was over, his voice had almost faded away, and his eyes seemed to have sunk right into his head.

"Any questions?" asked the army officer who was chairing the meeting.

A lot of hands shot up. The minister answered their queries wearily. After about a quarter of an hour, someone mentioned "the affair of the tanks". Arian's neighbour clutched at his arm.

The minister was saying, "Of course, it was a bad mistake . . . The more you examine it the worse . . ."

"Are any of the tank officers here?" asked the chairman. "Many of us would like to hear from one of them."

People started to crane their necks and whisper.

"Stand up," whispered Arian's neighbour. "What are you waiting for?"

"Is Arian Krasniqi here?" asked the chairman.

Someone said he was.

"Stand up, kid, and throw a scare into them!" his neighbour hissed in his ear.

Arian was in a daze. Afterwards, looking back, he couldn't

remember how he got from his seat to the rostrum. He sometimes thought he must have floated there in a trance.

"Well, Krasniqi," said the chairman, "tell us something about this affair of the tanks. You were there when the order arrived, weren't you?"

Arian nodded, and suddenly, more clearly than ever before, the famous afternoon came back to him – the afternoon when his whole life almost snapped in two: the tanks lined up on the plain, their turrets glistening in the rain, the muzzles of the guns like blind eyes. It all came back so vividly he wouldn't have been surprised to feel the rain falling on his shoulders. He started to speak, not focusing his eyes on anything in particular, as if he was afraid any distraction might make him lose that inner vision on which the truth, and his honour, depended.

Four days after Silva's return, the rest of the team from the ministry came back to Tirana.

In Silva's office, she and Linda swapped news for more than half an hour with the boss and Arian, who had come in that day with his sister. The weather was dull, so they'd switched the lights on, and this, together with their lively conversation, created a cheerful atmosphere.

The recent arrivals had had new stories to tell about the Chinese. Silva asked what was happening about the blast furnace, and was told that in two or three days' time it was going to be unblocked by means of an explosion – that was the only solution.

"I believe the person in charge is a friend of yours, isn't he?" said the boss, turning to Silva.

Silva thought she saw Linda avert her eyes on hearing this veiled reference to Besnik Struga's younger brother, as she had when Silva first told her about the projected explosion. (She had even blushed a little.) After a week's absence, Silva had noticed a change. Desks, filing cabinets, curtains, telephone – all were just as before. But even though it wasn't visible, the difference was unmistakably there. For a moment it seemed to Silva that she caught a glimpse of it in Linda's eyes, which were more beautiful now, even though they wouldn't meet her own.

"And what about here?" asked the boss. "Anything new here? We heard there was something, but it was all very vague . . ."

The other two relayed what people were saying about expulsions from the Party and the sacking of ministers. Every time a name was mentioned, the boss tut-tutted and said, "Dear me! Jolly good!" Then, as if to himself: "Well I never, all these plenums! What a turn-up for the book, eh?"

Scarcely twelve hours after the end of the plenum of the Central Committee, the names of those who had been expelled were announced. For the first time the words "putsch" and "putschist" were used as well as "sabotage" and "saboteur". The people concerned were said to have been put under house arrest. Some rumours had it that three or four had even been arrested as they came out of the last session, and that when they collected their overcoats from the cloakroom their epaulettes and stripes had already been ripped off.

Everyone now linked these events with the deterioration of relations with China. Some went so far as to hint that although he had been literally reduced to ashes a long time ago, Zhou Enlai had given the conspirators their instructions by means of a tape recording. Most people, however, thought the plot was a domestic matter, and that Zhou Enlai's exhortations were merely ideological. That seemed more probable: the Chinese certainly wanted a change in the Albanian Party line, as someone had said at an important high-level meeting, but it wasn't in their interests to overthrow the Albanian régime altogether.

One morning at the office, Silva looked out of the window and saw another crowd of Chinese in Government Square. Just as she'd done a few months before, she called to the others to come and see.

Next day, as if the crowd of Chinese in the square had been a sign, all the newspapers published the Peking government's announcement that China was cutting off all aid to Albania and recalling all its experts.

Brief group meetings were called for nine o'clock, where everyone was informed of the gist of the Chinese declaration and of Albania's reply. In the middle of the morning, everyone went down to the cafeteria as usual. It was hard to believe they'd heard about the Chinese note only this morning. It seemed quite stale already, as if it had been sent months ago, even as if it had existed for ever.

Silva could scarcely help laughing when she thought of what Skënder Bermema had said. She'd met him by chance near the National Theatre, and they'd walked together as far as the Street of the Barricades. He'd told her that the Chinese note had been accompanied by all kinds of weird documents, including an X-ray of a foot, which might have been the one Silva had mentioned to him some time ago.

"Of course," he said, "it may be apocryphal – that sort of thing always flourishes in situations like the one we're in now. But if they ever publish a white paper on Sino-Albanian relations in the past few years, they couldn't find a more appropriate symbol to put on the cover than that Chink's foot!"

Silva started to smile as she thought once again about Skënder's suggestion, but her laughter died away on her lips. She'd just caught sight of Linda and Besnik Struga on the other side of the street. She stared incredulously. But yes, it really was them – it was even pretty obvious that they hadn't met by chance. He had his hands in his pockets, and she was skipping along lightly by his side. She was smiling, too, but that was no ordinary smile: it radiated out over the world in general, and was clearly rooted in her whole being . . . Ah, thought Silva, now I see why she didn't want to meet my eye.

The other two didn't see her, and she felt a moment's resentment as they disappeared along the street. But she soon realized that the feeling wasn't directed against either of them. In fact, after a little, their being together seemed quite natural. They'd probably been seeing each other while she was away, and it was quite understandable that Linda hadn't said anything about it. It would be mean not to see their point of view, especially as both of them would probably confide in her eventually, if they really . . . No, her sadness was because of Ana: because Ana wasn't here any more, couldn't walk lightly along the street as she used to do, and yet something of her . . . But was that possible? Could Linda, who had never met Ana, be acting like her in some way, as if under some influence from another world? . . . Perhaps, after all, that was why Besnik . . .

Silva quickened her pace to try to control her emotion.

"Mother," Brikena whispered as she went in, "Aunt Hasiyé's here."

As she took off her coat, Silva saw signs of panic in her daughter's face, but pretended not to notice. She'd told Brikena so often not

413

to lose her head if a visitor turned up while she was alone in the apartment. As she'd told her the last time: it wasn't as difficult as all that to give whoever it was a cup of coffee and make conversation for a while. But Brikena must have got flustered again.

"What are you looking at me like that for?" said Silva. "It's nothing out of the way for Aunt Hasiyé to drop in!"

"But, Mother, she started talking like . . . like the last time . . ."

"Oh, Brikena, you know she's a bit strange in the head now," said Silva with a touch of annoyance. "People of her age can't always remember . . ."

"But she keeps rambling on, saying all sorts of odd things," Brikena answered. "She's asked me three times who I am – I was getting quite frightened."

"All right, all right," said Silva shortly, making for the living room and putting on a welcoming expression. "How are you, Aunt Hasiyé? How's everyone at home? Brikena, would you make Aunt Hasiyé a cup of coffee, please? And one for me too, if you will."

As soon as the old woman started to speak, Silva realized that her state had got worse. She mixed up the living and the dead, and confused time, place and everything else. Brikena, making the coffee, turned round and looked at Silva as if to say, What did I tell you?

"How's Ana?" said Aunt Hasiyé. "I haven't seen her for a long time."

Silva bit her lip.

"But Ana's passed on, Aunt Hasiyé," she said gently. But the old lady either didn't understand what she said, or else forgot it immediately.

"You hardly ever see your relations nowadays," she went on. "It used to be different in the old days. They used to come and see you of their own accord. But that's all over now. Fortunately I still see them in my dreams . . ."

Silva smiled sadly.

"Everybody has such a lot to do now," the old lady continued. "They're all involved with politics, too. In my young days, people took an interest in politics, but not as much as now. I remember the time when the Chinese were here – but you're too young to remember that! They had a very wicked sultan – a very, very wicked man with a name like a cat. Miao Zedong, he was called. But all the same he ended up breaking his neck!"

Brikena stifled a laugh.

"You two didn't know the Chinese – you can afford to laugh! They had eyes like this . . . like slits. But I can only just remember them myself. It's a long time since they went away – a hundred years perhaps, maybe more. I remember the day they went . . . A neighbour of ours, Lucas his name was, hanged himself with a luggage strap. Then the Germans came – I remember them very clearly. But they didn't like the Russians . . . I remember the Italians as well – they wore perfume, like women . . ."

Silva and Brikena both burst out laughing. Brikena handed round the coffee.

"I listen to the radio," said Aunt Hasiyé, "but I can't understand a word the modern politicians say. Who was it, now, that they were insulting on the radio yesterday? The Turks?"

"No, Aunt Hasiyé – the Chinese."

"No, no – not the Chinese. That was in my day. They took themselves off more than a century ago. No one can remember them. Now we're at daggers drawn with the Turks. You don't know what the Chinese are like – you've only dreamed about them!"

Aunt Hasiyé meandered on for some time, but Silva gradually stopped laughing. The way the old woman mixed up times and tenses might seem very funny, but if you thought about it, other people's attitude to time was no less absurd. There was something artistic about Aunt Hasiyé's way of talking: not only in her mixing up of time, but also in her abolition of the frontiers between reality, dream and imagination. She asked again about Ana, insisting that she'd met her last month in the street, carrying a string bag full of oranges. Silva decided there was no point in trying to explain. Hadn't she herself remembered her sister today? And was there really all that difference between the old lady's account of her meeting with Ana in the street and the description she herself might give of her impressions when she saw Besnik Struga and Linda an hour or so ago, and thought the dead woman had some how lent her colleague her light step?

Meanwhile the phone had rung and Brikena had run to answer it. It was Sonia, wanting to speak to Silva. She asked all three of them to go round that evening if they were free. Silva said it depended on Gjergj, but she'd talk to him when he got home, and call back.

Gjergj came in just as Aunt Hasiyé was getting ready to leave.

415

To the delight of Brikena, who was watching out for their visitor to produce more eccentricities, Aunt Hasiyé scarcely recognized the newcomer.

By the time all three of them set out for Arian's place an hour later, it was dark. Two fire-engines were rushing down Pine Street, sirens shrieking.

"The human brain is a very strange thing," said Gjergj. "We laughed at what Aunt Hasiyé was saying, but do you know, in her ramblings she mentioned something that actually happened today?"

Silva felt like exclaiming, "Telepathy!"

"She mentioned someone called Lucas hanging himself a hundred years ago. Well, he really did hang himself today. They were talking about it in the cafeteria at the ministry when I went in for a coffee."

"Who was he?"

Gjergj shrugged.

"I couldn't quite make out, to tell you the truth. One of the old guard, I think."

Hava Fortuzi reminded her husband for the third time that it was unlucky to go straight home after a funeral.

"What are we supposed to do, then? You know I don't feel like going anywhere."

"I know, darling, but we must go and see someone. It'll be better for you too. I know – the Kryekurts! What do you think?"

"All right," he grumbled. "I might have known we'd end up there. As usual."

"Better the devil you know . . ."

"Not necessarily . . . Oh, this suicide! I feel at the end of my tether!"

"Stop thinking about it."

"I can't, I can't!" he moaned. "It's not just Lucas himself – you know I didn't really know him very well. But there's something about his death that does seem close . . . familiar somehow . . ."

"You must just try to put it all behind you."

"It gave me a shock as soon as I heard how he'd died. I asked how he'd done it, and when they said he'd used a luggage strap I nearly yelled out, 'That was just how I thought I'd do it myself!'"

"Ekrem! You go too far!"

"The parallel is quite natural. We were both connected to . . .

416

Yesterday, when I read the Chinese note, my heart missed a beat. I expect his did too. It's all over now. There's nothing left. It's the end."

"Ekrem! Stop it!"

"It's the end. The last hope . . . the last gleam of hope . . ."

"You must be crazy! People will hear you!"

"The one little dream . . ."

The gate into the Kryekurts' courtyard was now in sight. Hava Fortuzi hurried towards it as to a haven. I only hope they're not talking about that wretch's death, she thought. But in the Kryekurts' living room that's just what they were doing. Apart from Mark and his fiancée, both of whom remained silent, the company included Musabelli, two more of the Kryekurts' acquaintance whom the Fortuzis hadn't seen for some time, and the doctor who had cut the unfortunate Lucas Alarupi down. They were all just back from the funeral, and Hava Fortuzi was surprised to see they'd all wiped their shoes so carefully they bore no trace of mud from the cemetery. She suddenly had a feeling that they, and for that matter the whole human race, spent all their lives going to funerals. So long as the doctor doesn't regale us with all the details! she thought, looking first at the fellow's short-cropped hair – a style he'd got the habit of in prison – then at her husband's tense expression. But of course the doctor – he'd always brought her bad luck – launched straight into a blow-by-blow account of the suicide. Hava Fortuzi listened absently to his account of the run-down area where Lucas Alarupi did the deed: a piece of waste ground near the disused railway station, covered with dust, clinker, like most such places. There were also lots of sheets of paper, which the poor wretch had looked at one last time before taking his own life. Everything was there: production diagrams, photographs of star workers, graphs showing the progress of the plan, telegrams congratulating the trade unions for beating deadlines. Hava Fortuzi watched her husband as the doctor spoke. He was listening with bated breath, and she was sure he was imagining his own feet dangling over bits of his translations of economic reports and other official documents, not to mention the poems of Mao Zedong.

As the doctor explained how he'd suspected for some time that Lucas's delusions would bring him to a sticky end, Hava Fortuzi thought with horror of her own Ekrem's fantasies: an invitation from Mao himself for the two of them to spend a fortnight at

Mount Kun-lin; long imaginary conversations in classical Chinese in which he gloated over Guo Moruo: "Tee-hee, now there's someone who knows more ideograms than you!" And so on.

It looked as though this cursed quack was going to blather on for ever. After trying several times to get a word in, Hava finally just interrupted.

"It may be stale news to everyone else, but I've heard rumours about a new rapprochement with the Soviet Union," she said.

"I don't believe it for a moment," declared the doctor.

"Neither do I," said Musabelli after a moment's reflection.

"What about a rapprochement with the West, then?" gabbled Hava, terrified lest the doctor go back to Lucas's death. If she hadn't been so concerned about her husband she would never have said such a thing: she and Ekrem had gone over it so often it made her ill just to think of it.

"Even less likely," pronounced the doctor.

"I agree," said Musabelli.

Ekrem Fortuzi sighed. Perhaps it was his sickly looks, perhaps the parallel between his own obsession and that of the departed – at any rate, his sigh seemed so momentous it made everyone else fall silent. He might not have intended to say anything, but as they seemed to be waiting for him to speak, he did so.

"Paradoxical as it may seem," he said faintly, "if I had to choose between China and the West, I'd choose China. Not because I dislike the West – on the contrary, because I love it, and should like it to exist in as safe a form as possible."

Looking round at his audience, he saw they hadn't understood.

"Let me explain," he said. "A West dressed up in socialist clothes would be safer, in my opinion, than it is in its naked form, as in Europe. Do you see what I mean?" He lowered his voice. "That's the kind of West we need – one wearing masks and disguises. Otherwise we shall always be in danger ... Anyhow, perhaps we don't need Europe at all any more ... We're older, we've changed, Europe isn't for us any more ... That's the point, you see ... Our only chance ... our only chance was China. That's why I wept, I admit, and I'm not ashamed to do so. It's more shameful not to weep. And so ... And so ... But what was I saying? ... Oh yes, I cried, I cried my eyes out yesterday when I heard them read out China's announcement on the radio ..."

As the others all gazed at each other, Ekrem got up and went out of the room. In the silence that followed, his wife went out after him. After a few moments she came back, looking relieved.

"He's in the bathroom," she said in a stage whisper. "I've been worried about him ever since yesterday. I think he's on the verge of a breakdown. The wretched Chinese language has driven him mad. They talk about an embargo on oil and chrome and I don't know what else, but that's nothing compared with what's happened to Ekrem. All the Chinese he learned, gone down the drain! What's chrome or oil beside that? They'll soon find another market for that sort of thing – but what about all that Chinese? Ekrem's quite right to be depressed, poor thing. Last night it quite broke my heart to look at him. I've already told you how he wept – more than anyone else outside China, I'm sure – when Mao died. But I thought that was all over. And then yesterday evening I heard him start up again! 'My poor Mao,' he was sobbing, 'they've all stopped loving you, they've all deserted you before your body is cold. The only one who still thinks about you and loves you is me, an Albanian, an ex-bourgeois. But let the others forget you, or curse you -- I shall go on translating you as before . . .' And so he went on, poring over his Chinese books. 'Now you're dead, the Word is dead,' he said. Oh, I'm so afraid something might happen to him, if it hasn't done so already! Alarupi's suicide was the last straw!"

Musabelli was about to speak when Ekrem came back into the room. Everyone would have liked to say something, so as not to look as if they'd been talking about him, but they were all lost for words. Perhaps they were paralyzed by the way he himself looked from one to the other, as if to say, "Well, you've been discussing me. What do you say? Have I gone completely bonkers?"

In the silence, Mark's fiancée whispered something in her young man's ear. He'd been staring down at the pattern in the threadbare carpet.

"*Il fait froid*," she said again, even more softly. Her pale blue eyes had darkened. And without waiting for the conversation to start up again, they both got up and went into the other room. Hava Fortuzi watched them enviously.

"Turn your collar up," Silva told Brikena, who could hardly keep her eyes open.

It was very damp as they walked back through the city centre just before midnight. A small group of roadsweepers walked along in front of them, talking.

"They're talking about the Chinese," said Silva.

"What can roadsweepers have to say about the Chinese?" asked Brikena sleepily.

On the opposite pavement a man dressed like a foreigner had stopped to listen.

"No, no," laughed one of the roadmen. "As sure as my name is Rem, you won't catch me again! You can say what you like about Mao Zedong, I shan't open my lips. I'd rather bite my tongue out than utter his name. I've already copped it once that way – I did fifteen years in jug because of Krushchev. And when, I ask you? When everyone was insulting him! Oh no, never again! Everyone else calling him all the names they could lay their tongues to, and me rotting behind bars! Just because I started cursing him a couple of hours before everyone else!"

The other roadsweepers laughed.

"You didn't go to jail for insulting Krushchev," said one of them. "They put you away for relieving yourself against the tree he planted in the garden opposite the Hôtel Dajti, in honour of Albano-Soviet friendship."

"So what?" said Rem. "What's the difference between a tree and the person who planted it? Don't talk to me about it – it makes me fit to be tied!"

"You mustn't lose your temper today, Rem – the last day before you retire! Thirty years sweeping the streets for the new man to walk along – isn't that what the union boss said? I tell you, it brought tears to my eyes."

"Yes, it quite upset me as well," said Rem.

"How amusing!" said Brikena. "I've never heard roadsweepers talking before. Don't walk so fast, Mother – I want to listen."

But by now they'd left the roadmen behind, and could hear only snatches of what they were saying.

"Come on, Rem! Wield your broom for the last time! You've swept some things away in your lifetime! Sweep the street clean for the last time! Sweep the whole surface of the earth clean!"

"What are they saying, Father?" asked Brikena. "I thought I heard one of them call out, 'Sweep the surface of the earth clean of everything to do with the Chinese!'"

"I shouldn't be surprised!" said Gjergj, slowing down. He looked

420

over at the roadmen, who at present were standing still. The man on the other side of the street, now quite clearly a foreigner, had also stopped to listen. But the roadmen had fallen silent.

"The one who's retiring really is sweeping the street for the last time," said Silva.

And in the distance they could see one of the men swishing his broom back and forth along the crown of the road, raising a cloud of dust and shrouding himself in mystery.

It was long past midnight, and messages from Europe were becoming few and far between. The observer at the Pole looked at his log-book: his notes were thinning out too. His superiors had pointed it out to him, but there was nothing he could do about it.

People said it was a kind of professional illness that afflicted everyone who did this job. After the first few months they gradually became indifferent. This aloofness brought about great changes in the way they perceived the universe: space, distance, time and events all assumed different dimensions. Many things that before had seemed important and established now seemed like ephemeral trifles; others arose out of nothingness and night to blaze like new planets. When people talked about the world's reserves of oil or coal or rock salt, he marvelled that no one ever thought about the world's reserves of malice, goodness and crime. History was written quite wrongly: a few battles and treaties, but all the most important things left out. Where for example would you find a single word about the twelve thousand girls in Europe who fell in love between five o'clock and a quarter to six on the afternoon of 20 September 1976? – in what annals, what diplomatic documents, historical or geo-strategic maps? And what about the sorrow of eleven generations of bald men between the end of the Middle Ages and the beginning of modern times? It was that kind of thing that was the real stuff of history, not that other squeaking of rats reeling home from some grotesque evening out, the tedious pastime of Lilliputians!

He realized that if he went on like that he'd end up neglecting his work and probably get sacked; but he'd given up bothering about that a long time ago. He'd find some other, less demanding job, or perhaps write his memoirs – *The Solitude of the World Listener*. His reminiscences would probably turn out as peculiar as the chattering radio messages, but perhaps they too would be punctuated by quieter passages, about the state of the ice, the temperature of the water, the barometric pressure . . .

He certainly wouldn't be writing about the everyday trivia of politics. The international monetary crisis was going to get worse, people said. And the next Pope would be a Pole – dear me, what a scoop! He looked at the time: he would be waking up his colleague in a few minutes. He'd jot down a few more notes, old chronicler of the planet that he was, like some medieval monk working by flickering candlelight; then he'd go to bed. A huge yawn blocked his ears for a moment and prevented him from hearing half of a sentence about China. Heavens, all the things he'd scribbled down on *that* subject lately!

But wait a minute! What they were saying just now was a bit out of the ordinary, more in the style of his own reflections. He leaned forward, hunching up his shoulders to bring the earpieces closer to his ears . . . *In Albania they think China should be swept off the face of the earth* . . . Good grief, thought the observer, who could have said such a thing? It was all very well for *him* to think it himself, sitting there on top of the world, but down there in that ridiculous mess, what far-sighted spirit was responsible for such a point of view? He concentrated, trying to hear more: *People walking the streets of Tirana at night express the opinion that Mao Zedong's China ought to be swept off the surface of the earth . . . This is the first time anyone had formulated in so radical and absurd a manner an idea so . . .* Well, my lad, thought the observer, inwardly addressing the unknown broadcaster, you may see it like that, but I agree with that sentiment entirely! And he suddenly longed to be having a quiet whisky somewhere with that anonymous passer-by from Tirana, peacefully discussing what countries seemed to them superfluous, what centuries they could do without, and how to rid the planet of such things, unfasten them and let them fall into the void. Just like that, he mused, aware he was about to lose the thread of his thoughts . . . The sadness of eleven generations of bald men hovered sadly, like a great condor, over the globe . . . I may be going round the bend, he told himself, but that doesn't matter either . . .

The headset, which was now dangling from his hand, was emitting poor little twittering noises. Drivel away, he told them – I'm not going to listen any more! He'd been gazing for some time at the wall, at the day's date on the calendar. There was a blue ring round it, picking it out as marking one of the only two dawns visible from here in the whole year. In six months of polar darkness, he had never once seen the sun rise. He had come there during that polar night, and now for the first time he was going to see the day. Mustn't miss this! he thought.

He dropped his headset on the floor, put on his anorak and walked over to the door. It did occur to him that he ought to wake his colleague to replace him, but he dismissed this insignificant thought from his mind.

The sun now really was rising. It was incredibly white, stunning as a cry, but constantly shrinking at the edges so as to let you pass. The monitor made his way across the ice in a kind of trance, not looking back. Except once: and when he saw the little building, so small and sombre in the distance, like a witch's cottage, with all that idiotic chatter inside, he felt like roaring with laughter.

I'm not mad, he told himself. It's just that my head is full of the light of a thousand mornings rolled into one. Or rather, with the light of a hundred and eighty-two dawns.

He walked on towards the pure expanses of ice far away from the noisy hut. If he'd turned back he'd only have heard a lot of ramblings about the two Germanies, the Roman Empire and the seventeenth century. It wasn't worth it. Such things weren't important enough to deserve a backward glance.

18

PROBLEMS WERE ARISING EVERYWHERE. A sudden drop in the temperature followed by two earthquakes in succession in central Albania seemed designed to complete the picture. The first green shoots of March and the open-air cafés opening up by the artificial lake outside Tirana – all the things suggesting holidays and the pleasures of the beach seemed shocking and incongruous, like a grin at a funeral.

The docks were cluttered up with heaps of chrome ore which the Chinese had deliberately omitted to load. As if the slump in oil production wasn't enough, the sudden fall in prices on the world market involved the country in considerable financial loss. But chrome and oil weren't the only sectors affected. The entire structure of foreign trade was shaken. Export agents hastened abroad in search of new markets, but European companies weren't in any hurry to oblige. The sound of telex machines was rarely heard these days.

Such representatives of European firms as did arrive at Tirana airport all had long hair and extravagant beards – some real, but some false, according to two or three Albanian sales reps who'd met their owners a couple of months before, since when there would not have been time for such beards to come into being naturally. This was confirmed by a brief report specially prepared by the Central Institute of Hygiene, which said that even in extreme circumstances a human hair cannot grow by more than one and a half centimetres per month.

There had already been grotesque scenes in the past between foreign visitors and Albanian officials, ever since Tirana airport had been equipped with a barber's shop. Newcomers were promptly taken there if their hair or beards "were an affront to the honour of the country of arrival." This gave rise to much resentment and sometimes to angry outbursts: one visitor took one look in the glass after his unruly mop had been shorn off, and burst into tears, sobbing "What have they done to my Sylvana?" But on the whole such disagreeable incidents were either avoided or hushed up.

Now, however, it was different. Both sides seemed to have decided to stick to their guns. The visiting sales reps refused to sit meekly down in the barber's chair, and the Albanian officials declined to make any concessions. The former protested loudly and threatened to go home on the planes they'd just arrived by, contracts or no contracts.

Some of them actually did so.

But only to return a fortnight later decked out even more extravagantly, their locks and whiskers longer than before (some even went in for "punk" – unheard-of!). Then the same scenes unfolded as before, with the same protests and the same refusals, and back the visitors marched to their plane, whose pilot already had the engines running. It was at this point that one of the foreigners, going up the steps to the aircraft, uttered the fateful words, "You see – the same as ever!" In this phrase lies the explanation of what followed.

This "The same as ever!", relayed to high places, together with all that it implied ("You're just as pigheaded as you were before," "You won't learn, will you?" "That's right – turn your backs on the outside world!"), soon brought a riposte, which duly made its way down again and exhorted the lower echelons: "Don't yield an inch!"

"You really are cracked!" exclaimed the agent of yet another foreign firm the next day. "You're the crazy ones!" replied the Albanian official who was dealing with him. What the official meant was: "You envoys from the capitalist world surely don't still expect us to change our policy and open up to the outside world?" etc. Meanwhile the barber had appeared in the doorway of his shop, brandishing his scissors menacingly.

The same as ever ... *Sempre gli stessi* ... So the visitors' behaviour was a stratagem, aimed at testing Albania and assessing the scale of its present difficulties. The news of what was happening soon spread by word of mouth all over the capital. One young literary lecturer who'd spent half his sabbatical rummaging through the archives found what he said was a parallel incident in a medieval chronicle. In the fifteenth century a certain Albanian fortress, which had been besieged by the Turks for so long that its supplies were almost exhausted and its inmates beginning to go hungry, gave a

425

mule a huge feed of corn and threw it over the ramparts. When the Turks opened up the mule and found all the undigested corn, they thought the people in the fortress must have plenty of food to spare, and gave up all hope of starving them into surrender. So they abandoned the siege and went away.

This tale gave rise to great controversy in literary circles. The analogy was considered very doubtful. The situation of present-day Albania bore no resemblance to that of the ancient fortress, which was suffering from a genuine famine, and the sending away of the sales reps was nothing like the throwing of the mule over the ramparts. But in the meanwhile the literary review which had published the text had come to the attention of foreign secret services, and though no one knew how they had interpreted it, the incident in question was repeated a week later. The same reps as before reappeared at Tirana airport – as obstinate as any mules!

Again they were asked to visit the barber's shop. Again they refused, turned on their heels, and made for the waiting plane.

Then for some days there was practically no traffic at the airport. Very few planes landed or took off, and if one did, the airport staff waited in vain for any hairy reps to disembark.

One rainy day an elderly customs official who'd been suffering for some time from high blood pressure, looked out and saw a kind of black cloud hovering over the landing strip. Now the official had seen the Chinese prime minister arrive here and appear in the doorway of his plane no fewer than four times. And since the cloud was hovering at about that level; and perhaps because the customs man had heard about the Chinese prime minister's ashes being scattered from a plane; and perhaps also because he'd been having dizzy spells lately – well, for some or all of these reasons, he thought the wandering black cloud was the tormented spirit of Zhou Enlai.

It was a boundless ocean, a galaxy of plots, secret machinations and bloody putsches. It was full of the names of monosyllabic victims, whose heads plunged down into the depths and then bobbed up again in a slow dance of death. Some were still red from the burning breath of the present, some dull, cold and covered by the dust of oblivion. They came and went as in a spiritualist séance, scarcely knowing themselves whether they sought revenge, victims or a return to the void.

426

Enver Hoxha turned the pages of his political journal one by one. He'd been keeping it for years, and it contained thousands of pages about China. A few hours ago he'd had it brought to the house on the coast where he was spending the weekend. He pushed the small globe away to make room on his desk for the journal. Through the window he could see the deserted coast, with its sand hardened by the winter. His glance came to rest now on one page, now on another, now on a date, now on a heading: Tuesday, 6 October 1964 – bad signs; Thursday, 10 November 1966 – explanations of Kan Cheng . . .

He'd known some of the people mentioned in these pages personally. Others, long swept away by the changes and chances of the age, were represented by words, intrigues or thoughts that had reached him through reports or radio messages. All this ought to be made available to the world at large, he thought.

His fingers went on turning the pages: Wednesday, 17 February 1971 – Chen Po-tah sentenced to death for treason; Monday, 15 November 1971 – Reflections on China; Durrës, Saturday, 28 July 1972 – The Lin Biao "plot".

He paused at this entry. He'd devoted several pages to the various versions of the marshal's death, and the doubts he'd had about it at the time . . . The plane had crashed . . . Caught fire . . . That's all anyone knew. According to an Ottawa paper, Kissinger had told the Canadian prime minister that ballistics experts had found bullet marks in the wreckage of the plane . . . Why should shots have been fired inside the cabin? Who had done it, and why?

He shook his head. An endless series of infamies, that was the only way to describe it.

He looked for his pen among the scattered pages, then underlined the words "Reflections on China". That was what he'd call his book. It was right that the world should have access to this testimony – it could only be of use to it. He underlined "Reflections on China" again: it would be hard, he thought, to find another country and another people who'd known China as closely as his own country and his own people.

From the corner of the table the small globe cast its shadow over the papers. Sometimes he'd harboured dark thoughts about that globe. Such terrible thoughts they might almost have made it fall out of its trajectory. But this hadn't happened.

Zhou Enlai . . . Tcheng . . . Tchang . . . They kept appearing and

427

reappearing, as to the summons of a gong echoing through time.

He looked up from his desk and gazed out again at the deserted coast. A telephone rang somewhere in the depths of the villa. When, after a short while, someone knocked at the door and told him the blast furnace at the steel complex had been unblocked by means of an explosion, he could still hear the echo of the telephone ringing in his ears. The messenger was hovering in the doorway.

"Anything else?"

The man's expression foreshadowed his answer.

"One man was killed in the explosion. Another was blinded. There were some other casualties."

Enver Hoxha sat motionless. The explosion had left one person dead and several injured. He looked at the journal as if the incident were already written there. He had a fleeting vision of war casualties, old comrades of his who had probably died of their wounds. They'd met their deaths during a period he'd described as "The Age of the Party", whereas the victims of the blast furnace, forty years later, were probably young, the same age as the earlier victims' sons. Their injuries would be different too – wounds caused not by bullets or shells, but by molten metal, the raw material of death . . . But it all came to the same thing in the end . . .

Yes, in taking up the torch, they all took upon their vulnerable shoulders the burden of sacrifice.

He looked out at the beach again to rid himself of the negative part of the news he'd just heard. The millennium was approaching its end, and his country was going to have to settle its accounts with a world it had never loved. He had done all he could to ensure that Albania should embark on the third millennium in the form he had imparted to it. But he still had to see to it that this form lasted for ever, that no one else ever altered it.

He looked back at his papers again, so fixedly that some of the Chinese names seemed to merge with some of the Albanian ones he'd just been thinking about.

Just as at the time of the break with the Soviets, many people would see the rupture with China as a farewell to communism – or to the East, as it was called in some parts of the world. These same people would expect to see the churches reopened and ordinary life liberalized – a general "opening up".

But they would rub their hands too soon, as before. And as before he would strike them down without mercy.

He reached for his pen to write these thoughts down. He thought them over for a while, in order to phrase them with suitable solemnity. When he'd set them down in black and white, he smiled.

Twenty-four hours before the unblocking of the furnace, at about two in the morning, a telegram arrived on the desk of the duty officer at Central Committee headquarters. It reported the discovery of oil in the area where test-drilling had been in progress for some months. But even before the good news had been transmitted by phone to all the government offices in Tirana, it had already been brought to the capital by the passengers on the early-morning train, who, looking out of the windows as they rolled across the plain, saw flames from the burning oil-well leaping up into the dawn sky. The engine-driver had tooted the whistle several times, and the passengers stood glued to the icy windows gazing spellbound at the column of fire on the horizon.

Ex-minister D—, handcuffed in his cell in Tirana, awaiting trial, heard those whistle blasts as a series of howls. O God, he sighed. What was the source of all his troubles? The examining magistrate had mentioned the "agitation" he'd felt during the famous telephone call that ill-fated evening – an agitation which he'd never mentioned to anyone, and which he was sure no one had suspected at the time. Apparently that was what it all started from . . . God, why hadn't he thought of it before? It was staring him in the face now . . . It must have been that visitor who never turned up, that minor civil servant whose name he couldn't even remember – he must be the one who told! Did he come back and lurk around his house like a ghost? . . . Judas! he groaned. Why didn't you choose someone else? Why did you have to pick on me?

Another whistle, longer this time, died away in the distance.

That same morning, at about a quarter past six, on a stretch of waste ground in the north-west suburbs of Tirana, not far from the railway line, where a week before the former factory owner, Lucas Alarupi, had been found hanging from an old telegraph pole (with newspaper cuttings, pages of statistics and all sorts of other papers scattered around over a radius of about twenty yards) – at this exact spot some municipal workers unloaded several crates from a van. On the crates, beneath some big Chinese characters, was written the word, "Fireworks".

The men had been instructed to attract as little attention as possible when destroying all these firecrackers and rockets, but when they'd selected this remote spot they'd forgotten that the railway line ran along beside it.

In the growing light of dawn they saw the waste lot was typical of those you get near big cities. The muddy ground, the scattered rubbish, the old tin cans, the dew as viscous as rain at night on a rubber cape – all combined to create a kind of lunar landscape. Not a real one, like what we see on our friendly old moon, but one of the sinister kind transmitted by cameras on space flights.

"Come on, let's get to work," said the man who appeared to be in charge, levering open one of the crates. "And mind it doesn't all blow up in your faces!"

He took a rocket out of the crate and carefully applied his cigarette lighter.

"Hell, it must be damp!" he growled. "Pass me another one."

The rocket suddenly started to sputter, then, to the shouts of the workmen, flew up into the air and landed a few yards away. It gave out a little flame, and a few sparks, then started to whirl round on its own axis with a stifled hiss. Another leap, and then it exploded, shedding a lurid glow all over the waste lot.

"Apparently they make all sorts of patterns – dragons and snakes – if you can get them to go high enough," said one of the men.

"That's why they decided to destroy them," said another.

"That's enough philosophizing," shouted the boss. "Get on with the job – we're already behind time. Only be careful not to get burnt!"

Cautiously at first, then more and more recklessly, the workmen let off the crackers and rockets, directed now by a couple of experts. The hitherto dreary waste lot began to glow with all kinds of wild and peculiar illuminations.

Just then the train whose passengers had seen the oil strike flaming in the distance was slowly approaching the central station. The workmen turned to look at it. The passengers all looked back out of the windows.

"What are you doing?" called a girl traveller gaily. The fireworks were reflected in her fair hair, streaming in the wind.

430

"We're destroying the Chinese fireworks," answered one of the younger workmen, forgetting they'd been told not to tell anyone what they were doing.

"What?"

He repeated his reply, but the train had moved on and the girl couldn't hear. Someone else waved at them from another coach. From the last coach but one a voice shouted:

"Have you heard? They've struck oil!"

The workmen stood discussing the good news for a while after the train had gone.

"I thought they might tell us something about the blast furnace," said one of them. "I've got a brother working there."

Then they returned to their labours, reflecting that the news of the oil strike ought to be celebrated with something less sinister than Chinese fireworks.

Meanwhile the train reached Tirana, at the same time as the news of the joyful column of flame.

The early part of the day was very tense. Rumours had reached the capital about the unblocking of the blast furnace and the finding of a new oil-field – perhaps the same train had brought both stories – but these mingled with the latest rumours about a plot said to have been discovered by Enver Hoxha in person. He was supposed to have surprised the putschists conspiring in a villa, or in the cellar of a villa, and they'd all flung themselves down on their knees and begged for mercy.

Far-fetched as all this was, one fact was corroborated by more or less reliable sources: the plot really had been discovered by Enver Hoxha. It was even said that at a meeting of the Politbureau he'd asked the Minister of the Interior why conspiracies were always uncovered by the Party and never by the state security services. The minister had turned pale.

By the beginning of the afternoon, everyone was talking about the plot, although the situation still wasn't clear. In the bar at the Dajti Hotel the foreign diplomats, who'd got wind of something, exchanged the latest news, vague and incoherent though it was. Even vaguer and more incoherent was the form in which the various embassies transmitted it by radio. Then, faster even than in the days when the ancient gods had their own messengers, the news spread far and wide through celestial space via spy satellites, some of which indeed bore the names of Greek gods.

What's happening? It seems very odd. Intelligence experts everywhere kept taking off their headsets and putting them back on again, just as perplexed as their superiors by seeing a national hullabaloo being made about such relatively trivial incidents as the discovery of a new oil-field and the unblocking of a blast furnace. But if you looked at it more closely – wasn't it really perhaps another plot? No, no, there was no possibility of confusion of that kind. It was really a question of property. What? What kind of property? Private property was consigned to the dustbin a long time ago . . . But I'm talking about public property, collective property . . . Oh, you still believe in *that*, do you? And so it went on, the satellites exchanging their strange cheepings and twitterings, like the cries of some prehistoric bird that had got stranded in time and was struggling to get back into the world.

The boss had been summoned to see the vice-minister. Silva and Linda had been looking forward to having a private chat. Yet they sat at their desks and said nothing. The more Silva tried to find a way to start a conversation, the more foolish she felt, which made her annoyed first with herself and then with her colleague . . . *I* can't talk to *her* as I used to since I saw the two of them together like that, she thought. But what's the matter with *her*? She might at least just behave as usual . . . Anything would be better than this . . .

But she found she couldn't be angry with Linda. Out of the corner of her eye she could see her profile – expectant, touching. And touching in a rare way: not because it was sad, but because it was happy. Silva decided she herself must take the responsibility for the present awkwardness. She had guessed Linda's secret, and must have given out waves which the other girl, anxious as she was, had interpreted as negative. In any case, the fact that Linda found she couldn't go on as if nothing had happened proved that she didn't want to be deceitful. Poor kid, it's not her fault, thought Silva. It's quite understandable that she shouldn't have told me about her affair, if that's what it really is. Any woman in her position would have felt embarrassed about it.

If only she knew I don't mind at all! On the contrary, it would be the ideal solution for Besnik. It had occurred to Silva more than once that perhaps she ought to broach the subject herself, quite plainly and straightforwardly. But she hadn't liked to.

In similar circumstances, before, she would have got out of such difficulties by some sort of polite evasion, like pretending she hadn't seen them that afternoon. She was just considering this, glancing occasionally at the door in the hope that someone would come in and help break the ice, when the silence was interrupted by the telephone. It sounded so loud she almost cried out. When she picked up the receiver and heard Besnik Struga's voice, she nearly exclaimed, "What a coincidence!" She would indeed have done so, if Linda hadn't been there . . . But there was something odd about his voice . . .

"Listen," he said. "The Bermemas are in trouble. One of the family, a young engineer called Max – perhaps you've met him – was killed this morning at the steel complex."

"What?" gasped Silva. "How . . . ?"

"And that's not all. Victor Hila . . ."

"What, him too?"

"He's still alive, but he's been blinded."

"Oh, how dreadful!" Silva cried.

The words were so flat, so inexorable, like the woes that prompted them. Death, blindness – things that stretched back to ancient tragedy.

"Silva," Besnik went on, "it's rather awkward for me to go and see the Bermemas, as you know, but I must. Max was Ben's closest friend . . ."

"Yes. I met them together at the complex, just as they were preparing to . . . How is Ben?"

"Just superficial burns. Several other people were injured too. Listen, this is why I'm calling you: are you going to go over? I know it's difficult for you too, because of Skënder Bermema, but . . ."

"Yes, but of course I'll go! If . . ."

"Victor's still there, in the local hospital. I'll tell you more about how he is later on."

"All right . . ."

"I'll call you at home, then, at about four o'clock, so that we can go together. I think they're bringing the body back around midday, and the funeral's due to take place late this afternoon."

Silva replaced the phone. She was shattered.

433

"Has something happened?" asked Linda, looking frightened. Silva nodded.

"Someone we know . . . died this morning at the steel complex."

"How awful," Linda murmured.

"And that isn't all." Silva paused, as Besnik had. "Victor Hila – you remember him, I'm sure – has been blinded."

Linda turned terribly pale.

"How dreadful!" she whispered, almost inaudibly.

"All those jokes about the Chinaman and his foot," said Silva, as if to herself. "Who'd have thought it would all end like this!"

"Oh yes, I remember!" said Linda. "He said it was all very well to laugh, but . . . It's as if he had a presentiment."

"Yes, it was that stupid story that started it all," said Silva. "If he hadn't had to leave his factory, he'd still be alive now."

It didn't shock Linda to hear Silva unconsciously equate blindness with death.

She sighed. Almost moaned.

"It was Besnik Struga I was talking to," said Silva. She didn't look at Linda as she spoke, thinking to spare her blushes. "His brother's one of the injured."

She thought of the stricken Bermema family. In the present circumstances, no awkwardness about past relationships ought to stop her going to see them. Besides, now that Ana was dead, the tension that once existed between the Bermemas, the Strugas and the Krasniqis had necessarily faded. And perhaps it would disappear altogether if . . . Silva turned towards Linda, and found Linda gazing back at her.

"Silva," she said faintly. "I've got something to tell you."

Silva could imagine how hard it was for her to speak: she sounded as if she might break down at any moment.

"I know, Linda," she said. Linda stared back out of beautiful, wide grey eyes. "I saw you out in the street together."

Linda flushed.

"I kept meaning to . . . but you see . . . I was so embarrassed . . ."

"I understand. But these things happen, and there's absolutely no need for you to feel uncomfortable as far as I'm concerned. It's perfectly natural, and as long as there are men and women . . ."

The words sounded so platitudinous, Silva changed the subject back to the accident, and what had happened to Max and Victor. It occurred to her that Linda, like everyone with a fixed idea, might still have preferred to go on talking about Besnik. But in fact she was listening intently to everything Silva said about the Bermemas. So much so, that Silva, by intuition rather than logic, found herself asking if Linda would like to go with her to see them.

Linda shrugged.

"Yes, I'd like that very much, if you really think . . ."

"If you want to come, come," said Silva. "It's not like an ordinary death. When there's a disaster of this kind, everyone comes to offer condolences, not only immediate family."

Then it struck Silva that Linda oughtn't to go if she regarded her relationship with Besnik as just a passing affair. Her decision as to what to do this afternoon might almost be regarded as a test . . .

"I wonder what Besnik . . ." stammered Linda.

"I think he'd want you to go," said Silva. "After all, his younger brother was injured . . ."

"Yes, so you said . . ."

And at this point their conversation ended, because the boss had just walked in.

To Linda's distress they didn't get another chance to talk all the rest of the morning, and so didn't finish their discussion about the afternoon. Even when she and Silva left the office, they weren't alone: a group of colleagues insisted in walking along with them. One called out, "I say, has anyone seen anything of Simon Dersha? I haven't set eyes on him for days." "Nor have I," someone answered. Yes, thought Silva, he does seem to have vanished without our noticing. But she didn't have time to pursue the subject, for Linda came up and whispered shyly: "So what are we doing about this afternoon, then?"

"I think it'll be all right for you to come," Silva reassured her. Then, after they'd walked on a few paces:

"It won't seem out of the way. We'll all be there."

Linda nodded a rueful goodbye to her colleagues and turned towards home. "We'll all be there . . ." What did that mean? Who were "we"? Why hadn't Silva suggested their meeting and going together? .

Linda felt hurt. The others still regarded her as an intruder. They were jealously protecting their own little circle. "We'll all be

435

there . . ." But she'd have to make her way there alone. Even Besnik hadn't said anything to her: he'd talked to Silva on the phone as if she, Linda, had never set foot in the office. Yes, for all of them she was still an outsider . . .

But as she walked slowly along, her bitterness gradually waned. I'm just being childish, she thought. How was Besnik to know she'd want to go to the funeral? From his point of view it was something she'd be glad to be spared . . . Linda sighed. How were any of them to know that if she wanted to go it wasn't to please anybody, still less out of morbid curiosity (ugh! she could hardly bear to think of it!), but simply because she was fascinated by them and their world. She longed to be close to everything that concerned them, whether joy or sorrow. No, they could never understand that! But Silva's feminine intuition must have given her an inkling, otherwise she wouldn't have suggested . . .

As Linda was helping her mother lay the table for lunch, the phone rang. It was Silva.

"Hallo," she said hurriedly. "Look, we didn't get a chance to arrange things properly. I didn't have time to tell you Besnik is going to ring me at four: you could come with us if you like . . ."

"Oh no," said Linda inadvertently. "Not with him!"

"Why not? But just as you like. You may be right. In any case, I'm sure it will be all right for you to come on your own. There'll be so many people no one will notice you . . . Do you know the address?"

"No," said Linda faintly.

Silva gave it to her. And she sat pensively down to lunch.

As Linda made her way to the Bermema's apartment, she told herself she could always have a look round when she got there, and then decide whether to go in or not.

She could see the crowd from some way off. It was larger than she'd expected: the pavement outside the apartment block was packed, and so was the pavement opposite. There was an ambulance among the cars parked all along the street. The nearer she got, the more slowly Linda went. When she got to the door she realized she could go upstairs without being noticed: two continuous streams of visitors were passing up and down. She started up without looking at anyone, reflecting that if she so decided she could turn round and come down again without setting foot inside the apartment itself.

Both the doors on the second-floor landing were open, and without knowing which was the Bermema's apartment, Linda went in through one of them. Fortunately the hall was crowded. She tried to make out which room had, in accordance with custom, been set aside for the men to deliver their condolences, and which for the women. Then she realized there was no such arrangement here.

She looked for some quiet corner from which she could look on without attracting notice. Her courage was ebbing away. In the end she decided she might as well stay in the hall: there were so many comings and goings, and no one seemed to be standing on ceremony. As Silva had suggested, in the case of a calamity like this, the usual forms were abandoned.

So far Linda hadn't seen anyone she knew. At one point she thought she glimpsed Silva's husband, but she couldn't be sure. And where was the coffin? she wondered.

About a quarter of an hour went by, and she might have stayed there indefinitely, but suddenly she saw Silva come into the hall.

"Oh, there you are!" Silva whispered.

"Have you just arrived?" asked Linda.

"No, we've been here some time. Have you presented your condolences to the family?"

Silva looked rather distraught, too.

"No," said Linda.

"Neither have I. Come on, let's go together – it's not easy for me, either . . ."

Linda gave her a grateful look, and clung to her arm as they made for the door. She longed to ask where Besnik was, but only said, "I'm so glad I found you!"

The room Silva led her into was spacious and heavily furnished, with chairs placed round all the walls. They chose a couple of seats in the row on one side, and sat down, Linda still clutching Silva's arm. The silence was broken only by murmurs too faint to be heard all the way across the room.

"Is that him?" Linda whispered, nodding towards a large photograph on the opposite wall.

Silva nodded.

Linda gazed absently at a big bronze clock with a statue of

Skanderbeg on top. Inscribed on its base were the words: "Albania's hour has come." She remembered learning it at school – the six-hundred-year-old maxim that could be applied as easily to national victory as to national disaster.

A new wave of visitors arrived, and a few of those already there, Silva and Linda included, stood up to make room for them and then went back into the hall. Some continued across into the other apartment, but:

"Let's stay here," said Silva.

Linda wanted to ask about Besnik, but didn't like to. It was as if Silva had forgotten their conversation that morning.

People kept passing in and out of the hall. One man with a very sad expression came up and greeted Silva. Linda thought she recognized him.

"A friend of mine," said Silva, nodding towards her. "This is Skënder Bermema – I think you know him."

"Oh, it's you!" said Linda, holding out her hand.

His response was friendly, but his sad expression didn't change. For a moment he looked at Silva without saying anything, as if he had been angry with her, but now was angry no longer.

"I was so shocked," said Silva. "I met him only a few days ago, at the complex, just as he was working to prepare the explosion. Just before . . ."

You could see him gritting his teeth.

"Who'd have credited it?" he murmured. "We thought that scourge would go away of its own accord. Who could have imagined it would take Max with it?"

"A scourge indeed . . ." echoed Silva.

"We split our sides laughing at their deceit, but it turned out to be more deadly than we thought."

Their laughter . . . Silva thought of Victor Hila. She couldn't imagine him blind. Laughter starts in the eyes . . . And that was where it had ended.

"Oh, here's Ben," said Silva, moving towards a tall young man whose face was partially covered with dressings held in place with sticking plaster.

He must be Besnik's brother, thought Linda. She'd have liked to go over, join in the conversation, perhaps even kiss him, but she was too shy. She was here, wasn't she? She mustn't ask for more. There were traces of tears on the young man's bandages, and again she felt like kissing him tenderly. My brother-in-law . . . God, was it possible?

"That was Besnik's brother," Silva said, coming back to her.

"Yes, so I guessed."

She suddenly felt she had to see Besnik himself. This was no mere wish arising from a fleeting passion, but something stronger, derived from the real affection that can only come into being gradually, maturing slowly like wine.

A stir of activity suggested that the journey to the cemetery was imminent.

"That's the dead boy's mother," said Silva, showing Linda a woman in deep mourning who'd just come into the hall. "Her husband was a minister just after the Liberation."

Linda was clinging to Silva once more, drinking in all she said.

"The man over there in the dark grey suit is the present husband of Besnik's first fiancée."

Linda looked at him until he seemed to notice he was being scrutinized. "Where's she?" she asked.

"I can't see her, but she must be here somewhere." Silva looked round. "Yes, I should think she *is* here."

The crowd in the hall and on the landing was getting denser. Besnik's brother went by again, with his tear-stained, black-streaked bandages. Then Linda felt Silva's hand on her arm.

"Look, there she is!" she whispered. "Zana . . ."

Linda trembled.

"Where?"

She was over by the door, in a black dress, with another woman who couldn't stop weeping.

"The one who's crying is the dead boy's sister. Her name's Diana . . ."

Silva went on talking, but Linda was scarcely listening now. She couldn't take her eyes off the first woman, Zana. That was more or less how she'd imagined her, except . . . The weight and coldness of the big silver comb in her hair seemed to be echoed in her eyes – but the coldness there, it seemed to Linda, was the kind men like. She felt a pang. Yes, she'd imagined her rather like that, except for the comb . . . Besnik had told her very briefly about their break-up. Perhaps it was really just a misunderstanding, he'd said after a moment's reflection. She had been sorry to hear it. People who split up over a mere misunderstanding can come to love one another

439

again. She would have been consumed with anxiety if it hadn't been for Ana. It was Ana who must have interposed between her, Linda, and Besnik's first fiancée, confronting Zana's power and neutralizing it. Linda, seeing Zana for the first time, with her seductiveness concentrated in that silver comb, marvelled at the thought of Ana and *her* saving power. Who was she, this dead woman who left behind her nothing but peace and light? How had she performed that miracle?

The crowd on the landing was parting. They were bringing out the coffin. Linda caught a glimpse of it, an oblong draped in red, being carried head-high. Then, further off, she saw Besnik, and Linda's husband. All the pall-bearers were gathered together now: Skënder Bermema, sad as ever; Besnik's brother, with his tear-stained cheeks; together with many more. A long, lugubrious procession. To Silva it suddenly looked like a whole generation, moving along mournfully to the strains of a hymn.

It was quite dark when Max's funeral was over, and some people who were there, and who had departed friends and relations of their own buried nearby, took the opportunity to visit their graves.

Silva and Linda were standing by Ana's tombstone when they saw Besnik approaching, followed at some distance by Skënder Bermema. The two women moved away a little. After a while, Besnik, who hadn't noticed them, left Ana's grave and walked over to the middle of the cemetery, where his father and aunt were buried. As they waited for him to be out of range – it was Linda who had asked Silva not to let him see them – Linda noticed the name of another Ana, on another tombstone, sumptuous and made of marble: "Ana Vuksani, aged 21, taken from her loving family and friends by an incurable illness . . ."

Then the two women moved back to the first Ana, their Ana. Skënder Bermema had stopped in an alley nearby to smoke a cigarette. Silva spent a little while arranging the flowers on the grave; she and Linda both stood for a moment in prayer; then she whispered, "Let's go now." Skënder was waiting for them at the end of the alley – unless he was there by chance – and all three walked back together to the bus stop.

Before reaching the city, the bus passed by a kind of dump on some marshy ground, and a lot of the passengers craned forward to see what was going on there. Bright streaks of light were shooting hither and thither in the gathering darkness, pursued by a little group not of urchins but of grown men.

"What is it?" Linda asked. But neither Silva nor Skënder Bermema replied.

Other passengers were curious too. The driver stopped the bus and stuck his head out of his window to ask what was up.

A passing pedestrian answered perkily, and the driver, winding up his window again, passed on what he'd said.

"They're destroying the Chinks' bangers!"

This produced some jokes and laughter, but all were drowned in the roar of the bus starting up again.

On the waste land the work of destruction went on. The men had hoped to finish before midday, but just as they were getting ready to leave they were told more stocks of fireworks had been found in a warehouse. They had to wait more than two hours for this batch of crates to arrive.

They were the same as those the workmen had dealt with in the morning, except that two of the cases had got very damp, and the rockets were difficult to ignite. But when they finally did go off, the men started emptying all the crates one after the other with the same mixture of resentment and jubilation as earlier in the day. As darkness fell, the waste lot was lit up with shafts of brilliance darting everywhere.

But where the rockets had once shot high into the sky, accompanied by the shouts of the populace, to celebrate grand and joyful occasions, they now fell back like wounded snakes, and after a few convulsive leaps, fizzled out miserably on the ground.

The destruction went on late into the night. An acrid smell of burned rubbish and singed cardboard hung over the whole neighbourhood. Sometimes a rocket, after squirming around for a while, would make a furious effort to lift off into the air, but then one of the workmen, carried away with excitement like all his comrades, would run after it, catch it, and grind it out underfoot, shouting "Snake, horrible snake!"

Some electricians working a few kilometres away, in open country, noticed, as it got dark, some many-coloured gleams and flashes in the distance. They were perched high up in the air, dismantling the superstructure of the radio station that until recently had transmitted news to Europe from the Hsin-hua news agency.

"What are those flashes?" asked one. "Perhaps we ought to climb down . . ."

"No, it's not lightning," said another, some way underneath him. "The sky's dark enough, but there hasn't been any thunder."

After turning to look again several times, they eventually got absorbed in their work once more and paid no attention to the distant lights. Expert as they were, they weren't too sure exactly what they were supposed to be doing. They'd thought when the job was first mooted that they were to take down the entire system, and had bragged to their friends that they were going to destroy the whole mass of wires and metal which had filled the world with Chinese. That's right, root up the lot! their friends had urged. But when they reached the site they were told they were only to disconnect certain parts of the system. To ensure that they weren't making any mistakes, they checked every so often against the diagrams they'd been supplied with, peering at them by the light of a lamp fixed to a girder.

"This must be it!" said the oldest engineer, just arrived from the northern provinces. He was a native of Doomed Heights, and although he hadn't actually lived there for a long time, he still had the typical local mentality. In his view, the part they had to remove was a particular piece of steel that understood Chinese. He wouldn't have been at all surprised if, by undoing the relevant nuts and bolts, he'd released a lot of hyperactive ideograms.

"Careful!" called the fitter who was working at the other end. "There's only a couple of bolts left at this end. What about you?"

"Same here! Hi, you down below – watch out!"

Ten minutes later the great mass of wires and metal collapsed with a deafening crash. The engineers climbed down and shone their torches to see where the wreckage had fallen. Only then did they realize how wet and muddy the ground was thereabouts. The fallen equipment had almost disappeared into it.

But it was late now. They collected up their tools and got ready to leave. No one said anything – a sure sign they each had something on their mind. Although they'd spent their whole lives erecting and dismantling this kind of equipment, they couldn't stop thinking about what they'd just seen by the light of their torches. Perhaps that bit of steel which could speak Chinese would lurk there in the mud, together with its drowned ideograms, then crop up every spring, until the new grass strangled it to death. Just as in people's minds the memory would fade of their friendship with China.

By the time she got home, Silva was exhausted. Gjergj wasn't back yet. Veriana had dropped in, and she and Brikena were chattering away in Brikena's bedroom. As she kissed her niece, Silva remembered Linda. Who could say? – perhaps she and Besnik really were in love?

Ten minutes later Gjergj came in. He was tired too.

"Would you like a cup of coffee?" Silva asked him.

"I certainly would!" he replied.

They sat down in the living room, and although it was getting dark, neither switched on the light.

Out in the hall the two girls could be heard busy with something, and suddenly Brikena appeared in the doorway.

"Mother – do you know what? The lemon tree has produced a lemon! It's absolutely lovely!"

"Really?"

"Come and look! It's only small still, but . . ."

"I'll come and see later on."

"Can't you come now?" said Brikena, disappointed at her mother's lack of enthusiasm.

Silva didn't like to let her down, so she followed the two girls out on to the balcony. It was all cluttered up, as such places tend to be during the winter: there was a deckchair that needed mending, lying around from last summer; some plastic containers; a pile of empty floor-polish tins.

"There!" exclaimed the girls, pointing to a tiny little lump, hardly distinguishable among the leaves.

"My goodness – yes!" cried Silva.

"Poor little thing!" said Veriana.

Silva did her best to smile. She remembered the day when the lemon tree had been delivered – on Brikena's birthday. Then that night, and the icy moonlight, and her fears about Gjergj on his way to China. How much had happened since then! Could so much have taken place in the time it took the lemon tree to produce a fruit?

She looked at the little plant tenderly. The world was full of

443

political meetings, plots, commotions and tragedies, while here in its little corner on the balcony, careless of everything else, the lemon tree devoted itself to its own raison d'être – bringing forth fruit. Compared with the tumult going on in the world as a whole, it seemed so frail, so lonely you couldn't help pitying it.

Silva smiled thoughtfully. Perhaps the lemon tree, if it had been able to think, would have pitied the rest of the world.

As she shut the door on to the balcony behind her, Silva for some reason thought of what old Aunt Hasiyé had said: "The Chinese? There have never been any Chinese here. You must have dreamt it."

Tirana, 1978–1988